A
STRANGER'S
GAME

A STRANGER'S GAME

JOAN JOHNSTON

POCKET BOOKS
New York London Toronto Sydney

Pocket Books
A Division of Simon & Schuster, Inc.
1230 Avenue of the Americas
New York, NY 10020

This book is a work of fiction. Names, characters, places, and incidents
either are products of the author's imagination or are used fictitiously.
Any resemblance to actual events or locales or persons, living or dead,
is entirely coincidental.

First Pocket Books hardcover edition March 2008

POCKET and colophon are registered trademarks of Simon & Schuster, Inc.

For information about special discounts for bulk purchases,
please contact Simon & Schuster Special Sales at
1-800-456-6798 or business@simonandschuster.com

Manufactured in the United States of America

10 9 8 7 6 5 4 3 2 1

Library of Congress Cataloging-in-Publication Data
Johnston, Joan
     A Stranger's Game / Joan Johnston.
          p. cm.
1. Sex addicts—Diaries—Fiction. 2. Children of murder victims—Fiction.
3. Judicial error—Fiction. 4. Murder—Investigation—Fiction. 5. United
States. Federal Bureau of Investigation—Officials and employees—Fiction.
I. Title.
     PS3560.O3896D53 2008
     813'.54—dc22   2007029117

ISBN-13: 978-0-7434-5438-4
ISBN-10:   0-7434-5438-3

For my friends
Claire Collins
and
Barbara McCleary

A
STRANGER'S
GAME

Prologue

~

"Merle Raye, get your lazy butt in here!"

"What's wrong, Daddy?" Merle Raye said, skidding to a stop on the waxed linoleum kitchen floor.

"I thought I told you to wash these dishes."

Merle Raye glanced at the coffee cup and saucer that sat alone in the white ceramic sink. "I—"

"I told her I'd do it, Big Mike," her stepmother said.

Merle Raye's father turned on her stepmother, his eyes narrowed and one meaty hand fisted. "If I'd wanted you to wash up, Allie, I'd have said so. I want her to do it."

"I only thought—"

"Don't think!" her father retorted, slipping his arms into the shoulder rig he wore as a cop with the Austin PD. "Just do what the hell I tell you to do!"

As he turned, Merle Raye shrank back, knowing what was coming, but also knowing there was no escape from Big Mike's fist. At the last moment, he opened his hand and slapped her across the face. Even that blow was enough to send her skinny eleven-year-old body flying. She hit the refrigerator with a thump, the "Remember the Alamo!" refrigerator magnet gouging her back and then falling to the floor along with her, where it broke in half.

"Goddammit! Now look what you've done!" her father bellowed.

Merle Raye pulled her knees up to her budding chest and put her hands up to protect her head and fiery face.

"Big Mike!" Allie cried. "Don't!" Her stepmother took a step forward and caught the punch meant for Merle Raye on her own shoulder, gasping at the pain of it.

"Get out of the way, Allie," her father snarled.

"It's only a cup and saucer," Allie said. "There's no need—"

"The girl needs to learn I mean what I say."

While Big Mike was diverted by her stepmother, Merle Raye scuttled out of the kitchen on her hands and knees. As soon as she was clear of them, she stood and ran down the hallway. There was no sense trying to hide in her room. Her father had already broken the latch by kicking down the door.

Merle Raye scampered for the linen storage closet in the hall, crawled behind the winter blankets stacked on the floor beneath the bottom shelf, and crouched there, curled up in the smallest ball she could make of herself. So far, this hiding place hadn't been discovered. But she was stuck here until her father left the house for work.

Merle Raye was always amazed—and grateful and guilt-ridden—whenever Allie stepped between her and Big Mike, taking the brunt of the beating intended for her, as though Merle Raye was her own flesh-and-blood daughter. The guiltier Merle Raye felt for escaping all that pain at Allie's expense, the more fiercely she loved her stepmother. She'd vowed to pay Allie back someday, although she had no idea how.

Merle Raye couldn't understand why Allie didn't leave Big Mike. Merle Raye would have given anything to be old enough to run away. She'd tried it once last year, but Big Mike had gotten every cop in Austin to hunt her down and then hauled her back home. She still hadn't figured out why he'd wanted her back. All he did when he got her home was yell at her and hit her and call her names.

Merle Raye shuddered when she heard Allie scream. One of these days Big Mike would end up killing one of them. Merle Raye's heart pounded as she heard her stepmother running down the hall to the bedroom she shared with Big Mike, and Big Mike roaring oaths as he chased after her.

Merle Raye knew how things were going to end. Big Mike's rage would find another outlet. Merle Raye put her hands to her ears to shut out the sounds of Big Mike doing what he did to her step-mother.

She wished her real mother hadn't died when she was born. Maybe if Big Mike hadn't been drowning his sorrows in beer, he wouldn't have named her after his two best friends. Lots of kids in Texas had two names—Jimmy John, Billie Sue, Bobbie Jo—so her name wasn't really that odd. But because Merle Raye had learned to keep her mouth shut unless spoken to, the other kids had pegged her as shy, and she'd gotten the unfortunate nickname Mertle the Turtle.

Being Mertle the Turtle was a heavy cross to bear. And because they'd lived in the same neighborhood in Austin her whole life, the nickname had stuck. Folks shouted "Hey, Mertle!" at her far more often than her real name. Merle Raye had vowed that as soon as she was old enough, she was going to change her name to something simple and elegant. Like *Grace*.

Nana Glory, her birth mother's mother, said her father hadn't got-ten drunk so much before her mother died, though she reckoned he'd always been a mean son of a bitch.

"Shows what happens when a female falls for a pair of broad shoulders, a headful of shiny black hair, and some twinkly blue eyes," Nana Glory had said.

Merle Raye didn't have her father's broad shoulders, but she'd definitely gotten his blue eyes and his straight black hair. She figured she'd gotten his short temper, too, because she sure got mad enough in a hurry when he got mean.

That's where the similarity ended. Merle Raye had never raised her hand against a soul, man or beast, and never planned to—with one exception.

She had thought long and hard about killing Big Mike.

Merle Raye had imagined a thousand ways of doing it, ways where she wouldn't get caught. She was smart and she kept her ears open every time Big Mike bragged about how he'd unraveled the clues and brought some killer to justice. There were some benefits to being a homicide detective's daughter, one of which was learning how to kill and get away with it.

Someday she'd be old enough to run away. Before she did, Merle Raye imagined the satisfaction of killing Big Mike. He surely deserved to die. It was bad enough that he beat her and her stepmother black-and-blue whenever he felt the mood strike him. But he'd done worse than that.

In a fit of rage, Big Mike had flushed her turtle—the one Allie had given her for her tenth birthday, which she'd named Mertle—down the toilet. Mertle was the first living thing that had ever been put in Merle Raye's care. For the two weeks she'd owned Mertle, she'd held her and loved her and fed her and taken the very best care of her she knew how.

When she'd realized the finality of what Big Mike had done, Merle Ray had felt an unbearable ache in her chest and a sudden knot in her throat. Tears had brimmed in her eyes. Then some sort of dam broke, and the sobs came so hard and fast she could barely catch her breath. Her eyes had swollen up and her nose had run.

She'd bawled like a baby for two hours, until Big Mike had kicked her door in, picked her up and shaken her so hard her head flopped on her shoulders, and said, "Shut the hell up!"

And she had. She hadn't cried over anything or anyone since.

Merle Raye bared her teeth as she thought of how many times Big Mike had disappointed her. And hurt her. And hurt those she cared about. Anyone who'd flush a poor, defenseless turtle down the toilet was just plain *mean*.

Someday, she vowed, as she listened to Big Mike slaking his meanness on her stepmother's body, Big Mike would get what he had coming. He'd be stone-cold dead. And no one would ever know it was his own daughter who'd done it.

1

Ten years later

FBI Supervisory Special Agent Breed Grayhawk was caught in the middle between two barnyard dogs, their neck hairs hackled and their teeth bared, warily circling, looking for an opening to rip out each other's throat. He didn't move. He hardly breathed. He didn't want to get noticed and maybe have both beasts turn their slavering fangs on him.

Or at least, that was how it felt.

In reality, he was leaning against the window ledge in his boss's office, listening to two opinionated, bullheaded FBI special agents argue over security for the upcoming visit of the U.S. president to the University of Texas at Austin campus.

"I understand that you want your team to be more involved in security during the president's visit, Vince," Special Agent in Charge Craig Westwood said. "But between the Secret Service, the Texas Department of Public Safety, and the SWAT team I'm bringing in from the regional field office in San Antonio, we have everything covered."

"So my agents are stuck doing previsit background checks on anarchists and white supremacists?" Assistant Special Agent in Charge Vincent Harkness retorted.

"It's necessary," Westwood replied in a steely voice.

"But peripheral," Vince persisted.

"Come on, Vince," Westwood said. "We're a team. Sometimes you don't get to pitch. You have to field balls."

"Shit, Craig," Vince flared. "My agents aren't even in the god-damn game!"

Breed tensed, waiting to see whether the San Antonio SAC, who was his boss's boss, would jump down Vince's throat. Breed gripped the hardwood window ledge under his hands, resisting the urge to thrust himself into the fray. It wasn't his battle, and Vince wouldn't thank him for interfering.

Breed watched as Vince's eyes darkened from brown to nearly black as he glared at Westwood, who stared right back. Vince's pale skin flushed, and his jaw worked.

Breed could understand his boss's point.

President John Coleman was giving the keynote address at the National Governors Association Annual Meeting—just five days away—in the LBJ Auditorium on campus. More than a thousand people were scheduled to attend. The nation's governors, the public, and the president were potentially at risk.

The Secret Service, now under the Department of Homeland Security, was in town to do the protective groundwork and provide security during the event, with the assistance of the Texas DPS and the FBI. At least, some of the FBI. The Austin "satellite" office, like an ugly stepchild, was being told, however nicely, to butt out.

Breed felt his body respond with a rush of adrenaline to the palpable tension between his boss and Westwood. He gritted his teeth, waiting to see who would blink first.

Westwood's hands were steepled beneath his chin, and the ankle of one leg was propped on the knee of the other, so he appeared deceptively relaxed in one of the two studded maroon leather chairs across from Vince's definitely-not-government-issue cherrywood desk.

Abruptly, Vince picked up a Montblanc pen from his desk, breaking eye contact with his boss. "You know we'll do our part," he said, before adding even more quietly, "however small it turns out to be."

"I appreciate that, Vince," Westwood said. "You're doing a fine job here." He dropped his foot to the ground and sat upright, his hands slapping his knees, signaling that the meeting was over.

Vince shoved an agitated hand across the flat top of his dark brown crew cut, before once again meeting Westwood's gaze with belligerence. "This might only be a satellite office, Craig, but I'd pit my agents against yours any day of the week."

"I'm sure your men are good at what they do, Vince. Langley doesn't let them loose on the world unless they're good. Like Grayhawk here, whose JTTF team has run down perpetrators of both identity theft and bank credit card fraud over the past year, if I'm not mistaken."

Breed found himself the object of Westwood's piercing blue-eyed gaze. He stood upright, his weight forward, as though to defend himself from physical attack. But Westwood was smiling at him. Breed wasn't sure how to respond to the SAC's compliment, which could just as easily have been construed as a slur, since the criminals his Joint Terrorism Task Force had apprehended weren't, in fact, the sort of domestic and foreign terrorists they were supposed to be hunting.

So he said nothing.

Breed knew he was only present at the meeting between his boss and the San Antonio SAC because, as Supervisor of the Austin JTTF, he was in a position to know whether there were any active threats to the president of the United States on the UT campus. He'd already made his report to Westwood: not only were there no active threats on campus, there hadn't been an active threat of domestic or foreign terrorism on campus during the entire two years Breed had been assigned to the JTTF.

"Anything else you want to mention about the situation on campus while I'm here?" Westwood asked Breed as he stood, his broad-shouldered six feet five inches towering over a still-seated five-foot-nine-inch Vince.

"No, sir," Breed said, broadening his stance and easily meeting the SAC's eyes. "There's no known threat to the president of the United States or to the governors of the fifty states, three territories, and two commonwealths who'll be on campus next week."

"No *known* threat," Westwood repeated, his gaze sliding from

Breed to Vince. "I'm relying on both of you to let me know if that situation changes between now and Wednesday, when the president shows up. I don't want any surprises."

Vince made a sound in his throat that might have been a grunt or a snort or a snicker.

Breed wondered if the same thought had occurred to his boss as had occurred to him. *Can anyone really account for the unexpected? Surprises are surprises precisely because no one anticipated them. Why are we going to be responsible if a disaster occurs, when we're so uninvolved in preparation for the president's visit? Are we being set up to take the fall if something goes wrong?*

Breed watched as his boss finally rose, as though he were the one dismissing Westwood and not the other way around.

"We're a first-rate resource, Craig," Vince said. "Use us."

"I will. If I need you."

Breed watched a muscle tick in his boss's jaw as Vince shook hands with the San Antonio SAC and imagined Vince biting his tongue to keep from making another retort.

"Don't be a stranger," Vince said to his boss. "Stephanie and I and the kids would love to have you and Emily and your kids join us at our cabin on Lake LBJ for a barbecue and waterskiing some weekend before it gets too cold."

"We'd enjoy that," Westwood said. "Let me have Emily give Stephanie a call and set it up."

As soon as the door closed behind Westwood, Vince said, "That son of a bitch!"

Breed grinned. "I can't believe you just invited that son of a bitch to spend the weekend at your cabin."

"He and I both know he's too busy to take me up on it," Vince said as he reached for a jacket on a hanger behind the door and slipped it over a stiffly starched white oxford cloth shirt. He shot his cuffs and adjusted a rep-striped tie. "Craig Westwood has been a thorn in my side ever since I joined the FBI."

"What did he do that was so bad?"

"Kissed a lot of ass on his way to the top."

The edge in Vince's voice kept Breed silent.

"Aw, hell," Vince said, suddenly grinning and slapping Breed on the back. "I'm just pissed because when Craig and I went through the FBI Academy at Quantico a thousand years ago, I graduated five spots ahead of him, and now the son of a bitch is my boss."

Breed laughed because Vince laughed. But the bitterness in Vince's voice told him it wasn't really a laughing matter.

Breed strode out of the Friday-night-empty FBI office ahead of Vince and got blasted by the lingering South Texas heat. He looked at Vince in his standard FBI dark suit and tie and was grateful for the work he did on campus that made it possible for him to wear a Stetson, an open-throated, Western-cut shirt, blue jeans, and cowboy boots.

"What did Westwood do that got him promoted ahead of you?" Breed asked.

As Vince's car remote chirped to open the door on his black SUV, he said, "It wasn't so much what he did as what I didn't do."

Breed lifted an inquiring brow.

"Stephanie's mother got sick," Vince explained. "I had to ask for a transfer from the Southwest region, where things were hopping, to a satellite office in Georgia near Stephanie's mom—a place where things were definitely *not* hopping. Craig stayed put, then went to Langley and made a name for himself, before returning to South Texas as regional SAC."

"Tough luck," Breed said.

Vince shrugged. "That's the way it goes." He glanced at his watch and hissed in a breath as he settled onto the hot black leather seat. "I'm late. I promised Stephanie I'd be home by six to take her and the kids to the cabin this weekend. Which I shouldn't have the time to do, if Craig were using the manpower in this office the way he should."

"I guess that means you can't join me for a drink," Breed said as he stood by the door to his pickup.

Vince shook his head. "Not tonight," he said as he started up his car and rolled down the windows. "See you on Monday, unless a terrorist threat rears its hydra head over the weekend. If you need me, you know how to reach me."

"Yes, sir." Breed watched Vince drive away, then got into his cobalt-blue Dodge Ram and headed west on U.S. 290 out of Austin. It had been a helluva day. With the president's upcoming visit, he'd better enjoy the weekend, because it was likely to be a helluva week.

He needed a drink. And a woman. Preferably in that order. And he knew just where to find both.

2

Breed hit his brakes and skidded sideways to avoid a deer scampering across U.S. Highway 290 west of Austin. He grinned as the adrenaline that kicked in sent his thumping heart up into his throat. And grimaced as he acknowledged that missing a deer caught in the headlights was about the most excitement he'd had in a month of Sundays.

Breed had been ready to bust balls when he'd been appointed as one of six FBI special agents on the JTTF two years ago. For the first year, he'd posed as a graduate student in business, son of the governor of Wyoming, King Grayhawk.

Not that King had ever been a father to him. Breed's mother Sassy had been married to King when he was born, all right. But his father had taken one look at his supposed offspring's crow-black hair, odd silver-gray eyes, and copper-hued skin, named him Breed for the half-breed he appeared to be, and started divorce proceedings.

The truth would have been easy enough to prove with DNA, if anyone had bothered. But King was too proud, Sassy was too drunk, and Breed was too angry.

Nevertheless, in the name of patriotism—and because it was the politically correct thing to do—King had been persuaded by the FBI to allow Breed to use his wealthy father's oil connections and influence to help him get introductions to rich Saudi and Egyptian and Iranian sons attending UT, in hopes of uncovering an al-Qaeda operative.

It had all been for naught. As the San Antonio SAC had pointed out, the worst offenses Breed had rooted out were identity theft and bank credit card fraud. And those thieves had been strictly American. So much for heroically saving the country from foreign and domestic terrorism.

Breed likened his work with the JTTF to a shepherd watching his flock. The wolf might not come around for months at a time, but the shepherd had to remain vigilant. If he let down his guard, the wolf could—and would—slip in amongst the flock and slaughter them.

Breed hadn't told anyone the fanciful analogy he used to describe what he did for a living. But it kept him committed and made him feel his work was necessary and important. Especially when there hadn't been even the whiff of a terrorist threat in the two years since he'd become a member of the Austin JTTF.

He groused to his friend, Texas Ranger Jack McKinley, about the inaction and redundancy, and sometimes downright boredom, of his work. But he would never, ever abandon his watch for the wolf.

Which was why the meeting today with the San Antonio SAC had left him feeling antsy. Anxious. Like a creature that smells fire in the wind, sensing danger, ready to run, but unsure in which direction safety lies.

All his life, Breed had known when trouble was on the way. It was a survival mechanism, a sixth sense that warned him that his mother was headed into alcohol rehab again, and he was about to be pawned off on another relative.

Or that some lush she'd met in rehab and married didn't want her son around, so he'd better make himself scarce.

Or that she'd found a guy to pay a plastic surgeon to give her a new face and a more bosomy figure, and she would be leaving him with yet another distant relative, or even a "friend," while she went away to recuperate.

He'd survived being abandoned again and again by his mother. He'd even thrived. Because he always prepared himself for the worst, and therefore was never disappointed, no matter what happened.

He pulled into a spot in front of a ramshackle cowboy bar called

Digger's and shut off his engine. He was hoping for a cold drink. And a warm woman. With any luck, he wouldn't be disappointed.

The heat of a sunny October day in South Texas had dissipated, but when Breed stepped inside Digger's, the smell of sweat hung in the air. And despite the national obsession with not smoking, a haze of burned tobacco clouded the turquoise-painted interior.

An old Waylon Jennings tune was playing on an equally ancient jukebox, forcing the voices inside Digger's up a notch, so twenty-five people sounded like forty. Everyone wore cowboy hats and belts and boots, and Wranglers like the Texas Rangers wore, with rivets in the right places and seams that didn't chafe on horseback.

Breed was a regular, and the bartender nodded at him and set an ice-cold and dripping bottle of Dos Equis beer in front of him on the scarred wooden bar.

By the time Breed said, "Thanks, Jimmy Joe," the bartender had already shuffled away to fill another order.

Breed stared into the mirror over the bar, which was crowned with a curving set of Longhorn steer horns that had to be ten feet from point to point. He'd purposely sat down next to the female at the end of the bar who looked shapely from behind. He felt his heart jump when she lifted her stunning blue eyes and met his gaze in the mirror.

The attraction was immediate. And powerful. He recognized it without giving in to it.

Breed didn't do relationships. Didn't believe in romantic love. Didn't believe in anything that ended happily ever after. It wasn't part of his experience. When he wanted a woman, like now, he found one willing to satisfy his needs. In exchange he offered mutual satisfaction—or money. Nothing more.

He perused the woman beside him at his leisure, recognizing that she was pretty, rather than beautiful. Her eyes were too far apart and her nose was a little crooked, but her mouth looked very kissable, the lips full and pink without lipstick. Her complexion was unbelievably light and creamy, and he wondered if the rest of her was as smooth and touchable. She had straight black hair that fell halfway down her back. He was amused to find her staring boldly back at him in the mirror.

She was drinking tequila shots. One upside-down shot glass sat in front of her, and she was nursing a second glass that was half full. He felt a strong tug in his groin when she smiled at him in the mirror, revealing nearly perfect white teeth. She lifted her shot glass in a toast and tossed the rest of it down without making the sort of face females usually made when they drank straight liquor.

She turned the glass upside down and set it carefully on the bar without a sound. In a husky voice that felt like a warm hand caressing his flesh, she said, "Another one, Jimmy Joe."

Breed's body hardened like a rock. So much for subtle interest in the female sitting to his right. He was already imagining himself deep inside her when he felt her hand on his thigh. He jerked at the touch, but managed to hang on to his beer without spilling it as he turned to her, easing his leg free.

"I'm Grace," she said. "What's your name?"

Breed usually liked to do the chasing, but somehow he didn't mind getting caught by this particular she-wolf. "Breed Grayhawk," he replied.

Her eyes narrowed, and he watched as she noted the copper hue of his skin, the high cheekbones and blade of nose, the narrow lips and chiseled chin. He felt himself flush when she nodded, acknowledging without a spoken word what his name likely meant.

Half-breed.

He was disconcerted when her inspection didn't stop with his face but drifted to the breadth of his shoulders, his lean waist, and—he couldn't believe she was actually doing it—the hard ridge in his jeans, before skimming down the length of his legs.

He didn't much like being sized up like a prize bull. So he gave her back what he'd just gotten, starting with her striking, wide-spaced blue eyes, a nose that should have been aquiline, but now had a bump that proved it had been broken once upon a time, and a mouth with lips so full they made a man wonder how they would feel in a lot of different places. The mouth was scarred, too, with a small white mark on the upper right edge.

Abusive husband? he wondered. Abusive father, maybe? Car accident, more likely. She had a self-possession that he couldn't make fit with a cringing victim.

She smiled, a bare curve of her lips he would have missed, except it was reflected as a twinkle in her blue eyes. Then she lifted a finely arched brow—another barely-there scar slicing through the right edge of it—to ask if he was done yet.

He wasn't.

Breed let his eyes follow the length of her neck to milky white shoulders and a pair of breasts that were amazing, if they weren't fake, outlined in a low-cut, lace-trimmed white sleeveless top. A narrow, cowboy-belted waist flared into the kind of hips that made a woman good at childbearing, and slender, jean-clad legs. He imagined them naked, wrapped around him, and felt his mouth go dry.

He couldn't believe the invitation he saw in her eyes when their gazes met again. He wondered for a moment if she was a hooker—beat up by her john one too many times?—and realized he didn't give a damn. He wanted her any way he could get her.

He hadn't noticed Jimmy Joe bringing her another drink, but she turned from him, licked some salt from her hand, drank half the shot glass of tequila, then bit into a slice of lime.

He felt that lick in the place he wanted it most. His whole body tensed, and he must have looked—and smelled—to her like some sort of beast in rut, because she glanced sideways at him before shoving her silky black hair back across her shoulder in a gesture that reminded him of a doe flicking her tail at a stag.

He glanced at the two shot glasses upside down in front of her and the third half-empty one and realized he didn't want her senses dulled any more than they already must be.

"What would it take to get you into bed?" he said in a low, guttural voice.

For the first time she looked less than supremely self-confident. "What?"

"How much to have you?"

Her eyes flickered with some emotion he couldn't name before she said in a cool voice, "More than you can afford, Cowboy."

"Name your price," he said, determined to have her, whatever it cost him.

"I don't want your money." She did a perusal of his body that made his blood feel like lava in his veins, then said, "I need a favor."

"Name it."

"After," she said. "Agreed?" She held out her small hand for him to shake.

Her grasp was surprisingly strong as he caught her hand in his own. "Sure."

"You won't back out?"

Her rasping voice made the hair on his arms stand up, as though he'd been stroked. At that moment, he would have promised anything to have her.

"I won't back out." The rough voice he heard didn't sound like his own. She wasn't a very good businesswoman if she was willing to put off getting money in advance, or something in writing about that promised favor. Once he had what he wanted from her, he'd be glad to help her out. If what she wanted was reasonable. And didn't cost him more than he thought she was worth.

"Where can we go?" he asked.

"How about your truck?"

He snorted. It was a pretty good guess that he drove a pickup. Most cowboys did, and he was certainly dressed like one. But he had no intention of trying to copulate like some teenager behind the gearshift of his truck. "There's a motel across the street. We can get a room there."

She shook her head. "No vacancy," she said, pointing back out the year-round Christmas garland–festooned front window of Digger's to the flickering block-lettered sign across the street, which read NO V-CANC-, two of the red lights having burned out.

Breed swore under his breath. "Where, then?" he said, irritated that she'd agreed to this, if she had no intention of following through.

"We could drive back into town."

"Too far." He couldn't wait that long.

"I have a blanket in my car," she said. "We could go down by the creek behind the bar."

"Sex under the stars?" Breed said cynically.

"Why not?"

Breed didn't trust her, but he was sure he could take care of himself even without the Glock 22 he'd left in his glove compartment. He was supposed to keep the weapon with him at all times, since technically, an FBI agent was never off duty. But that would mean he shouldn't be drinking, either. Breed figured if he was going to break the rules, it was better not to be in a position where he could drink—and shoot.

He certainly wasn't going to let a little worry over her ulterior motives keep him from enjoying that luscious, well-endowed body. He threw enough money on the bar to cover his drinks and hers and said, "You ready?"

She eyed the money he'd left, shrugged, downed the last half of her drink, very quietly turned the glass upside down on the bar in front of her and rose to her feet.

Breed was 6'4" tall, and when he stood, she barely came to his shoulder, even wearing cowboy boots, which gave her an extra inch or so of height. For an instant, he wondered how old she was. Another look at the cleavage so blatantly displayed silenced his qualms. He slipped a hand under her elbow and said, "Let's go get that blanket."

The air outside had cooled as night fell and felt refreshing. He followed her to a cheap, dark blue, foreign-made car with a dent in the right front fender. Without thinking, he noted the out-of-state Michigan license plate number as she opened the trunk to retrieve the blanket. Actually, it was a patchwork quilt, a pretty nice one, from what he could see in the yellow neon light from the DIGGER'S sign attached to the whitewashed adobe wall.

He took it from her and tucked it under his arm. He reached out a hand for hers, but she ignored it, closed the trunk, pocketed the car keys in her jeans, and headed toward the creek that ran behind the bar.

It was a good thing there was a three-quarter moon, or he might have lost her in the shadows of the cottonwoods along the creek. The shallow water rushed over the rocks and a breeze rustled the yellowing leaves overhead. A hundred feet from the bar, they lost the sound of the jukebox, and it was late enough that there was no traffic to be heard on the isolated county road.

She stopped at the edge of the creek and turned back to him, her arms crossed protectively over her breasts. He had the sinking feeling she'd changed her mind.

He was annoyed at how relieved he felt when she said, "How's this?"

"Fine by me." He swung the quilt out from under his arm in a furling movement that opened it so it spread out before it hit the ground.

She dropped to her knees on the quilt and straightened the two corners closest to her. He dropped to his knees on the other side but reached for her, rather than the quilt, sliding an arm around her waist and pulling her close, feeling the infinite softness of her breasts—God help him, the real thing—pillowed against his chest.

He felt her body stiffen as his arms closed around her, and he lifted her chin with one finger to search her face in the moonlight. She looked vulnerable. And anxious.

For a single instant, he considered releasing her. But she closed her eyes, shutting out the look of innocence, and he lowered his head and found her mouth with his.

He expected resistance, but she welcomed the intrusion of his tongue and sucked on it as her body surged against his. Her hands knocked off his Stetson and sieved into his hair, holding his head against her mouth as they feasted on one another.

He yanked her lacy top up over her head, swearing at even that momentary break in contact with her mouth, then latched on again as he reached behind her for the clasp on her plain white bra, pulling it down off her arms and throwing it away before his hand cupped one large, creamy orb.

She gasped at his touch in the midst of unsnapping his Western-cut shirt and shoving the soft cotton off his shoulders with hungry hands that sought out his flesh. He reached for her belt, and she wasn't far behind him, undoing his belt buckle, then grabbing for the snap and zipper on his jeans, which sounded loud in the quiet of the night, broken only by his heavy breathing and hers.

"Dammit!" Breed wanted more movement than he could get with his jeans around his hips. He abruptly let go of her to sit back and yank off his boots. He looked up and caught her grinning at him as she yanked off her boots at the same time, then lifted her hips to scoot out of her jeans, slipping off barely-there white lace panties.

She was naked before he was and launched herself at him with a laugh, pinning him beneath her as he toed off the last of his clothes. He grinned up at her, and the instant his feet were free, rolled her beneath him, settling himself between her thighs and feeling her legs wrap possessively around him.

Which was when he remembered the condom he'd stuck in his jeans pocket. His jeans that were clear the hell on the other side of the quilt. Time enough to retrieve it later. He had more important things to do right now. Like enjoy her mouth. And her long, elegant throat. Her ears with the tiny sapphire studs. Her milk-white breasts with their rosebud tips.

She writhed under him as he took pleasure in tasting her satiny, salty flesh and moaned as she arched her body, pushing her hips against his in a demand for more.

He rolled her on top of him, edging them closer to his jeans and giving her the freedom to move as she sat up, straddling his hips. She scooted back and grabbed on to his erection, smiling slyly as she used her hands to good effect, and then her mouth, making him groan with the exquisite pleasure of what she was doing.

He caught her by the shoulders, knowing that he was losing control and wanting to put himself inside her—but not without a condom. He didn't intend to have a child of his out there somewhere without a father. He knew too well what that was like. He rolled aside to grab for his jeans, found the condom, and tore open the package with his teeth.

And realized he'd torn the rubber, making it useless. "Shit! Have you got a—"

"I'm protected," she said.

Before he could stop her, she slid onto his body, sheathing him in a move so deft that they were joined before he realized what she'd done. He grasped her hips to disengage them, but she began to move in an age-old rhythm that made him groan with the sheer pleasure of feeling, for the very first time in his life, his bare flesh sheathed by female flesh.

She leaned down and joined their mouths, and he was caught in a cocoon of sensation, with the flowery smell of her hair draped over his shoulders and chest, the lime and tequila taste of her mouth, and the exquisite feel of her warm, wet body surrounding him, squeezing him, torturing him with delight.

She brought him to the brink again, but he wasn't ready to end it so quickly, so he pulled her under him. He looked down on her closed eyes, her languid, shivering body. She moaned and lifted her hips, tightening her legs around him, and he felt himself harden and pulse within her.

He gritted his teeth to delay his climax. He wanted more. He was determined to have more.

She opened her eyes and looked up at him.

He drowned in those dark, limpid pools as he sank into her, thrusting once and feeling her response, thrusting again and feeling her exquisite resistance. Her eyes were focused on his, daring and demanding.

He met her dare. And acquiesced to her demand.

He pressed his mouth fiercely against her throat, finding soft flesh and sucking hard. He growled when he felt her teeth sink into his shoulder. Then he felt her body spasm and uttered a harsh, guttural cry, arching his back with an ecstasy that verged on pain, as he spilled his seed.

As he slid off of her onto his back, staring up at the leaves above them and the moon beyond that, he heard only his own bellowing lungs and her gasping breaths beside him.

At last she sighed and turned on her side to face him, raising herself on her elbow and perching her head on one hand, so she could look down at him.

He slid one hand under his head and turned his face to observe her. He hadn't forgotten about the reckoning. She wanted something from him. A favor. He was about to find out the price she'd set on the use of her body.

Whatever it was, it had been worth it.

She cleared her throat and said, "How's it goin', cowboy?" Her voice was raspy when she spoke, giving him that same impression of having his body stroked. He felt himself quiver, like a stallion presented with a mare in heat.

He wouldn't have believed he could be aroused again so soon, but his body was knotted with unbearable tension and he felt a blind craving, an unquenchable need to plunge himself into her again. It hadn't taken much on her part to incite him. A few husky words. A look of invitation. He could see from the satisfied look on her face that she knew the effect she was having on him.

Breed didn't like feeling manipulated, especially when he wasn't sure what else she was going to ask for, now that she'd given him what he'd wanted—and gotten him to forgo the condom he never forgot to use. He sat up and brusquely demanded, "What is it you want? What favor is it I owe you now?"

He held his breath as he waited for her answer, certain he wasn't going to like it one damn bit.

Instead of answering, she sat up, her back to him as she reached for the clothes she'd strewn across the quilt.

"Well?" He grabbed his own clothes and began dragging them on, staring at the smooth, graceful line of her back. Waiting. Wondering. "What is it you want?"

She looked at him over her shoulder and said, "When the time comes that I need your help, cowboy, I'll be in touch."

3

~

Grace Caldwell had come into Digger's tonight because she'd discovered that FBI Supervisory Special Agent Breed Grayhawk sometimes stopped at the bar to wind down on Friday nights. She'd wanted to see what he looked like, maybe even strike up an acquaintance. She hadn't intended to have sex with him. She still couldn't believe she had.

Her few previous experiments with sex had been rushed, because she and Clete had been afraid of getting caught. But Clete had known what he was doing, and she'd both liked him and been curious, so the sex had been pleasant. But nothing like this.

Tonight had been . . . transcendent.

Which wasn't at all what she'd intended to achieve by seducing a stranger. Still, she'd gotten exactly what she'd wanted from the experience. Now the lawman owed her a favor.

Considering how she'd spent the past year, she was going to need it.

Breed was swearing violently and creatively under his breath. "You'll be in touch?" he said, zipping up and snapping his jeans, then buckling his belt in jerky movements.

"If you give me a number, I'll be in touch."

"What if I don't want to give you my number?" he retorted. "What if I never want to see you again?"

She slipped into her underwear and jeans, which were still lumped together on the edge of the quilt. "You agreed to do me a favor," she reminded him.

"I didn't know what the hell you had in mind, or I never would have—"

"You could have asked what I wanted."

"I thought you wanted a potload of money," he shot back.

"You were wrong." She sat down to pull on her socks and boots as she watched him put his own on standing up, hopping on one foot, and then the other. "Are you afraid I'll ask you to do something illegal? Or immoral?"

He glared at her, but she didn't ease his mind by telling him what she wanted or reassuring him that she didn't intend any such thing. The truth was, she didn't know yet what she might need from him.

He picked up his black felt Stetson from the grass and slapped it against his jeans. "Why me?" he said, tugging his hat down tight and low on his forehead.

She wondered how he would feel if he knew she'd stalked him. Plotted to meet him. Seduced him. What she said was, "You have compelling eyes."

He snorted and rolled his eyes, which looked frustrated, angry, and disgusted.

What Grace really thought was that he'd looked lonely sitting at the bar, but she didn't think he wanted to hear that. And that she planned to use him to find out more about his boss, FBI Assistant Special Agent in Charge Vincent Harkness. And she was sure he didn't want to hear that.

"Who are you?" he said. "What the hell have I gotten myself into?"

She scooped up the quilt and looked at him significantly until he stepped off of it, so she could gather the rest of it up in her arms. "My name is Grace. And you've agreed to help out a woman in need."

"How can I reach you?" he said.

"You can't. I don't have a phone." She expected him to question that statement, but to her surprise, he didn't.

"I'm just supposed to wait around until you call me and start making demands?" he said irritably.

"Unless you intend to renege on your promise."

"Look, lady—"

"I think we've finished our business." She slung the quilt over her arm and started back toward the parking lot.

He grabbed her arm so she was forced to turn around. She lifted her chin and sneered at his hold on her until he let go. She found herself facing a man whose temper was tightly leashed, his hands fisted at his sides, his jaw clenched.

Grace stood her ground, refusing to cower. She wasn't a child anymore. She'd promised herself she would never again be a helpless victim of someone larger and stronger. If this feral male tried to strike her, he might find himself facing a wildcat with claws.

"Tell me what you want from me. Right here. Right now."

She felt a shiver run down her spine at the ferocity of his voice, the danger in his eyes. "I don't need a single thing from you right now."

She tensed, ready to defend herself. It soon became apparent that, even though he may have had the urge to grab hold and shake her within an inch of her life, he wasn't going to give in to it. She wondered if he would keep his word to help her if—when—the time came that she needed him. "May I go now?"

"Tell me how to reach you."

"There's no need for you to contact me," she said, hurrying to get to her car, anxious now to escape. "Don't waste your time trying."

"There's nowhere in Texas—nowhere on earth—you could hide from me if I wanted to find you."

"I thought you never wanted to see me again," she said with the hint of a smile.

"I don't like games," he said through tight jaws.

She opened the driver's-side door, threw the quilt across to the passenger's seat, and said, "Then you shouldn't have agreed to play."

He caught her arm again and said, "Do you really intend to drive, as much as you've had to drink?"

Grace hadn't considered how drunk she was. Which was the

problem with drinking so much. You weren't really thinking straight afterward. Witness her spur-of-the-moment decision to have sex with a virtual stranger, a lawman who was now arguing with her over whether she ought to be drinking and driving.

The reason she'd been drinking—celebrating—came to mind. She was so close to her goal. So close to finding out answers that had eluded her for a very long, very difficult year.

"I'll give you a ride home," Breed said, taking her arm and leading her toward an enormous dark blue pickup, the bed of which seemed to be full of building supplies, which were partially covered by a tarp.

"I'll stay at the bar until I sober up," Grace replied, trying to pull free.

"I'll take you home," he insisted.

She wasn't about to let Special Agent Breed Grayhawk anywhere near where she lived in Austin. When she left here she planned to disappear. He wouldn't be hearing from her again until she needed his help. "Let go!" she cried, struggling to break free.

"Hey, you there! Let go of the lady!"

Grace blessed the Code of the West, which required a cowboy to come to the aid of any female in trouble. Three large men who'd just left the bar were headed in their direction. "Help!" she called. "Please, help me!"

Maybe this wasn't her best moment, Grace thought, as Breed shot her a dark look. What she was doing wasn't quite honest, but she was willing to use her wits to win free. She saw rescue in three sets of brawny shoulders and tough, bearded faces.

Breed was still holding on to her arm when the three men arrayed themselves across from them. The one on the left said, "Let go of the lady."

"This is a private argument, gents," Breed said.

"You want us to leave, ma'am?" the one on the right said.

"I want to go home," Grace said, "and this man—"

"Sweetheart, you know I can't let you drink and drive," Breed said.

The three big men exchanged glances. The one in the middle said, "Is this your man, ma'am?"

"He is *not!*" Grace said.

"I saw her at the bar with him," the one on the right said. "She was pourin' down the shots."

"We are *not* together," Grace protested.

"Seems like you are now, ma'am," the one on the left said.

"Are you going to help me or not?" she said.

Breed bared his teeth in a grim smile and said, "Honey, you don't want these three fellows to pound on the man who's pledged to help you through thick and thin, do you?"

"Yes, I do!" Grace said, then realized how her response might sound to the three cowboys. She turned to them and said, "I am *not* his *honey!*"

The three brawny men glanced at one another. One smiled. Another chuckled.

"You got yourself a feisty little filly there," the one on the left said.

"Glad it's you and not me," the one on the right said.

"Time to get home to my wife," the one in the middle said. "She'll have my hide for being out so late."

As the three men separated and headed for their trucks, Grace glared at Breed. "You're not driving me anywhere."

"How about if I follow you, then? To be sure you get home safe."

Grace figured that was the best deal she was going to get. So she took it. "Fine." She stared down at his hand where it secured her elbow, and he let go. She took the few steps to her car as fast as she could walk—she refused to run like a scared rabbit—and saw that he was getting into his pickup as she started her engine.

Once she was behind the wheel, Grace realized she had no business being there. Driving while intoxicated was no joke. She drove the speed limit with both hands on the wheel and made herself focus, as well as an inebriated person could, on the empty road in front of her and the persistent headlights behind.

It took almost an hour to get back to Austin, which gave Grace

plenty of time to figure out how she was going to lose her unwel-
come tail. She couldn't simply pick an address. Special Agent Grayhawk would probably insist on seeing her inside the house. The best
choice was to head for one of the big dorms on campus, where he'd
be unlikely to follow her.

Grace had a friend who lived in Jester East, so that was where she
decided to go. She parked in a tow-away zone, gambling that she'd be
gone before a campus cop came around.

Breed pulled his pickup in behind her and got out. "Won't you
get towed parking there?"

The man was too damned observant. "They usually stop towing
at midnight," she prevaricated. "I'll be gone tomorrow before they're
out hunting down violators."

He frowned but didn't dispute her. "What's your last name,
Grace?"

She wasn't sure whether to give him no name or a false one. She
decided on the latter. "Smith."

"Let me see your ID," he said, putting out a palm.

Too obviously false, she realized. "Good night, Breed," she said,
turning and heading for the stairs up to the dorm. The lights there
beckoned like salvation. She didn't have an access key for the dorm,
so she timed her arrival at the door just right, so she could tailgate
inside with a group of students, one of whom opened the door for
everyone else heading inside.

"I'll be in touch," Breed called after her.

She heard the threat in his simple statement. She didn't think he
could find her, not with all the precautions she'd taken with her new
identity. But it was worrisome to wonder what he might do when he
realized she could not, in fact, be found.

Grace glanced over her shoulder one last time at the man she'd
allowed inside her body. He looked tall and strong and ruggedly
handsome. She couldn't regret what she'd done. Sacrifices had to be
made for the greater good. She couldn't help it if he happened to be
one of them.

Once inside, Grace ducked into the stairwell, in case Breed came into the lobby. She waited there, peering out through a crack in the door. A moment later, Special Agent Grayhawk tailgated inside with another group of students. He looked around, then checked the elevator to see which floors it was headed to. While he watched, the elevator stopped at the fifth, sixth, and tenth floors.

Which ought to leave him guessing where she'd ended up.

Grace waited for the lawman to leave the building, which he did within the next minute, then stood out of sight near the front door until she saw his truck leave. She waited another ten minutes after that, watching to make sure no campus cop showed up to tow her car, to ensure he was good and gone.

Even so, Grace was nervous—make that even more nervous than usual—when she headed back outside. She searched the shadows to see where Breed might be hiding. She jumped when she heard a small branch break off and fall to the sidewalk and shivered when the breeze hit the sweat on her nape.

But she didn't have the luxury of giving in to her fears. Grace got into her car, buckled her seat belt, and started the engine. She had a house to burgle tonight.

4

Grace Caldwell had been careful over the past year to live in the shadows. She'd never had an easy life, but it was better now than it had ever been when she was Merle Raye Finkel. That naive, battered thirteen-year-old girl had been accused, tried, and convicted of the horrific double murder of her father and stepmother.

Merle Raye had felt a dark thrill of pleasure when she heard—from the cops who'd arrested her for the crime—that her father was dead. And been devastated when she learned that her stepmother had died along with him. Anyone who knew her, and it was her own fault nobody really did, would have known that she revered her step-mother, and that she would never have done anything to hurt Allie.

Unfortunately, Merle Raye had made no secret of the fact that she detested her father. It had been mere coincidence that the day her father and stepmother had been shot to death with her father's service weapon, her father had beaten Merle Raye badly enough that she'd finally gotten the courage to run away again.

When she'd been caught, she'd been wearing sunglasses to cover a black eye and had wrapped a scarf around her face to cover her puffy lip where it was split. Her mussed black hair had hidden the large knot on her head, and her cracked ribs and the belt-buckle wounds on her back were covered by several layers of clothes. She'd put her wrist in a sling, knowing the injury was more than a sprain but afraid of the questions that would be asked if she tried to have it treated at a clinic.

She was sitting in the back of a Greyhound bus headed to Phoenix when the police intercepted her in El Paso, believing her to have taken flight after murdering her father and stepmother.

The .45 caliber Glock 30 she'd supposedly used to kill her parents was never found. However, several years earlier, her father had used his Glock to kill a felon in the line of duty, and Austin PD records for that incident had been matched to the bullets recovered from her parents' bodies, confirming that Big Mike Finkel had been killed with his own gun.

Because of the heinous nature of her crimes, the State of Texas had wanted to put Merle Raye Finkel behind bars for the next forty years, something allowed by new Texas laws on determinate sentencing for juveniles, who were moved to an adult prison when they turned twenty-one to serve out the rest of their life sentences.

Nana Glory had hired one of the best criminal attorneys in the state to argue that Merle Raye had been acting in self-defense, and that her stepmother's death had been incidental and accidental, since it appeared a stray bullet aimed at Big Mike had killed Allie.

Nana Glory had sworn that she believed Merle Raye when she'd protested her innocence. But the defense attorney had convinced her grandmother that Merle Raye should admit to the murders, plead self-defense, and ask for mercy from the court, since the circumstantial evidence against her was overwhelming.

So she had.

Merle Raye's cracked ribs, belt-buckle scabs, black eye, and broken wrist had gone a long way in convincing the judge that she'd been a battered victim, not a cold-blooded killer. So she'd been tried—but convicted, of course—as a juvenile offender.

Merle Raye Finkel had spent the next eight years, from age thirteen to twenty-one, in the Texas Youth Commission's high restriction facility at Giddings, barely an hour east of Austin. Giddings had locks on the doors and strict rules and more violence inside than she'd ever experienced in all her years as an abused child on the outside.

At Giddings, Merle Raye Finkel had shed her chrysalis and be-

come a new person, *Grace Elizabeth Caldwell.* The name had been
the easy part. She'd always wanted to be called *Grace.* To her, the
name sounded elegant and quiet and serene. *Elizabeth* was for a
girl she'd met in juvie who'd saved her life—at the cost of her own.
Grace had figured she owed Lizzie that much. *Caldwell* was from
the phone book. She'd opened the book, put her finger on a name,
and taken it for her own.

Merle Raye Finkel's eight years inside hadn't been wasted on
Grace Elizabeth Caldwell. Merle Raye had absorbed a great deal
about how the criminal mind worked by listening to her father, the
homicide detective. At Giddings, Grace had learned how to be a
criminal.

Juvie had been a school of hard knocks, and Merle Raye had graduated with honors. She'd learned all there was to know about lying,
stealing, intimidation, handmade weapons, picking locks, boosting
cars, and faking identities. Most important of all, she'd learned pa-
tience. How to wait for what she wanted.

Grace Elizabeth Caldwell had come out of Giddings with a mis-
sion: to find the son of a bitch who'd killed her beloved stepmother
and framed her for a double murder—and make him pay. She hadn't
yet decided the form her vengeance would take. That could wait
until she found the bastard.

Unfortunately, Nana Glory, the only person left on this earth to
whom Grace was attached, had died a year before Merle Raye's sentence was completed. But Nana Glory had bequeathed Merle Raye
an amazing gift.

In her grandmother's will, which Grace had received a copy of
when she turned twenty-one and was released from juvie, Nana Glory
had written: "I'm leaving this money to help you in your search for
the man who killed Allie and that mean son of a bitch who was your
father. I know how much you loved Allie, and how much she loved
you—as though you were her very own daughter.

"The fact Allie didn't have a mark on her, while you'd been beaten
black-and-blue, makes me certain your stepmother must have come

home after you'd gone. Otherwise, Allie would have put her body between you and your father, as she always did."

Grace would have cried then, if she could. But she'd gotten out of the habit in juvie, and her tear ducts no longer seemed to be working. She'd fought the lump forming in her throat and the physical ache in her chest. Feelings made you vulnerable. Feelings could get you killed.

It was the clue left in her grandmother's will that had set Grace on the path to finding the man who'd set her up.

"Allie told me your father had some big case he was working, something that was finally going to get him noticed, get him a medal, get him promoted. He wasn't going to share the glory with his partner. He was doing it all on his own. All I can think is that it must have gone bad."

That was the only help Nana Glory had offered. That and the $3,575,432.31 she'd left to her "beloved granddaughter Merle Raye Finkel" in her will. Nana Glory's gift—once it was deposited, with the help of an attorney, in an untraceable offshore account—gave her the financial wherewithal to search for the person her father had been tracking down. The person who'd apparently turned on him and become the hunter, rather than the prey.

Instead of reporting to the adult parole officer who'd been assigned to her by the Texas Department of Criminal Justice, Grace Elizabeth Caldwell had created false ID to back up her new identity, then carefully killed and buried all traces of Merle Raye Finkel. She didn't want the real murderer to be able to find her once he realized she was looking for him.

Grace had started her search almost a year ago with the papers and notes her father had left behind, which she'd stolen out of storage. That had been a dead end. She'd then used newspapers to find out who'd been murdered in Austin in the two years before her father's death, and which of those crimes had been solved and by which police officers. By process of elimination, she'd come up with five unsolved murders that her father had been investigating at the time of his death.

Over the past year, Grace had posed as a UT student by day. And become a thief by night.

Her first break-in had been at the home of her father's partner, Merle Hogart. It turned out Merle drank every bit as much as her father had when he came home at night. And left his work papers at the office.

Then she'd burgled the home of her father's other best friend, Ray Simms. That was where she'd struck pay dirt. It seemed Ray planned to become Joseph Wambaugh someday and write a book about his life as a policeman, because he'd copied all the murder books for every case that had been opened in the department over the past ten years. He kept them hidden in boxes in chronological order in the closet. Or had, before Grace stole them.

Using the stolen murder books, Grace learned how evidence was collected to solve a crime. She'd followed every lead on the cases over the two years before her father's death that had been concluded successfully, that is, where the criminal was now behind bars, to see if any of them were connected to her father's death.

They had all been dead ends. Nowhere could she find a link to Big Mike's murder.

It was the unsolved cases that had intrigued her. Slowly but surely over the past year, Grace had solved four of the five "cold" cases her father had been working on at the time of his death. Grace had anonymously provided the information she'd uncovered in each case to the Austin Police Department, so the murderer could be apprehended and brought to justice.

Grace knew she'd been dubbed the Angel of Death by the Austin PD, who'd been working to find out who she was as hard as she'd been working to find out which homicide might be linked to whoever had framed her for murder.

She had one final homicide left to investigate—the death of FBI Special Agent Harve Thompson, in what the papers had dubbed the Cancer Society Murder. Her father and his partner were the homicide detectives assigned to what eventually became a joint Austin PD–FBI murder investigation.

By process of elimination, it had to be someone involved with Harve Thompson's murder who'd killed Big Mike and Allie. She even had a suspect, someone whose behavior in relation to the Cancer Society Murder bore further scrutiny.

Which was why she'd decided to break into the home of Breed Grayhawk's boss, FBI Assistant Special Agent in Charge Vincent Harkness.

5

～

Grace had discovered that when Big Mike was investigating the Cancer Society Murder, the FBI had presented him with a suspect they believed had "killed one of their own," a drug addict and FBI informant named Cecil Tubbs. But neither Big Mike nor the FBI had found enough evidence against Tubbs to bring him to trial.

Looking at the evidence against Tubbs ten years later, Grace was convinced that someone—perhaps the man who'd stabbed Harve Thompson?—had framed Cecil Tubbs the same way she'd been framed. Tubbs had just turned out to be a little bit luckier than she was and had escaped prosecution.

When she'd gone hunting for Tubbs, it turned out he wasn't as lucky as she'd thought. He was dead, the victim of a hit-and-run accident. So much for getting off scot-free. Whoever had framed her was tying up loose ends.

Grace had often wondered if the man who'd framed her ever worried that she might come looking for him when she got out of juvie. Whether he was still afraid of getting caught all these years later. And whether, if Grace got too close, he would arrange an "accident" for her, like the one that had killed Cecil Tubbs.

After discovering Tubbs's fate, Grace wasn't taking any chances. Even if the killer came looking, he wouldn't be able to find her. She was a person who didn't exist. And she intended to catch him before he could eliminate her.

Which was why she'd taken the time to carefully study Vincent Harkness's home before trying to break into it. As an FBI agent, Harkness likely knew the statistics on burglary—one occurred every 13 seconds—so she expected to find closed-circuit TV surveillance outside and a wireless monitoring system inside.

To her surprise, there was no outdoor CCTV monitor, and the wireless system inside was a Keepsake SSD-16 with PIR (passive infrared sensors), which Harkness had likely installed himself, and connected to a WEMA (We Monitor America) central monitoring station. They had no pets.

Her investigation also revealed that Mrs. Harkness liked the bedroom window open at night, and that on at least two occasions over the past three weeks it hadn't been closed when the family—Vincent, his wife Stephanie, and their two teenage kids Brian and Chloe—left the house for work and school.

Earlier this evening, Grace had watched the entire family drive away in a black SUV packed full of stuff they'd need to spend the weekend at their cabin on Lake LBJ, an hour or so west of Austin. She had shaken her head in disbelief when she realized the bedroom window had been left open!

Which meant the Keepsake SSD-16 monitoring system wasn't engaged, since it would have beeped to alert whoever was setting it that the window wasn't secured.

Grace knew a good opportunity when she saw one. She'd gone to Digger's and had a drink—*and sex*—with Breed Grayhawk, then returned to the Harkness house in the middle of the night—it was nearly 3:00 a.m.—when the neighbors were likely to be sound asleep.

She picked the lock on the back gate, stealthily crossed the backyard, and slipped inside the open master bedroom window. She moved quickly through the house, using a flashlight with a directed beam, looking for a home office where Vincent Harkness might keep records. She was seeking anything that might connect Harkness to the unsolved Cancer Society Murder, to FBI informant and murder suspect Cecil Tubbs, or to her father, Big Mike Finkel.

She found Harkness's office off the family room. She was encouraged to find it locked. That might mean he had something to hide. She looked for additional monitoring security but determined Harkness's office was connected to the house system, which wasn't engaged. Grace had a set of lock picks with her, and the dead bolt on the office door was open in a matter of seconds.

She paused and listened for any sound out of the ordinary. The house was silent except for the hum of the refrigerator.

And the pounding of her heart.

Grace had to admit, she was a nervous criminal. There was just too much at stake if she made a mistake and got caught.

Her freedom. Her future.

Grace had become a fugitive the day she decided not to show up for her first meeting with her parole officer. If the police caught her breaking and entering, it wouldn't take them long to fingerprint her and determine she was Merle Raye Finkel—a felon in violation of her parole. If that happened, she was going back to prison for a very, very long time. And since she was now an adult, it would be *prison*.

Grace had gambled that she would be able to find the man who'd committed the crime for which she'd been convicted before the police could find her. And not only that she'd find the perpetrator, but that she'd uncover enough evidence against him to prove his guilt and clear her name.

If she failed, she would be labeled a felon—and be a fugitive on the run—the rest of her life.

Assuming she could stay one step ahead of the law.

With the stakes so high, with so much at risk, Grace was not just careful, she was meticulously careful.

She worked quickly and methodically going through the papers on Vincent's desk. Then she searched the drawers, which weren't locked. She checked the closet for a false back, rifled the file cabinets, looked under the desk for a secret compartment, knocked on the walls to see if there was a hiding place she'd missed. She found nothing.

Grace felt a rising sense of desperation. This was the last "cold case" connected in any way to Big Mike. Vincent Harkness had

seemed such a promising suspect to have killed her father and stepmother, because he was such a promising suspect for having committed the Cancer Society Murder.

Harkness had sat at the same table as the Cancer Society Murder
victim, who'd lived right down the street. He'd worked in the same
office as the victim. They'd obviously known each other. And he'd
been mentioned on the list of people who'd been questioned about
the murder by Big Mike.

Sitting at the dinner table each evening as a child, listening to
Big Mike, Grace had learned that most murders were committed
by someone who knew the victim. Big Mike would surely have suspected Harkness. Had Harkness taken the initiative and silenced Big
Mike?

*What if it wasn't Harkness? What if Big Mike and Allie were mur-
dered by some random killer? What if you've wasted the past year and
thrown away your chance at a somewhat normal life and you never
find the real killer?*

Grace couldn't face that possibility, because it was too grim. She
headed for the master bedroom and searched the walk-in closet.
Vince's side was neat and the clothing had been hung with almost
military precision. All the garments faced the same way and were
grouped together by type.

Stephanie's side was equally neat, but she had an intriguing ar-
rangement of shoe boxes on a shelf stacked as high as Grace could
reach. She began opening them to see what she could find.

Grace knew it was important to get in and out of a house she was
burgling in a hurry. But the hot pink, silk-covered diary she found in
the fourth shoe box down, an anomalous splash of color in the beige-
toned house, was irresistible.

Since she hadn't found anything else that might help her, she
sat down on the sand-colored chaise longue in the master bedroom
and examined the diary she held in her gloved hands. She flipped
through the rag-weave book to a random page, focused her flashlight
on the small, loopy handwriting, and began reading.

*I met him at the Squealing Pig in Amarillo. I was hav-
ing a Salty Dog at the bar when he asked if he could
buy me another drink. I liked the contrast between his
bleached-blond ponytail and the depth of his dark brown
eyes. He was a big man. Not fat. Muscular and tall.
He had a five o'clock shadow, which made me wonder
whether he had dark curls on his chest. When he asked if
I'd like to sneak away somewhere with him, I said yes.*

*I couldn't help giggling when he took me to a van in
the parking lot! He had a mattress on the floor in back. I
lay down on it, and his heavy body came tumbling down
on top of me. He shoved my legs apart so we were belly to
belly, and I could feel how hard he was down there. He
kissed me, pushing his tongue deep—*

Grace slammed the book closed. Her heart was pumping hard,
and she licked at the sheen of sweat that had formed above her upper
lip. Now she knew why she'd found the diary hidden in a shoe box in
the closet. She wondered if this was the story of how the woman of the
house had met her husband. Or whether it was the record of an affair.
She opened the diary to a different page and started reading again.

*His blue eyes were striking as he looked up at me, his
long blond hair draped across the pillow and spilling over
broad, bronzed shoulders. His hands slid over my bare
buttocks and down between—*

Grace slapped the book closed, breathing hard. Okay, so the wife
had engaged in at least one affair. Maybe two. Surely that was all.
She opened the diary one more time.

*His skin was like onyx, shiny and dark, and the brush
of his mustache as he leaned down to kiss my naked breast
was—*

Maybe they were fantasies, Grace thought, as she tried to still her frantically beating heart. Wishes for encounters that weren't real. And yet, Grace found the accounts compelling. And arousing.

Time she got the hell out of here. She headed for the walk-in closet to return the book but hadn't taken more than two steps when she heard the garage door going up.

Grace wanted to run, but her feet felt rooted to the floor. She tried to breathe, but her throat was too constricted to draw air.

The family was supposed to be at their cabin on the lake. Who'd returned early? Why hadn't she heard the sound of the tires on the brick driveway? She bolted for the open window. Thank God she didn't have to reset a security system! She stopped abruptly when she realized what she still held in her hand.

Her sweaty palm inside the medical glove tightened reflexively on the diary.

Grace grimaced as she realized why she'd been caught so un-awares. The pulse hammering in her temples as she'd read all those erotic passages had pretty much blocked everything out. Damn, damn, damn! There was no time to put the vile thing back. She'd have to take the diary and run.

6

Vincent Harkness had been ASAC of the Austin office of the FBI for four years. He'd also been tasked with setting objectives and determining investigations for the local JTTF. Generally, he considered himself a happy man. But he'd gritted his teeth through every day of his professional life since Craig Westwood had become the San Antonio SAC last year—and his boss.

Vincent was forty-three. He was hanging on till retirement, annoyed and irritated every time he watched from the sidelines as Craig managed another splashy takedown, like his recent joint operation with the DEA to intercept a drug shipment from Afghanistan intended to finance al-Qaeda operations in the United States.

The closest Vincent had come to a terrorist was a case of identity theft by a Korean-American student on the UT campus. Sure, he was bitter. As many commendations as he'd gotten early in his career, he should be in charge of a regional office by now. He shouldn't be stuck in godforsaken Austin, Texas.

Not that everyone thought Austin was such a bad place to be. It was the site of the state capitol and home to the University of Texas, with a student body of nearly fifty thousand. Thanks to Lady Bird Johnson, the hill country around Austin turned purple with bluebonnets every spring. A vibrant country music and movie industry flourished in Austin, and the high-tech community was constantly growing.

It just didn't have any goddamn terrorists. And the only way to get noticed in the FBI these days was to uncover an al-Qaeda plot to harm innocent American citizens.

Maybe if he'd been less resentful about the course of his professional life, Vince wouldn't have overreacted when he'd caught his wife fucking another man. Maybe he would still be operating on the right side of the law. Maybe he never would have crossed over to the dark side.

Telling his family that al-Qaeda retribution was a constant danger to anyone in the FBI, Vincent had impressed upon his wife and two teenage kids the idea that his safety, and more importantly, the safety of the nation, depended on their discretion. If anyone ever contacted them as to his whereabouts, they were always to say, "He's not here right now. Can I take a message?" They were not to offer any further information.

The truth was, his safety did depend on their discretion. But not for the reasons he'd given. His activities when he was gone from his family on weekends had nothing to do with the FBI. When the rest of the world thought he was out of town relaxing with his family, Vincent was doing something he'd never imagined himself doing. And doing it so well that he'd never been caught.

It was amazingly satisfying to, literally, be getting away with murder.

After work today, Vincent had escorted his family to their cabin, driven the Chris-Craft while Brian and Chloe water-skiied on Lake LBJ, barbecued some chicken on the grill, then kissed his wife and kids good-bye and driven away.

Now he sat in a narrow alley in his black government SUV— bearing stolen plates, of course—as though he were on an FBI stakeout. He was watching the front door of a bar in Spring, Texas, a suburb north of Houston, a bare three hours east of Austin on I-10. Vincent had done FBI stakeouts often enough to know that boredom was his greatest enemy. However, the excitement of tracking prey kept him awake and aware, despite the late hour.

He was waiting for one particular man to come out of the bar.

He'd know the unsub—the unidentified subject—when he saw him, even though his only means of identifying the man was a passage written about him in his wife's diary.

Vincent had first discovered Stephanie kept a diary nine years, three months, and twenty-two days ago, when he'd accidentally knocked a shoe box off the shelf in their walk-in closet. He'd been surprised when a pink, silk-covered book had fallen out of the box, rather than a pair of the expensive, very high heels his wife favored.

He would never have invaded her privacy by reading what appeared to be a diary filled with Stephanie's distinctive handwriting, except it had fallen open, and he'd seen the word *orgasm* along with *his hairy chest*. Vincent had about three hairs on his chest, which he shaved off, because he figured it was more manly to have a bare chest than one with three measly hairs.

He hadn't left the closet for three hours. He'd been violently ill in the bathroom afterward. His wife had a sex addiction. To feed it, she'd been having sex with anonymous men she picked up in small-town bars while she was traveling on business, instructing some hospital how to implement medical software sold to it by MedWare, Inc., the national conglomerate that employed her.

Every sexual encounter had been faithfully recorded, complete with the name of the town to which she'd traveled, the name of the bar, and a description of the man—and what she'd done with him.

Vincent might have gone through the rest of his life keeping his wife's shameful secret, but once he'd known for sure that Stephanie was cheating on him, he couldn't help watching her closely. He wasn't certain what he would do if he ever caught her in the act. He loved her. They'd dated all through high school and college, and he'd married her when they were both twenty-one. She was a good mother to their two children. He'd expected to grow old with her.

Vincent hadn't realized how holding in all that anger and disgust and humiliation would affect him. Hadn't understood the danger of it. Had never fathomed how a human being could explode under unbearable pressure.

Until it had happened.

Not long after he'd discovered Stephanie's diary, he and his wife had attended a Cancer Society benefit at the Four Seasons in downtown Austin. They'd sat at a table full of FBI agents and their wives, all of them present to applaud when Craig Westwood received his Volunteer of the Year award.

Stephanie had said she was going to the ladies' room, but it was taking her a long time to come back. When he'd gone hunting for her, he'd seen her coming out of a storage closet in a hallway near the ballroom. Her lipstick was gone, and she was trying without much success to smooth her blond hair. She was headed, finally, for the ladies' room.

He'd felt the adrenaline pumping as he stared at the brass door handle, knowing what he was likely to find inside. He was afraid to look in that closet. But he'd been unable to walk away.

Vincent had yanked the door open in one swift move and stepped inside, letting the door close silently behind him. He'd stood staring, stunned to find a fellow FBI special agent and neighbor—Harve had borrowed his leaf blower earlier that day, for Christ's sake—in the storeroom. His nostrils had flared at the strong, musty smell of sex.

Harve hadn't yet buttoned his starched blue oxford cloth shirt, and the knot of his navy print tie was caught in curly black hair at midchest. His suit trousers gaped open, revealing flaccid pink flesh. Harve's expression was startled at first, but soon changed to a smirk that insinuated *You haven't been satisfying Stephanie, so what do you expect?*

Vincent didn't remember hitting Harve in the mouth with his balled right fist. Or stabbing him in the chest with a steak knife he'd grabbed from a collection of kitchenware stacked on a nearby shelf, while Harve lay half conscious on the floor. Eventually, the knife had gotten caught on a rib and Vincent hadn't been able to yank it free.

He remembered the slippery feel of the blood on his hand and the meaty smell of it, the gurgling cries coming from Harve's broken-toothed mouth, along with a gush of blood that was filling his lungs.

Most alarming and upsetting were the shock, disbelief, and horror in Harve's eyes.

Vincent had stood there for a few moments, chest heaving, heart pumping, before he looked down at what he'd wrought and sobbed with rage and sorrow. He'd tried once more to dislodge the steak knife, then grabbed one of the neatly folded black napkins from another shelf and frantically wiped the handle of the knife.

He looked around to see what else he might have touched, but other than the knife and the napkin—and the bloody body, clothes still disheveled, lying dead on the floor—the room was as he had found it. He wrapped a clean napkin around his bruised knuckles, folded the bloody napkin as best he could, and stuffed it in his suit pants pocket.

He glanced in both directions before he let himself out into the empty hallway, then wiped the shiny brass door handle clean.

The next morning, Vincent had kept his bruised knuckles in his pocket, not shaking hands with the Austin homicide detective who'd shown up at his front door to investigate Harve's murder, letting him assume it was FBI superiority that made him unsociable. A guy named Mike Finkel.

Vincent had breathed a sigh of relief when Harve's murder had been solved shortly thereafter. A snitch named Cecil Tubbs had been arrested. And then gone free. And then died in a hit-and-run.

Vincent didn't know himself why he'd killed the second man. Or the eighth. Or the twenty-eighth. But the immense satisfaction of killing one of his wife's lovers, he believed, had led to his decision to kill all the others.

Because Stephanie had taken a transfer with MedWare, Inc., every time the FBI had transferred Vince, her sexual encounters had begun in Texas, Arizona, New Mexico, and Oklahoma, continued in Georgia, Florida, Alabama, and South Carolina, and migrated, along with the family, to Washington, D.C., Virginia, West Virginia, and Maryland, before returning to the Southwest.

Vince's trail of murders had followed the same track. It was sheer luck his victims were spread out over so many states, in suburbs of big cities, where bar brawls were common.

Over the past nine years, Vincent had watched the papers, and other than Harve's death, which was dubbed the Cancer Society Murder, only one other killing—someone who'd turned out not to be one of Stephanie's lovers, after all—had even been reported locally.

Ever since the day he'd discovered the existence of his wife's diary, Vincent had continued reading the one-hundred-fifty-page pink silk-covered book. Because Stephanie wrote briefly and concisely about her lovers, she'd never filled it up. He'd decided that, when she did, he would buy her another one for Christmas. Pink. The color of all those penises.

Vincent hadn't killed all her lovers yet. Wasn't even close. But every one he did kill made it possible for him to tolerate his wife's addiction.

He was jarred from his thoughts by the cacophony of violin and electric guitar music that spilled out when the door to the Black Leopard bar opened. He studied the two men staggering across the parking lot. The first was short. The second bald. Neither was his man.

Vince never had complete names to identify the men he sought and had to rely on Stephanie's descriptions of her lovers in her diary. But they usually had some identifier that made it possible for him to locate his target. Since men were creatures of habit, especially when it came to their drinking haunts, Stephanie's lover would inevitably return to the bar named in her diary.

And meet his death.

The description in Stephanie's diary of the lover Vincent had come here to kill was seared into his brain.

> *I met George at the Black Leopard in Spring. I was*
> *halfway through a Salty Dog at the bar when he asked if*
> *he could buy me another drink. I liked the chestnut color*

*of his shaggy hair, the almond shape of his dark brown
eyes, his dark, full beard. He was a big man with thick
biceps. Muscular and tall—a couple of inches over six
feet.*

*He was wearing a plaid shirt and jeans with a Western
belt with a huge rodeo buckle. George swore he'd won it
for being the best bareback bronc rider in East Texas.*

*I told him I knew a little filly he might like to ride and
saw a fire in his eyes that made me wet down there. When
he asked if I'd like to follow him back to his place, I said
yes.*

*He had a ratty apartment that smelled of stale bacon
and beer, but I didn't have a chance to do much more
than wrinkle my nose before he pressed me back against
the door with the weight of his big, powerful body and
kissed me hard, pushing his tongue deep—*

Vincent groaned. It was painful to remember any more than that.
The thought of his wife's soft, fragile body in the arms of some sweaty,
hairy man was torture. He'd often thought it would have been a lot
smarter to have killed Stephanie than all the men she'd gone to bed
with.

But the husband was always the first suspect when a wife was murdered. And Stephanie was so . . . normal at home that if he hadn't
found her diary all those years ago, he would never have known about
all the men she'd screwed.

When he came to some sleazy bar in the worst part of town hunting prey, like he had tonight, Vincent made sure his bowie knife was
razor sharp. He'd learned, after the first couple of kills, how to avoid
the human ribs and collarbone, so it didn't get stuck.

He wished he didn't have to kill at night in dark alleys, so he could
see their eyes better. He'd never forgotten the shock and disbelief and
horror in Harve's dying gaze. But he wasn't stupid. He didn't want to
get caught.

The point here was payback. They'd done him wrong—fucking his wife—even if they were the ones who'd been seduced by Stephanie. They deserved to die. It was as simple as that. He took their wallets and watches so it would look like a simple mugging gone bad.

All he kept was their driver's licenses. He had twenty-eight of them. Tonight would make twenty-nine.

He'd discovered that the best way to catch his victim unawares was to intercept him coming out of a bright, noisy bar, which compromised his visual and aural senses, after he'd been drinking for several hours, which dulled everything else. Giving Vincent an easy shot at him with a Taser stun gun.

When Vincent's prey fell to the ground, struck by 50,000 volts of electricity, his body spasming, muscles not responding to commands from the brain, he was as vulnerable as a newborn kitten. Vincent usually struck the mortal blow first, then stabbed his victim in the chest several more times so it would appear as though he'd accidentally gotten the heart.

A coroner who looked closely enough might have found the two marks left by the stun gun darts. But Vincent shot for the crotch, and he usually hit where he aimed. Pubic hair hid the marks, unless someone was looking close, which mostly, with the kind of alcoholic bums he was stabbing, they didn't.

He'd seen his mark head into the bar around 9:30. It was nearly midnight. It wouldn't be long now.

7

It was the middle of the night by the time Vincent arrived home. He headed to the backyard to hide his bowie knife and George Hansen's driver's license in the underground space beneath the shed where he kept his garden tools. Everything else he'd stolen had been dropped in various Dumpsters around Spring before he'd left town.

Vincent was careful to clean himself up after each killing and dispose of his clothes, which he would drop at various Goodwill and Salvation Army locations around Austin. Investigative techniques were so good these days, a killer couldn't be too careful.

When he came out of the bathroom after his shower—and the ritual sterilizing of the drains—wrapped in a towel, Vincent headed for the hidden video camera that was secreted behind a pastoral oil painting of bluebonnets that hung over his and Stephanie's king-size bed. He took out the videocassette and put it in the VCR in the TV at the foot of the bed and fast-forwarded through the tape to see if anyone had been in the bedroom since they'd left town for the weekend.

Vincent had made a deal with himself that so long as his wife never brought one of her lovers home, he could handle her continuing antics on the road. He wasn't sure what he would do if he ever discovered she'd brought someone into their marital bed. Fortunately, the situation had never arisen.

But he had remained vigilant. There was no telling when Stephanie might cross the line. He pulled on his pajama bottoms, glancing at the tape every once in a while to make sure there was no move-

ment of any kind in the bedroom. He had just buttoned the last button on his pajama top when he saw someone appear on the screen.

Vincent leapt for the remote control and hit the pause button.
On the screen he saw a woman in his bedroom who was not his wife.
She was dressed in a dark T-shirt, jeans, and tennis shoes and wearing rubber medical gloves. Her face looked vaguely familiar. He focused on her eyes, nose, and mouth, trying to remember where he'd
seen her before. He played the videotape in real time and watched
with fascination as she sat on the chaise longue and opened his
wife's diary.

Vincent felt an electric shock that nearly stopped his heart. Other
than the twenty-eight—now twenty-nine—driver's licenses, which he
kept buried, there was nothing to link him to the random killings
outside bars in cities and towns across the country.

Except his wife's diary.

Anyone in possession of that diary would know for sure that his
wife had fucked the Cancer Society Murder victim. If that person
bothered to check further, he would discover that more than a few—
twenty-nine—of his wife's lovers had met an untimely end.

Then his shock turned to horror.

He saw the woman rise abruptly, as though she'd heard a noise,
and look toward the door. She started for the closet, as though to
return the book, then halted and ran for the *wide-open bedroom
window*—with the diary still in her hand.

"That bitch!"

Vincent remembered his sixth sense telling him, when he'd come
in through the garage door to the kitchen, that someone had been
in the house. He'd checked the alarm and sworn aloud when he'd
realized his son hadn't engaged the alarm system, which was Brian's
one responsibility when they left the house each day. He'd decided
on the spot to take away Brian's iPod and his Xbox for two weeks and
see if that helped his son learn to be more responsible.

He'd looked over the entire house before he'd come into the bedroom to change. His office had still been locked up tight, and noth-

ing had been moved or missing in the rest of the house, as far as he could tell. The trophies from his kills weren't even in the house. So he'd felt relieved.

By then she'd been long gone. With Stephanie's diary.

Vincent stopped the videotape and ran to the closet. He didn't want to believe what the tape was telling him. He yanked out the shoe box where his wife kept her diary, dislodging several other shoe boxes, which tumbled to the carpeted floor, spilling expensive Manolo Blahniks and Jimmy Choos—his wife was a fan of *Sex and the City*—all around him.

An agonized sound escaped his throat when he saw the shoe box that had held his wife's diary was, indeed, empty. His pulse was throbbing so hard in his head that he could feel it reverberating with the force of a hammer on an anvil.

In order to restore some measure of calm, he bent down and began to put shoes back into pairs and replace them in boxes, and then to replace the boxes in order on the shelf. He knew their order by heart. When he'd replaced all the shoes, he put the lid back on the empty diary shoe box and slid it between the tuxedo Chanels and the suede Cole Haans.

Vincent left the closet, closing the door behind him, and crossed back to sit on the foot of the bed to think. He knew his wife wasn't scheduled to leave town again until Wednesday. She only made notations in her diary after her trips. Which meant he had five or six days to recover the damned thing before she went looking for it and found it gone.

And began to wonder if her husband had discovered its existence.

He couldn't afford for that to happen. He didn't want his wife confronting him. Or admitting the truth to him. He didn't want to have to leave her. Or kill her. He loved her.

Vincent took a deep breath and huffed it out, trying to calm his nerves. He held up his shaking hands and willed them to be still. He had all the resources of the FBI at his disposal to find the bitch who'd stolen Stephanie's diary, even if he would have to use them covertly. He had less than a week to find her. Kill her. And get the diary back.

He picked up the remote and rewound the videotape to the spot where the woman had first appeared. He had the best shot of her when she was coming out of the closet. He stared hard at her face. He knew it from somewhere. He looked for distinguishing marks and saw the tiny scar on her mouth. The broken nose. The break in the arch of her eyebrow. Accident? Domestic abuse?

"Oh, my God," he whispered. "That's Merle Raye Finkel."

Vincent remembered her from the mug shots that had been passed around the FBI office after she'd shot her stepmother and her father, Big Mike Finkel, the homicide cop who'd interviewed him about Harve's murder. Everyone in the office felt vindicated that they hadn't helped the cop more in their joint investigation of Harve's death, because it turned out he beat up on his kid, who'd finally shot him with his own gun.

The mug shots had pictured the girl with some pretty serious cuts and bruises, apparently from the beating her father had given her the same day she'd murdered him. Vincent remembered she'd been tried in the juvenile justice system, which meant she would have gotten out when she was twenty-one. Just this past year.

What was she doing in his home? Was it a coincidence she'd chosen to rob his house? He frowned. She'd had no bag of any sort with her to carry away jewelry or other loot. So what had she been hoping to find?

Had she known about the diary before she'd come here? That didn't seem possible. But why else would that be the only thing she'd taken?

Vincent sat himself down at the computer in his home office, which was connected by modem to the computer at his FBI satellite office, and started doing the research necessary to locate Merle Raye Finkel.

Over the next two hours, Vincent discovered that Merle Raye

Finkel had been released from Giddings eleven months ago, collected an exorbitant inheritance from her maternal grandmother, and failed to show up at the first meeting with her adult parole officer. Efforts by the Texas Department of Criminal Justice to locate her had come to naught.

Merle Raye Finkel had ceased to exist.

Vincent knew better. She was right here in Austin. The problem was how to make sure that once she was in custody, he would be the person to interrogate her. He needed control of the situation. But how to get it?

The idea that suddenly came to him was brilliant, even if he did say so himself. He would have the right to apprehend and question Merle Raye Finkel if she were being hunted by the JTTF as a terrorism suspect.

All he had to do was make sure she became one.

It would be easy to phone in an anonymous tip pointing a finger at the girl. Vincent snapped his fingers. Of course! She could be planning to kill the president when he came to town on Wednesday. After Virginia Tech, no anonymous tip about some crazy woman running amok on campus was going to be taken lightly.

And once the JTTF found her—and with all the resources they had available, how could they fail?—Vincent was certain he could convince Breed to turn the suspect over to his boss for interrogation.

Vincent knew it wouldn't take much to convince Breed that, rather than immediately informing the FBI regional field office about the anonymous tip, as regulations required, they ought to keep it to themselves. He could point out that, if they told the San Antonio SAC about this threat to the president, Craig Westwood would surely have his agents take over the investigation.

And their office would once again be out in the cold.

Oh, yes. That argument would work.

When Breed found Merle Raye Finkel, Vincent would make sure he brought her to a federal holding cell, where Vincent would be waiting to interrogate her, recover the diary, and arrange her death.

Shot while attempting to escape? Suicide?

He had plenty of time between now and her capture to decide which would be best.

Having satisfied himself that his plan would work, Vincent went to bed and slept for six hours. He was always tired after he killed one of Stephanie's lovers. At first, he'd tried to resist the urge to sleep. But he'd learned there was no denying his body's need to decompress.

When he woke up, he quickly dressed and grabbed a granola bar for breakfast. He left the house around ten o'clock and parked a block away from a convenience store, where he used a ball cap to conceal his face from the surveillance camera and bought a throwaway phone. Then he drove to the UT campus, in case the FBI traced his call to the nearest cell phone service tower, and called his own FBI office, using a device to mask his voice.

Merle Raye Finkel is planning to blow up the LBJ Auditorium when the president is speaking.

He ended the call and drove to another part of town where he broke the cell phone into pieces and dropped them in Dumpsters.

Then he headed for his cabin on Lake LBJ. He hoped the kids planned to be out on the boat this afternoon. He wanted to make love to his wife.

8

‿

Grace had jogged the entire three blocks from the Harkness residence to where she'd left her car parked, as though she were out for a little evening exercise. Driving home, she'd forced herself to go the speed limit and to come to a full stop at stop signs. Luckily, she didn't have far to go to get "home."

She was living in a lovely town home, one of several over the past year where she'd agreed to house-sit for corporate types who traveled overseas on business. With no residence or utilities or cable in her name, she became an invisible person. For added safety, she bought disposable cell phones and threw them away after each use.

The dark blue Toyota she'd driven to Digger's, and then to the house she'd burgled, belonged to the homeowner. However, whenever she was investigating, she used license plates she picked up from cars in a junkyard, so the car couldn't be traced back to where she was living.

Grace had felt sick when she finally arrived home, aware that if she didn't find something incriminating in the diary she'd stolen, she might have made her job a lot harder. She wondered how long it would take before the theft was discovered. How long she had before Vincent Harkness realized someone might once again be looking—all these years later—to see whether he'd been involved in the Cancer Society Murder.

And suspected him of silencing the cop who might have suspected him of the deed.

Grace went around the house turning on soft lamps. After the dark years at Giddings, the lights made her feel safe. Then she headed back to the kitchen, where she poured herself a shot of tequila. With the diary in one hand and the shot glass in the other, she settled herself in a wing chair in the study. The diary fell open on its own in her lap.

Grace found herself staring at a yellowed newspaper clipping. She carefully set down the shot glass on the side table, then unfolded the worn newsprint and read the inch-high headline: "Cancer Society Murder at Four Seasons."

"Oh, my God," she said. She'd read the article before. It detailed what information was known about the murder of FBI Special Agent Harve Thompson.

Her gaze slipped to the writing in the diary, which was dated the day before the article.

I had my eye on Harve all evening, but I still couldn't believe it when he winked at me, with Peggy sitting right there beside him and Vincent sitting right next to me. I felt that familiar itch, and I left the table and headed for the ladies' room, where I hoped to scratch it.

Imagine my surprise when Harve caught up to me just outside the ballroom door! And gave my rear end a familiar pat. And suggested we find someplace where we could be alone.

God, it was amazing! I came twice before he did. I think it was the fact that our spouses were, literally, right outside the door, and the terrifying possibility that we might be discovered by someone at any moment, that made it so hot.

I really did go to the ladies' room when we were done and used a wet wipe from my purse to remove the smell of him and repaired the damage to my hair. My bra strap was ripped, and I pinned it up. There was nothing I could do about the glow of satisfaction I could see in my eyes.

Luckily, when I got back to the table, Vincent wasn't there. Harve's wife Peggy said Vincent had gone off to chat with some of his FBI buddies. By the time he returned, I could feel the flush was gone. As was that lovely feeling.

Vincent asked if I was ready to go, and I said yes, of course. As usual, he wasn't talkative on the way home. And he didn't want sex when we got into bed. It really isn't all my fault that I need it so much from other men.

Oh, God. I can't wait till the next time!

There was a subsequent entry, with the same date as the newspaper article.

I can't believe Harve was murdered last night! His body was found in the closet where we fucked like minks. Did someone see us go in there? Was it Peggy? Or, God forbid, VincDient?

A homicide detective, Mike Finkel, came to the house first thing this morning to ask us what we knew, since we were sitting at the same table as Harve and Peggy at the banquet and we live right down the street from them.

I thought my heart was going to burst right out of my chest, I was so scared. I almost blurted out that I'd been in that closet with Harve, but Vincent kept an arm around my shoulder the whole time, and all I could think was how humiliated he would be if I told what happened.

So I stayed quiet. Vincent told the detective we didn't know anything, and he went away.

I would die if Vincent ever found out the truth about my . . . problem. I can never tell anyone about me and Harve. It would kill Peggy. Oh, that's not funny. And it would kill Vincent. And it would ruin all our lives. Thank God, my secret is safe here in my diary.

Grace drank the shot of tequila. She needed it. Here, at last, was a real connection between the Cancer Society Murder victim and Vincent Harkness—or at least his wife—to follow. Had Vincent committed the murder? Had Big Mike figured it out? Had her father been killed because of what he knew? Was her stepmother's death simply collateral damage?

Grace paged quickly through the rest of the diary, hoping for another newspaper article, anything that would provide concrete evidence that Vincent Harkness had killed his wife's lover that night.

There was nothing.

Grace leaned back in the chair, turned to the very first page of the diary, and began to read. If there was a clue to the truth in here, she was going to find it.

She was two-thirds of the way through the diary when she read an entry where Stephanie Harkness recounted how she had slept, which was a euphemism if Grace had ever heard one, with a man named John Dickson in Norman, Oklahoma.

Beneath Stephanie's account of the incident were several sentences written in a different color of ink, apparently added later, in handwriting that was less readable—more agitated—than the first entry.

> Today I saw a photo of a man I knew as John—his last name is Dickson—in a copy of the Norman Transcript which I found on the hospital administrator's desk. John was murdered outside the bar where we met in Norman, OK. This is the second time this has happened! A guy I knew as Ray—his last name turned out to be Turner— was murdered a year ago outside the bar where we met in Amarillo, TX. Can this be just a coincidence? If so, it's totally creepy!

Grace closed the diary and considered what the entry might mean. Why would Stephanie think John Dickson's or Ray Turner's deaths—

a year apart—had anything to do with her? Had Vincent been acting differently toward her? Did she think her husband might have been the one who'd killed Harve Thompson? Did she think jealousy might have provoked him to follow her, and to kill two of her other lovers?

Grace had a sudden thought: *Just how many of Stephanie's other lovers have suffered a similar fate?*

She would have to check it out on the computer. A glance at her watch showed it was nearly 5:00 a.m. The computer would have to wait. She needed some sleep. She was exhausted.

Even if it turned out Vincent Harkness *was* the Cancer Society killer, Grace had no idea how she was going to prove he'd come after her father and ended up somehow also killing her stepmother. Without the gun used in the crime, which was probably long gone down some sewer, or a confession—fat chance of that!—she was going to have a hard time clearing her name.

And if you're wrong about Harkness? If this is all a wild goose chase?

That thought was too terrifying to consider. If it wasn't Harkness who'd killed her parents, she had nowhere else to turn.

Grace lay down on her bed and tried to get some sleep, but her brain was too busy running possible scenarios for how Big Mike might have been killed.

What if Stephanie-the-sex-addict had ended up in bed with Big Mike? And Allie had come home and let Vincent in and *blam! blam! blam!* But that would mean Stephanie *knew for a fact* her husband was a killer. And her diary didn't seem to bear that out.

Grace realized she wasn't going to be able to sleep until she'd finished reading the diary. She got out of bed, went to the study, and sat down again with the book in her lap.

She read until the sun came up and seared her tired eyes, but there were no more comments by Stephanie in different-colored ink. There was nothing to suggest that Vincent Harkness was guilty of anything more reproachful than ignoring his wife in bed.

It was time to ask Breed Grayhawk for help.

9

Breed's curiosity about Grace *Smith's* identity had kept him from getting a good night's sleep. He'd resisted the urge Friday night to go straight to the JTTF computers to find out who she really was. He wasn't going to give a perfect stranger that much importance in his life.

He woke up Saturday morning with the same urge but resisted it again. He picked up a late breakfast at a drive-thru window, aware that even if he headed to the office, he couldn't stay long, because he had a two o'clock birthday party to attend an hour's drive south in San Antonio. A birthday party that put a knot in his stomach, because his supposed biological father, King Grayhawk, would be there.

But Breed had promised Kate Grayhawk Pendleton's twin boys, Lucky and Chance, that he would be there to celebrate their eighth birthday. No matter how unpleasant and uncomfortable the day was going to be, he intended to keep his promise.

Kate was the daughter of Breed's elder half sister Libby, and thus his niece, even though, at twenty-nine, she was a few years older than him. They'd become friends after his mother dropped him off at his elder brother North's ranch near Austin when he was sixteen—and forgot to come back for him.

It was bad enough that King was going to be at the twins' party, but he wouldn't be alone. A plethora of Kate's relatives—who barely tolerated each other—were also planning to attend.

Breed was nearly to I-35 South, which would take him, in about an hour, from Austin to San Antonio, when he saw the JTTF office from the corner of his eye. He'd promised to come early to help Kate set up for the party, so he didn't have time to satisfy his curiosity about Grace *Smith*.

At the last second, he jerked the wheel to make the turn to the JTTF office, swearing as he nearly sideswiped a car parked on the corner. He'd never make it through the day if he didn't find out the truth about Grace. Once he'd solved the mystery of who she was, he could put the damned woman behind him once and for all.

To his chagrin, when he did a National Crime Information Center computer search at the JTTF office, the Michigan license plate on Grace's car turned out to be stolen. It was registered to a white Ford Bronco in Detroit.

"Shit," he said.

He felt the knot in his stomach tighten as he wondered what he'd gotten himself into. A stolen tag? A phony name? What was she trying to hide? *Who was she?*

Luckily, the JTTF had an MOU—Memorandum of Understanding—with the university that allowed them access to campus databases.

Breed went through every college photo of a *Grace—middle or last name*—on file but saw no one who looked like his Grace. Which was when he conceded with disgust that *Grace* was probably a phony name, too. With more than fifty thousand students registered for the current school year, it wasn't going to be easy to find her through a search of the campus computer without a photo to use for comparison.

She'd had a stolen plate. She'd taken him to a place she didn't live. She didn't have a phone. She'd apparently given him a false name. The woman clearly didn't want to be found. Maybe he ought to let the whole thing go.

Then he thought about what else she'd told him. What else she might have lied about. *I'm protected.* The damned woman might be running around right now with his child growing inside her!

Thinking back, Breed realized how little information Grace had revealed about herself. Not that he'd asked for any. He'd wanted one thing from her, and she'd given that to him in a more than memorable way. Leaving him in her debt.

And her—maybe—pregnant.

But honestly, what were the chances one stupid act on his part would have the kind of consequences he was imagining? He ought to forget about her. Forget about the evening. File the whole episode under "strange but inconsequential."

Breed growled in frustration. If there was any chance at all he had a kid growing in that woman's belly, he wanted to know about it. He would never condemn a child of his to life with a mother who got pregnant during a one-night stand. He knew way too much about how an unwanted child might suffer.

He swore and sat bolt upright. He had another source of information about Grace as close as the phone.

Breed called information on his cell and let the service connect him to Digger's. He glanced at his watch and saw it was eleven o'clock in the morning. He wondered what time Digger's opened. When Jimmy Joe picked up on the first ring, he wondered if it ever closed.

He cleared his throat and said, "This is Breed Grayhawk. Last night I was sitting at the bar with a woman named Grace. Can you tell me her last name?"

"You didn't get it?" Jimmy Joe asked.

Instead of responding with the sarcasm on the tip of his tongue, Breed said calmly, "No, I didn't."

"Too bad. 'Cause I don't know it either."

"What about the name on her driver's license? You must have carded her when she came into Digger's."

"Of course I did," Jimmy Joe said. "The first time. But that was almost a year ago. And I don't look at names, just dates."

"How old is she?" Breed asked.

"Best I can recall, she was twenty-one when I carded her."

At least she wasn't jailbait, Breed thought with relief. Unless the driver's license was phony, too.

"Was the ID fake?" Breed asked, knowing that the bartender might have accepted an ID he recognized as fake, just to have the extra business.

Jimmy Joe snorted, aware, Breed suspected, of what he was asking him to admit. "Didn't look it to me," the bartender said.

"Anything you can tell me about her?" Breed said.

"Why're you so interested?" Jimmy Joe asked. "She steal something from you?"

My self-respect. "I just want to contact her."

"She's only been in here maybe a half-dozen times over the past year," Jimmy Joe said. "Never talked much. Just drank shots, like she did tonight. Then left."

"Left with other men?" Breed asked, feeling his stomach knot at the thought.

"Naw. Never before. Just last night. With you."

"She ever come in with anybody?" Breed asked.

Jimmy Joe paused, then said, "Yeah. Once, about three months ago. I remember 'cause he was in a wheelchair, and they sat at a table instead of the bar."

Well, Breed thought. That was something. He could check the various governmental databases for handicapped students, for handicapped permits for parking, and for handicapped driver's licenses.

"What did he look like?" Breed asked, grabbing a pen and a piece of paper to write down a description. "You get a name?"

"She called the kid Troy. No last name mentioned. I remember the name," Jimmy Joe said, " 'cause of the Dallas Cowboys quarterback. You know, Troy Aikman?"

"She was with a *kid?*" Breed said, focusing on the adjective the bartender had used for Troy.

"He seemed a lot younger than her. Fuzz for a beard. Black hair, dark brown eyes. Maybe 160 pounds. Don't know how tall. Average height maybe. T-shirt, jeans, and tennis shoes. Very polite."

"But he was old enough to drink?" Breed asked, hearing the skepticism in his voice.

There was a long silence on the other end of the line. "He was in a wheelchair," Jimmy Joe said at last.

"So you didn't card him." Breed made it a statement rather than a question.

"I'm not admitting anything," Jimmy Joe said.

"I'm not out to bust you, Jimmy Joe," Breed said. "I just want to find the girl. What else can you tell me about Troy?"

"He's a paraplegic, not a quad. And the wheelchair was new."

"Did he do the driving? Or did she?"

"I saw her get the wheelchair out of the trunk of her car."

"The dark blue, foreign-made—"

"Naw. This car was red. A Pontiac, I think. The one she's driving now is dark blue. Some little foreign thing."

Breed gritted his teeth. So much for getting the make and model of her car from Jimmy Joe. Had she been driving a stolen car last night, to go along with the stolen plate? What had happened to the red Pontiac? "Anything else you can remember?"

"Every time she was in here, she seemed to be celebrating something," Jimmy Joe said.

"Celebrating?"

"Yeah," Jimmy Joe said. "Heard her mention 'another one biting the dust.' "

"That's all you've got?"

"Maybe you can ask her what she meant when you find her," Jimmy Joe said.

"If she comes in again, don't tell her I asked about her, just call me," Breed said, giving Jimmy Joe his cell phone number.

"Why should I?" Jimmy Joe said.

Being undercover on campus, Breed never mentioned his FBI or JTTF connections. He used the one reason he thought might make Jimmy Joe call him if Grace showed up. "She might be carrying my kid."

Jimmy Joe chuckled. "Must have been some night last night."

"Good-bye, Jimmy Joe."

Breed pulled up the Texas Department of Motor Vehicles database and did a driver's license search for a male with the first or middle name Troy. Breed suspected a lot of kids in Texas had been named Troy after the Dallas Cowboys quarterback became popular, but only a few of them would be old enough to be driving.

The results were encouraging. Only 142 Troys with Texas driver's licenses. He limited the search to those under thirty, with black hair and brown eyes, who were also handicapped. To his surprise, that left him with three males.

Breed looked at the first driver's license photo, which featured a smiling, clean-shaven boy with too-close-set brown eyes and a large, bulbous nose. Troy Grover was eighteen, 5'6" and weighed 220 pounds. Jimmy Joe had said the boy was "average." He might have missed the close-set eyes, but nobody would have forgotten that big nose. Probably not his boy.

He checked the second, Troy Carter. He was 5'8" and weighed 165. A little more average. His brown eyes were so light they were almost hazel, and his black hair had been streaked with a white blond. He was wearing a nose ring and an eyebrow stud in his photo and had a Chinese tattoo visible on his neck. Definitely not his boy.

The third photo pictured a solemn boy with peach fuzz on his cheeks and chin and under his nose. He had short, curly black hair and eyes so dark brown he seemed to have no irises. Troy McMahon, despite his ordinary American name, had a faintly Middle Eastern appearance, with a hawk nose, skin a dark shade of brown, and heavy black brows.

Breed made a face. These days, he saw terrorists everywhere. He reminded himself that the kid was in a wheelchair and went through the rest of the information on the license. Troy McMahon, 5'10", 160 pounds, brown eyes, black hair, lived in Austin, Texas. In Jester East.

Well, well, well.

Maybe Grace had stopped by to see Troy last night. He would have to make a visit himself to Mr. McMahon. And see if the young man—he was only twenty—could help him find the mysterious Grace.

Breed heard a beep that meant a fax was coming through the JTTF machine. He didn't even glance up, because he figured Steve, the UT cop assigned full-time to the JTTF force, who was manning the office over the weekend, would pick it up. He saw on his computer that he'd received an instant message from Vince Harkness. He was about to open it when he heard Steve shout, "Holy shit!"

Breed called out, "What's up?"

"You gotta see this!"

Breed headed for the fax room, but Steve met him in the hall holding up two faxed pages.

"Someone phoned in an anonymous tip to the FBI here in Austin," he said. "A woman named Merle Raye Finkel is planning to blow up the president when he comes to town. We've got an honest-to-God terrorist threat to investigate!"

Breed could understand Steve's excitement. Contrary to what the public might think, terrorist threats didn't come across their desks every day. As Breed's report on JTTF activities to the San Antonio SAC had made clear, the JTTF hadn't come across a single terrorist threat in two years.

This was something new. This might be the "real deal."

Breed read the fax again and frowned. "This is a threat against the president's life. Why are we getting this? Why isn't this going straight to the Secret Service?"

"Maybe they got it, too. There's a cover note here from Vince," Steve said.

Breed took the fax pages from Steve and read the handwritten note from Vince on the bottom of the cover page.

> *I figure this falls under our "background on anarchists and white supremacists" assignment from the San Antonio SAC. I don't see why we should have to take a backseat on this one, so it's all yours.*

Good luck! Keep me in the loop and let me know if you find anything—anything at all—that makes it look like this woman might be a genuine threat to the president. Vince.

"I guess we've got work to do," Breed said.

"All right!" Steve said, pumping his fist.

Breed slid the second fax page aside and realized that what he'd thought were two pages of information was really three. He froze when he saw the enlarged photograph on the third page. He recognized the mug shot. It was the woman with whom he'd enjoyed carnal knowledge last night.

Her real name was Merle Raye Finkel.

And she was a convicted double murderer.

10

The girl in the mug shot was much younger than the woman Breed had met last night, and her face was bruised and cut. He put a finger on the cut at her eyebrow. And the one by her mouth. And the bump at the bridge of her nose. It was his Grace, all right.

Breed felt physically ill.

Merle Raye Finkel had been convicted of the double murder of her father and stepmother and had spent eight years at Giddings. She'd been released on adult parole. And then disappeared.

Not quite, Breed thought. She'd spent the past year in the Austin area, visiting Digger's every time "another one bit the dust." Another *what?* he wondered.

Grace hadn't struck him as the killer type. *But she was.* Or the type to blow people up. *But maybe he was wrong about that, too.* He would have to find her to find out the truth.

Breed felt bile rise in his throat as he realized—suddenly and certainly—that it was no coincidence that he'd run into Grace Smith last night.

She set me up! Merle Raye Finkel knew exactly who I was when she offered sex in exchange for a "favor." What the hell does she want from me? Is she hoping to blackmail me into helping her with whatever crazy scheme she has in mind? She can dream on. That isn't going to happen!

But at the very least, his position as SSA of the JTTF was compromised. He should call Vince immediately and put him on notice about his sexual encounter with Merle Raye Finkel.

Which would likely get him—just as immediately—excused from participation in the search for the woman, Breed realized. Despite all his grumbling about Craig Westwood, ASAC Vincent Harkness ran his satellite FBI office every bit as much by the book as the San Antonio SAC.

Besides, Breed wanted to be the one to find Merle Raye Finkel. He didn't like being manipulated. Or made to play the fool. He was going to take great relish in snapping the cuffs on her. The icing on the cake was that when he brought her in, he'd be doing his small part to protect the president of the United States.

Breed had learned long ago that it was easier to ask for forgiveness than permission. He already had a lead on Merle Raye Finkel. The moment he handed her over to his boss would be soon enough to tell Vince how he'd met Merle Raye Finkel, aka Grace Smith.

"Did the caller give us any clue where to start looking for her?" Steve asked, studying the faxes over Breed's shoulder.

"Nope." But Breed had a good idea where he was going to start looking. He had an address on his desk for Troy McMahon. He headed down the hall, laid the fax pages in the Xerox machine, and ran himself a copy of both the photo and the information that had come with it.

"I wonder what she did to get herself noticed," Steve said.

"Who knows? What difference does it make?" Breed took the copies and handed the fax pages back to Steve.

"I mean, did she try to buy nitrate fertilizer or steal some C-4 to make herself a bomb, or what?"

"Guess we'll find out. Call up the whole team, Steve," Breed said. "Get them in here and get them to work."

"Will do," Steve replied. "You want me to call in reinforcements from anywhere? We've got access to CIA, DIA, Air Force OSI, ATF, Secret Service—"

"God, not the Secret Service!" Breed said. "Or anyone else, for that matter. Not yet. Unless you want to find yourself sitting here twiddling your thumbs, while somebody else grabs the ball from us and trots off with it. Vince wants us to handle this. So we're going to handle it. There'll be time enough to call in everybody else on Monday, if we can't find this woman."

Breed intended to do some snooping on his own. Especially since he had a source who might be able to tell him where to find Merle Raye Finkel.

He stopped long enough on his way out the door to open the instant message from Vince, which turned out to be the same information that had just been faxed to the office. With another note appended: *Contact me immediately when you locate Merle Raye Finkel. I'm counting on you.*

Breed grabbed his Stetson from the antler hat rack and headed for the door.

"Where you going in such a hurry?" Steve asked.

"Birthday party for two eight-year-olds," Breed called back. With a quick stop to ask a few questions about Merle Raye Finkel on the way.

"At least you've got your priorities straight," Steve said with a grin.

"Always," Breed shot back. He intended to find Merle Raye Finkel without interference from a half-dozen other special agents and a dozen other law enforcement agencies. He wanted her all to himself long enough to ask some questions. Then he'd be happy to turn her over to the FBI.

He couldn't believe he'd had sex with a convicted murderer last night. A woman suspected of being a terrorist. Who might also be the mother of his child.

He had to find Grace Smith before someone else did and ask her how the hell she'd ended up on a terrorist watch list.

And what the hell she wanted from him.

11

～

Breed wondered if Troy McMahon would be in his room this close to lunchtime. He had his answer when he knocked on Troy's Jester East door and a male voice called out, "Come in!"

Breed had already chambered a round in the Glock 22 he carried in a special holster in his boot. He took a deep breath and let it out, to calm his racing heart, then let himself into the room. The young man inside, who sat in a wheelchair, didn't match the description he had of Troy McMahon. "Troy?" he said.

The blond-headed boy, who wore tortoiseshell glasses, gave him a wide, guileless smile. "I'm Harry Gunderson," he said. "Troy's meeting with his group at the Union."

"His group?" Breed questioned.

The smile disappeared, and a frown formed on Harry's brow. "Was Troy expecting you?"

"I'm a friend of a friend of his," Breed said.

The kid waited expectantly and Breed said, "Grace."

The smile returned. "Oh, yeah. It's Grace's group he's meeting with."

Breed barely resisted saying, "Grace's group?" If he was Grace's friend, he should know about her group. *Terrorist group?* he wondered. "How long ago did Troy leave?"

"Oh, you're not late. They're meeting at the Union Underground at eleven thirty for lunch."

"Thanks," Breed said. "Guess I'll see him there." Breed could see another question forming on Harry's lips and let himself out before the kid could ask. His heart was beating a hard tattoo and his hands had knotted themselves into fists.

He told himself he was making mountains out of molehills. What kind of terrorist group met out in the open for lunch? What kind of terrorist group had a nonmember who knew they existed and told perfect strangers where and how to find them? It had to be some other kind of group. But what kind? Greenpeace? Bridge? Or the kind that fomented insurrection and solved problems by setting off bombs?

Breed's gut told him it wasn't something innocuous. Not when Grace Smith—a convicted double murderer who'd given him a false name, a false address, and had a stolen plate on what he assumed was a stolen car—was its leader.

Breed walked the four blocks to the Texas Union building, site of the infamous Texas Tower, where a lone sniper had terrorized the campus in the sixties, wondering what he would find when he got there.

Universities had always been a source of radical thought and militant behavior, and UT was no exception. Students were the right age to be idealistic enough to pick up a banner and march for a revolutionary cause. That was why a JTTF had been created on campus, to observe and infiltrate, if necessary, any groups on campus that might be a breeding ground for terrorism—foreign or domestic.

Breed wondered how large Grace's group was and why he'd never heard of it, especially if they met in the Union. The six FBI members of the JTTF, along with Steve, the one campus cop currently assigned to the team, took turns eating at the Union to familiarize themselves with the students who gathered there, and to identify any groups that met on a regular basis.

He wondered if someone else on the JTTF had noticed Grace's group in the past. Perhaps there was even a record of it on file. He would check on that later. Right now, he intended to see for himself.

As he turned the corner onto Guadalupe Street, also known as the

Drag, his cell phone rang. He saw on the caller ID that it was Vince Harkness.

He answered the phone with, "What's up?"

"I called because we've got work to do," Vince asked. "I sent you an IM, but I wanted to make sure you were aware that we got an anonymous tip—"

"I'm working on it now."

"I thought you were off today," Vince said.

"I've got—" Breed didn't want to admit he had a lead, because he was certain Vince would send someone—make that a helluva lot of FBI special agents—to help him explore it. "I thought I'd take a look around campus, see if I can spot her in any of the usual gathering spots. Weren't you supposed to be at your cabin on Lake LBJ this weekend?"

"I'm not completely out of the loop when I'm not in the office," Vince replied. "With the president in town on Wednesday, I figured I'd better check this out."

"I'll let you know if anything breaks," Breed said.

"This may be nothing, Breed. But if it's something, I want it handled right. Let's not foul it up."

"I hear you."

"If you locate her, give me a heads-up," Vince said.

"You got it." Breed hung up the phone. Now he was keeping crucial information from the guy at the top. And Vince was not only his boss, but his mentor and friend.

When he'd been trying to make up his mind whether or not to join the FBI or opt for the Texas Department of Public Safety, which was the route he needed to travel to become a Texas Ranger, it was Vince who'd convinced him to go with the FBI. He'd spent time with Vince and Stephanie and the kids at their cabin on Lake LBJ, and Vince's family had come with him to Grayhawk Fourth of July picnics at his older brother North's ranch west of Austin.

Breed hated like hell keeping anything from Vince. But he had a feeling he was going to find himself in a shitstorm when the truth got out about his amorous interlude with a woman who'd turned out to be a terrorist suspect. And the later he had to face it, the better.

Because it was Saturday, the Texas Union wasn't busy, and it was easy to pick out several tables of students that might be the ones he was looking for. He didn't see Grace at any of them. He headed for the only group that included a student in a wheelchair.

As he approached the table, the boy in the wheelchair, who matched the description of Troy McMahon, said, "Is there something I can do for you?"

"I'm looking for Grace," Breed said.

"Did she send you here?" Troy asked.

Breed sidestepped the question. "Do you know where I can find her?"

"We're in the middle of a meeting," he said. "If Grace sent you, you're welcome to join us."

Breed glanced from innocent-looking teenage face to innocent-looking face and asked, "What kind of group is this?"

"We're called the Victims for Vengeance," a blond girl said.

Breed wondered how long the group had been meeting, and why, with a name like that, he hadn't heard of it before. Surely one of the JTTF guys must have noticed them if they met in the Union on any kind of regular basis. It sounded like a group that might foment exactly the kind of violence the JTTF had been created to thwart.

"Would you like to sit down?" the blond girl asked, gesturing to an empty chair beside her.

"I'd be interested to hear what you have to say," Breed said. "If you don't mind."

"No problem, man," Troy said. "Any friend of Grace's is a friend of ours."

Breed found a chair across the table from the blond girl, which put his back to the wall and gave him a good view of the rest of the Union, in case Grace showed up. He turned to Troy and said,

"Would you introduce me to everybody?" Might as well get names, if he could.

"I'm Troy McMahon," Troy volunteered. "Victim of a hit-and-run. Cops never found the guy who ran me down and left me paralyzed."

"I'm Christy Wheatland," the pretty blond said. "Victim of rape. He hasn't been caught."

"Rudy Franklin," a freckle-faced redhead said. "Gunshot victim. Convenience store robbery. Never caught the guy." He held up a hand with three fingers missing.

"ATM robbery and aggravated assault victim," a brunette with one apparently glass brown eye said, focusing on Breed with the other, not quite matching, brown eye. "Son of a bitch got away clean. Oh, and I'm Susan Garrity."

"How did you all meet Grace?" Breed asked.

"She kind of found us, one at a time," Troy said. "Got us all together. Gave us a goal."

"Which is?" Breed prodded.

"To find the people who victimized us and bring them to justice," the blond girl said.

"I'm surprised Grace isn't here," Breed said.

"Oh, she doesn't come all the time," the brown-eyed brunette said.

"Why not?" Breed asked.

"She's busy investigating leads," the freckle-faced boy said. "Doing the job the cops didn't finish."

Breed frowned. *Grace, the convicted double murderer, is playing cop?*

"I can see you're skeptical," Troy said. "We all were at first. But Grace is good. She's found leads the cops didn't find in every one of our cases."

"What happened to you?" the freckle-faced boy said.

Breed realized they were waiting for him to reveal how he'd become a victim. "Uh." He shoved his shirt collar aside and revealed the ugly scar from a wound he'd gotten when he was ten and one of his drunken mother's many drunken boyfriends had accidentally shot him. "Carjacking," he said. "Cops never found the bastard."

"Bummer," Troy said.

"Grace didn't make it clear to me. What, exactly, is the purpose of the Victims for Vengeance?" he asked.

"We're a support group for each other," the pretty blond said.

"That's all?" Breed said.

"Until we find the criminals who committed the crimes against us," Troy said.

"And when you do find them?" Breed said.

"An eye for an eye," the brunette with the glass eye said.

"A chance for the guy who hit me and ran to see what it's like to spend his life sitting instead of standing," Troy said.

"Or what it's like to play the piano without all your fingers," the redheaded boy said, waggling his two-fingered hand.

"I see. You want vengeance," Breed said. *Maybe vengeance against the government that hasn't protected them? So they plan to bomb the president—and the nation's governors, and a thousand or so others who'll be there to hear him speak—to smithereens, to make some sort of statement?*

"Grace has been teaching us investigative techniques," Troy said.

"Such as?" Breed asked.

"How to go door-to-door and ask questions," Troy said.

"How to research DNA evidence," the pretty blond girl said.

"How to review video evidence of a crime," the freckle-faced boy said.

"How to trace the origins of a weapon," the brunette with the glass eye said.

"I see," Breed said. "She's made junior cops out of you."

Troy took an indignant breath and said, "We wouldn't have to do the cops' job for them if they'd done it themselves."

"Are you saying your crime wasn't investigated?" Breed asked.

"They quit looking when they didn't find the doer," Troy said.

"But you won't stop looking," Breed said.

The girl with the glass eye shook her head. "Not ever."

"No matter what you have to do?" Breed said.

"We're not doing anything illegal," Troy said.

Breed looked at them, one at a time, and said, "You're talking about vigilante justice."

"You have some problem with that?" Troy said.

Breed avoided the question by asking, "How many of you are close to finding the offender who victimized you?"

"None of us," Troy admitted.

"That's why we're a support group," the pretty blond said.

"I really just want to find Grace," Breed said.

"You can't," Troy said.

"You must have some way of reaching her. A phone number, an e-mail—"

Every head at the table was shaking no.

"You don't find that a bit odd?" Breed asked.

"She has her reasons for staying under the radar," Troy said.

"Which are?" Breed watched as the Victims for Vengeance exchanged glances, apparently deciding if they were going to tell this newest member—a perfect stranger—what they knew about their leader.

At last the freckle-faced boy said to the others, "She wouldn't have told him how to find us if she didn't intend to tell him everything."

Breed sat forward on his seat, but he didn't rush them.

"Grace spent time in prison—" Troy began.

"In juvie," the brunette corrected.

"In Giddings," Troy amended, not bothering to hide his annoyance. "For the murder of her father and stepmother."

"Sounds to me like she was the criminal, and the cops found her and put her away," Breed said. "What's she doing in a group like—"

"Grace was *innocent*," Troy interrupted.

"She was convicted on circumstantial evidence," the freckle-faced boy said. "The gun used to commit the crime was never found. The police never even looked for another suspect. They went after Grace because she'd run away from home after her father nearly beat her to death."

Breed's disbelief must have shown on his face, because Troy's eyes narrowed and he continued, "For the past year, since she got out of jail—juvie," he corrected, glancing at the brunette, whose mouth was already open to correct him, "she's been hunting for the real murderer."

"And she's getting close to finding him," the pretty blond said.

Breed wondered just how much of her story Grace had shared with them. For instance, whether she'd told them her real name. And that she was violating her parole.

Had one of them sent the anonymous message to the FBI? Did one—or more—of these Victims for Vengeance know that Grace was planning to bomb the LBJ Auditorium during the president's visit? Were they in on it with her?

If so, he couldn't imagine why they were meeting so publicly, or why they'd invited a stranger to join their group. He needed to report back to Vince what he'd discovered so far and get help from the rest of the JTTF to surveil the group. "Is everybody here today?" Breed asked. "I mean, have I met all the Victims for Vengeance?"

"All except Grace," Troy said.

"You didn't bring lunch?" the pretty blond said, holding up a brown paper sack.

"I can't stay today." Breed glanced at his watch. "I'm already late for a birthday party. When and where is the next meeting?"

"So you want to join?" Troy asked.

"Yeah. Sure," Breed replied.

"Grace called to say she wasn't coming today, because she found some new evidence that affects her case," Troy said. "She promised she'd tell us all about it tomorrow afternoon."

"Where?" Breed said.

"She's supposed to call me sometime today," Troy said. "I'll get the word out to everyone. Be sure I have your cell number before you take off."

Breed gave it to him, then stood and said, "I'm looking forward to the next meeting." *When I will see Grace Smith again face-to-face. And take Merle Raye Finkel into custody.*

The Victims for Vengeance smiled and waved as they sent him on his way.

12

～

"I thought this was going to be a *small* family celebration, Kate. Now I find out you've invited not just one of your illustrious grandfathers, but both of the sons of bitches."

Kate Grayhawk Pendleton ground her teeth, then unclenched her jaw and managed a smile for her mother-in-law, Texas Governor Ann Wade Pendleton. Kate avoided looking in the direction of the Texas DPS officer on the governor's protective detail who stood at the edge of her backyard patio, looking outward to make sure no one snuck up and assassinated the governor.

The man was clearly looking in the wrong direction, Kate thought, as she resisted the urge to strangle the woman who'd been the bane of her existence for the past nine years. Ann Wade had come early for the twins' birthday party but seemed disinclined to help.

Her mother-in-law had to be too warm in the black St. John knit suit, nylon stockings, and Chanel pumps she was wearing, but Kate had never seen her dressed any less formally. Her short, naturally blond hair was perfectly coiffed, and her makeup, on a surgically enhanced face, was subtle and impeccable.

Ann Wade made Kate, who was dressed in a white blouse with a red V-neck sleeveless sweater pulled over it, Levi's, and white Keds without socks, feel like a frump.

Kate tried to keep the resentment out of her voice as she explained, "Grandpa King would have had to leave Wyoming for Austin in a few days anyway, for the NGA Annual Meeting. So he decided to come early to be here for the twins' birthday party."

"I would gladly have postponed my meeting with King Gray-hawk," her mother-in-law drawled in the East Texas accent she'd ac-quired growing up in the piney woods near Houston, "and greeted him as one governor to another in Austin. What's the other son of a bitch's excuse for leaving that South Texas ranch the size of Vermont he's so attached to and showing up here?"

"I wish you wouldn't use that word to—"

"Don't tell me you're happy they're both coming," Ann Wade in-terrupted. "When King Grayhawk and Jackson Blackthorne are in the same room together, it's like standing bare-assed in a nest of rat-tlers. You don't know which way to jump."

"I love them both very much," Kate said, cutting off her mother-in-law's rant. "And Lucky and Chance are over the moon that both of their great-grandfathers will be here."

But Ann Wade was not far wrong in her estimation of the behavior Kate expected from the two powerful adversaries. Ever since Black-jack had stolen Eve DeWitt away from King when they were young men, marrying her to get his hands on her dowry of fifty thousand acres of rich DeWitt grassland, they'd been mortal enemies.

Over the years, King had married four times looking for some-one to replace Eve. None of the marriages had taken. Kate's mother Libby, and her uncles North and Matthew, were the children of King's first wife, Jane. The marriage to his second wife, Leonora, didn't really count, because it had been annulled.

Sassy had come next. She'd borne Kate's uncle Breed Grayhawk.

King's fourth and last wife Jill had presented him with three kids in five years before she'd run off with one of King's cowhands. Taylor, Gray, and Victoria were better known for their youthful escapades in Jackson Hole, Wyoming, as King's Brats. Kate hardly knew the Brats, who were now in their twenties. They pretty much stayed around Kingdom Come, King's ranch in Wyoming.

It seemed to Kate that Grandpa King had lived most of his life mad and miserable. She'd been directly affected by his vow of re-venge against Blackjack when King had prevented Kate's father,

Clay Blackthorne, from marrying Kate's mother, Libby Grayhawk, when she was pregnant with Kate. It had been King's aim to deprive Blackjack of his grandchild. But it was her mother who'd suffered the most, by being separated from the man she loved.

Grandpa King had gone nearly insane with rage and grief when Eve DeWitt, threatened with divorce by Blackjack, had committed suicide. Grandpa Blackjack had asked for the divorce in order to marry the true love of his life, Ren Creed, which he'd done. There was more to the story than anyone had told Kate when she was a child, but things had pretty much gone downhill from there between her grandfathers. Putting them together in the same room was asking for trouble.

To complicate matters, her parents, who'd finally gotten married nine years ago—after spending twenty years apart—were coming to the twins' party, too. The tension was always palpable whenever her mother confronted Blackjack or her father confronted King. Her parents had promised to be on their best behavior, but they'd warned her they couldn't be held responsible if her grandfathers provoked them.

Needless to say, Kate hadn't slept much last night.

She'd begged Breed to come and help referee. He'd snorted at the suggestion that he could be of any help. She hadn't needed to force the tears of stress that had fallen. Breed had hidden any sympathy he felt behind a stoic face, but he'd agreed to come to the party and do what he could to keep murder from being done.

Kate hoped to do Breed a favor in return. She'd long ago vowed to reconcile her uncle with his father, King Grayhawk. It had not only been difficult. It had been impossible. The two men managed never to be in the same place at the same time. She'd wanted Breed to come to the twins' birthday party because her house was so small he wouldn't be able to avoid King.

Kate had spent enough time haranguing Breed that she'd heard all the reasons why he wanted nothing to do with his father. First and foremost, King Grayhawk had abandoned him at birth. Kate knew for a fact that King had experienced second thoughts about kicking the baby out with the bathwater, so to speak.

He'd been in a jealous rage when he'd abandoned Breed, thinking Sassy must have cheated on him. After the damage was done, King had remembered the great-great-grandfather who'd taken a Sioux bride, and realized it was entirely possible Breed might be his own get.

Kate hoped to bring the two men together for a few minutes at the party to see if some fence could be mended.

Kate sighed. Sometimes she wished she didn't have so much family. Especially family with so much animosity toward one another. Then she'd remember the years when she was growing up, and her mother was estranged from King and her father and everyone else, and she was grateful for what she had.

This was the twins' first birthday party since their father had died, and she was glad her sons would be surrounded by so much family. Even if at times, like now, she felt like tearing her hair out.

Ironically, at exactly the point when her parents had finally married each other, providing a perfect ending to their fairy-tale romance, her life had tumbled into a state of chaos when she'd precipitously married J. D. Pendleton.

Sometimes it was hard to be around her mom and dad, they seemed so happy with their two late-in-life children, Kate's eight-year-old half brother Houston and six-year-old half sister Dallas. Especially considering what a big mistake Kate had made choosing her own spouse.

She'd been ashamed to admit to her parents that they'd been right when they'd advised her not to marry so young, or so soon, after a handsome, blond-haired, blue-eyed campus stud had swept her off her feet. Which advice had, of course, caused her to rebel in a typically stupid teenage fashion.

In a fit of pique and resentment, Kate had married the wrong man—University of Texas quarterback J. D. Pendleton—when the right one—Texas Ranger Jack McKinley—had married someone else.

It hadn't taken her long to realize that J.D. had lived a spoiled, privileged life. And that he felt entitled to have things handed to him, rather than having to work for them. He'd cheated on her, discreetly, of course, with women too numerous to count. When she'd turned twenty-five, and he could get his hands on her trust fund, he'd gambled—and lost—it on risky ventures.

Kate would have continued to endure those humiliations without complaint if J.D. had been a good father to the twins. He was not. He'd considered his sons, who'd loved him dearly, a bother and a nuisance. Kate had felt responsible for the pain and confusion in their eyes when J.D. was "too busy" to spend time with them, because she was the one who'd chosen this man to be the father of her children.

When Kate had finally filed for divorce, J.D. had made it clear he would fight her. He wasn't about to let go of the steady stream of money and influence he expected her very powerful, and very rich, grandfathers to keep providing for their beloved granddaughter and her loving husband. J.D. had figured he would need their support someday when he ran for president of the United States.

He'd attacked the one area where she was most vulnerable, declaring that if she tried to divorce him, he would seek sole custody of the twins. "You'll be lucky if you see them again before they're twenty-one!" he'd threatened.

Of course, there was no guarantee J.D. could actually get sole custody. But the battle would have been nasty. And she had a secret that could ruin her if it was discovered. Besides, by then, J.D.'s mother was the governor of Texas and had as many powerful Texas state judges in her pocket, some of which she'd appointed, as Grandpa Blackjack did. Kate had backed off, resigned to her fate.

Then, suddenly and unexpectedly, she'd become a widow.

J.D. had been killed—in an explosion so devastating that his remains had needed to be identified using his DNA—while performing the military service he'd believed would help his candidacy. Kate had felt every bit as much relief as grief. And lived with a heavy load of guilt as a result.

Kate turned to face her mother-in-law and said, "I feel blessed that so much family is willing to be here to celebrate the twins' birthday. Especially this year. With J.D. gone."

Ann Wade exhaled a mouthful of smoke and stabbed out her cigarette in an ashtray on the patio table at which she sat. "We know who's to blame for those two boys being fatherless, don't we?"

Kate felt an ache in her chest and wasn't sure whether it was guilt or shame or just plain anger. Instead of making some retort, she finished hanging the donkey piñata from the porch beam and carefully came down the stepladder to the stone patio.

It was true that the day J.D. died, he and Kate had argued on the phone about huge Internet gambling losses J.D. had incurred while in Afghanistan. After J.D.'s death, Ann Wade had discovered e-mail evidence of the quarrel and blamed Kate for her son's distraction that day, which seemed to have led to the accident at the ammo dump that had caused his death.

"The fact my sons are fatherless," Kate finally replied in an even voice, "is all the more reason to want Grandpa Blackjack here, even if he's mean as a molting sidewinder to Grandpa King."

"Speak of the devil," Ann Wade muttered, staring at the sliding glass door that opened onto the patio.

Kate turned and found her grandfather Blackjack standing in the sliding glass doorway with his wife Ren beside him.

"Didn't expect to see you here, Blackjack, Ren," Ann Wade said, eyeing them over the filtered menthol cigarette she was lighting.

Blackjack was tall, with impressively broad, square shoulders at an age when most men had brittle bones that left them bent over. His face was deeply tanned and filled with crevices that seemed hewn from stone. His thick head of black hair had turned completely silver with age.

Ren's auburn hair was streaked with silver and captured in a French braid that ran halfway down her back. From the lines of experience on her face, no one would ever accuse her of using Botox or Restylane. Both were dressed casually in Western shirts, jeans, and boots.

"Ann Wade," Blackjack said with a curt nod, as Ann Wade squinted at him through a stream of exhaled smoke.

No love lost on either side, Kate realized.

Blackjack's piercing gray eyes searched Kate's face, and she quickly put on the mask she wore to conceal her feelings of failure from her family. She watched Blackjack's eyes narrow and his brow furrow and put a smile of welcome on her face to complete her disguise of well-being.

Fortunately, her grandparents were soon bracketed by Lucky and Chance, who were clamoring for attention. The eight-year-old boys were tall for their age, which was to be expected, considering their forebears were tall on both sides of the family. They had black hair and bright blue eyes that matched hers and were mischievous and fun-loving and bright.

"Tell us what you got us for our birthday, GeePa," Lucky begged.

"Did you get us our own horses, GeeMa?" Chance asked.

"Lucky! Chance!" Kate admonished. "Give your GeePa and GeeMa a chance to get settled before—"

"We gotta know, Mom," Lucky interrupted.

"We gotta know if we got horses," Chance said, as the two boys followed their grandparents outside onto the patio.

"You promised, GeePa!" Lucky said.

Kate had nowhere to stable horses in the city and no money to pay for their board and feed and all the other expenses that went along with owning not just one, but two horses. She was sure Blackjack and Ren would provide any financial support that was required, but she hated being any more indebted to them than she already was.

She'd tried to discourage her grandfather from buying the boys horses, but she'd known she was talking to a brick wall. Once he'd made up his mind to do something, it was as good as done. Blackjack looked at her, asking with his eyes for permission to tell her sons what they wanted to hear.

Kate tried to relax her smile, so it wouldn't look as brittle as it felt, and said, "Go ahead. I know you're dying to tell them."

He pulled pictures out of his breast pocket and handed one to each boy. "Big Doc," he said to Lucky, the elder twin by five minutes. "And Little Doc," he said to Chance. "Two of the best quarter horses in Texas."

"Yippee!" Chance said, leaping off the ground.

"Thank you, GeePa. Thank you, GeeMa," Lucky said as both boys threw themselves into the arms of their great-grandparents.

Kate kept the smile on her face with effort. "I presume you're keeping Big Doc and Little Doc at Bitter Creek, so the boys can ride them when they come visit."

"Hell, no!" Blackjack said. "What would be the point of that? I've got them boarded at a stable fifteen minutes from here. There's a nice covered arena where the boys can ride year-round."

When was she supposed to take them there? Kate wondered. She loved her work as a physical therapist at Brooke Army Medical Center, where she helped young soldiers, all veterans of the war in Iraq, learn to function without the limbs they'd lost fighting for their country. But by the end of each day, she was physically and emotionally exhausted.

And when she was done at work, her day was far from over. She still had to pick up the boys from after-school day care, supervise their homework, prepare dinner, do laundry and dishes, and get clothes and lunches ready for the next day.

The twins also had soccer, football, or baseball practice or games, depending on the season. Which didn't leave much time for horseback riding. It seemed a shame to give them horses that would sit in the stable getting fat.

But seeing the joy on the faces of Blackjack and Ren and her twin sons, she didn't have the heart to complain. "You've given the boys a wonderful gift. Thank you."

"Can we go see our horses now?" Lucky asked.

"Please?" Chance said.

Kate looked at her watch. It was about an hour before the party was scheduled to start, and if Blackjack and Ren left with the boys, she'd have a chance to smooth the waters between Ann Wade and her parents and King before they returned. "Do you mind taking them?" she asked Blackjack. "Just be back before the party starts."

"Aren't you coming, Mom?" Lucky said.

"I've got things to do here," she said. "You can tell me all about it when you get back."

Chance shot a look at her from worried eyes, but when Lucky grabbed his hand, he ran after him.

Once the sliding glass door was closed behind them, Ann Wade said, "Trust that son of a bitch to give your kids something that makes more work for you."

Kate was surprised because she didn't think Ann Wade gave a damn how much work Kate had to do. Then she realized her mother-in-law was jealous because Blackjack and Ren had managed to give the twins something better than whatever she was intending to give them. "I thought it was a very appropriate, generous gift," she said.

"Sure it was," Ann Wade said. "Oh, hell. The other son of a bitch is already here."

Kate whirled to see her grandfather King having trouble getting the sliding glass door open. She realized Blackjack must have accidentally locked it when he left. She wondered if the two men had run into each other in the house and realized she would have heard the commotion if they had.

"Where are my boys?" King demanded as he finally shoved the door open. He headed onto the patio trailed by a Wyoming Highway Patrol sergeant, one of the detail of bodyguards, known simply as the Detail, assigned to protect the Wyoming governor. Kate knew King had more than one bodyguard and assumed he'd left the rest of the Detail out front, where they'd be shooting the bull with the rest of Ann Wade's bodyguards.

"Lucky and Chance have gone out for a while before the party," Kate said as she hurried across the patio to hug her grandfather.

"I've got something for them out front," he said smugly. "Something they're going to want to see."

"What is it?" Kate asked.

"Two of the best quarter horses in Wyoming. Had them trailered down here for the occasion."

Ann Wade laughed, raised a brow, and said to Kate, "I'd like to see how you're going to get out of this one."

"Oh, dear," Kate said. Better to get the truth out now, so she could soothe ruffled feathers before the boys returned. "Blackjack had the same idea. The boys are off with him and Ren now," she said ruefully, "looking at two of the best quarter horses in Texas."

"Guess those boys'll have a choice which mount to ride," King said. "No doubt mine will become their favorites."

"Grandpa King, would you consider—"

"Just let me know where Blackjack has his nags stabled and I'll arrange to have these two magnificent animals stabled at the same place."

"Lucky and Chance don't need—"

"Are you telling me you're going to let Blackjack give my great-grandsons horses for their birthday and not me?" King demanded.

"I only thought—"

"I'll be damned if I allow that to happen!" King said.

"Hello there, King," Ann Wade interjected. "Welcome to Texas."

"I'm busy, Ann Wade," King said, not even glancing in her direction.

Kate raised her eyebrows in alarm at her grandfather's rudeness and made small, jerky gestures with her head toward Ann Wade, urging him to acknowledge her mother-in-law. She had to roll her eyes and mouth the word *Please* before King gave in.

King shot her a pained look, then turned to the Texas governor and said, "How're they hanging, Ann Wade?"

"Just fine," she replied, blowing out a stream of smoke.

King turned right back to Kate, who gave an exasperated sigh at her grandfather's suggestion that Ann Wade Pendleton had a set of male balls—which pretty much every opponent she'd ever faced in the political arena would concede she did. Kate laid a hand on her grandfather's forearm and said, "I know Lucky and Chance will—"

"They'll love my gift, that's for damned sure," King said.

Kate realized she'd lost the war before she'd even fought the first battle. She should have known better than to argue. "You're right," she said, tightening her grasp before releasing his arm. "They'll be delighted with your gift."

Which meant she was going to spend a lot of time driving back and forth to that stable. Maybe the boys would be willing to lease two of the horses to people who couldn't afford to buy one. And she felt sure Lucky and Chance would be willing to make all four horses available for one of the handicapped riding programs they participated in through Cub Scouts, extending their great-grandparents' generosity to benefit others.

"Hello!" she heard from inside the house. "Where are you, Kate?"

Kate felt a warm rush of feeling as she spied her father and mother. Clay Blackthorne was a federal judge in Austin, and she saw as he reached the sliding glass door that he had a deputy marshal with him for protection. She hated the thought of her father being in danger. It seemed he was always trying some high-profile case where his life was threatened. The deputy joined the other two bodyguards at the edge of the patio while Kate rushed to embrace her father.

She could feel the tension in his body as he eyed King over her shoulder and gave him a tighter hug. A hug that said "Please don't make trouble."

"Hello, King," her father said.

"Hello, Daddy," her mother said.

"Hello," King said. His reply could have been intended for either or both of them. Neither her parents nor King made a move any closer to the other. No one was shaking hands. No hugs were exchanged. But so far, everyone was being cordial.

"Ann Wade," her father said, nodding his head at the Texas governor.

Ann Wade nodded back.

"It's so nice to see you again," her mother said to Ann Wade.

Her mother smiled.

Ann Wade smiled back.

Kate breathed a silent sigh of relief. And stiffened at her father's next words.

"Who parked the horse trailer out front?"

"That would be Grandpa King," Kate said, slipping her arm through her father's, in case it was necessary to haul him away to avoid a confrontation. "The horses are his gifts to Lucky and Chance."

"Aw, hell," her father said, shooting daggers at King with his eyes. "I ought to be allowed the chance to buy my own grandsons their first horses, not have to battle it out with their great-grandfather."

"Great-grandfathers, plural," Ann Wade said with a chuckle.

"What?" her father said.

"Seems Blackjack had the same idea as King here," Ann Wade said, gesturing in King's direction with her cigarette. "Lucky and Chance are off right now taking a look at the quarter horses he's given them for their birthday."

"What about the two out front?" her father asked.

"I'm having them stabled at the same barn," King said. "It'll give the boys a choice of mount."

Her father turned to her and said, "Isn't that an embarrassment of riches?"

Kate shrugged. "What can I say? Which horses would you suggest I return?" She held up a hand when her father opened his mouth to reply. "Lucky and Chance love their great-grandfathers equally. They wouldn't want to hurt either one of them by rejecting his gift."

"How about not accepting either gift," Ann Wade suggested. "Send all four animals back where they came from."

Kate resisted the urge to glare at her mother-in-law, who was slinging barbed comments like a wayward child standing at a safe distance and poking a chained-up dog with a sharp stick. Kate felt furious but helpless, unable to snap back. If she didn't maintain her calm, all hell might break loose. She absolutely refused to let Ann Wade spoil the twins' birthday party.

"I didn't know about Grandpa King's gift when I let the boys accept Grandpa Blackjack's gift," Kate said. "It would be cruel to tell them now that the horses have to go back."

Besides which, the horses, while in no way able to replace their father, would help keep the boys busy and distracted from the empty chair at the supper table.

"Where did Mom go?" Kate asked her father, looking over his shoulder into the house.

"I'm right here," her mother said, stepping back onto the patio.

"Oh, no!" Kate said, staring at the adorable calico kitten her mother held in her arms.

"Oh, yes," her mother said, smiling sheepishly. "I thought the boys might like to have—"

"A cat," Ann Wade said derisively. "Along with a litter box, I'm sure, to stink up the house."

"Oh, I don't think—" her mother began. She stopped herself and turned to Kate. "I thought the boys might like to have a pet, and a cat seemed like less work for you than a dog."

"Thank you, Mom," Kate said, taking the mewing kitten from her mother's arms. "I know Lucky and Chance will love him."

"Her," her mother said.

Ann Wade snickered. "Naturally. Which means kittens in nine months or a year. This is priceless."

Kate turned to her parents and King and said, "Why don't you all go inside and get yourselves something to drink? The boys will be back in a little while. Here," she said, grabbing for the wriggling kitten, which had nearly escaped her grasp, and passing it back to her mother. "You'll want to have her nearby when the boys show up."

After she'd shut the sliding glass door behind her parents and King, she turned to her mother-in-law. "I don't appreciate the running commentary on my family's gifts to Lucky and Chance."

"I call them as I see them," Ann Wade said.

"I suppose you've come up with a better gift?" Kate snapped.

"The best," Ann Wade said.

Kate ground her teeth, telling herself she wouldn't ask. But when Ann Wade didn't speak, she finally said, "Well? What is it?"

"Ah. Here he is now."

Kate's heart missed a beat when she turned toward the sliding glass door and saw who'd arrived. "Jack!" she gasped.

Kate couldn't seem to breathe right. She'd only seen Jack McKinley in passing over the past nine years. Jack and Breed were good friends, but she'd made a point of avoiding any place Jack was going to be. Once upon a time, when she was a naive young girl of nineteen and Jack a mature man of thirty-two, she'd been in love with him.

That was before they'd both married other people.

At first, she'd been angry with Jack for marrying his high school sweetheart so soon after rejecting her. Then, she'd been ashamed of her ramshackle behavior, getting married to the first person who'd shown an interest in her after Jack's marriage. Finally, she hadn't wanted to hear how wonderful his life was. Or lie about her own.

It was shocking to see him in her home. On her patio. He'd been thirty-two the last time she'd seen him. She knew all his physical stats from the days when he'd been a pro football quarterback—6'3" and 212 pounds, with sun-streaked chestnut hair. Nine years later, he looked harder. More remote. Even less approachable than he'd been all those years ago.

He was in uniform, or as much of a uniform as the Texas Rangers ever wore—a crisp, white, long-sleeved Western-cut shirt tucked into Wrangler jeans, a black bolo tie with a silver and turquoise clasp, and black ostrich cowboy boots. His badge, a circled star pounded out of a silver Mexican *cinco peso* coin, was pinned over his heart, and a SIG-Sauer P226 rested in a tooled leather slide holster at his waist.

"Hello, Kate," he said. He touched his finger to the brim of his gray felt Stetson and said, "Governor."

"Hello, Sergeant McKinley," Ann Wade said. "I'm glad you could come."

Kate glanced at her mother-in-law, then back at Jack. "Have you brought Ann Wade's present for the boys?"

Ann Wade laughed. "Jack *is* the boys' present."

Kate put her hands on her hips as she confronted her mother-in-law. "What kind of joke is this?"

"With all due respect, Governor Pendleton—" Jack began.

"I suppose I should have explained what I wanted when I called your captain and told him to send you here," Ann Wade said to Jack. "But I wanted to surprise my daughter-in-law."

"What am I missing?" Kate asked. "Why is Jack here? What does he have to do with my sons?"

"Meet the newest member of the governor's protective service detail," Ann Wade said, gesturing toward Jack. "Assigned to protect the governor's grandsons."

"Are you out of your mind?" Kate said.

Ann Wade leaned back in her chair. "My grandsons need a male figure in their lives. I can't count on you to marry anytime soon. The only men around here are Grayhawks and Blackthornes, constantly at each other's throats. Sergeant McKinley is—"

"A Texas Ranger, ma'am," Jack said.

"I'm aware of that," Ann Wade said. "You're a hero, in fact. Both as a Texas Ranger—your exploits are legendary—and as a former pro quarterback. There is that blight on your reputation, when you were accused of shaving points in the Super Bowl. However, I believe if those accusations were true, the Rangers would never have made you one of their own. What I'm left with is a man who reminds me of my son. A male role model my grandsons can admire."

"I don't babysit," Jack said. "Ma'am," he added.

"I know about your almost-ex-wife taking your little boy off to Kansas," Ann Wade said. "That's a shame. But now that they're gone, you don't have any personal obligations to keep you from watching my grandsons twenty-four/seven."

"My sons don't need a bodyguard," Kate protested. She couldn't have Jack around night and day. They had a romantic history that would make Jack's presence not just uncomfortable but unbearable.

Ann Wade reached for another cigarette. "It's a done deal."

"What if I refuse?" Jack said.

"I suppose if you want to leave the Texas Rangers, that's your choice," Ann Wade said implacably.

Kate saw a muscle work in Jack's tightly clenched jaw. Ann Wade had him hog-tied, ready to burn her brand on his flesh. Kate didn't dare appeal to her father or grandfathers for help. If she did, all hell would break loose.

"How long do you see this assignment lasting, ma'am?" Jack asked.

"I've got another year to serve as governor," Ann Wade said.

"A year?" Jack said.

Ann Wade nodded. "Or until my daughter-in-law remarries. Whichever comes first."

"That's outrageous!" Kate said. "You're forcing me—"

"You're free to do as you like," Ann Wade said, rising at last. "I'm simply providing my grandsons with the protection they need, now that my son is no longer here to take care of them. It's hot out here. I hope you've got the air conditioner on inside."

"When does this assignment begin, ma'am?" Jack asked.

"Right now." Ann Wade tipped her head toward the boisterous sound of children's voices coming from the house. "If I'm not mistaken, the party is about to start."

13

~

Breed phoned his report in to Vince while driving south to San Antonio. "I assigned the six JTTF special agents to surveillance of the Victims for Vengeance. I figured if we want to keep the Secret Service and the San Antonio SAC from stealing this investigation away, it's better if I use only my own men.

"They have something to prove to the Feebees in San Antonio, who've kicked them aside this past week," Breed said. "They'll keep their mouths shut because they're glad to finally be seeing some action.

"I made sure they understood that if they say anything to anybody about the anonymous tip we got regarding Merle Raye Finkel, especially an FBI agent from another office—or anyone, for that matter— who might let slip what we're doing, they'll lose their chance to do some good."

"You're amazing," Vince said with a laugh.

"I had a good teacher," Breed said.

"I had a good student," Vince replied.

Breed wondered what Vince would say when he found out Breed had had a head start investigating Merle Raye Finkel. And that he knew her *real* up close and personal.

"Where are you now?" Vince asked.

"I'm headed for the twins' birthday party in San Antonio. I'll be back on the job in a couple of hours."

"Keep me in the loop."

"I will." Breed closed his cell phone and put the pedal to the metal.

It wasn't the balloons tied to the mailbox and waving in the wind that told Breed he'd arrived at Kate's house. It was all the Texas DPS and Wyoming protective detail cars and SUVs—and the pickup with horse trailer—parked in front of the modest three-bedroom home on live-oak-shaded Mulberry Street.

Breed was in awe of Kate because she'd invited her sons' powerful grandparents and great-grandparents, none of whom got along, to celebrate the twins' birthday this year. Even more amazing, they'd apparently showed up. Because of J.D.'s death, the gathering was fraught with a lot of emotion for Kate, so he'd agreed to come to support her. And the twins. He was sorry to be late, but it couldn't be helped. Kate would understand. He hoped.

Over the past year, Breed had gone along with Kate to the twins' T-ball and Pop Warner football games. He'd seen more cartoon movies than he could count. He'd been there for Lucky and Chance because their father hadn't—and never would be again.

And because he'd figured he owed them.

Breed had never told Kate how he'd taunted J.D. about how much harder it would be to get elected as the next president of the United States if he'd never served his country in the military. Not that it couldn't—hadn't—been done. But a few medals never hurt a candidate. J.D. had lapped it up. It had appealed to his vanity to imagine himself as a hero.

Breed hadn't counted on J.D. dying.

As he stepped onto the covered front porch, he checked in with the Texas governor's DPS bodyguard, who had Breed's name on a list of approved visitors, and said, "Would you mind keeping an eye on this fellow for a little while?"

Breed handed a leash to the DPS sergeant, at the end of which was a cavorting, sniffing, inquisitive black lab puppy Breed had brought as a gift for the twins. "I think he'll cause less havoc out here."

"That's for sure," the DPS bodyguard said with a grin as he took the leash. "Especially considering the calico kitten I saw being carried in there an hour ago."

"Oh, shit," Breed said.

"Yeah, bound to be lots of it, until the two of them get house-broken," the bodyguard said with a laugh.

"What's with the horse trailer?" Breed asked.

The bodyguard shrugged. "I can make a guess."

"Another gift," Breed said flatly. He'd talked to Kate before he'd gotten the boys a dog, worried about the extra responsibility it would mean for her. She'd said the boys were old enough to care for the dog themselves, with a little supervision, and that she thought it was a good idea. But they'd also been given a cat? And a couple of horses?

Breed realized he should have called Kate sooner to apologize for not coming early to help her set up. But he couldn't honestly say he was sorry to be spending less time with a dozen shrieking eight-year-olds. But even with everything going on at the JTTF, he would never have let the twins down by not showing up.

He followed the noise through the house, stopping in the kitchen for a beer, then slipped through the open sliding glass door onto the patio, hoping to go unnoticed. One of the eight-year-olds—he realized it was Lucky—was blindfolded and wildly swinging a stick at a donkey piñata full of candy that was hanging from the patio eaves.

Breed tensed when he saw King sitting at a patio table with Kate's parents, Clay and Libby Blackthorne, who were smiling and clapping encouragement. Their daughter Dallas was sitting in Libby's lap, while their son Houston was standing in the line of children waiting to hit the piñata.

At a separate patio table sat Jackson Blackthorne and his wife Ren. And a woman he'd seen altogether too much of over the past year, Ann Wade Pendleton. Judging by the full ashtray in front of the Texas governor, she'd been chain-smoking. From the bored look on her face, she wasn't having much fun.

As though she felt his eyes on her, Ann Wade's mocking gaze met his. He'd tried to make nice with the woman for Kate's sake, but he figured the apple didn't fall far from the tree. If J.D. Pendleton had been a son of a bitch, he'd learned at the foot of the master. Ann

Wade had proved herself to be ruthless in politics. From the way she'd ridden Kate's shoulders the past year, Breed had become convinced she had a heart of stone.

While he was warily eyeing Ann Wade, he felt his neck hairs prickle and turned to find his "maybe" biological father, Wyoming Governor King Grayhawk, staring at him. Breed managed not to shiver, but he felt his skin crawl.

This was the man who'd made sure his life was a living hell by sending him out into the world as a babe in the arms of an alcoholic mother. Lions killed the young of other males. Breed wasn't altogether sure that that wouldn't have been more merciful.

He'd been rescued by other members of King's pride. And had grown into an adversary worthy of his father, if he'd cared to fight him. Breed believed that ignoring King was a more fitting punishment. Purposefully, he turned his gaze away.

Kate was laughing and reaching to take the stick from Lucky before removing the blindfold and putting it on another child. Lucky turned and spotted Breed over her shoulder.

Breed felt his heart lurch as the little boy yelped with excitement and raced toward him, launching himself into the air at the last moment so Breed had to juggle his beer bottle to catch the boy in his open arms.

Kate's sons had managed to do what he'd thought impossible. Make him feel again. Make him care. Those two grieving boys had slowly but surely battered away at the wall he'd built around his heart to protect himself, leaving chinks in it.

Which was how that damned Grace Smith had managed to get under his skin. He didn't want to feel anything for her. Not sympathy. Not pity. Not even frustration or anger. But Kate's sons had created a breach so wide he was having trouble protecting his heart.

Or maybe he didn't want to. Being alone was safe. But being alone was damned lonely.

"Uncle Breed!" Lucky cried as he nearly strangled Breed with an exuberant hug.

Breed laughed and hugged the boy back, then dropped onto his knee and set his beer bottle behind him as he put his other arm out to collect Chance, who was two seconds behind, and much more controlled in his greeting, than his twin.

"You'd better get back over there," Breed said, urging the boys back toward the group around the piñata. "That piñata could break at any moment."

Kate had already put the blindfold on a little girl and was turning her in a circle so she wouldn't know in which direction to strike out.

The boys held onto him, clamoring to know what he'd gotten them for their birthday.

"Was I supposed to bring a present?" Breed asked.

"It's our birthday!" Lucky said.

"We're eight now!" Chance said.

Breed grinned and ruffled their hair. "You can have it after you open your other presents."

At that moment, the little girl hit the piñata hard enough to break it, and wrapped candy flowed from the break in the papier-mâché donkey. Hearing the other children's excited cries, the little girl tore off her blindfold.

A moment later, Breed was alone, as Lucky and Chance raced back to get their share of the candy spilling onto the stone patio.

While the kids were busy, Kate came over to give Breed a hug. "I was afraid you weren't going to make it."

"I wouldn't dare miss this party," he said. "Otherwise I'd be stuck with the twins' present."

Kate made a face and laughed. "Where is he?"

"I left him out front with one of Anne Wade's bodyguards."

"I'll bet he appreciated that," Kate said.

"I'm sure he'll cope," Breed said. "How's the party going?"

Kate glanced worriedly at her parents and grandparents and mother-in-law. "No blood has been spilled. Yet."

Breed slid an arm around her shoulders. "You're a born diplomat."

"I haven't managed to get you together with your father," she said. "Despite my best efforts. Have you even said hello to him?"

"King Grayhawk was a sperm donor. That's as close to a father as he's ever been to me."

"He wants to change that," Kate said.

"I don't."

"Won't you talk with him?" Kate pleaded. "For me?"

Breed made a frustrated sound in his throat. "It's a little late for me to start playing dutiful son. I wouldn't know how. Give it a rest, Kate. For me?"

"Fine," she said, pretending to pout. Then she brightened and asked, "How's your love life?"

Breed laughed. And then groaned. "If you only knew!"

Kate grinned. "Is there someone special? Really? Finally? I can't believe it!"

"She's special, all right," Breed muttered.

"Tell me about her."

"Maybe later. How about your love life?" he said, turning the tables on her. "Jack McKinley's free again. His divorce should be final any day now."

Breed watched Kate's face blanch and tightened his grasp on her shoulder to steady her. "Hey! You okay?"

"Fine. I gotta go," she said, pulling herself free. "I can see a fight about to erupt over candy. Stick around. You're just in time for cake and ice cream."

"Goody," Breed said.

Kate laughed. "I happen to know you love chocolate ice cream."

Breed grinned, but Kate had already turned back to separate two boys who were both claiming ownership of the same handful of candy.

"Time for cake and ice cream," she announced. "Everybody inside!" The children raced inside with Kate, leaving the rest of the adults on the patio.

Which was when Breed realized Jack had been standing with his back to the patio, along with two uniformed bodyguards and a deputy marshal. "You're here!" he said as Jack approached him. "I didn't see you out front, so I assumed you must have had to work."

Jack was in his face, close enough that their voices couldn't be heard. "Did you have anything to do with this?"

"I thought you and Kate might enjoy—"

"I'm talking about this assignment from the governor," Jack said furiously.

"I don't know what the hell you're talking about."

"I'm talking about Governor Pendleton assigning me as a bodyguard for Kate's kids for the next year."

Breed was shocked. "How can she do that?"

"That's what I'd like to know," Jack said. "But I called my captain, and it's just like she said. A done deal."

Breed didn't apologize. He wasn't responsible for what had happened. "How did she end up choosing you, of all people?"

"She obviously doesn't know about that stupid crush Kate had on me when she was nineteen," Jack said.

Which she never got over, Breed thought, eyeing Jack. Kate had been convinced that even though Jack denied feeling anything for her, he'd been equally smitten. She'd been proved wrong when Jack had married his high school sweetheart.

But they were both free again to love. And who knew what might happen if they were thrust together day in and day out, as Jack's assignment would require.

"It's only a year," Breed said.

Jack groaned.

"The twins are a lot of fun," Breed said. "Speaking of which, we'd better head inside."

Breed felt a hand on his shoulder and when he looked, found himself facing King Grayhawk. He knocked the hand away and snarled, "Keep your hands to yourself, old man."

"How do you like working for the FBI?" King asked, apparently unperturbed.

"Let's go, Jack," Breed said, turning his back on his father and stepping inside.

Jack said, "Excuse me, Governor."

When Jack caught up to him he said, "What happened to 'honor thy father'?"

"Screw him. He was never my father."

"Looks like he might want to change that."

"It's too late," Breed said. "It wouldn't bother me if King Grayhawk got himself blown to smithereens at the NGA Annual Meeting next week."

Jack raised a brow. "Is there a chance of that?"

"Oh, hell," Breed said, huffing out a breath of air. "I have no business mentioning that."

Jack immediately looked concerned. "If I'm going to be protecting Governor Pendleton's grandkids, and there's any chance they're going to be at that meeting to say hello to their grandmother, then it is my business."

"You want a beer?" Breed said as he opened a cooler full of drinks in the kitchen.

"Sure," Jack said.

Breed handed Jack an ice-cold Pearl and said, "Let's go out front where we can hear ourselves talk."

Breed waved at Kate as they crossed the living room, where a dozen eight-year-olds sat at kid-size tables eating cake and ice cream. When they reached the front porch, he pointed to the black lab and said, "My present for the twins."

Jack smiled. "I would have gone for a Border Collie."

"Good thing you didn't," Breed said as they moved to the far end of the porch. "I think Kate already has her hands full."

"I know how she feels," Jack said. "I'm going to have to get some guidance on this bodyguard business, especially when it involves a couple of kids."

"Wherever the twins are, Kate isn't far behind."

"That's what I was afraid of," Jack muttered.

"What's the problem?"

Jack was silent.

Breed sighed. He liked Kate and he liked Jack and he thought they would make a great couple. But he wasn't going to push it. It looked like they'd have plenty of time together in the next year to discover whether they really belonged together.

Breed leaned against the porch rail and said, "The reason you might want to keep the kids away from Ann Wade at the NGA Annual Meeting is because the Austin FBI got an anonymous phone tip this morning that a woman plans to bomb the LBJ Auditorium when the president's making his keynote speech on Wednesday."

"Does the Secret Service know about this?" Jack asked.

Breed shook his head. "The Austin ASAC assigned it to the local JTTF—which means me. At least for now."

Jack raised a brow. "So you don't think the tip is credible?"

"Who knows? The caller—whose voice was disguised, and who called from somewhere in Austin on a throwaway cell phone—gave us the name of the supposed bomber. Merle Raye Finkel. Juvie record for the double murder of her parents. Served eight years, got out last year when she turned twenty-one, then skipped out on her adult parole. Just disappeared."

"That sounds ominous," Jack said.

Breed grimaced. "I had sex with her last night."

Jack released a startled bark of laughter. "You're kidding, right?" When Breed remained silent, Jack said, "What did your ASAC say when you told him that?"

"I haven't told him yet."

"At least you know right where to find your suspect," Jack said.

"I wish. She gave me a false name and she was driving a car with stolen plates. I followed her to a dorm on campus, but it turned out she didn't live there."

"You get her phone number?"

Breed shook his head no.

"The sex was that bad?"

"The sex was—" Breed cut himself off. "I don't do relationships."

"Yeah, I know," Jack said. "So how are you going to find her?"

"I found a known associate, a guy in a wheelchair who went with her to the bar where I met her. Turns out Merle Raye Finkel—aka Grace Smith—is the leader of a group called the Victims for Vengeance."

"That sounds equally ominous," Jack said.

"It's a bunch of undergrads, all victims of violent crimes, who feel like they never got justice because their crimes weren't solved by the cops. Their goal is to find—and get vengeance against—the people who hurt them."

"Does that rise to the level of domestic terrorism?" Jack asked.

"Only if they act against the public in general or the government, as opposed to, say, the individual against whom they have a beef," Breed explained.

"How is this Merle Raye—"

"Grace," Breed corrected. "She's calling herself Grace Smith."

"How does Grace Smith fit in with the Victims for Vengeance? I mean, she committed the crime, and the police sure as hell caught her."

"According to the group—I attended a Victims for Vengeance meeting today before I came here, using Grace's name as my entrée and pretending to be a victim myself—Grace never murdered her parents. She's looking for the guy who really did the crime."

"Grace wasn't at the meeting?"

"She's called another meeting of the group tomorrow. One of the kids, Troy McMahon, is supposed to call and tell me where and when to show up.

"I had the JTTF special agents start a surveillance the moment the Victims left the Texas Union, and they'll be watching them until the group meets up again tomorrow."

"When you'll be there to take Merle Raye Finkel into custody," Jack said.

"Yep." Breed headed back across the front porch. "I'll take the puppy," he said, relieving the DPS sergeant of the leash. "It's time to give the twins their gift."

Jack was right behind him but stopped when his cell phone rang. Breed watched as Jack checked the caller ID and then swore.

"I have to take this." Jack listened, then said, "I'm on my way."

"Did someone not get the word that you're a bodyguard now?" Breed said.

"I have to take some personal time," Jack said. "Tell Kate I'll be back as soon as I can."

That was all the explanation Jack gave before he headed for his pickup. Breed watched him go, wondering if something had happened to Jack's nearly ex-wife or his son. But the old cowboy rules still applied in Texas. You never asked a man his business. If he wanted you to know what was going on, he would tell you.

But Breed wondered. And he worried about his friend.

14

⁓

Jack McKinley stepped inside the kitchen door to his parents' small home on the outskirts of the pricey Alamo Heights district in San Antonio and found his tall, once-elegant mother standing hunched at the sink in a plain cotton dress, her dark brown eyes huge and red-rimmed, remnants of tears on her pale cheeks. "Where is he?" Jack demanded.

Rose McKinley reached out in supplication. "Jack, don't. He can't help—"

"Don't apologize for him!" Jack snarled.

His mother shrank from him.

Jack took a step back and put his hands out in front of him to show he was keeping his distance. It broke his heart to think his mother could feel threatened by him. He wasn't his father. He'd tried very hard all his life to be *nothing* like his father.

"I thought he was over this," Jack said. "It's frustrating to be going through all of this again. Still."

"It's a disease, Jack."

Jack snorted in disgust. "That's just an excuse for—"

"He's a gambler, Jack. He can't help himself."

"What about the drinking? And the shouting? And the lamp out on the lawn and the broken bedroom window. I suppose he can't help that, either."

"He's ashamed," his mother said. "And embarrassed."

Jack felt the blood pounding in his throat, crawling up his cheeks, revealing the anger he always felt when his mother made excuses for

his father's behavior. It wasn't as though his father's gambling problem was something new. Jack had grown up in a household where
they'd been flush one week and out in the streets the next.

What he'd hated most were the broken promises. *I'll quit. It won't
happen anymore. That was the last time. We'll never have to move
again.*

But here Jack was—nearly twenty years after he'd left home
for college on a football scholarship, thinking he was finally free
of his father—repeating the old familiar pattern. His father gambling, and losing, and taking out his frustration—and shame and
embarrassment—on his family. Or what was left of it.

Only his mother remained at home. Both of his younger sisters had
married unreliable men to escape. Jack seldom saw Jessica or Joleen,
unless one of them called him to rescue her from an irate husband,
whom she subsequently forgave and returned to the next day.

Jack felt sick inside. He wanted to rescue his mother, just as he'd
wanted to rescue his sisters. He'd even wanted, once upon a time, to
rescue his father. But nothing Jack had been able to do had cured his
father of the addiction that had robbed him of his dignity and cost
Jack, at one time or another, all the things in his life that he'd held
most dear.

Jack hated his father. Hated him for what he'd done. And what
he'd asked Jack to do.

*"They're going to kill me, Jack. Slit my belly and let my innards
fall out. You have to do what they want. You have to shave points in
the Super Bowl. It's the only way they'll forgive my debt and let me
live."*

"How much do you owe?" he'd asked his father, his stomach roiling.

"Three hundred twenty-one thousand eight hundred dollars."

The amount had been staggering. Jack couldn't imagine how
anyone could have given a compulsive gambler that much credit.
Except, his father had an asset he could use for collateral: a son who
was a pro football quarterback. A wealthy pro quarterback who made
millions each year.

Jack had tried to pay his father's gambling debt with cash, but the man holding his father's marker didn't want money. He'd wanted much more. He'd wanted Jack to fix the results in the Super Bowl, to rig the game so the big gambling syndicates could cash in.

Jack had refused.

But he'd fumbled the ball on the opposing team's five-yard line. And gotten an intentional grounding call on fourth and short. And thrown an interception in a spot where he had no receiver within a dozen yards.

And they'd lost the game.

Soon afterward, the rumors had started that he'd lost on purpose, that he'd thrown the game. His teammates had refused to play with him. No one could prove anything, but he'd been forced to quit football. He'd purchased a restaurant in Austin called the Longhorn Grille and tried to make it work. He'd been on the verge of losing it to the IRS when the Texas Rangers had come calling.

Because of his smirched reputation, they thought he could more easily infiltrate a statewide sports gambling syndicate. The Rangers wanted him to find the gamblers who were manipulating the results of sports in Texas, everything from football to horse racing.

Jack had jumped at the chance to redeem his honor. To stifle the rumors. To find the men who'd corrupted his father and ruined his life.

He'd never found the culprits, of course. The simple fact that the syndicate had left his father alive was proof that they thought Jack had fulfilled the deal he'd been offered. There'd been no one to whom Jack could plead his innocence. No one would have believed him. Especially when the tabloids discovered the huge bet his father had made that the opposing team would win.

That had been the final, fatal betrayal. That had been the day Jack washed his hands of his father once and for all.

Except, it hadn't been that easy.

Jack still came when his mother called. He couldn't abandon her. So here he was. Again. In a house devoid of any kind of amenity, a barely livable place where his mother suffered his father's outrageous behavior after he'd lost everything yet again.

"Where is he?" Jack asked.

"You aren't going to—"

"I'm not going to hurt him," Jack said in a sinister voice that made it clear he could happily break every bone in his father's body.

His mother was clearly reluctant to tell him where he could find his father, but the house was so small, it wouldn't take long to locate him. As Jack headed down the hallway, she called after him, "He's locked himself in the bathroom."

Jack pounded on the bathroom door with his fist and shouted, "Come on out, Dad."

"I'm sorry, Jack," his father sobbed from behind the flimsy door. "I'm so sorry."

Jack swore under his breath. He took a step back and took a deep breath. His father wasn't just pitiful, he was pitiable. Jack had never gambled on anything in his life. He'd been too afraid he might be afflicted with his father's vice.

He wondered whether his father had bet the house this time, and whether his parents would end up living out of their car again. Assuming his father hadn't bet the car, as well. They'd moved into the Y before, men's and women's, until his father got another stake, made another killing, and found another place to live with Jack's mother.

Jack made his voice less threatening and said, "I want you to come out, so I can make sure you're all right."

"I didn't mean to do it, Jack," his father said. "I couldn't help myself."

Jack clenched his teeth to keep from responding.

"They told me to give you a message, Jack."

"What are you talking about, Dad?"

The bathroom door eased open a crack, and he saw his father's grizzled face in the stark light spilling over the sink. "They said you have to back off your investigation, or they're going to slice me in half, eyebrows to balls."

Jack jerked as though he'd been punched in the face. He'd thought he was invulnerable to intimidation. He'd sworn fifteen years ago that he'd never let his father put him in a position again where he had to make a choice that put him in the wrong. He'd told himself that if the situation ever arose again, he'd let the sons of bitches kill his old man, who deserved whatever they did to him.

In the face of this new threat, he realized he could do no such thing. Even hating his father as he did, he couldn't let him be murdered in cold blood. Not if he could save him. But he wasn't going to be forced into doing the wrong thing, either. He would die first.

His father choked back another sob and said, "They said you can lead the investigation away from them and do it in a way that no one will ever know."

Jack realized he must have been getting pretty damned close to the man who'd threatened his father all those years ago, for him to make such a coldblooded threat.

Jack tasted the bile in his throat and realized the syndicate was going to think he was kowtowing to them again. Because he'd just been pulled off his investigation and assigned as a bodyguard for the governor's grandsons.

Damn it all to hell!

He would have to talk with his captain and see what he could work out. He wasn't going to let the syndicate think they had him in their pocket.

"Not this time, Dad," he said, shaking his head. "It isn't going to happen."

"But you have to—"

"I don't have to do a damn thing but move you and Mom some-place safe until this blows over."

It wasn't easy to see the look of terror in his father's hazel eyes and know he was partly responsible for putting it there. But he'd learned a lot of lessons since that threat fifteen years ago. He wasn't going to let his father's fear keep him from doing his job this time. He wasn't going to betray everything he believed in to save a man who really didn't deserve saving.

"Put some things together. You and Mom are coming with me."

"I don't need my son to take care of me or my wife," his father retorted.

"I'm not giving you a choice," Jack replied. "Put some things in a bag or don't, it's all the same to me. But you're leaving this house."

Jack saw the moment when his father realized his son wasn't going to be swayed. The old man's shoulders sagged and his chin sank. He rubbed his hands over his two-day-old beard and said, "Fine. Have it your way."

Jack realized his mother was hovering in the hall near his shoulder and turned to her. "Pack a bag, Mom."

"Where are we going?" she asked.

"To my ranch."

When he'd gotten the divorce papers from Gayle a year ago and realized his marriage was really over, Jack had used his share of the proceeds from the sale of his restaurant to buy half ownership with Breed Grayhawk in a quarter horse ranch a half hour west of Austin.

The main ranch house was an enormous white two-story wood frame structure with black shutters. It was fronted by four Doric columns, with a second floor gallery porch over a lower porch that ran the entire length of the house. Majestic magnolias on either end of the house gave it the feel of an old southern mansion and led to its name, Twin Magnolias.

Jack thought they'd gotten a bargain when they'd bought Twin Magnolias, but the house, with its peeling paint, leaky ceiling, frayed wallpapered walls, and worn hardwood floors had needed a lot of work. Jack and Breed had put a lot of sweat equity into the property. They'd made the most necessary repairs, but after nine months of hard work, it was still far from being transformed into anything approaching its original beauty.

Jack had taken the upstairs, which consisted of two bedrooms and two baths, while Breed, who also had a condo in town, had taken the bedroom and bath on the first floor. They shared a combination study and library downstairs, which they used as a business office, the kitchen, and the great room, which had a cathedral ceiling with a two-story stone fireplace.

Jack figured his parents could sleep in the second upstairs bedroom. Entry and exit to the ranch was along a single dirt road that could be easily watched and guarded. That would keep his parents out of the line of fire if bullets started flying.

He stood back as his mother passed by. She touched his arm— comfort? acceptance? understanding?—but she didn't look at him on her way to the back bedroom. His father took advantage of the distraction to sneak out of the bathroom and follow his wife down the hall.

Jack was still shaking his head in disbelief at what he was being forced to do when his cell phone rang.

When he picked up, his Ranger captain said, "I assigned your syndicate investigation to Dave Randall. He tells me your paperwork is so out of date, there's nothing in writing for him to review."

Ever since Gayle had left Texas and taken six-year-old Ryan with her, Jack had barely managed to make it to work in the mornings. He missed his son. The judge had said Ryan could visit him on alternate Christmases and Thanksgivings. It felt like way too little time. Soon, his young son wouldn't know him. And he wouldn't know his son.

Jack had tried to explain to the family court judge that he couldn't leave Texas without losing his position as a Texas Ranger. He'd tried to explain the history of the elite force of lawmen, which went back to the days when Texas had been a Republic, with its own president and its own army and navy. How being a Ranger meant he could work independently to bring wrongdoers to justice. He hadn't wanted to give up his syndicate investigation—the same investigation that had, unbelievably, just been taken away from him.

After his speech in court, the judge had replied that there were cops in every city. He wasn't willing to require Jack's wife to stay in

Texas. She was free to take their son and return to her family in Kansas. Jack could ask for more visitation when his son was older.

Lately, his life seemed to be full of unpleasant surprises.

"Tell Dave to call me," Jack said, "and I'll catch him up on everything I've been doing. Unless you'd like to get me out of this babysitting job, in which case I won't need to bring anyone else up to speed."

"Do the paperwork," his captain said. "Governor Pendleton was pretty specific about who she wanted guarding her grandsons. I don't see how I can get you out of that. Especially with this threat to the governor's life."

"You mean the phone threat to set off a bomb during the president's speech on Wednesday?" Jack asked.

"What?"

"Apparently some woman named Merle Raye Finkel is planning to set off a bomb at the LBJ Auditorium during the president's keynote at the NGA Annual Meeting."

"Where did you hear that?" his captain asked.

"I've got friends in low places," Jack said.

"Ah," his captain said. "Your FBI buddy. We didn't get a named suspect. Just an e-mail saying Governor Pendleton is going to be blown into pieces too small to find."

"An e-mail? Not a phone call?"

"Yep."

"I find it interesting that there have been two separate threats on the same day," Jack said. "Is it possible this Finkel woman is responsible for both?"

"Anything is possible," his captain said.

"Did you know the FBI was investigating a bomb threat?"

"Now I do," his captain said.

"Are you planning to share your e-mail tip with the FBI?" Jack asked.

"Did they share their anonymous phone tip with us?" his captain said. "The protective detail will take care of the governor, Jack. You just keep an eye on her grandkids. And their mother."

And their mother, Jack thought as he snapped his phone shut. This wouldn't be the first time he'd kept an eye on Kate to keep her safe. He'd been acting as her bodyguard—unbeknownst to her—when they'd first met.

A vision of Kate naked, her pert breasts peeking from between locks of long black hair, appeared in his mind's eye. Jack felt his body responding and swore. He wasn't even close to being "over" her. Seeing her today, he'd realized that she was even more beautiful than she'd been when she was nineteen and he'd first met her.

Her father had been the federal judge assigned to try "Bomber Brown," a lunatic accused of blowing up the federal courthouse in Houston. Kate's uncle North, who was a good friend of Jack's, had asked him to keep an eye on her, since she'd been kidnapped the previous year by someone trying to manipulate her father, who was then the U.S. attorney general.

In order to stay close to Kate, Jack had agreed to help her in a harebrained matchmaking scheme she'd come up with to get her parents together. Her mother had been living in Wyoming, while her father was working in Austin. Kate was certain that if they were together long enough, they would realize that they loved each other, marry, and live happily ever after.

She wanted Jack to pretend that they were lovers. Since he had a reputation as a ladies' man, a shady past that had forced him out of football, and was being pursued by the IRS, her mother was bound to come running if she thought Kate was involved with him.

Because of his promise to Kate's uncle North, Jack had gone along with Kate's game of pretend. The practice kissing they'd done had convinced Jack he was in over his head. The chemistry was so good it was scary. Kate had gotten a schoolgirl's crush on him, but he'd known she was way too young for him to be fooling around with her. And besides, she was his best friend's niece.

It had taken every bit of willpower he had to resist her charms when she'd tried to seduce him.

It was a fluke that he'd run into his high school sweetheart at a reunion, just when Kate was trying to make him jealous by dating the UT quarterback. He'd forgotten how much fun Gayle was. He'd forgotten how good she felt in his arms. He'd wanted a family. And he'd wanted to escape the temptation of going after a woman who was too young to know what she wanted.

So he'd proposed. And Gayle had accepted.

Jack hadn't realized how much he loved Kate Grayhawk until he heard she'd married J. D. Pendleton. The pain in his chest, in the region of his heart, had told him the truth. By then it was too late. They were both married to other people.

Jack figured the past was the past. Whatever magic might have been between them would be long gone by now. He would rather not head down that road, even in his imagination. He'd tried marriage. It hadn't taken.

He would keep the governor's grandkids safe. And keep his hands off Kate Grayhawk Pendleton.

15

~

Breed realized the time had come to tell his boss—and friend and mentor—Vincent Harkness, that he'd had sex with the JTTF's terrorism suspect, Merle Raye Finkel. He wasn't relishing the thought. It was going to be a humiliating admission. Not to mention potentially career-ending.

He called to ask if he could stop by Vince's house and arrived Sunday morning about the time he knew Vince and his family usually got home from First Baptist Church services. During football season Vince usually went to the early service because he liked to be home in time to watch the ESPN pregame show.

Breed had spent more than one afternoon sitting in Vince's living room drinking beer, eating nachos, and watching the Dallas Cowboys on TV. He wished he had something that mundane planned for this afternoon.

Stephanie opened the front door to his knock, turned her cheek for his kiss, smiled and said, "I'm so glad to see you, Breed. He's in his office and asked if you'd join him there."

Stephanie had large blue eyes set far apart and a petite, nicely curved figure that always made Breed think of a cheerleader.

She was wearing a white, button-down oxford cloth shirt tucked neatly into belted jeans with a crisply ironed crease and shined penny loafers without socks. He'd seen her wearing the same outfit, or something very similar, so often it might have been a uniform. Her naturally honey-blond hair was cut even with her jaw, and she wore it in a pageboy with bangs that just touched her eyebrows.

Vince's home office was down the hall, and as Breed walked past the family room, he waved at Brian, who was sitting on the floor with his back against the beige Natuzzi leather couch watching ESPN, and at Chloe, who was lying on the couch with her head on the armrest, texting on her cell phone.

"Hi, guys," he called out.

"Hi, Breed," Chloe said.

Brian absently waved back at him without looking in his direction and said, "Hi!"

Vince's office door was closed, so Breed knocked.

"Come in," Vince called.

Breed let himself in and closed the door behind him. He found Vince seated at his desk with his computer on. The wrinkles on his forehead seemed more pronounced and there were dark circles under his eyes that suggested he hadn't slept well. He was dressed as conservatively as his wife in a polo shirt, neatly creased khaki pants, and boat shoes without socks.

"What's the latest word?" Breed asked.

Vince rolled himself backward in his ergonomic desk chair so he was facing Breed and said, "According to the JTTF surveillance reports, all the Victims for Vengeance members are still at home. Nobody's left for McMahon's dorm room. You'd think at least one of them would have an errand to run before the meeting there this afternoon."

"You'd think," Breed agreed.

"I'd give my left nut to know what Merle Raye Finkel is doing right now," Vince said.

Breed felt the same way. He pulled up the captain's chair near the desk and sat down. During his brief career with the FBI, Vince Harkness had always been the one he'd gone to for professional advice. He needed some now.

"There's something I haven't told anyone that I need to get off my chest," Breed said.

Vince was instantly attentive. "You know I'm here for you, Breed."

"You always have been." Breed felt a knot in his throat. He didn't want to disappoint this man. But he knew he was going to have to admit the truth sooner or later. And in this case, sooner was better than later. He took a deep breath and said, "I had sex with Merle Raye Finkel night before last."

Vince exhaled a loud gust of air and shoved a hand across his crew cut. At last he said, "That's quite a confession. Care to elaborate?"

"I didn't know who she was at the time. She called herself Grace. I met her at a bar—Digger's, about an hour west on U.S. 290—and, well, we hooked up."

Vince made a *hmm*ing sound.

Breed felt a flush creeping up his cheeks.

"What time was this on Friday?" Vince asked.

"Around eight, I guess."

Vince *hmm*ed again. "You didn't ask for her phone number afterward?"

"She said she didn't have a phone."

"You didn't question that?"

"Not at the time," Breed admitted ruefully.

"Did you get a last name?"

"Smith," Breed said. "I knew it was phony, but she wouldn't show me her ID."

"What about the car she was driving?" Vince asked.

"A dark blue foreign model, stolen Michigan plates."

"At least your training wasn't totally wasted," Vince said.

Breed looked down at his hands, which were clasped on the arms of the chair. He'd known he was going to be taken to task. But when someone whose opinion you cared about put the spurs to you, it hurt a lot worse than when a stranger did it.

"You didn't ask where she lived?" Vince continued.

"I followed her back to Austin, hoping I'd discover just that," Breed said, meeting his mentor's piercing, dark-eyed gaze. "She went to a dorm on the UT campus, Jester East. But she doesn't live there."

"And you know that because . . . ?"

"I spent most of yesterday morning trying to track her down. And found nothing," Breed said. "The bartender at Digger's gave me the lead—the connection to Troy McMahon—that sent me to the Victims for Vengeance meeting. You know the rest."

Vince leaned back in his rolling chair and eyed Breed as though he were some lower form of life. "I'm disappointed in you."

"Yes, sir. I—"

"I'm *Vince* to you outside the office," Vince interrupted. "I'm your friend. Which is why I'm so disappointed you didn't come to me with this information yesterday, Breed. As soon as you knew it was relevant to the bomb threat we're investigating."

Breed didn't excuse his behavior. He knew from his FBI training that there was no excuse for not doing the right thing.

"Is there anything different about Merle Raye Finkel's present appearance compared to her mug shot that would be useful to us in trying to locate her?" Vince asked.

"She looks very much the same. Older, of course."

"No new scars? Anything about her hair—"

"Her hair is still black, and she wears it long, parted in the middle. No new scars that I saw."

"I take it you saw everything," Vince said with a raised brow.

Breed felt the embarrassing flush return. He nodded without speaking.

"Have you told anyone else what you've just told me?" Vince asked.

"No," Breed replied, shaking his head. Then he remembered he'd told Jack. But Jack would be discreet. And he didn't want to contradict himself.

"I think we can keep this between us," Vince said. "No need to advise anyone up or down the FBI chain of command, as far as I'm concerned."

Breed gave an inward sigh of relief. He wouldn't have wanted his sexual escapade bruited about the JTTF office, or to have something like that in his personnel file. He wanted a career in the FBI. He would never live it down if it turned out he'd had sex with a terrorist on the eve of her attempt to bomb the U.S. president into oblivion.

"The thing is," Breed said, "once we catch Merle Raye Finkel, she might say something about what happened between us."

"I'll take care of Merle Raye Finkel. Just make sure when you take her into custody that she doesn't talk to anyone before I get a chance to interrogate her. I'll give her a reason to keep her mouth shut about you."

"But—"

Vince held up a hand. "I'd give my life to protect you in the field. I'm glad I can help you out. You do your part and find the woman. I'll take care of everything else."

Breed felt a niggling sense of unease at Vince's willingness to cover up the truth about his relationship with a woman who might turn out to be a terrorist. He wondered if it really could be kept secret. And what would happen if it came out later that Vince had helped him cover the whole thing up. It was always the cover-up that seemed to get politicians into trouble, rather than the initial crime.

"Maybe I ought to write up a report to explain—"

"Explain what? That you had sex with a suspected terrorist?"

"She was just some woman I met at a bar!" Breed protested.

"You think the FBI—not to mention the public, when the press gets hold of this, and it will—is going to believe your meeting was totally accidental? You want to keep a very tight lid on that can of worms."

"But—"

"Give yourself a break," Vince said. "Nobody has to know about this but the three of us. I'll make sure Merle Raye Finkel keeps her mouth shut. And I'm not going to tell anyone your secret. Just bring the girl in, and I promise you, this will all go away."

There was a knock on the door and Stephanie opened it and stuck her head in. "Can I get you boys something to drink?"

Breed was already on his feet. "Not for me, Stephanie. I have somewhere I have to be."

"Thank you, honey," Vince said. "I'll have a Coke." He stood to shake hands with Breed. "Be careful this afternoon. I'll be waiting for your call. Remember, she's not to speak with anyone—"

"What about a lawyer?"

"Terrorists don't get lawyers," Vince snapped. "You should know that. Your job is on the line here, Breed. Do what needs to be done. When the girl shows up, clap a pair of cuffs on her and bring her to me."

"And if she doesn't show up?"

"We'll cross that bridge when we come to it."

16

After he left Vince's house, Breed went by the JTTF office to pick up the wire he planned to wear to the Victims for Vengeance meeting scheduled later that afternoon. According to the special agents surveilling the Victims, they'd begun leaving their residences around half past one. They were all headed, apparently, for Jester East, where the meeting was scheduled to begin at 2:00 p.m. in Troy's room.

Breed wondered if Grace would show up. He was sure Troy would have told her that Breed had come to the Victims meeting on Saturday using her name as an entrée. Which meant she would know he'd gone looking for her. And almost found her.

What would she think? How would she react?

Breed supposed it depended on whether Grace had, in fact, known all along that he was an FBI agent. Whether she was, in fact, planning some act of domestic terrorism. And what it was, in fact, she'd wanted from him when she'd asked him for that "favor."

He wondered who'd sent the anonymous tip accusing Grace of plotting an act of terrorism. He would have been a lot more likely to discount it if he didn't have his own bizarre experience with Grace, who'd given him a phony name and address and been driving a car with a stolen plate.

Not to mention the fact that she was a parole violator who'd apparently slipped off the grid. Why all the deception if she wasn't planning something sinister?

Did she have accomplices who were getting cold feet? Or was it one of the Victims for Vengeance, who'd decided Merle Raye Finkel was planning to carry her vengeance a little too far? What if the Victims for Vengeance were part of the plot? Would Grace have told Troy that Breed was an FBI agent? Was he walking into some kind of trap?

This was one time he wasn't sorry the FBI tended to use ten men when two might have done the job. He would have plenty of backup if he needed it.

"You guys out there?" Breed said, holding his cell phone to his ear as though he were making a call, in order to check the tiny microphone attached to his Levi's jacket. The wire was being monitored by Steve and a couple of JTTF special agents in the Jim's Plumbing van parked in front of the dorm.

"We're here," he heard in the tiny bud in his ear. "Think she'll show up?"

"It's anybody's guess," Breed said. "Stay on your toes. I'm not sure how this is going down today. If I need you at all, I'm gonna need you in a big damned hurry."

"We're ready," he heard in his ear.

"Any sign of Finkel down there?" Breed asked.

"Nope."

"Let me know if she shows up," Breed said.

Breed wouldn't have bet money on Grace showing up at the meeting today, except she had to contact him again sometime to get whatever favor it was she wanted from him. So why not today?

Especially if she didn't know someone had ratted her out.

He wanted her to come. Otherwise, he and Vince were going to have to turn this whole mess over to the San Antonio SAC and the Secret Service bright and early tomorrow morning and let them have a whack at finding her.

At which point, his ass was going to be grass.

He closed his phone as the pretty blond Victims member joined him where he stood at the elevator in the Jester East lobby. "Hey, Christy," he said. "Nice to see you again."

"You, too," she said with a broad smile.

"What's on tap at the meeting today?" he asked as Christy pushed the button for Troy's floor.

"Don't know. Grace just said she had a surprise for all of us."

Breed felt the hairs on his arms prickle. He had his Glock with him, but he didn't want to end up shooting Grace in a roomful of kids. He didn't believe the Victims for Vengeance wanted anything more than vengeance against the individuals who'd injured them. But what if he was wrong?

What if he'd underestimated everyone, including Grace? What if they were planning to obliterate the president of the United States and everyone who showed up in the LBJ Auditorium to hear him speak?

Breed remembered the innocent faces around the table in the Texas Union. He looked at the pretty blond to his right. She winked at him when she caught his eye. Flirting, he realized with some astonishment. Terrorists? If they were, he was a horse's ass.

Of course, he'd had sex with a woman who turned out to be a terrorist suspect, so that horse's ass label might be pinned on him yet. Better to catch Merle Raye Finkel and get her delivered to Vince before he dismissed the danger to the public—and the president and the nation's governors—from the Victims for Vengeance.

Breed had purposely come early so he could greet each Victims member as he or she arrived. He and Christy were the first to show up.

"Glad you could come," Troy greeted him from his wheelchair. He pointed to his bed, which was one of only a few places to sit in the small double-occupancy room, which had a bed headed by a desk on each side, two closets and built-in chests at one end, and two windows at the other. Breed sat down on the hard mattress, and Christy sat down next to him.

Breed noticed Troy's roommate, Harry Gunderson, was lying on his bed, his back to the group. His empty wheelchair stood in the spot where his desk chair would be. Breed didn't think it was his place to ask why Harry was still in the room when Harry wasn't a member of the group. But he wondered about it.

When Troy saw the direction of Breed's gaze he said, "Harry's sacked out. Late night at the books. He won't bother us."

But he was one more person for Breed to worry about. He didn't want the kid waking up and freaking out if things got loud when he was taking Grace into custody.

The plan was for him to leave the room with Grace before he arrested her, but if she wouldn't come willingly, he'd have to take her here. Of course, a half-dozen FBI special agents were waiting—in the van below and in the lobby and the stairwell—who could be here within moments after he made his move on Grace.

The biggest problem he expected to have was keeping Grace to himself while he escorted her to lockup, where Vince would be waiting to question her.

It took another fifteen minutes before everyone arrived. Everyone except Grace, that was.

"What do you suppose is holding Grace up?" the freckle-faced boy asked.

Troy looked around the room, focused his gaze on Breed, and said, "She's not coming."

"Why not?" the brunette with the glass eye asked. "She arranged this meeting, and I canceled—"

"Because of him," Troy said, pointing at Breed.

Breed was instantly wary. His eyes searched the room, looking for threatening gestures or a weapon that might be used against him. What he saw were perplexed expressions on innocent faces.

"He's not who he said he was," Troy said.

Every eye in the room turned toward Breed.

"Grace told me he's an FBI agent, the one in charge of the JTTF," Troy continued. "That's Joint Terrorism Task Force, for those of you not in the know. He's here looking for Grace. Who prefers to remain hidden."

Breed sat frozen. Grace had certainly done her homework on him. Which made him even more certain that she'd known exactly who he was when they'd met Friday night.

How the hell was he going to find her now? Unless these kids knew how to find her and just weren't telling him. He eyed the group surrounding him, who looked more confused than confrontational.

"Why would the FBI be after Grace?" Christy asked.

"That's what Grace would like to know," Troy said. "Why did you really come to our meeting yesterday? What is it you want from Grace?"

Breed hesitated, then said, "Somebody phoned in a tip to the FBI accusing Merle Raye Finkel—that's Grace's real name—of plotting to blow up the president when he comes to town this week."

He saw slack jaws around the room. Heard gasps. Exclamations of protest.

"The call was anonymous," Breed said. "I thought it might have come from one of you."

He saw surprised eyes and shaking heads all around. Breed rose and kept his eye on everyone's hands as he backed his way to the door. "Anybody want to tell me where Grace is? Troy?"

Troy's eyes narrowed, and his lips pressed flat. "You know what I think? Somebody's framing Grace. Maybe she's getting too close to the man who really killed her parents, you know?"

Breed made a disgusted sound in his throat.

"Yeah," the blond girl said. "I can't believe Grace—whatever her real name is—would be involved in anything like what you're suggesting."

"So why didn't she come here today to defend herself?" Breed asked.

The Victims for Vengeance exchanged glances.

"Maybe she knew you'd stick her in jail again and this time throw away the key," Troy said.

"Look," Breed said. "This isn't a game. I need to know how to find Grace. I need to talk with her. Isn't there some way I can reach her? Troy?"

"No. Really, man. There's no way."

"You're not lying, are you? That's obstruction of justice."

"No, I'm not," Troy retorted. But his features were mulish rather than frightened.

"If she calls you again, Troy, and I'm betting she does, you need to call the FBI and tell them—"

"I'm not finking on Grace," Troy said.

"Then you become an accessory to whatever she does. And the word is, she's planning an act of domestic terrorism. You willing to help her incinerate a lot of innocent people?"

"Of course not!" Troy protested. "I don't know where she is. She's never told any of us where she lives. She just . . . shows up. I told you before. We don't call her, she calls us."

"Anybody here got any idea at all where I can find Merle Raye Finkel?" Breed asked, meeting the eyes of each kid, one at a time.

"No."

"Not me."

"None at all."

"Uh-uh!"

"If you hear from the woman who's convinced you what a good idea vigilante justice is, give me a call."

Breed dropped cards with the JTTF number in each kid's lap. He looked at each of them one last time and said, "You all might want to rethink the whole Victims for Vengeance idea." Then he backed out the door and let it close behind him.

As he headed down the hall toward the elevator he said into the mike, "You get all that?"

"Yeah," he heard in his ear. "Stupid kids. Where is this mystery woman?"

Breed shook his head at the way Grace was manipulating him. Manipulating the FBI and the JTTF. Manipulating all of the lawmen who'd let her suffer for something she supposedly hadn't done. Making them do her will, like puppets on string.

"What do you suppose she's planning?" the voice in his ear said.

Breed disconnected his mike before he said, "That's what I intend to find out."

He admitted, as the elevator opened and let him out in the lobby downstairs, that he had no idea where to start looking for her. All he could do was wait for Grace to contact him.

He was afraid she'd already sent the only message—through the Victims—that he was going to get: *I know who you are. And you don't scare me.*

She was starting to scare him. Who was Grace Smith, really? A woman wronged by the justice system? Or someone guilty as sin and crazy as a loon? Crazy enough to plant a bomb to blow up the president?

There was one part of his Friday night with Grace that Breed had neglected to mention to Vince. The favor he'd promised her in exchange for sex.

Breed was waiting now for the other shoe to drop.

Vince might have been able to keep Breed's sexual romp with Grace a secret if she were in custody. But Grace was running free. She could betray him—or further involve him—at any time. And likely would, if it suited her purposes. Whatever they were.

Breed gritted his teeth so hard a muscle jerked in his jaw. What, exactly, was she planning to ask him to do?

17

~

"How the hell did you get in here?" Breed demanded.

Grace found herself facing a Glock that was locked and loaded. She was sitting at Breed's kitchen table in his condo in Austin. It had been a toss-up whether he would show up here, or at the ranch he owned with Jack McKinley, when he returned home after the Victims for Vengeance meeting. She'd guessed right.

She put her hands up to show she was no threat to Breed and said, "I broke in."

"Why?"

"I need your help."

"You're wanted for questioning by the FBI. You're a convicted felon in violation of your parole. The only help you're going to get from me is a ride to federal lockup. You will not pass GO, you will not collect two hundred dollars."

"Vincent Harkness murdered my father and stepmother."

"Bullshit."

"It's true. I can prove it," Grace said. That wasn't precisely true. But she hoped it would keep her from getting shot or whisked off to jail, where Vincent Harkness would be sure to arrange an accident to silence her.

"Stand up," Breed ordered, grabbing a plastic cuff from a kitchen drawer.

She remained seated. "I'm not going to allow you to handcuff me, Breed."

He gave a nasty laugh. "I'd like to see you try and stop me."

"May I show you something?"

"Keep your hands where I can see them," he said, training the Glock on her center mass.

She pointed with a finger that was still high in the air. "It's right there. The pink book on your kitchen table."

When she started to reach toward the diary, he snapped, "Hold it right there."

"It's a diary," she continued. "It belongs to Stephanie Harkness."

"Vince's wife?" Breed said incredulously. "You *stole* a *diary* from an FBI ASAC's wife? Are you out of your mind?"

"I think you'll find it very interesting."

"I'm not reading my boss's wife's diary," Breed snarled.

"Even if it contains evidence that Vincent Harkness is a murderer?"

"If you stole that, you're going to have trouble using it in court to prove—"

"I don't intend to settle this in court."

"Oh, yeah, you're one of the Victims for Vengeance," Breed said viciously. "Since when is vigilante justice the answer to anything?"

"You aren't the one who spent eight years locked up for a crime you didn't commit," Grace snarled back.

"Every criminal I ever met was innocent," Breed said with a sneer.

"I *am* innocent," Grace said. "That diary proves it!"

"You're telling me Stephanie Harkness knows her husband is a murderer, and she wrote about it in her diary?"

"Look for yourself," Grace insisted.

Breed stared at the diary. But he didn't reach for it.

"You remember the Cancer Society Murder?" Grace said.

"Vince knew the guy who was murdered," Breed said.

"Vince *killed* the guy who was murdered."

"You are some piece of work," Breed said disgustedly.

"It's all in the diary," Grace said. "Stephanie cut out a newspaper article about the murder and kept it with the entry where she explains how she had sex with the murdered guy the night he was killed. She and Vince were at the banquet. They were questioned by my father, Big Mike Finkel, who was an Austin PD homicide detective investigating the murder."

"Assuming everything in Stephanie's diary reads the way you say, how do you get from that set of facts to Vince murdering the victim. Or your father, for that matter?"

"May I put my hands down?" Grace asked.

Breed swiftly crossed to her, stood her up, and patted her down—embarrassingly thoroughly—to make sure she didn't have a weapon, and said, "You can put them down now."

"I could talk more easily if I didn't have a weapon aimed at my palpitating heart," Grace said.

She watched as Breed seemed to come to a decision. He put the Glock back in his boot holster and crossed to sit on the opposite side of the table from her, with the pink diary between them.

"I think my father figured out what Vince had done," Grace said. "Or suspected him of the Cancer Society Murder. Vince killed him to protect his dirty little secret. My mother happened to come home at the wrong time and saw or heard too much. So she had to be killed, too."

Breed reached for the diary and paged through it until he found the newspaper clipping Grace had mentioned. She watched the emotions come and go on his face as he read the entry. Disbelief. Dismay. Disgust.

"Stephanie doesn't come to a conclusion one way or the other," he said at last.

"I know it's all circumstantial," Grace said. "But you must admit, it's also compelling."

"Where's the proof you said was in here?" he said, flipping through the pages.

Grace stood and held out her hand for the diary. "Do you mind?"

He handed the book to her, and she flipped through until she found an entry in different-colored ink. "Read this page."

Breed's face showed his distaste as he read about Stephanie's sexual encounter. His brow furrowed when he read the lines she'd written below it, which noted the oddity of two of her lovers being murdered outside the bars where she'd met them. The lines were still drawn on his face when he looked up. "Even Stephanie doesn't come out and accuse Vince of murder. And I have to tell you, the idea that my boss—my *friend*—is a serial killer seems too farfetched to be true."

"After I stole Stephanie's diary on Friday night, I read—"

"Did you break into Vince's house before or after you met me?"

"After you drove away from the dorm—"

"Where you don't live," Breed interjected.

"I went home to change clothes, then waited for it to get late enough for folks on Vince's street to go to bed and fall asleep. Then I broke into his house. I wouldn't have taken the diary," she said, "but I was reading it when he came home and—"

"Vince was at his place on Lake LBJ Friday and Saturday with his family."

Grace shook her head. "Someone came home. If it wasn't him, I don't know who it was."

"Vince didn't mention coming back to Austin," Breed mused. "I wonder . . ."

"If there was another murder somewhere over the weekend?" Grace said, finishing his sentence with the thought that had come to her mind. "I didn't check that. But we could."

"We could?"

"I've already done some checking on my own," Grace said. "To see if there were other deaths in the cities where Stephanie took lovers."

She waited for him to ask. She wanted him to ask.

"Well? Were there?"

"I only checked the first fifteen—the eighty-two entries in the diary go back nine years, in eleven states and the District of Columbia. But—"

"Out with it," Breed said irritably. "What did you find?"

"A lot of men with first names and descriptions that matched those in Stephanie's diary have been killed outside the bars where she met them. They were also robbed. At least one of the crimes I researched has been solved."

"How many dead?" Breed asked.

"Ten of the first fifteen men Stephanie took as lovers."

"Do you realize what you're suggesting?" Breed said.

Grace nodded.

"You can't really believe—"

"No," Grace interrupted. "*You* can't really believe Vincent Harkness is a serial killer."

"It's too fantastic to believe," Breed said, rising and pacing the length of the kitchen. "I was in Vince's home just this morning. I spoke to Stephanie and the kids. Everything was so . . . normal. All you have as proof is a diary—"

"Harkness must have known about its existence," Grace said, rising and perching one knee on the chair, leaning toward Breed, urging him to accept the truth of what she'd discovered. "He must have been reading it all along. That's the only way he could know his wife was taking all those lovers. He must have been jealous, maybe even went a little crazy. So he killed them."

"I—" Breed shoved his hands through his hair, leaving it standing on end. "I don't know what to say."

"Will you help me?"

She saw a startled look on his face. Followed by a look of chagrin. "You knew exactly who I was when you met me, didn't you? You planned all along to—"

"Ask for your help in tracking down a killer?" Grace interrupted sharply. She lifted her chin and said, "You damn bet I did!"

"So, you *planned* to seduce me?"

Grace felt a blush rise on her cheeks. "I only wanted to meet you. I never intended—"

"Don't bother lying!" Breed said. "The whole point of that interlude was to leave me owing you a favor."

"I'm not for sale," Grace retorted. "I wanted you. You wanted me. I simply made the most of the situation."

"You sure as hell did," Breed said.

"Can we stick to the point?"

"What about the bomb threat?" Breed said. "What is that all about?"

"I have no idea what you're talking about."

"Yesterday morning, the FBI received an anonymous phone tip saying that you—that is, Merle Raye Finkel—intended to set off a bomb when the president speaks at the LBJ Auditorium on Wednesday. Vince put me in charge of the team of agents out hunting for you."

Grace couldn't catch her breath. "He knows!"

"What are you talking about?"

"Harkness must have figured out somehow that I was in the house. He knows I have the diary. He wants me caught so he can make sure I don't tell what I know."

Breed dropped into a kitchen chair, rubbing his forehead. "Vince told me he wanted to be the first one to question you. He made sure I'd want to deliver you to him, and him alone."

"You can't take me in, Breed. If you do, he'll kill me."

"You're exaggerating—"

"He killed the snitch he set up to take the fall for the Cancer Society Murder," Grace said.

"Vince told me that guy died in a hit-and-run," Breed said.

"Yeah. I know."

"Are you blaming Vince for that, too?"

"Yeah. I am," Grace said.

"What is it you expect me to do?"

"He's your friend. You'd know best how to trap him."

Breed snorted. "The only way to trap him would be to catch him in the act."

Grace sank into the chair across from Breed. She looked into his eyes and said, "Maybe you'll just have to take me in for questioning after all. And be there to save my life when Vincent Harkness tries to kill me."

18

⁓

"I've found Merle Raye Finkel," Breed said, holding his cell phone so Grace could hear Vince's replies. He still thought her story was bullshit, but he'd let her talk him into making this call.

"Good work," Vince said. "Where is she? Do you have her in custody?"

"Not yet," Breed said. "She called and asked me to meet her."

"I want to be there," Vince said.

Grace exchanged a "What did I tell you?" look with Breed, who grimaced and replied to Vince, "No problem."

"Where are you meeting her?" Vince asked.

"She's been house-sitting. Not far from where you live, actually," Breed said.

"So that's how she disappeared," Vince mused.

"I was thinking we ought to get SWAT—"

"No SWAT," Vince said.

Grace arched her eyebrows, another wordless "Am I right? Or am I right?" and Breed grimaced.

"I want her alive," Vince said. "SWAT has a tendency to shoot first and ask questions later."

"What did you have in mind?" Breed asked.

"Where are you now?" Vince said.

"At my condo in town," Breed lied. Grace had convinced him to make the call from the home where she was house-sitting, in the belief that Vince would head there the instant he knew where she was to interrogate her on his own. By the time all their plans had been made, it had gotten dark outside.

"Do you have someone sitting on the house, watching the girl?" Vince asked.

"Not yet," Breed said as he glanced at Grace.

"Give me the address where the girl is, and I'll meet you there in an hour," Vince said.

Breed recited the address.

"That really is practically around the corner," Vince said. "Too bad I can't go right now."

"You sure you don't want me to call for backup?" Breed said.

"I think the two of us can handle this," Vince said. "Don't you?"

What Breed thought was that Vince's behavior was suspicious. Way outside usual FBI protocol for apprehension of a suspect, which was pretty much the more special agents, the better. "I was thinking she might have bomb-making paraphernalia on-site. Maybe the bomb squad—"

"At a place where she's house-sitting?" Vince said skeptically. "Not likely."

But not impossible, Breed thought. If Merle Raye Finkel really had been a terrorist, she might very well have loaded the garage with ammonium nitrate fertilizer. Or C-4. Or even TNT. Which made Vince's behavior even more questionable. "I can get there in half an hour," Breed said.

"I can't," Vince said. "And I want to be there when you take her down."

"You want me to go now and watch the house until you get there?" Breed asked.

"If she was going to bolt, she'd already be gone. Just meet me around the corner on the south side of the house in an hour," Vince said.

"You got it." Breed closed the cell phone, but it took him a moment to meet Grace's eyes. She didn't look particularly happy to be vindicated. Relieved, maybe. Anxious, certainly.

"You know what he's planning," she said as she dropped into the wing chair in the study.

"I'm not a mind reader like you," Breed said as he crossed to the swivel desk chair and sat down. "What is he planning?"

"Your friend Vince is already out the door on his way here," Grace said. "When he gets here—in the next ten to fifteen minutes—he plans to catch me unawares, interrogate me to find out what I did with his wife's diary, and then fix it so it looks like I killed myself.

"Or he might take me somewhere and stab me to death—which is how all his other victims died—and drop me in a Dumpster," Grace finished.

"I still can't believe—"

"You can stand behind the door when he gets here and listen, if that's what it takes to convince you Vincent Harkness is a murderer," Grace retorted.

Breed realized he was starting to believe what Grace was saying. It made him sick to his stomach. A man he'd admired as a friend and mentor, a man he'd brought into his own and his brother's home, a man who had a wife and kids who adored him—well, maybe Stephanie wasn't so adoring—might be a serial killer.

If it was true, how could he not have seen the signs?

Then he remembered how Ted Bundy had deceived his friends, including author Ann Rule, for years. The BTK killer was a beloved deacon in his Kansas church. And John Wayne Gacy, who'd murdered thirty-three boys and men and buried them in his basement, was selected as an escort for President Carter's wife, Rosalynn, when she came to Chicago for a political event.

It was obviously easier than anyone believed for a man to hide the evil inside him.

Breed still had doubts that Vince was what Grace said he was. He glanced at her with narrowed eyes. What if she was lying? What if all she wanted was to get Vince here so she could kill him, even without the evidence she needed to prove he'd done the things she'd accused him of doing?

Maybe it was pure coincidence that Stephanie had screwed the victim of the Cancer Society Murder.

The same night he died?

And of course Big Mike Finkel had questioned Vince about the murder. He and Stephanie had been sitting at the same banquet table with the victim. That didn't mean Vince had killed anyone.

What about all of Stephanie's other dead lovers?

You have only Grace's word for that. You haven't checked the first thing for yourself.

But Grace had given him a way to find out the truth. If she was right, Vince would show up here alone. Soon. Which meant he needed to work out the details of where he was going to hide so he could both protect her from Vince—and protect Vince from her.

"Do you suppose Vince is simply going to knock at the front door?" Breed asked.

Grace shot him a disdainful look. "I doubt it. He'll try the back door, which has a lock so cheap he can open it with a credit card."

"Where are you going to be?"

Grace rose from the wing chair and crossed the study, opening a cupboard to reveal a TV set, which she turned on. "I'm going to be sitting in that chair"—she pointed to the wing chair she'd just vacated—"watching TV." She used the remote to find the *food* channel.

She returned to the chair, which had its back to the door, and sat down. Breed realized that when she was sitting in the chair, she wasn't visible from the study doorway.

"I don't want him to think I'm expecting him," she said. "So I'll be innocently sitting here watching Rachael Ray prepare a 30-minute meal."

The show had just started. Breed wondered if it would still be playing when Vince arrived. If he arrived.

He looked around the room, from the wall of bookshelves behind the desk, to the wall with the cabinet containing the TV across from the doorway, to the final wall, which contained the doorway and a bi-fold closet door. "I suppose I'm going to be hiding in the closet."

Grace eyed the louvered bi-fold door. "Yep. You should be able to see and hear everything that happens from there."

Breed crossed to the closet and opened the bi-fold door. "This closet is full of crap."

Grace hopped out of the chair and helped Breed move the shelves of office supplies to the other side of the closet and then remove two of the shelves, so Breed would have a place where he could stand concealed.

When they were done, Grace closed Breed inside the closet, crossed to the wing chair, sat down, and said, "Can you see me?"

"Yeah. But I can't see the doorway. What if Vince decides to simply shoot you from there and forgo the questions?"

"He won't," Grace said confidently. "He wants that diary. The only way to get it is to ask me where it is."

Breed realized that he hadn't seen the diary since they'd left his condo. "Where is it now?"

Grace glanced up at him past lowered lids and said, "I hid it."

"I've been with you every moment—"

"Not every moment," Grace said with a small smile.

Breed realized that when they'd first arrived, after he'd done a perusal of the house to make sure they were alone, she'd told him she had to use the bathroom. He'd gone back to the living room and waited for her to return. Which she had.

Without the diary.

"Aw, hell," he said. "Are you going to tell me—"

"I'm telling you nothing," she said fiercely. "The same way I'm telling him nothing. That diary is the proof I need to clear my name. It's staying hidden where only I can find it until Vincent Harkness confesses to the murder of my father and stepmother."

"You're kidding yourself if you think he's going to admit to anything."

"He can't afford to kill me until he gets the diary back," Grace said stubbornly. "And now you know what he's done—what he's probably still doing—too."

"All I know is what you've told me," Breed said.

"Even without the diary, you could get Stephanie Harkness to tell you what bars she was in and find out whether the guys she hooked up with are alive or dead," Grace pointed out.

Breed was having trouble wrapping his head around the fact that he might soon find himself in a situation where he would have to kill Vince—or be killed. Because if Vince showed up here, it meant that at least some of what Grace had told him was true.

He checked his Glock to make sure he had a round chambered, then pushed at the bi-fold door to make sure he knew how to get it open. He realized he had to push in the center, rather than at the side. The door was half open when he heard a familiar voice. And froze.

"Hello there, Miss Finkel. We meet again."

Again? Breed thought, feeling his flesh prickle. *When had Merle Raye Finkel met Vincent Harkness? And why hadn't Grace told Breed she knew him?*

As Breed stared out from between the louvers, he saw Vincent Harkness enter the study. Vince had a Beretta pointed at Grace's head. And a smile on his face.

19

Grace squared her shoulders and lifted her chin as FBI Assistant Special Agent in Charge Vincent Harkness stepped into view. She restrained a gasp when she saw the Beretta in his hand. She could do nothing about the shiver that ran down her spine when she realized he had a suppressor attached to it.

"How did you find me?" she demanded, staring defiantly into his dark, obsidian eyes.

"Where's the diary?"

"I don't know what you're—"

Vince moved so fast, Grace never had a chance to protect herself before he swung the metal barrel of his gun. She cried out as her cheek exploded with pain. She saw the closet door start to move and shot a frightened warning look in that direction. She needed Vince to confess. She wanted no question left in Breed Grayhawk's mind that Vince Harkness had killed her parents. And maybe a lot of other people besides.

The copper taste of blood filled Grace's mouth where her teeth had cut her lip, and she felt a warm dribble of blood on her cheek where the skin had broken. She looked up at Harkness with all the hate she felt inside and taunted, "Such a big, strong man. Too bad you can only get off by hurting defenseless people. Like my step-mother."

"I only want to hear one thing from you, bitch. And that's where you hid my wife's diary."

Grace made a gesture with her hand toward the doorway. "You're welcome to search the house. But you'll never find it. I'm going to use it to bury you."

Vince raised his hand to strike her again, and the closet door exploded off its hinges.

"Breed, no!" Grace cried.

She watched in horror as Breed got caught up in the broken wood, giving Harkness time to flee through the study door.

Breed finally got free and ran after him, calling out, "Stop, Vince! Or I'll shoot!"

Grace sat where she was, listening for a gunshot. Which never came. Instead, she heard shattering glass. And screeching tires.

A few moments later, Breed reappeared in the doorway. Grace looked up at him and said, "Couldn't kill him, huh?"

"He's my friend. *Was* my friend." Breed crossed and knelt beside the chair to look more closely at the damage to her face. "How are you?"

"You should have let him hit me again," she said bitterly. "I know how to handle that kind of pain. And that kind of man. I've had enough experience with it."

"He would have killed you."

"You didn't save me by playing hero," Grace said. "You only prolonged the agony. I didn't have a chance to provoke him into confessing. I'm no further ahead than I was before."

Breed shook his head. "I saw him come to this house by himself when he said he'd meet me first. I heard him ask for the diary. I saw him point a gun at you. And strike you."

"So what?"

"So now I know he's worried about what Stephanie's diary might reveal. Which means we need to find out what's in there that he's so scared will come to light."

"*We*, kemo sabe?" Grace said.

"Come with me," Breed said, sticking his Glock in his boot holster and taking her hands in his.

Grace let him lead her to the bathroom, where he settled her on the toilet seat, then yanked open medicine cabinet doors until he found what he was looking for. He pulled out a bottle of alcohol, a tube of Neosporin, and a box of SpongeBob SquarePants Band-Aids.

"There isn't time for this," Grace hissed, as Breed dabbed alcohol on her bleeding cheek and lip with a cotton ball he found in a glass jar on the counter. He squeezed some Neosporin on his forefinger and swiped that across her cheek, then wiped his finger on his jeans.

"When did you meet Vince Harkness?" he said brusquely.

"I can't believe he remembered that," Grace said, wincing as Breed pressed the Band-Aid over the wound on her cheek.

"Answer the question!"

"I think we need to get out of here," Grace said. "Harkness could still call in SWAT to take both of us out and hope the diary stays buried."

Breed grasped her arms and hauled her to her feet, bringing them nose to nose. "What is it between you and Vince Harkness? When did you meet?"

Grace felt her heartbeat ratchet up a notch. She forcibly calmed herself before she spoke. "Harkness stopped by my parents' house when the FBI came up with a suspect they believed had committed the Cancer Society Murder. He said the FBI was taking over the investigation into the death of one of their own. Big Mike argued that the Austin PD wasn't going to be shoved aside. That's when we met."

Breed let her go. "That was a long time ago. That's it?"

Grace brushed a hand absently across the scar on her right eyebrow. "Almost."

"What else?" Breed demanded.

"When he left, my dad beat the shit out of me." She looked up at Breed and said, "It was nothing personal. Big Mike was just pissed off at Harkness. Maybe he already suspected him of the murder."

"Son of a bitch," Breed muttered. "Why didn't you tell someone what your father was doing to you?"

"My dad was a cop. Who was I going to complain to?"

"Your mother—"

"My stepmother loved me. She protected me whenever she could." Grace shrugged. "But she loved Big Mike."

"You're right," Breed said suddenly. "We'd better get the hell out of here. Pack what you need for a couple of days."

"Where do you suggest *we* go?" Grace said, heading for the bedroom. She opened the bedroom closet, slipped the backpack she found there on her shoulder, and said, "I'm ready."

"That was quick."

"I wasn't sure when I might have to get out of here in a hurry. You still haven't told me where we're going," she said as she followed Breed down the hall.

He made a stop in the kitchen, where he opened the freezer, shoved packages around, and came out with a plastic bag of frozen peas. "Hold that against your jaw," he ordered brusquely. "It'll keep down the swelling."

Without another word, he headed out the back door.

They passed through the backyard fence and down an alley to where Breed had left his pickup.

"Where are we going?" Grace asked, the bag of frozen peas molded to her aching cheek.

Breed glanced at her and admitted, "I have no earthly idea."

20

~

Once Breed had the engine started and they were on their way, he glanced at Grace and said, "I wish I knew what Vince is going to do. Whether he's going to run. Or whether he's going to try and bluff it out with the FBI, maybe tell everyone you're an even bigger threat than anyone thought, and come after you. After us," he corrected.

"Couldn't you call someone and explain the situation?" Grace asked.

Breed flipped open his phone and called the JTTF office. "Hey, Steve," he said.

That was all he got out before Steve said, "You'd better get your ass in here and explain what the hell is going on!"

Breed glanced at Grace, then said, "What did Vince tell you?"

"That you're emotionally involved with Merle Raye Finkel. That you've gone over the edge."

"Vince is the one who's over the edge," Breed retorted. "He's in some kind of deep shit, Steve. I'm not sure just how bad—"

"Vince said you'd say something like that," Steve interrupted. "He said you're on the run with Finkel, and that you have no intention of bringing her in. Is that true?"

Breed said nothing. What could he say? The only proof, if you could call it that, of Vince Harkness's *maybe* murderous activities was his wife's diary. Breed stuck the phone under his hip to muffle the sound and asked Grace, "Where's the diary? Do you have it?"

She unzipped her backpack and showed him the pink silk cover. "Right here."

Breed pulled the phone back to his ear and said, "I have Stephanie's diary, Steve. She's a sex addict. It seems Vince has been killing her lovers. Grace—" Breed stopped and corrected himself. "Merle Raye Finkel stole the diary from Vince's house and found out what he's been doing. I know for a fact that he's trying to shut her up."

Breed heard silence on the other end of the line.

"Where are you?" Steve said. "I want to see this stolen diary. Where can we meet?"

Breed hesitated, then said, "Did Vince ask you to set me up, Steve?"

Silence again.

"Come in, Breed. Every FBI special agent on the JTTF is out looking for you right now. It won't be long before we find you—and the murdering terrorist you're protecting."

"I'm not protecting a *murdering terrorist*," Breed protested, rattled by the fact Steve obviously didn't believe a word he'd said. What had Vince said or done to convince a man Breed had worked closely with for two years that he was deranged, unbalanced, or worse? "I'm protecting a woman I think might have been unjustly convicted of murdering her parents."

"I suppose Vince killed them, too?" Steve said sarcastically.

"I don't know whether he did or not." Breed glanced at Grace, noting the scar on her brow she'd stroked when she'd described how her father had beaten her after Vince Harkness had shown up at her father's door. "But it's possible."

"Your best bet is to turn yourself in," Steve said. "We can clear all of this up once we have the girl in custody."

"Merle Raye Finkel is *not* a terrorist," Breed insisted. "Where's the evidence to connect her to a plot to blow up the president? Tell me that!"

"Vince found the bomb, Breed. The jig is up."

Breed's mouth went dry. "What *bomb*?"

"The van full of nitrates parked in the driveway of the house where the girl's been house-sitting," Steve said. "Vince said the girl told you where the bomb was, and you told him, but when he tried to take the girl into custody, you knocked him down, grabbed the girl, and the two of you ran."

"I'll call you back." Breed turned off his cell phone, knowing it could be traced if it was on, and certain Vince would have thought of that, too. Breed frowned. He recalled now seeing a white van in the driveway when he was chasing Vince. He knew it hadn't been there when he and Grace arrived at the house, but he'd been too focused on catching Vince to realize its significance.

Breed tasted bile in his throat. It was hard not to admire the way Vince had snapped the trap shut on them.

Breed knew now that Vince had intended to kill Grace once he'd retrieved Stephanie's diary. The shooting would be justified in light of the van of explosives in the driveway. He would simply be taking out a terrorist.

Breed marveled at the logistics it must have taken to find a van and fill it with ammonium nitrates—which weren't that easy to come by these days—in the thirty-six or so hours since Vince had discovered the diary missing and made his plan to catch and kill Merle Raye Finkel. Vince had apparently parked the van in Grace's driveway and fled on foot.

With that van of nitrates in the driveway, Breed was going to have a difficult time convincing anyone that Merle Raye Finkel wasn't a terrorist.

His best bet was to call the San Antonio SAC directly and tell him everything that had happened. Westwood just might listen to him. But since Breed was on the run with Grace, Vince would have the opportunity to do some fast talking first. The San Antonio SAC and Breed's boss went back a long way, and by the time someone decided to believe Breed's story, he and Grace might be dead.

He dialed the JTTF office again, and when Steve picked up, Breed said, "Call the San Antonio SAC, Craig Westwood, and tell him what's going on. You know me, Steve. You know I'm not crazy. Just call Westwood and—"

"That's not going to happen," Vince said.

"Have you been there all along?" Breed asked.

"I have," Vince said. "You're on speakerphone. Everyone in the office can hear us. Everybody's here, Breed. We're all concerned about you. We want to keep you from making an even bigger mistake. Come in. Let's talk."

"When we do, the truth about you—whatever it is—is going to come out, Vince."

"The truth is, you've gotten yourself emotionally involved with an unstable woman. This investigation is going to remain confined to the Austin FBI and the JTTF, so we can do damage control."

"I'll call Craig Westwood myself and—"

"I wouldn't do that," Vince warned. "For the sake of those you care about."

Breed heard Vince's unspoken threat to Kate's life. To the lives of the twins. To his brother North's life.

Vince continued speaking as though the people Vince had been referring to that Breed "cared about" were the men in his office. "You're an embarrassment to me, to the men you've led, and the FBI. I urge you to come in on your own."

"You're not going to get away with this, Vince. You can't convince people I'm crazy. Because I'm not."

"Then why don't you come in?" he heard Steve ask, his voice sounding as though he might be on the other side of the room from the speakerphone.

"Because I don't—" Breed cut himself off. He was about to say he didn't trust his own men. Which did make him sound crazy.

"You don't trust us," Vince finished for him. "We can do this the hard way, Breed. Or the easy way. But rest assured, we'll find you. And we'll find the woman. Why not turn yourself in?"

"So you can kill us?"

"See what I mean?" Vince said, as though speaking to the agents listening in on the call. "He's delusional. Seeing enemies where he should see friends."

Breed made a disgusted sound and said, "Steve, if you believe—"

"I don't believe you're a bad man, Breed," Steve said. "But you need help. I agree with Vince. I think you should turn yourself in."

Breed snapped the cell phone shut with an oath. With a hand he realized was shaking, he dropped the phone on the car seat beside him.

"We're in trouble," he told Grace.

"What was all that about a bomb?" she asked.

"Vince set us up. Actually, he set you up, and I got caught in the trap."

"What are you talking about?" Grace said.

Breed felt a mounting frustration at the situation he found himself in. The way Vince was manipulating things, Breed doubted he and Grace would have a chance to turn themselves in. Somehow Vince would make sure they never lived to tell what they knew. They were going to be shot by sharpshooters. Or commit suicide in their cells, if they were captured alive.

Thank God he knew someone who would believe him. Someone who could be his eyes and ears on the ground while he figured out how to survive this fight to the death.

With a steady hand, Breed reached for his cell phone, hit speed dial, and waited for Texas Ranger Jack McKinley to answer his phone.

21

~

Jack McKinley wasn't the only person assigned to protect the governor's grandkids. But he was the one assigned to protect them overnight. Which meant sitting in a vehicle outside the house and making perimeter searches from time to time to ensure no one was lurking in the bushes. He had too much time alone to think. Too much time alone to remember. It seemed like a thousand years since he'd first met Kate Grayhawk Pendleton.

But it was only nine.

He'd gone to her parents' wedding reception at the Castle, the legendary South Texas ranch house that had been the home of Kate's paternal grandparents, the Blackthornes, and their ancestors, ever since the Civil War. The fathers of the bride and groom, King Grayhawk and Jackson Blackthorne, were never pleased when members of their respective families got along. But every single person he saw looked happy. Except Kate.

Which was odd, because she'd manipulated and schemed like crazy to get her parents together. It had been an almost impossible task, because when she'd started, her father had been engaged to another woman.

He'd watched Kate's eyes search the crowd at the backyard barbecue, looking for someone. Until they lighted on him. He was nearly hidden by the wall of morning glories on one end of the covered back porch. He saw her hands bunch into fists and then watched her consciously unclench them.

He saw how nervous she was. And how beautiful she was. And how young she was. Nineteen to his thirty-two.

If it had only been their ages, he might have let his attraction to her grow. But there were other reasons he wasn't the right man for her. Things about himself that he would never share with anyone. Things about himself he kept buried deep, in hopes they would never be discovered.

He'd fallen in with Kate's scheme to get her parents together without realizing how easy it would be to love her. Kate's plan had required them to pretend they were engaged. To pretend they were lovers.

It hadn't been easy turning away from her when she'd finagled it so they spent the night together in the same bedroom—with her parents under the same roof. She'd done a half-naked striptease, enticing him to make their romance the real thing, and let her eyes rest on the proof of his arousal.

He'd turned his back on her and managed to keep his distance that night, but seeing her at her parents' wedding reception had brought all those feelings back. Making his body yearn for her. And his heart ache.

He watched Kate approach him where he stood on her grandparents' porch, watched her buck up the courage to speak.

All she said was, "Hello, Jack."

He turned hard as a rock in thirty seconds flat. He had to angle his body away so she wouldn't see what she'd done to him. But he didn't take his eyes off her. *Couldn't* take his eyes off her. He felt the wind riffle his hair. Saw how it made the chiffon she was wearing flutter.

She'd been her mother's bridesmaid, and she looked fresh and lovely in a full-length, peach-colored gown with a ruffle up top that did nothing to conceal her womanly bosom.

She held out the chiffon skirt in the wind, smiled and said, "I feel like a teenager in her prom dress."

He smiled, because he could feel the tightness in his face and needed a way to ease the tension he felt inside. "Cute as a button," he said.

Her smile disappeared. "I'm not a child, Jack. Don't talk to me like I am one."

"I was hoping to avoid you," he admitted.

He saw the look of anguish that crossed her face and watched her swallow hard.

"I thought Texas Rangers weren't afraid of anything," she said.

"You're more formidable than some of the critters I've taken into custody."

"Come see the freak," she said bitterly. "The formidable Kate."

"Don't," he said.

But it was too late. Her eyes were already brimming with tears.

"Aw, Kate." He resisted the urge to take her into his arms. Fiercely resisted it.

He watched her blink back the tears and clamp her lower lip in her teeth in an unsuccessful attempt to keep her chin from quivering. He nearly reached for her then, but she whirled and ran.

Some predator instinct sent him after her. In two steps, he caught her shoulders, turning her into his body, holding her fragile softness in his arms. She clung to him, her arms gripping his waist.

He could feel her trembling and said in an unsteady voice, "I'm no good for you, Kate."

She kept her cheek pressed against his chest, where he could feel his heart thumping erratically.

"I love you, Jack," she said.

"I know," he managed to get past the lump in his throat.

But he made no corresponding declaration. He gently caressed her long black curls with one hand while he held her close with the other. He tipped her chin up and looked into her sky-blue eyes. It was impossible to mistake her feelings. And impossible to return them.

"It wouldn't work, Kate," he said, answering her unspoken plea. "There are things in my life—"

"Why can't it work?" she said angrily. "I don't care about anything you've done. I only care about being with you."

"You're being naive, Kate. You have no idea—"

"I love you, Jack! Please. Please—"

He used his mouth to shut her up but kept his lips closed as he kissed her. She moaned against his mouth, wanting more. He heard an agonized sound come from his throat as he opened his mouth to her and thrust deep, staking his claim.

Then he remembered where they were. And that he had no intention of letting this go any further. He ended the kiss, grasping her shoulders so hard she made a sound of protest as he forced the two of them apart. He looked into her glowing eyes and said, "I'm not the white knight you think I am."

"I don't believe the rumors, Jack," she said earnestly. "No one can make me believe you're a bad person, that you shaved points, that you cheated on your taxes. I don't believe any of it."

He didn't argue with her, just let his hands drop and took a step back. "You're too young to know what you want. And I'm old enough to know better. This isn't going to happen, Kate."

"Why not?" she demanded. "You know you want me."

"That's lust," he said brutally. "Not love."

"I don't believe you," she argued. "You do love me. I know you do."

"If I did, that would be all the more reason to keep my distance."

"That doesn't make sense!"

"You deserve better. You deserve—"

"I want *you*!"

"We don't always get what we want," he said flatly. "Or what we deserve," he added.

"I'm not going to wait around for you to come to your senses," she threatened. "I've got a life to live, and I'm going to live it. You'll be sorry—"

"I'm already sorry I showed up here," he said. "I've given my regards to the bride and groom. I'm outta here."

"Go! See if I care," she said. "Don't expect me to come running after you. Grayhawks don't beg. Or plead. Or go down on bended knee for anyone!"

She was shouting by the time she finished, panting with fury and frustration, tears streaming down her cheeks.

Jack never hesitated. He never looked back. When he reached his pickup, he jumped inside, slamming the door as he gunned the engine, his tires burning asphalt as he roared away.

"Do you really have to sit out here alone?"

Jack started when he realized Kate was standing at the open driver's-side window of his Ford Explorer. He couldn't believe she'd snuck up on him. He was supposed to be protecting her and her kids, not daydreaming. Especially about her.

"Why don't you come inside?" she said.

"Because this is where I'm supposed to be."

"The biggest danger to Lucky and Chance is Ann Wade hinting she'd like to have full custody of them. Since she's not here, I believe my boys are safe. Come inside, Jack."

"It's late," he said.

"I know," she replied.

She stepped back as he opened the car door. He followed her into the house, noting that her arms were wrapped tight around her chest. Maybe it was the chill in the night air. Or maybe it was the fear of what might happen if the two of them were alone in the dark.

She turned on the lamps from a wall switch as they entered the living room, giving the room a soft glow. "Can I get you something to drink? Some coffee?"

"My back teeth are floating," he said. "I wouldn't mind using your bathroom."

She pointed down the hall, and he made himself walk slowly, as if he weren't fleeing the hounds of hell, which it felt like he was.

Temptation.

He wanted her. And they were both free.

Or as good as. He was waiting for Gayle to send him the papers that would make him a divorced man. He wasn't sorry to end the marriage. Gayle hadn't wanted much to do with him toward the end of it. But he was sorry he'd hurt the woman he'd married. And he deeply missed his son.

Jack made use of the facilities and flushed the toilet, hoping Kate wouldn't realize he'd been running from her, keeping his distance, because that was the only way he thought he could keep his hands off her.

When he got back to the living room, he saw she'd poured them each a drink.

"Jack Daniel's, neat," she said. "That's what I remember you drinking. Okay?"

"I'm on duty," he said.

"Take it, Jack."

Jack took the drink.

She clinked her glass against his and said, "To happier times."

Did she mean the past? Or her hopes for the future? Either way, it was something he could drink to.

She gestured to a well-worn brown leather chair and said, "Have a seat, Jack." She seated herself on the peach-colored sofa opposite him, then slipped out of her tennis shoes and curled her legs under her.

Jack shoved the footstool out of the way and dropped into the leather chair, grateful to have the distance of the room between them.

The house was quiet. Neither of them spoke.

Jack felt the tension arcing between them. The awareness that they were alone.

"I've always thought Ann Wade was diabolical," Kate said. "She would be very happy to know how uncomfortable we both are right now."

"I couldn't get out of it," Jack said. "I tried."

She held up her glass in a toast to his efforts and drank deep. She cradled the glass of whiskey in both hands and said, "This has become my comfort over the past year since J.D. was killed.

"It doesn't help that I spend every day working with boys—young men—whose bodies have been torn apart by IEDs. It's amazing how many of them survive with horrendous injuries. It's the Kevlar vests they're wearing. They aren't eviscerated the way GIs were during the Vietnam conflict. They come home missing eyes and ears, hands and feet, arms and legs. But they come home."

She drank deeply again. "I keep imagining J.D. . . . There wasn't a piece of him left big enough to identify, except with DNA."

"Don't do this to yourself, Kate."

She shoved an agitated hand through her hair, rubbing her scalp and making an irritated sound in her throat. "I wish I missed him. But I don't."

When she met his gaze again, he saw her blue eyes were liquid with unshed tears.

"I tried to divorce him. Did you know that?"

"Kate, don't—"

"He threatened to take Lucky and Chance away from me, so I backed down." She started to drink, realized her glass was empty, and headed to the dry bar in the corner of the living room to refill it. "Now I have Ann Wade breathing down my neck, asking me if I wouldn't be happier letting her take the boys every summer. And over Thanksgiving. And Christmas."

When she turned to face him, he saw her glass was filled so close to the brim that it would likely spill if she tried to walk with it. She lowered the level of whiskey by an inch before she headed back to the couch.

Jack wondered how often she indulged this way. And whether her drinking was the impetus for her mother-in-law's efforts to gain custody of her grandsons. "Men die in war, Kate," he said.

"We argued on the phone the day he died. Over his gambling, if you can believe it," she said.

"Gambling?"

"He gambled on the Internet. More than we had to lose."

"I'm sorry," Jack said.

"I don't need your pity, Jack. I've managed to feel sorry enough for myself over the past year." She took another drink.

Jack was concerned about how much she was drinking but realized he had no right to say anything. He wasn't a part of her life. Never had been, really. "I'd better get back outside," he said.

He'd already stood and set his nearly full glass on the end table when she said, "Wait."

She set her glass on the coffee table and crossed to him. She stood directly in front of him, close enough that he could feel her body heat and smell the flowery shampoo she used. She reached out and took his hand.

"Come with me."

She started toward the hall, which led back to the bedrooms. He was so surprised, he'd walked a few steps before he stopped. She was drunk. She didn't realize what she was doing.

She turned and searched his face, perhaps seeing his confusion. And his reluctance. "I've been alone for more than a year, Jack. I thought we might offer each other a little comfort."

Before she'd even stopped speaking, Jack was shaking his head. "I'll be glad to talk," he said, "and listen. Or give you a shoulder to cry on," he added, realizing his heart was pounding. "But I don't think you and me making love—"

"Having sex," she corrected. "We don't love each other. I might have loved you once, Jack," she said. "But that was a long time ago."

Jack felt bruised, as though she'd sucker-punched him. "If you're looking for a fuck buddy," he said harshly, "I'm not your man."

She looked shocked at his verbal assault. And wounded. "I only thought—"

"You're drunk," he said, attacking, because she'd hurt him, and he wanted to hurt her back. "I doubt the sex would be worth the time and trouble it would take. I've got a job to do," he said, heading for the door. "Don't bother—"

"Jack!" She ran to intercept him, going up on tiptoe as he turned, so her body slammed against his and her arms clasped him tight around his neck. "I'm sorry, Jack. I'm so sorry." She was crying, holding on to him as though someone was trying to drag her away. "I do love you, Jack. I always have. Always. Even when—"

"Don't say it!" he warned.

"Even when I was married to someone else," she said, looking into his eyes, her own vulnerable and glistening with tears.

Jack kept his arms at his sides. For about two seconds. Then he was holding her tight against him, feeling the soft female curves against his body, pressing his nose into her hair, blinking hard as his eyes stung and watered.

"I've missed you so much, Jack. I've wanted you so long. I'm sorry, Jack. I'm sorry. I'm—"

"Don't," he said. "Baby, don't."

He tried to resist, but her mouth was on his throat, on his chin, on his cheeks, on the side of his mouth. He turned a hairsbreadth and found her mouth with his.

He'd tried to deny how much he wanted her. How much he needed her. How much she was a part of him and always would be. But he couldn't do it anymore. He kissed her the way he'd imagined kissing her for too many years.

His hand was already under her blouse feeling warm flesh when she stepped back. He stared at her for a moment, confused, until she took his hand and began leading him toward the bedroom.

He'd already taken a few steps after her when he stopped. "I'm on duty," he reminded her.

She smiled. "You can watch over all of us just as well from inside the house, don't you think?"

Jack knew his mind wasn't going to be on his work if he followed Kate into her bedroom. He was fighting against his better judgment when his phone vibrated at his hip. He was tempted to ignore it. But he was a Texas Ranger. And he was on duty.

He checked the ID and saw it was Breed. He considered letting the call go to voice mail. Then he remembered he'd left his mother and father at the ranch, and that there might be some crisis because of it.

He pulled Kate close with his free hand and felt her arms slide around his waist as he flipped the phone open. In a voice that showed his irritation at being interrupted, he said, "What's up?"

He pulled Kate's arms free and stepped back as he listened to what Breed was saying. A few moments later he snapped the phone shut and met her questioning gaze.

Jack knew Kate and Breed were good friends, that she would want to know if Breed was in a scrape. But he wasn't about to lay any more trouble on her already overburdened shoulders.

So he simply said, "I've got to go. I'll call someone to come replace me."

22

~

Kate was staring at the closed front door, still trembling, still trying to pull herself together after her emotional encounter with Jack, when she realized there was someone else in the room. Her heart thumped even harder in her chest, if that was possible. What if Ann Wade was right and there really was some danger menacing her sons?

Jack was gone. She was the only one standing between Lucky and Chance and whatever threat had come into her home. She would gladly give her life to defend her sons. Kate moved her weight to the balls of her feet, ready to attack, and slowly turned to confront the danger, whatever it was.

At first, all she saw was the shadow of a man in the dark kitchen doorway. That was enough to raise the hairs on the back of her neck and constrict her throat, making it impossible to scream for help, even if help had been close by.

But there was no one to save her. No one to protect her children but her.

How had this stranger gotten into the house? How long had he been standing there?

He was terrifyingly tall. His eyes were dark, sunken hollows in a pale, gaunt face. His hair was light-colored, long and lank. He was wearing a torn chino shirt and dirty khaki trousers so large they were gathered at the belted waist. Her gaze shot to his hands, which he held at his sides, looking for whatever weapon he might be wielding. They were empty.

She searched his features again, her mind trying to make sense of what her eyes were telling her. She nearly fainted when he spoke.

"Hi, honey. I'm home."

23

"Is it really you?" Kate asked.

"Yes, my loving wife, it's me," J.D. replied. "I see you haven't wasted any time finding someone to replace me."

Kate recoiled, stung by J.D.'s unfair accusation. "I thought you were dead!" She was still reeling from his sudden appearance, so dizzy she thought she might vomit. She pressed a hand flat against the wall to keep herself upright and swallowed the bile in her throat.

"How is this possible?" she gasped. "There was proof—DNA evidence—that the remains I buried were yours."

He shoved up his folded shirtsleeve and showed her a missing hunk of muscle, a gouge in his forearm that had scarred over, then pulled up his pants leg and showed a corresponding scar on his calf. "There was a chunk or two of me in the mix, all right." He rubbed his fingers together, the universal sign for money, and said, "It's amazing how persuasive cold, hard cash can be when you need lab results to turn out a certain way."

"Who was it I buried? Who was it my sons mourned?"

"It seems the same day I was KIA—killed in action—another guy from my unit went MIA—missing in action. Turns out he was the one who was KIA. And here I am." He spread his arms wide. "Back from the dead."

"You *faked* your death? Why, J.D.?" she cried in anguish.

"You want the truth? Or the official version?"

Kate's head hurt. She closed her eyes and pressed her hands against her pounding temples. "Oh, my God. This is a nightmare."

She opened her eyes again, but J.D. was still standing there. "Where have you been all this time, J.D.? It's been a year since we held a memorial service for you."

"Officially, I've returned to hearth and home after a heroic escape from the Taliban in Afghanistan, followed by a harrowing cross-country trip through Pakistan to the coast, and then across the sea to Mexico, and finally overland to Texas and my loving wife. Whom I found in the arms of another man," he reminded her nastily.

"And the truth?" Kate asked as she dropped her hands and glared at her husband.

J.D. shrugged. "The Texas Rangers were getting a little too close to the truth about my gambling activities. I figured it was better to disappear for a while. The hassle I had getting back to the good old USA is pretty much the way it was."

Kate shuddered. J.D. had put her and her sons through the agony of believing him dead because the law was after him for illegal gambling activities? "How could you let us believe you were dead? Lucky and Chance are just now starting to get over the loss of their father. I can't imagine how they're going to react to the fact you're back from the dead. Surely your escape didn't take an entire year. Why didn't you come home sooner?"

"Do you want the official version? Or the truth?" he said as he sauntered over to the living room chair that had been his favorite and settled himself in it, setting a worn pair of combat boots on the footstool as he pulled it close.

"The truth, dammit!"

"Okay, okay. I've been hiding out."

Kate's knees kept threatening to buckle as she made her way to the couch. Her legs finally collapsed, and she landed awkwardly on the edge of it. She leaned forward, her hands on her knees, because she had to hold on to something or fly into a million little pieces. "What are you doing here, J.D.?"

"I came back for my boys. Who knew 'Mommie Dearest' would be so unhappy to see me alive. Seems Ann Wade got a little power-hungry while I was gone. She's decided to run for president herself. Which makes my return from the dead a bit of a nuisance."

"Ann Wade knows you're alive?" And then, "You visited your *mother* before you came home to your *wife and children?*"

"Can you imagine my own mother warning me away from my sons?" he said angrily. "I told her I had it all worked out so I could return from the dead. I would have been MIA all this time, and the DNA identification would be a mistake. My comrade-in-arms would have been KIA and buried in my place.

"Turns out Ann Wade wants me to stay dead. Turns out she thinks my connections to the Mexican Mafia would come to light if I returned and put a serious crimp in her efforts to get elected president."

"Your connections to the *Mexican Mafia?*" Kate hardly knew what she was saying. Everything she'd heard so far was so unbelievable she was having trouble processing it.

"It's a California prison gang. At least, it started out that way. Now it has very long, dangerous, tentacles." J.D. grimaced. "The less you know, the better for you," he said, avoiding her question.

"How long have you been in Austin?"

"A week or so, I guess."

"Where have you been staying?" Kate asked, amazed and appalled to think J.D. was just now making his presence known to her. If he'd come even an hour earlier she would have been saved from revealing her feelings to Jack, whom she was no longer free to love. Because she wasn't a widow. And never had been.

"Does it matter where I've been?" J.D. asked irritably. "I'm here now."

"For how long?" Kate demanded.

"I told you, I came for the boys."

"What does that mean, exactly?" Kate said. "Are you still planning to make a miraculous return from the dead?"

J.D. was already shaking his head. "I'm headed to South America as soon as I can get the boys—"

The horror of what J.D. was suggesting began to sink in. Kate tried to stand, but her legs wouldn't hold her, and she toppled back onto the couch. Her whole body was trembling with fear and anger. "You're not taking my sons anywhere. You can't do it, J.D. I won't let you!"

"You're welcome to come along," he said.

"What makes you think I'd go anywhere with you?" she snarled.

"Look, honey," he shot back, "I had to take this kind of crap from my mother. I don't have to take it from you."

Kate wished Jack were here. Wished anyone with a gun was around so he could point it at J.D. and keep him away from Lucky and Chance. "My sons are staying at home. Where they belong."

"Aren't you forgetting something?" he said.

"What?"

"They're my sons, too."

Kate bit her lip to keep from blurting the truth: *They're not your sons!* That might stop J.D. momentarily. But it would give him too much power in the game they were playing right now. And it was a game. He wanted something from her. And it wasn't her sons.

Kate straightened her spine as she realized why he'd really come. "How much do you need?" she said with a sneer. "Or maybe I should ask, how much do you want?"

J.D. laughed. "You always were a bright one. I need a quarter million. To start."

Kate was shaking her head. "I don't have that kind of money."

"Your grandfathers do."

Then Kate realized what else J.D. had said. *To start.* If she paid the first time, he would be imposing on her, and her grandfathers, for as long as any of them were alive.

"What if I refuse to pay?" she said.

"Then I'll steal the boys and disappear."

As threats went, it was a pretty good one. The protective detail Ann Wade had ordered for her grandsons was going to end when she was replaced as governor in a year. Kate could hire a private bodyguard, and she could warn the boys to stay away from their father if he contacted them. But the bald truth was that, unless Kate paid J.D. off, she would spend the next ten years or so looking over her shoulder, wondering when her sons would be kidnapped.

She stared at her husband, sitting there in his chair, alive and well and as selfish as ever. "I want you out of my house. I want you gone. Now."

"You know what you have to do to get rid of me."

Kate no longer wondered, as she had when she was working with wounded soldiers who'd used lethal force to defend their lives and the lives of others, whether she could actually kill another human being. She knew now she could. It was just too bad she didn't have a gun in the house.

Which was when she realized that J.D. had given her a powerful weapon she could use to be rid of him. One that would take him out of her life for good. Or at least, for a very long time. J.D. was a deserter. All she had to do was make sure the military knew how to find him.

"Where are you going to be?" she asked J.D. "I have to know where to deliver the money."

He shook his head. "I can see your mind working, my dear, going around like a hamster in a cage. I'm not about to let you call the government down on me. Once I leave this house, you won't be able to find me. I want the money deposited in an offshore account. I'll leave the account number with you. When I confirm the money's there, I'll disappear from your life. Until I need some more," he added with a malicious chuckle.

"I hate you," Kate said.

"You're not the first bitch to say that. And you won't be the last," J.D. replied in an equally cold voice.

"I want a divorce."

J.D. shook his head. "Uh-uh. I'm not about to get rid of the goose that lays the golden eggs."

"Then I'll divorce you," Kate said.

"You can't divorce me," he said with a grin. "I'm legally dead."

Which meant she was free, legally, to go on with her life. Except she knew J.D. was alive. Which meant she was still a married woman. In seven years, she could have J.D. declared dead—again—and be legally free. But spending the next seven years knowing he was alive, that he was wanted by the law and extorting money from her, would be a living hell.

"Put the account number on the kitchen counter on your way out," she said.

"I appreciate it, honey. I'll just get out of your hair."

Kate glared at him, at the shit-eating grin on his face. She might have been naive at nineteen when she'd married J. D. Pendleton, but she'd grown up since then. She had no intention of letting J.D. take advantage of her. Or put her sons in danger. "Good-bye, J.D."

"So long, honey. Be seeing you."

As he headed for the back door, Kate stood on shaky legs and made her way down the hall toward her bedroom, holding on to the wall to stay upright. The bedroom she had almost shared with Jack tonight.

Kate yearned for Jack's kisses. The strength of his arms. The tenderness of his gaze. She wanted a future with Jack. Which meant she needed to be free of J. D. Pendleton.

The question was how to accomplish that.

Her first thought, as she lay down on her bed with the lights off, in a room as black as J.D.'s heart, was to call her father. Clay Blackthorne had been U.S. attorney general before he became a federal judge. He'd gone after the baddest bad guys in the land for a living and put them all in prison. He would know how to handle J. D. Pendleton.

But if she called on her father to hunt down J.D., it was likely Ann Wade would be forced to come to her son's defense. Kate didn't want her father fighting a war with such a powerful opponent. The Texas governor had long, strong arms. There was no telling what harm she could do to Kate's father.

She knew her grandfathers, both Blackjack and King, would be happy to tackle Ann Wade Pendleton. But again, at what cost?

Wouldn't it be easiest, in the long run, just to pay off J.D. and make him go away? With any luck, the bad guys he was hiding from would find him and take care of the problem for her. At the very least, paying him off would buy her time to figure out how to resurrect him from the dead long enough to get him out of her life for good.

So who should she ask for the cash to pay off J.D.?

Her father was out, because as soon as he found out the situation, he would want to go after J.D. directly. Likewise with Grandpa Blackjack. He would never agree to pay blackmail.

Which left Grandpa King.

Should she try to get him to give her the money without telling him why she wanted it? Or should she admit why she wanted it and swear him to secrecy? If she told him the truth, he might be more likely to give her the money and stay mum precisely because it was a secret she was keeping from her father and Blackjack, both of whom he hated.

Or should she just tell everyone, including the military, that J.D. was alive, pay a bodyguard to protect her sons, and let the chips fall where they may?

Could Lucky and Chance be kept safe from their father 24/7? Would J.D. persist in trying to kidnap his sons when he knew they were being protected by an armed bodyguard?

Yes. He would. Because he knew she would pay anything—do anything—to get them back.

Besides, did she want her sons to have to live their lives behind protective glass? Wouldn't Lucky and Chance, as they got older, want to know why they needed a bodyguard? Would they accept whatever explanation she came up with to avoid telling them the truth? And wouldn't they find a way, as mischievous boys did, to sneak away from the man watching them, and perhaps be stolen away by J.D. in an unguarded moment?

Kate chewed a thumbnail in the dark. There was no easy answer to her dilemma. No certain "right" course of action.

She had some thinking to do.

24

~

Breed was still reeling from the knowledge that Vince Harkness was very likely a serial killer. Why else would he go through the trouble of framing Merle Raye Finkel as a terrorist and including Breed in the elaborate charade?

He was lucky Vince wasn't willing to call on the full resources of the FBI to find him. Yet. But when Vince got desperate enough, he would. Before that happened, Breed needed to get himself and Grace someplace safe.

Unfortunately, he had no idea where that might be.

Knowing Vince, he would have all six JTTF special agents checking out Breed's regular haunts. Which was why Breed had asked Jack to meet him at a busy truck stop west of Austin where they'd eaten once and decided the food was so bad, they'd never go there again.

"Who was that on the phone?" Grace asked.

"I've got a friend with the Texas Rangers I can trust, Jack McKinley. We own a ranch together called Twin Magnolias."

"I know," Grace said.

"I should have known you'd know," Breed muttered. "Anyway, I'm hoping Jack can talk one of the JTTF guys into telling him what's going on with the van full of nitrates that was left in your driveway."

"Why would an FBI agent tell a Texas Ranger his business?"

"Jack knows all these guys. He's gone drinking with them. They've been to the ranch. More than that, one day soon, this situation will be resolved, and someone on the JTTF is going to need something—

some information or a favor—from the Texas Department of Public Safety.

"If he helps Jack now, Jack will repay the favor later. That's how it works in law enforcement. Tit for tat. So I'm betting—"

"My life," Grace interjected.

Breed conceded the truth of her statement with a nod. "Your life. And mine," he added, "that Jack can get someone to cough up the truth about what's going on. Once he finds out what the JTTF knows about that bomb in your driveway, he can follow the trail of the ammonium nitrates, and the van, back to their source. Which, with any luck, will be Vince Harkness."

"How long is that going to take?" Grace asked.

"I don't know. A couple of days maybe. After that, the situation's going to get dicey." Breed pulled into the Burger Heaven truck stop and parked his pickup where it would be hidden from the road between two sixteen-wheel rigs.

"What's going to change to make the situation suddenly dicey?" Grace said.

"Vince can't count on keeping your existence—and the existence of that nitrate truck bomb—a secret for long. He's going to run into a time crunch."

"Time crunch?" Grace said, hop-skipping to keep up with Breed's long strides as they headed into the truck stop together.

"It's Sunday night. The president is coming to town on Wednesday. If Vince doesn't catch us in the next day or so, I guarantee you someone on the JTTF is going to get nervous about all this secrecy and call in their own anonymous tip to the Secret Service or the FBI in San Antonio."

"How does that help us?"

"I'm not sure it does," Breed admitted. "It might make our situation a whole lot worse. Unless we have proof by then that someone besides you turned that van into a bomb."

Breed headed for a wooden booth near the back exit of Burger Heaven. The clatter of dishes and silverware was the predominant sound, because the men, truckers who traveled alone, weren't doing much talking. And the jukebox at Burger Heaven, which had been "Out of Order" when he and Jack had been here seven months ago, was still broken.

Breed sat down on the red leather seat of a booth facing the front door, and Grace sat down on the other side. Breed felt relatively safe here, because Burger Heaven was full of truckers who didn't know and didn't care who sat to the right or left of them.

A waitress in a short-skirted, short-sleeved black uniform with pink trim and a pink apron appeared and asked, "What can I get for you folks?"

Breed looked at Grace, who said, "Do you have apple pie?"

"We sure do, honey," the waitress said with a deep Texas accent. "You want that heated up with a scoop of vanilla ice cream on top?"

Grace's smile was blinding. "That would be great!"

"Make that two," Breed said.

"Coffee?" the waitress asked.

"Water for me," Grace said.

Breed remembered the last cup of coffee he'd drunk at Burger Heaven and said, "Water for me, too."

Once the waitress was gone, Grace leaned over and said, "I can see a scenario where the FBI sends a SWAT team with very big guns out to find me. And you turn me in to save yourself."

"If I was going to turn you over to the FBI, Grace, I would have done it long before now."

"You might change your mind when you see all those loaded guns pointed at you."

"You still don't trust me," Breed said.

"Oh, it isn't just you," Grace replied, unwinding her silverware from the napkin it was wrapped in and spreading it on the cigarette-burned, knife-cut, laminated red tabletop. "I don't trust anybody. I can't afford the luxury."

Breed leaned across the table until their noses were nearly touching. "You don't seem to get it," he said through gritted teeth. "I'm on your side. I want to help you."

She glared back at him. "No, *you* don't seem to get it. I can get along fine without help from you or anybody else!"

Breed froze as he suddenly felt a presence behind him. He watched Grace's eyes go wide, and realized that whoever was standing at his right shoulder had the drop on him.

25

～

"Am I interrupting something?"

Breed huffed out a gust of air and said, "Jesus, Jack! You scared the shit out of me."

"You're the one who sat by the rear exit," Jack said. "You should have been watching it."

"Sit down," Breed said, shoving the Glock he'd palmed, which was hidden under the table, back into his boot.

Grace scooted over to the wall to make room, and Jack sat down beside her.

The waitress showed up a moment later with their apple pie à la mode. "How 'bout you, honey?" she said, winking at Jack. "You having pie, too?"

"Coffee," Jack said. "Black."

Breed took a bite of the pie and nearly gagged. The apples were mushy and the dough was greasy. He swallowed the stuff in his mouth and set down his fork.

"What kind of trouble are you in that's so secret you couldn't tell me about it on the phone?" Jack said. "And so important it couldn't wait until I got off duty?"

"Meet Merle Raye Finkel," Breed said as he gestured to Grace. "Convicted murderer. And accused terrorist."

Jack eyed Grace warily, then looked at Breed and said, "You're just full of surprises."

"My name is Grace Caldwell," Grace corrected, setting down her fork and extending her hand to Jack. "It's nice to meet you."

Jack hesitated, then took her hand and said, "Great to meet you, too. I hope you know what's going on here, Grace, because I'm not getting much that makes sense out of my friend here."

"You'll tell him your name, but you wouldn't tell me?" Breed said to Grace in an aggrieved voice. "I knew I should—"

"Hey!" Jack said, interrupting Breed. "Why the hell am I here?"

Breed turned on him and said, "Because Vince Harkness planted a truck bomb full of nitrates in front of Grace's house and told the FBI that Grace put it there."

Jack frowned in confusion. "You're saying Vince Harkness is a terrorist?"

Breed shook his head. "He only did it to frame Grace, to make it look like she's a terrorist."

"What would be the point of that?" Jack asked, keeping a cautious eye on Grace, who was forking down her apple pie like there was no tomorrow.

"So I can't point the finger at him for murdering my parents," Grace said through a mouthful of pie dough. "And stabbing a whole lot of his wife's lovers to death."

Jack stared at Grace as though she were a two-headed calf. He turned back to Breed and said, "I'm lost here."

"Grace believes Vince Harkness is a serial killer," Breed said. "That he's been murdering Stephanie's lovers."

"She has affairs when she's on the road on business," Grace explained. "And a bunch of her lovers have ended up dead."

Breed said, "Show him Stephanie's diary, Grace."

Jack's hand went to the SIG at his waist as Grace opened the backpack on the bench seat beside her and didn't leave it until her hands came out bearing only a pink silk book. She laid it on the table in front of him, open to a page that contained a yellowed newspaper clipping.

She pointed to it as she said, "This is the entry where Stephanie Harkness describes how she had sex with the Cancer Society Murder victim the same night he was killed. My dad was a homicide cop in

Austin at the time and investigated the murder. I think he suspected Vincent Harkness."

Jack read the entry as she continued, "When I checked the first fifteen of these entries, I discovered ten murders had been committed corresponding to the first names and locations where Stephanie took lovers."

Jack turned to Breed, disbelief clear on his face, and said, "You really think Vince killed all those men?"

"His wife speculated that he did," Grace said, turning pages and showing Jack the entry in different-colored ink. "And someone— besides me—killed my parents."

Jack stopped speaking when the waitress showed up and said, "Here's your coffee, honey. Oh, what a pretty book," she said, eyeing the pink silk diary.

Grace mumbled, "Thanks," and quickly returned the diary to her backpack.

"You sure you don't want a little pie to go along with that coffee?" the waitress asked Jack.

"No, thanks," Jack said. "Just the coffee." When she was gone, he turned to Breed and said, "That diary she showed me is it? That's all the evidence you have that a man you've admired—and emulated— for years is a murderer?"

"If it isn't true, why was Vince so anxious to have the diary back that he met Grace in secret and pistol-whipped her when she wouldn't turn it over to him?"

"To protect his wife—and himself—from the humiliation of having Stephanie's affairs become public," Jack said.

Breed glanced at Grace. "He has a point."

"Are you sure Vince parked that truck bomb in Grace's driveway?" Jack asked. "I mean, couldn't someone else have left it there?"

Breed glanced at Grace, who was eyeing him warily. Hesitantly, he said, "The van wasn't there when I went into the house with Grace. But it was parked in the driveway when I chased Vince back out again."

"Were you watching the driveway the whole time? Did you hear the van arrive?" Jack asked.

"I had the TV on," Grace admitted. "And we were talking. But who else could have put it there except Vince Harkness?"

"One of your Victims for Vengeance," Breed said softly.

"None of them knows where I live," Grace said.

Breed's eyes narrowed. "You could have been followed."

"I was too careful for that." Grace eyed his uneaten pie and said, "Are you going to eat that?"

Breed shook his head. He couldn't have swallowed anything past the constriction in his throat.

"Do you mind if I eat it?" Grace asked.

Breed shoved the plate of melting vanilla ice cream and Dutch apple pie across the table and watched Grace dig in. She ate like she might never see another piece of apple pie à la mode again. And maybe, he thought, for the eight years at Giddings, she hadn't.

"Besides," Grace said past a mouthful of pie, "the Victims don't want to blow people up. That's not what we're about."

"No, you just want to put a bullet between their eyes," Breed said.

He was staring hard at Grace, because Jack had put doubts in his mind.

Grace stared right back. "I didn't have anything to do with that van in the driveway," she said. "And I'd vouch for the fact that none of the Victims for Vengeance did, either."

"The group's name doesn't leave me feeling particularly convinced they're harmless," Jack said.

"They're *victims*!" Grace retorted.

"Yeah, I get that part," Jack said. "It's the *vengeance* part that worries me."

Grace made a frustrated sound in her throat as she forked in the last bite of apple pie.

"You know, Breed, you could straighten this out just as easily if Grace were in custody," Jack said. "And if you bring her in, you won't end up in prison yourself as an accomplice to God knows what."

Grace swallowed without chewing. She looked around and Breed thought she was noticing for the first time that she'd allowed herself to be trapped in the booth.

"Tell Jack about Vince's threat to kill me," she said. "Tell him about Cecil Tubbs."

"Vince threatened to kill you?" Jack said. "And who the hell is Cecil Tubbs?"

"I watched Vince point a Beretta at Grace's head," Breed said. "He meant to kill her, Jack. He just wanted the diary back before he shot her."

Jack looked skeptical. "But he didn't shoot her."

"Because I came crashing out of a closet where I was hiding." He held up a hand to avoid further explanation and said, "Don't ask."

"So, who's Cecil Tubbs?" Jack asked. "And what does he have to do with all this?"

"Cecil Tubbs is the man arrested, but never tried, for the Cancer Society Murder," Breed said. "He was later killed in a hit-and-run accident that Grace believes was arranged by Vince."

"You don't think someone else could be responsible for all these murders? Or that hit-and-run?" Jack said. "That it might be coincidence that a few men Stephanie Harkness had sex with died?"

"Ten deaths isn't a few," Graced shot back. "And they didn't just die, they were all stabbed to death—outside the exact same bars where they met Stephanie."

"We need your help, Jack," Breed said.

"You want a Texas Ranger to investigate murders committed by an FBI ASAC?" Jack said incredulously.

"No, Grace and I will take care of that," Breed said.

Jack snorted and rolled his eyes. "Of course. I should have known."

Breed held on to his temper with effort. He met Jack's gaze and said, "I need you to track the ammonium nitrates and the van that were left at Grace's house." He glanced at Grace and added, "I think the trail will lead back to Vince."

Jack grimaced. "Even if Vince did park that van there—and I'm still not convinced he did—do you think he hasn't covered his tracks so well they'll never be found?"

"You may be right," Breed conceded. "But if the van and the nitrates can be traced, you're the one who can do it. Will you help us?"

Breed realized too late he'd said "help *us*"—and Jack had noticed the slip.

Jack eyed him speculatively, glanced at Grace, and said, "Sure. Why not? How do I reach you when I need to get in touch?"

"Better let me call you," Breed said. "I don't know where we'll be."

"Have you got a place to go?"

"I'm still working on that."

"You should turn yourself"—Jack glanced at Grace—"yourselves in."

Breed shook his head. "I want proof that Vince set up Grace to take the fall for the van full of nitrates before I go to the FBI with his wife's diary."

Jack eyed Grace, who was wiping up the last of Breed's apple pie with a sticky forefinger, and said, "I take it there's no real threat to the president from Merle Raye Finkel?"

"Absolutely not," Breed said. "I don't know for sure, but I'm guessing Vince was the source of that anonymous tip to the Austin FBI naming Merle Raye Finkel as a terrorist suspect."

"You think Vince was responsible for both bomb threats? The one to the FBI and the one to the Texas DPS?" Jack said.

Breed looked hard at Jack. "What threat did the Department of Public Safety get?"

"According to my friend in the Criminal Investigation Division," Jack said, "the DPS got an e-mail threat that said Governor Pendleton was going to be blown to smithereens. It didn't mention Merle Raye Finkel."

"Does the FBI know about that warning?" Breed asked.

"Did the FBI tell the DPS about Merle Raye Finkel?" Jack replied.

"She was a terrorist suspect," Breed said. "The JTTF is supposed to handle suspected terrorists."

Jack snorted. "A bomb threat is a bomb threat. It doesn't have to be terrorism. It can just be a pissed-off constituent. Besides, the State of Texas has its own people to deal with domestic terrorism. We don't need the FBI to do it for us."

"The FBI has better—"

"Don't go there," Jack warned. "Texas has plenty of resources to manage a bomb threat. Not to mention the help we can get from the Secret Service, which has been all over the LBJ Auditorium with a fine-tooth comb. By the time everybody shows up Wednesday night for the president's keynote, it'll be the safest place in town."

"Unless that second threat is the real deal and somebody else out there is determined to blow up the president," Breed said.

"Actually, this threat was against Governor Pendleton. But since she's going to be in the LBJ Auditorium with the president, the threat also includes him and the rest of the governors," Jack said. "Which includes your dad."

"He can get blown up for all I care," Breed said.

"It also includes Kate's mother-in-law. And Kate and the twins," Jack said.

"What?"

Breed was waiting for Jack's explanation when the waitress appeared at the booth with a pot of coffee and said to Jack, "More coffee, honey?"

"No thanks," Jack said.

Breed noticed he hadn't drunk the first sip. They'd agreed the last time they were here that Burger Heaven coffee could have been used as tar on a roadway.

"Could you bring us a check?" Breed said.

"One check or two?" the waitress asked.

"One check, please."

When the waitress was gone, Breed said, "What does that bomb threat against Governor Pendleton have to do with Kate and the twins?"

"Last I heard, Governor Pendleton was arranging a photo op where she shakes hands with the president while her dead-war-hero son's kids look on," Jack said. "In which case, Kate will be there. And I'll be there to keep an eye on all of them."

"Let's get this sorted out, Jack. I don't want anything happening to Kate or the kids."

"Or your father?"

"King Grayhawk can go hang!"

"I'd better get moving," Jack said. "I have a lot to do and not much time to do it."

He went out the way he'd come in, through the rear exit. Grace had watched him the entire way out the door. When he was gone, she turned to Breed and said, "He doesn't trust me."

"He doesn't need to trust you," Breed replied. "He trusts me."

Breed dropped enough money on the table to cover the pie and coffee, along with a generous tip. "Ready to head out?"

"Almost," Grace said. "I just have one more question."

"What's that?"

"Where are we going?"

26

~

Grace had feared a day might come when she would need a bolt hole, a place where she could escape from danger. Sitting with Breed in Burger Heaven, with nowhere else to go, she'd realized that day had come. Staying in the open meant becoming an FBI target. Like a wild, hunted animal, she knew it was time to go to ground.

"I own a house in the hill country no one knows about," she told Breed. "I think we should go there."

Breed said only, "Point me in the right direction."

They headed west and traveled another hour, deep into the Texas hill country.

As Breed drove down a bumpy, narrow dirt track that had been created by wagon wheels more than a century before, Grace breathed deep through the open truck window and said, "Can you smell it?"

He looked at her and said, "Smell what?"

"The mesquite. The scrub oak. The land."

Breed suddenly swore and hit the brakes, as a large, bristly animal dashed across the road right in front of them. "Was that a *pig*?" he said incredulously.

"Wild boar," Grace replied. She watched in the headlights as the grunting animal crashed back into the overgrown thicket of mesquite and scrub oak and cactus that covered her property. "I've also got deer and rabbits and wild turkeys and—"

"Great hunting," he quipped.

"Nothing gets hunted on my land," she shot back. "My home is a refuge. For me. And for them."

An awkward silence fell between them, and Grace realized she'd overreacted. But when you were the one who'd been hunted, as she'd been hunted over the past year, you had a different perspective on the deadly sport.

"How much longer till we get to your house?" Breed asked.

"I've got seven hundred acres," Grace said. "The house is smack-dab in the middle of it."

"I haven't seen any power lines," Breed said. "What about electricity and running water?"

"I prefer oil lamps and candles, but I've got a generator for electricity. I get my water from a well, and somebody put in plumbing at the turn of the century."

"Is the FBI going to be able to trace you to this place through property records?"

Grace shook her head, then realized the headlights had revealed a herd of white-tailed deer grazing beside the road, and Breed's eyes were focused on them. "After I found this place, I consulted a lawyer in New York. He created an offshore corporation and engaged a couple of intermediaries to help me buy it—with cash."

The road opened onto a grassy glade, and when Breed flicked on the brights, Grace caught sight of the deer antlers over the doorway of her single-story, sunshine-yellow wood-frame house. The house, an enormous live oak draped protectively over its eaves, had stolen her heart the first moment she'd seen it. The wilderness surrounding it fed her soul.

Grace felt her throat thicken painfully with emotion, as it did every time she came here. Her voice croaked when she tried to speak. She cleared her throat and said, "That's my home."

Breed stopped his pickup at the rail in front of the covered front porch, on which Grace had hung a wooden swing, and said, "You have the key?"

"It isn't locked," Grace said.

Breed lifted a brow in disbelief. "Why not?"

"There's nothing inside that can't be replaced." She hesitated before adding, "And I don't like locked doors."

Breed glanced at her, and she knew he understood what she was saying without further explanation. The years at Giddings had left a lot of scars that didn't show. Grace would never willingly lock herself in again.

The truck lights stayed on after Breed turned off the ignition, and Grace used the time to go inside and light a kerosene lamp. Then she gestured Breed inside.

She watched him as he took in the Western furnishings, which included two burled wood side chairs, an overstuffed couch with a Southwestern print, and a cowhide accenting the original pegged oak floor.

There were no curtains on any of the windows. Privacy wasn't an issue, and after the windowless walls at Giddings, Grace felt like she could never get too much sunshine or moonlight. The kitchen, dining room, and living room comprised the main room. "There's a bedroom through there," she said, pointing to an open doorway, "and a bathroom with a claw-foot tub."

Grace went around the room opening windows, letting in a refreshing evening breeze. With Breed helping her, it didn't take long before her home was filled with the soothing rustle of the live oak overhead, and the croaks of the frogs and chirps of the crickets along the creek that ran behind the house.

Grace lit more lanterns as Breed crossed the room to examine the floor-to-ceiling stone fireplace. She'd often imagined the mothers and fathers, husbands and wives, children and grandchildren who might once have sat in front of it. She'd put her own spindle-backed rocker there to become a part of its history.

He pointed to the stack of firewood in the grate and said, "Would you mind if I light this?"

"Please do," Grace said. "Matches are—"

He'd already found them, and Grace heard the scratch of sandpaper and smelled sulfur as he touched the match to the kindling she'd laid before she'd left the house the last time.

Grace felt a sense of homecoming as the fire began to crackle. And realized she was imagining another rocker. And Breed Grayhawk sitting in it.

She abandoned the reflection as quickly as it rose in her mind. She didn't want or need a man in her life. She was managing just fine on her own. But the tempting thought—the fantasy, and she believed the *fiction*, of a man who was loving and caring—came back. Maybe if Breed was gone from the house, he would take the fantasy with him.

"You can park your pickup in the barn," she said.

Breed turned with an engaging, rueful smile on his face and said, "I suppose the barn's not locked, either."

Grace smiled back, then realized how good it felt, and who she was smiling at, and wiped the expression off her face. "No, it's not locked. If you don't mind, take a lantern along and crank up the generator out back. Then I can cook us a late supper."

"I'm starving," Breed admitted. "But I can't believe you've got room for any more food in that skinny stomach of yours, after all that pie."

Grace smiled. "I always eat dessert first. Then, if anything goes wrong, I didn't miss it."

While Breed was gone, Grace looked through the cupboards for something she could make for a late supper. They both might be dead tomorrow, but tonight they needed to eat.

She searched the cupboards and found spaghetti in a box and some marinara in a jar. That would have to do. She set a pot of water on the stove and turned on the burner when she heard the generator start.

A few minutes later, Breed was back inside. He looked at the pot of water on the stove and the marinara sauce she was dumping in a second pot, then turned his attention to the stripped pine dining room table.

"I see you've been busy," he said, nodding his chin toward the stacks of papers and the laptop computer on one end of the table.

"It's been a long year," she admitted, crossing to the table. She stared at everything for a moment before she said, "And there's more work to be done. But not right now." She began shoving everything to one end, to make a space where they could sit down to eat.

"Anything I can do to help?" Breed offered.

Grace paused in what she was doing, looked him in the eye, and said, "What I'd really like you to do is call the FBI SAC in San Antonio and tell him how I'm being framed—again—for something I didn't do."

Breed picked up a stack of books and moved them to a nearby counter. "I wish I could."

"Why can't you?" Grace said.

"Vince threatened to hurt my friends, my family—anybody I care about—if I call Craig Westwood." Breed turned to help her move another stack of papers. "And since I'm hiding out with you, I can't protect my family if he retaliates."

"How would Vince Harkness even know?" Grace asked.

"He'd know because the first thing the San Antonio SAC is liable to do is confront him. Right now, Vince is in a position to explain away any accusations I make. He and Craig Westwood are old friends. They went through Quantico together."

"So what do we do now?" Grace said, looking around at the stacks of research papers, books, bankers boxes, and notes crowding her kitchen, which had finally led her to Vincent Harkness.

"I think maybe you should put the spaghetti in that pot. The water's boiling."

Grace made a face but did as he asked. While she was watching the spaghetti go limp in the water and moving it around in the pot so it wouldn't stick together, she said, "Really. What happens now?"

Breed stuck a finger in the marinara, hissed, and stuck it in his mouth. "We wait. And see what Jack turns up."

Grace nudged him aside with her hip, opened the cupboard

that contained the plates, and handed two of them to him. "We just *wait?*"

"At least we have a place to lay our heads for the night." Breed set the plates on the table and started looking through drawers for silverware. "I just have one more question," Breed said, mimicking her words at Burger Heaven.

"What's that?" Grace asked.

Breed glanced toward the single bedroom door, then at the short, overstuffed couch, and said, "Where am I sleeping tonight?"

"Anywhere you like," Grace replied. "So long as it's not in my bed."

27

Breed kidded Grace all through dinner about his sleeping accommodations. "I'm six foot four. That couch is five foot three, if it's an inch. I don't think that's going to work."

"Actually, I believe it's six feet long," Grace said. "But you can always sleep on the cowhide in front of the fire."

"On that hard wood floor?"

"Over the years, I'm sure lots of folks have slept on that hard wood floor," she said. "You'll be in good company."

"I'm a guest. Shouldn't I get the bed?"

"I'm the woman. Shouldn't I get the bed?"

After Breed helped Grace wash the supper dishes, he settled in one of the two burled wood chairs across from the couch. Grace wrapped herself in the quilt they'd lain on when they'd made love Friday night, and made herself comfortable in the rocker in front of the fire.

The generator was off, and the only light came from the fireplace, the moonlight, and several kerosene lanterns around the room.

Breed was anxious. And uncomfortable. He shifted in his chair. And shifted again.

"You can stretch out on the couch if you're tired," Grace said, rocking slowly and steadily.

"I'm not tired," Breed said irritably. "I need to be doing something. It's too damned quiet here."

Grace closed her eyes. "If you think it's quiet, you're not listening."

"I can hear the wind rustling the leaves just fine. And the crickets. And the wood popping and snapping in the fire. And I hear the floor creaking every time you rock in that ancient collection of wood. Maybe I should have said it's too damned peaceful."

Grace angled her head to look at him and said, "What's wrong with peaceful?"

"I can think of better things to do when I'm alone with a pretty woman than sit quietly on the other side of the room."

"Oh." Grace smiled. "You're talking about sex. No thanks."

Breed laughed. "How about something to read? You have any books around here?"

"Just a bunch of research books I stole from the library when I was studying serial murderers."

"That sounds like great bedtime reading," Breed said dryly.

Grace laughed. "I know for a fact it'll put you to sleep."

Breed chuckled. "It's too early to go to bed. Talk to me. Tell me about yourself."

"I will if you will," Grace replied.

"You go first."

"What would you like to know?"

Breed thought about the question. "Why didn't you just meet with your parole officer when you got out of Giddings and get on with your life? Why this great epic search for a killer you may never find?"

"I was glad when I heard my father was dead," she said pugnaciously, as though she expected him to judge the statement. "My whole life, all he ever did was yell at me and hit me." Her voice softened as she added, "Unfortunately, my stepmother was murdered along with him. The simple answer to your question is, I wanted justice for her."

"I take it she wasn't the stereotypical wicked stepmother, the kind you see a lot in Disney movies and Grimm's fairy tales."

"Not at all," Grace said. "My biological mother died when I was born. Big Mike married Allie when I was so young, she's the only mother I ever knew. She loved me like I was her own flesh-and-blood daughter."

"Sounds nice."

Grace nodded. "It was. At night, Allie would read to me. Winnie-the-Pooh is what I remember best. She would make pancakes for me with faces on them. She taught me how to ride a bike. She bought me a turtle for my tenth birthday."

Grace rocked for a moment before she said, "My father flushed it down the toilet."

"Big Mike sounds like a real son of a bitch."

"From what I heard earlier tonight, you don't think your father is such a prize, either," Grace said. "I believe your exact words were, 'King Grayhawk can go hang.'"

"I hate him."

"Why?" Grace asked.

Breed hesitated, then said, "He threw me out—threw me away—the day I was born."

"Why?"

"Because I have these odd, silver-gray eyes and this copper skin. Because neither of those features came from my blond-haired, sky-blue-eyed mother, with her milky white skin. He thought my mother cheated on him with one of the Sioux hired hands breaking horses for him at his ranch in Wyoming, Kingdom Come. He threw me out with my mother the day I was born."

"Did you ever go hunting for your real father?" Grace asked.

"Hell, no!" Breed said. "Why would I want to do that?"

"Maybe he didn't know about you. Maybe he would have wanted to be a father to you."

"Judging from my mother's behavior when I was old enough to watch her in action, my father was just another one-night stand."

"I'm sorry."

"You don't have to feel sorry for me. I never needed him. I've managed fine on my own."

"Where have I heard that before?" Grace said.

Breed glared at her, then twisted his lips in a rueful grimace. "Doesn't make it any less true."

"You didn't have it so bad. I think having no father would be better than having one who used you for a punching bag."

"There are worse things than physical punishment," Breed said.

"Like what?"

"Being abandoned," he blurted.

"Oh," Grace said. "Your father—"

"Not him. My mother. She abandoned me. Again and again."

Grace's silence encouraged him to say more.

It took Breed a moment to put his thoughts into words. He'd suffered terribly at times during his life. He'd never spoken to anyone about that suffering. He'd simply endured.

"My mother was an alcoholic," he began. "When she was sober, which wasn't often, she'd swear she never cheated on my father. That the drinking—and the one-night stands—started after he threw her out."

Breed snickered. "She swore to me, all my life, that King Grayhawk *is* my father. That if I look this way, it's because there was a Sioux bride on my father's side going back a few generations."

"Is that true?" Grace said, her eyes wide.

Breed shrugged. "Yeah. So what? Kind of strange those Sioux genes didn't show up until I was born—to a blond-haired, blue-eyed mother."

"What does King look like?"

"He has black hair and blue eyes."

"You have black hair. And gray—silver-gray, I suppose—eyes."

"But my skin—"

"Is beautiful," she said, her eyes glowing in the firelight. "It looks like it would be warm to touch." She hesitated and said, "And it is."

Suddenly, the room was charged with electricity. Grace kept her gaze on the fire, avoiding Breed's attempts to get her to meet his gaze.

"So, you see, you could be King Grayhawk's son."

"What difference does it make now?" Breed said. He was hard as a rock again. How the hell did she do that to him? And she seemed to-tally disinterested in anything having to do with sex. "King threw my mother out," he said in a voice made harsh by desire. "And turned her into a lush."

She drew her legs up under her and crossed her arms around them. "You blame your father because your mother started drinking? That sounds like her problem, not his."

"It was his fault. She told me she begged him not to turn us out, be-cause I was his son. He wouldn't believe she was telling the truth."

"You don't believe yourself that you're his son, because of your physical characteristics. Seems to me you could understand his doubt."

"He destroyed my mother," Breed said stubbornly. "She was in and out of alcohol rehab her whole life."

"She's dead?"

Breed nodded, because his throat was too constricted to speak. He hadn't grieved his mother's death. But he must have loved her, because whenever he remembered her, his throat would tighten up, so it was painful to swallow. Then he would remind himself of what his life had been like with her, and the tightness would go away.

It had been a relief when his mother died driving drunk. He didn't have to feel guilty anymore about being happier living with his brother North during the last years of her life, instead of traveling around the country with her and her latest boyfriend-lover-paramour-gigolo-husband.

"Why do you say your mother abandoned you? Sounds like you were both kicked out of King's house."

"Every time she went into rehab, she left me with whatever kind friend or poor relation would take me in," he said. "It must have been going on even when I was a baby, but the first time I can remember it happening, I was five. She left me with someone she called Aunt Gertie. Aunt Gertie stuck me in a back room and left me there. I remember being hungry a lot.

"The last time it happened, I was sixteen, and she dropped me like an old tissue with my older brother North, at his ranch west of Austin. She told him I was fourteen. I let him believe it, because I was afraid he wouldn't let me stay if he knew I was sixteen. And I had nowhere else to go."

"I think that's why I bought this place," Grace said. "Because, after Giddings, I wanted a place I could call home."

"I bought part ownership of Twin Magnolias with Jack McKinley for the same reason," Breed said. "I have a condo in town, but it's just a place to hang my hat. I needed—"

"Land. Something that lasts forever and will be there long after you're gone."

Breed glanced at her and said, "Yeah. That's right."

"Did you love your mother?" Grace asked.

"Did you love your father?" Breed shot back.

"I hated him," she said vehemently.

"I pitied her," Breed said. "Because she could never get over him. And I was mad at her. Because I was never enough for her."

"It must have been awful to love someone who kept leaving you like that," Grace said quietly. "At least I had Allie."

"Who stayed with Big Mike and let him keep on beating you."

"That's not fair!" Grace said. "I wasn't legally her daughter. There was no way she could have taken me away from him."

"She could have told someone he was beating the hell out of you."

Grace opened her mouth—Breed was sure to deny the truth of what he'd said—but closed it again.

"I always wondered why she never ran away," she mused. "I ran away once, but he brought me back. I dreamed about killing him. And getting away with it."

"That's a strange thing to admit. Under the circumstances."

She focused on the flickering fire and said, "I never got the chance. Somebody else beat me to it."

Breed yawned.

"Sorry I'm boring you," she said tartly.

Breed grinned. "All this talking has worn me out. I think it's time I hit the sack."

She lowered her feet and stood. "I'll get you a blanket and a pillow."

Breed stood and glanced at the couch. "That's a really short couch."

She smiled and gestured to the expanse of floor in front of the fire.

"How about sharing the bed with me?" he suggested.

"It's an antique—a standard-size bed. There wouldn't be room for both of us."

"There would be if we cuddled up together."

"Forget it, cowboy."

Breed followed her to a linen closet in the hall that led to the bedroom and bathroom, still making his case. "I thought we were good together."

"What does that have to do with anything?"

"What happened with us, it doesn't happen all the time."

"I wouldn't know about that." Grace stopped abruptly and turned to stare at him.

He was staring back and saw the blush rise on her cheeks. "You weren't a virgin," he said.

"No, I wasn't," she replied, closing the subject.

But Breed was fascinated by what he'd discovered. "You were only thirteen when you went into juvie. And you've only been out a year. I should have realized—"

"Keep your conjecture to yourself," Grace said as she shoved a pillow, pillowcase, sheet, and blanket into his arms. "Sleep wherever you like. Just not in my bed."

She marched toward her bedroom without looking back.

"Wait a minute!" he called to her.

Grace stopped and glanced back at him over her shoulder. "What is it?"

"I have a question," he said as he struggled to gather the linens into his arms.

She turned to face him in her bedroom doorway, her legs spread wide, her arms folded protectively over her chest. "Well? I'm waiting."

"When we had sex, and the condom tore, you said you were protected. Grace, are you on the pill? Or some other kind of birth control?"

She took a step backward, put a hand on the door frame, and said, "No."

Then she slammed the door in his face.

28

Grace realized a moment after she slammed her bedroom door that if Breed wanted in, there was no way she could keep him out. She'd removed every lock in the house, and she'd never been sorry for it. Until now.

She braced her back against the door and spread her legs to give her leverage if he tried to break in. At least she could put up a good fight.

But there was no need. She heard Breed's retreating footsteps on the hardwood floor.

Grace waited a little longer to be sure he wasn't trying to trick her. When she heard him mutter "Son of a bitch!" from the other room, and imagined him trying to fit his long, lanky body on her too-short, overstuffed couch, she relaxed, levered herself off the door, and crossed the room to her bed.

Grace loved her bedroom. Everything was frilly, the way she'd wished her bedroom had been when she was a little girl and Big Mike hadn't been willing to spend money on all that "girly stuff." And it was as different as it could be from the spartan accommodations she'd endured as a young woman at Giddings.

Grace wasn't so foolish as to think she could relive her childhood. She wouldn't have wanted to. But she could indulge herself with some of the things she'd missed.

So she had a canopy over her bed and a half-dozen lacy pillows on the ruffled seafoam-green and rose-print bedspread. She even had a couple of stuffed animals, including a turtle she'd named Mertle.

Grace shoved everything except a single pillow onto the braided rug at the foot of the bed and pulled down the covers. She was tempted to sleep in her clothes, but she undressed and put on something else she'd missed at Giddings. A lovely, feminine nightgown.

There was nothing girlish about Grace's nightwear. It was meant to be worn by a woman—to attract a man.

Grace didn't know why she'd bought such filmy, provocative nightgowns, when the last thing she wanted in her life was a man. She found it hard to imagine one who wasn't like her father. But the truth was, she hadn't been immune to the romance novels she'd gotten out of the library at Giddings.

Women in those books always found true love and lived happily ever after. The men they met were strong but gentle. They were noble and kind and thoughtful and caring.

They never shit or spat or cursed.

Which definitely made them a fantasy.

Grace had never imagined she could have a discussion with a man like the one she'd had tonight with Breed Grayhawk. In fact, she'd only talked like that with one other person—Lizzie Harmon.

Lizzie had been Grace's confidante in juvie. With Lizzie, she'd discussed whether she ought to have sex with Clete, who was serving a life sentence—that began at Giddings—for a gang shooting.

Grace hadn't been sure whether to give in to Clete's entreaties or not. Lizzie had told her to go for it. Afterward, she'd told Lizzie all about it, and the two of them had giggled through the night.

Not long after that, Lizzie was stabbed with a homemade shiv and died in Grace's arms. The pain of losing Lizzie had been a hard lesson. But Grace was a fast learner. She'd never made another close friend in juvie. And it had been too dangerous to confide her deepest feelings to anyone over the past year.

So why had she talked so openly tonight with Breed Grayhawk?

Because he reminded you of one of the heroes in those silly romance novels you read at Giddings, the ones who never shit or spat or cursed.

Well, not exactly. He did curse. A lot. And she'd heard him flush the toilet after supper. She'd even seen him hawk and spit, when he'd gotten a little oil from the generator up his nose when they'd shut it down for the night.

Breed Grayhawk was real, all right.

But he made love like the men in the novels she read. Her body quivered at the memory of how it had felt when he caressed her. When he pressed his mouth to her breast. When he put himself inside her.

So why did you say no when he suggested having sex?

Grace frowned. The answer she came up with confused her.

I said no because I wanted him. A lot.

Which made no sense. Grace turned down the kerosene lantern on her bedside table and got into bed. Moonlight streamed in through the uncurtained windows.

Grace turned on her side, tucked her hand under her cheek, closed her eyes, and breathed slowly and deeply, which was how she'd gotten herself to sleep every night she'd spent at Giddings.

It didn't work.

Grace sat up and pulled her knees to her chest. She rested her elbows on them, then perched her chin on her hands and stared at the door to her bedroom while she had a conversation with herself.

Why shouldn't I have sex with him if I want him?

You might fall in love with him.

So? What's the problem with that?

Then you'd end up like Allie, if he turned out to be like Big Mike.

I'd never stay with a man who beat me!

You would if you loved him.

So I won't fall in love with him. I'll just have sex with him.

You sure you can keep the two separate?

Men do it all the time. Or so I've heard.

Fine. Go for it. Just don't say I didn't warn you!

Grace had only one problem, now that she'd argued herself into having sex with Breed. And that was how to get him to participate.

Grace glanced down at the pert nipples she could see through her sheer black peignoir.

Surely that wasn't going to be a problem.

Grace opened and closed her bedroom door as quietly as she could, then tiptoed barefoot down the hall and stood at the entrance to the living room.

Breed was snoring.

She put a hand to her mouth to cover her snicker. Heroes in romance novels didn't snore, either. But her real man did.

Don't forget he's an FBI agent. Don't forget he could turn on you in a heartbeat. Don't ever trust him. Don't ever fall in love with him.

Grace shook off the warnings. She was not just a felon and a fugitive. She was a young woman who wanted—who needed—to be held and touched. And loved.

She crossed the room silently and stood over the snuffling lump under the covers on the couch. She moved Breed's Glock, which he'd left within easy reach on the end table, onto the floor, just in case he woke and grabbed for it. She didn't want to get accidentally shot.

"Breed," she said.

He jumped up as though she'd shouted his name and grabbed for his Glock. A second later she was on her back on the floor with Breed on top of her, his hand at her throat.

"Where the hell is my gun?"

She scratched at his choking hand until he loosened his hold, then grated out, "I moved it, so I wouldn't get shot when I woke you up."

He suddenly realized what she was wearing. Or not wearing. That his naked chest was pressed against her almost naked breasts. That his hard body was pressed against the softness of her belly. And forgot about the gun.

As quickly as he'd put her down, Breed was off her and had her back on her feet. He took three steps backward and stared at her, his chest heaving.

Grace stared back. She was still gasping air to ease her tortured lungs and put a hand to her injured throat as she let her eyes roam his body.

He'd stripped down to thigh-length gray Jockeys, and Grace couldn't take her eyes off his broad chest, his ripped abs. He'd been naked in the moonlight when they'd made love for the first time, but he'd been lying down, not standing up. He looked strong in the firelight.

She ate him with her eyes. And watched his body respond. She lifted her eyes to his face and smiled, like a cat who'd found a pot of cream.

"What's going on, Grace?" he said suspiciously.

She held out her still-trembling hand to him and said, "I wondered if you might like to share my bed after all."

Grace had a moment of uncertainty when she thought Breed might refuse. Then he took her hand and headed for her bedroom, dragging her along behind him. Not that she was at all reluctant. He was just moving so fast, she had to trot to keep up with his long strides.

Once he was across the threshold, he turned and scooped her up in his arms and carried her the rest of the way to the bed.

Grace threw her head back and laughed. This was a romance fantasy come to life. And a great deal of fun.

A moment later Breed dumped her unceremoniously on the bed. And stalked away toward the door.

"Where are you going?" Grace asked, sitting up, startled by his abrupt about-face.

He didn't stop until he'd reached the doorway. "I don't know what your game is, but—"

She scooted to the edge of the bed and started toward him.

"Stop right there!" he ordered, putting out a flat hand like a traffic cop.

"I'm not playing games, Breed," Grace protested. "I just changed my mind."

His eyes narrowed. "Just like that?"

She took another step toward him. "Just like that."

"Why?"

Grace laughed and lowered her lashes, looking up at him from beneath them playfully, teasingly. "Does there have to be a reason?"

"With you, I figure there probably is," he said bluntly.

"I want you," she said, her voice low, seductive. "Isn't that enough?"

She took another step, which brought her close enough to extend her hand and lay it on his bare chest.

She felt his flesh quiver, watched his nostrils flare for the scent of her. But he held his ground.

"I can see you want me, too," she said, letting her eyes slide down his body to the proof of his arousal.

He lifted her chin gently with a forefinger and said, "This would be sex, plain and simple. I want that understood up front. I don't do relationships."

"Neither do I," Grace said, putting her body against his.

"And I don't have a condom."

"So?"

"Grace, have you thought you might get pregnant?"

She bowed her head so her chin almost touched her chest and said, "I can't have a baby. Big Mike . . ." She swallowed hard. "Big Mike kicked me and tore . . ." She couldn't go on.

Breed was silent so long, Grace finally looked up at him.

He was gritting his teeth. His eyes shimmered in the moonlight.

Grace pressed her face against his throat, as he slid an arm around her waist and lifted her off the ground. He nudged her head up and his mouth came down to capture hers. His tongue thrust deep, as his palm slipped down to cover her womb.

She was overwhelmed by powerful sensations and grabbed hold of anything she could find. Her fingers thrust into his hair. Her palms cupped his face, as she forced his head up to look into his eyes

Grace saw an agony there that mirrored her own

She lifted her mouth to meet his and held on tight as he made love to her with tenderness. And took away the pain.

29

~

Grace couldn't sleep. There was a man in her bed. Snuffling. Shifting. Sprawling. She'd spent every one of her nearly twenty-two years sleeping alone. It felt strange to share her bed with someone. Especially someone so determined to sleep on so much of it.

Grace had loved making love—*having sex*, she corrected—with Breed. But she had no experience dealing with what came afterward. She hadn't figured he'd hook an arm around her waist, pull her close, and fall fast asleep. She felt . . . imprisoned. She wanted . . . escape.

She inched closer to the edge of the bed, but even as she did, Breed's leg hooked over hers. She shivered as his coarse male hair brushed against her skin. His hand curved around her rib cage and pulled her naked body snug against his. She could feel his warm breath on the back of her neck, the rasp of his day-old beard on her shoulder.

Then she realized his breathing had changed.

"You awake?" he whispered.

"Mm-hmm."

"Me, too. I'm not used to sleeping with someone else in bed with me."

Grace laughed. "You've been doing a pretty good imitation of it, then."

Breed chuckled. "Why are you awake?"

"I can hear you breathing. The sheets rustle when you shift. You're taking up the whole bed. Sleep is impossible."

"Then you won't mind if I keep you up a little longer." He turned her onto her back in the moonlit room, cupped her breast in his hand, and suckled it.

Grace caught fire. She grabbed his hair and held his head where it was as her hips bucked upward, seeking contact with his.

"Breed," she begged. "Please."

He laid a hand on her belly and slid a finger down between her legs. But that wasn't what she wanted. She shoved his hand away and gripped his hips and scooted herself under him. "I want you inside me," she said. "*Now!*"

She was grateful he didn't play games. Grateful he didn't use his greater strength to do this his way. She wasn't sure why she wanted him so much. Wasn't sure why his weight felt so good on top of her. Or why it felt so good when he thrust deep inside. She wrapped her legs around his hips and arched her body upward, seeking the rhythm that would bring the most pleasure.

She found his mouth with hers and thrust her tongue inside, mimicking his intrusion below. Loving the taste of him, wanting to be joined to him, feeling his hands on her breasts, pinching enough to tease and titillate, sending frissons of desire arcing through her.

She returned the favor, using her fingernails to scratch his nipples and tantalize muscle and sinews along his thighs, between his legs, between his buttocks.

She bit his shoulder and felt his mouth latch onto her throat and suck hard enough to cause exquisite pain. She writhed beneath him, feeling the tension building inside her, waves climbing higher and higher, until there was no escape from the tumult that followed.

"Breed!" she cried.

"Grace!" He arched his body as he joined her ecstasy.

The moment of exhilaration stretched. And broke. And cascaded over them both.

Grace was slick with sweat and panting hard and welcomed the sudden breeze she felt from the open window, as Breed lifted himself away from her and lay on his back beside her.

She looked in his direction, half expecting his eyes to close again, for him to fall back asleep. But he slid a hand behind his head, and she could see his silver-gray eyes shining in the moonlight.

She didn't want to talk. Didn't want him to talk. She wanted to bathe in the glow of satisfaction from their lovemaking. Their *bout of sex*, she corrected.

She hadn't expected Breed to want her again. Hadn't expected to want him so fiercely. But she wasn't sorry. It had felt good.

As her body cooled, the breeze began to chill her, and she reached down for the sheet to cover herself.

Breed turned on his side and helped her pull the sheet up over her shoulder, but he said, "It's a shame to cover something so lovely."

"I'm not—"

He kissed her.

It wasn't a passionate kiss. It was different from any kiss he'd given her so far.

Tender.

The word popped into her head, and she squeezed her eyes tight as though to shut it out. She didn't want him to care for her any more than she wanted to care about him. This was all about the *sex*. Nothing else.

"Hey," he said. "Are you all right?"

She opened her eyes and found herself looking into a face filled with concern.

She wasn't aware she'd raised her hand until she saw her palm cup his whiskery cheek. She watched as her thumb played across his damp lower lip. She traced his dark brow with a forefinger that slid down his nose and touched the bow on his upper lip.

"Grace?"

He was asking what she was doing. Hell. She didn't know herself. How could she tell him?

Playing with fire.

"Hold me," she whispered.

He gathered her into his arms, the sheet between their naked bodies, and lay back down. He kissed the scar on her eyebrow and said, "Sleep, Grace. I'm here to watch over you."

Grace closed her eyes. And slept.

30

A burst of sunshine in his eyes woke Breed, who groaned and rolled over. He realized he wasn't in his own bed. And that he was alone.

Grace was gone.

He bolted upright, panicked for an instant, then heard her humming in the kitchen. She was probably making breakfast.

He lay back in the soft bed, in the feminine room, as the night before came back to him. In living color and 3-D. Every sight and sound and scent. Every taste and touch.

He'd had her twice last night. And woke up before dawn and had her a third time. He wanted her now.

Breed groaned and pressed his forearm to his brow. But there was no getting her out of his head.

It had been an unforgettable night. An unbelievable night. He'd been insatiable. And so had she.

Why her?

If he were choosing a woman to want for more than a night, it wouldn't be Grace Caldwell. She had every bit as many hang-ups as he did. She wanted no more to do with him than he wanted to do with her. Not to mention she was a convicted double murderer. And a thief. He was pretty sure she wasn't a terrorist.

But not absolutely certain.

Breed groaned again.

He had to be out of his mind having sex with her. He should have refused her offer. He should have gone back to the living room and wrapped himself up in a blanket and crammed himself into the confines of that too-damned-short couch and gone back to sleep. But she'd told him that story about Big Mike, and all he could think to do was hold her. And kiss her. And make love to her.

Shoulda, coulda, woulda. It was too late now. He had Grace Caldwell's scent in his nostrils. The taste of her in his mouth. The feel of her on his fingertips.

"Breed, breakfast is ready! I've got pancakes with blueberry syrup. And hot coffee."

Breed groaned. It sounded wonderful.

He got up and hunted down his shorts, which he found in the corner of the room, and pulled them on. He headed straight for where he'd left his jeans draped over a chair in the living room, wanting more clothing between his naked body and Grace before he laid eyes on her again. He dressed himself in haste, in case the last of his good sense decided to fly out the window when he caught his first sight of her.

Grace was setting plates piled with pancakes on the table when he joined her. She had her hair in a youthful ponytail. She was wearing a sleeveless T-shirt that left her midriff bare and hip-hugger jeans with tennis shoes.

He'd kissed every inch of that exposed skin last night.

"Anything I can do to help?" he said, tucking his shirt in and zipping up his jeans, then buckling his belt. Tight.

"Enjoy your pancakes." She sat and poured blueberry syrup on her pancakes, then pushed the bottle in his direction.

He sat down across from her and dug in. They both ate voraciously for a while. A natural result, he supposed, of all that physical activity last night.

"These pancakes taste delicious!" he said. "What's in them?"

"Pecans and applesauce. How's the coffee?"

"Good." It was great, actually. Hot and strong.

He didn't want to find any more virtues in Grace Caldwell. He didn't want to get any more involved than he already was. He didn't want to start imagining what it would be like to wake up every morning to Grace in his bed. And Grace across the breakfast table.

"What's on tap today?" she asked.

"Since you have a computer here, we should do some more research on the lovers in Stephanie's diary. See if we can find any more premature deaths."

Grace reached for a stack of papers at the other end of the table, sorted through them, then said, "Ah, there it is," and pulled one out. "I've already made a list of Stephanie's lovers by name and location."

Breed took one look at the lengthy list and said, "Busy little bee, wasn't she?"

"Very," Grace agreed.

"I'd really like to check this list out on the TCIC and NCIC and ViCAP."

"What are all those initials for?" Grace asked.

"Texas and National Criminal Investigation Centers, where data on crimes is collected," Breed explained. "And ViCAP—the Violent Criminal Apprehension Program. Every participating law enforcement agency submits data on violent crimes, which allows the system to come up with behavior-based crime analysis.

"For instance, if all Vince's murders were committed the same way—with a knife, near a bar—a search using those parameters would cough up similar murders across the country."

"Is there someone you could call to do it for you?" Grace asked.

"I can do it myself," Breed said, "if I can sneak into Twin Magnolias without getting caught. My computer there is connected by modem to the FBI databases."

"Won't Vince have someone watching your ranch?" Grace said.

"Yeah, he probably will. But I have a way to get in after dark without being seen."

"You aren't planning to leave me behind, are you?"

"I was, yeah."

"I want to come, Breed. I want to help."

"Your being with me doubles the chance we'll get caught. I need to go alone."

Grace made a face, but she didn't argue further. Which made Breed suspicious. He was going to have to figure out a way to make sure that when he left tonight, she stayed behind.

"I have an idea how we can keep the JTTF busy—keep some of their agents busy—so there won't be as many left to watch for us tonight," Grace said.

"What's that?"

"I can ask the Victims for Vengeance to help us out."

Breed opened his mouth to object, but she cut him off.

"You told me they're already being watched. What if they start moving around? Traveling, actually, around the state. That would draw FBI attention toward them. And away from us."

"It might work. If you had a way to contact them without the JTTF tracing the calls back to you. By now their phones are tapped and their computers are compromised."

Grace smiled. "No phone calls necessary. Just a message to an Internet site they'll know to access at a computer-not-their-own."

"How are they going to know to do that?" Breed asked.

"All I have to do is phone the bagel shop where Troy has breakfast every morning. I tell the manager there, who's a friend of Troy's, to have Troy get an extra cinnamon-raisin bagel with a schmear. When he hears that message, Troy will call everyone to let them know there'll be a morning meeting of the Victims and ask who wants what on their bagels." Grace spread her hands. "Voilà."

"Everyone knows to contact the site," Breed finished for her. "When did you set that up?"

"I wasn't sure whether I might have to go into hiding if my parents' murderer found out I was looking for him and came after me," Grace explained. "I suggested it to the Victims. They agreed it was a good idea. The option to communicate that way was there for any of us who might need it. It turns out I do."

"Go for it," Breed said, gesturing toward her laptop.

Grace posted her e-mail on MySpace. "I suggested they leave Austin for a few days and visit friends or family. Do you suppose that'll be enough?"

"It'll send up a red flag Vince can't ignore," Breed said. "Hopefully, he'll think at least one of them intends to get in contact with you. That's going to stretch the agents he has available to him—even if he decides to include agents in the Austin office who work directly for him—to the limits. And give me more freedom of movement."

Grace noticed the change of pronoun and said, "All we have to do is stay put until they start moving, which should start happening later today."

"I assume you also have a plan for how to make an untraceable phone call to the bagel shop," Breed said.

Grace crossed and opened a kitchen drawer and pulled out a disposable phone. She leaned back against the sink and dialed a number from memory.

"Hi, Todd. Could you please tell Troy when he shows up to bring back a cinnamon-raisin bagel with a schmear? Thanks."

Grace hung up the phone and pitched it into the trash can in the corner. "Done."

Breed tried not to watch as Grace stretched her arms over her head and leaned from side to side. She winced as she stretched her neck and put a hand to her bruised cheek.

"You okay?" He rose and crossed to her. He reached out a hand and gently angled her head to survey the bruise Vince had left on her face.

"I'm fine." She smiled at him from beneath lowered lashes and added, "Just a little tired."

Breed felt himself flushing. His thumb traced her lower lip, which was swollen from his kisses. "I didn't mean to keep you up."

She met his gaze and said, "I didn't mind."

Her lips were irresistible. He leaned over to taste her, and she opened her mouth to him.

Breed cupped her breast, heavy and rounded in his hand, and flicked his thumb across the tip.

Grace moaned.

Breed took a quick step back and stared at her. "This is crazy."

"I know," she agreed, her blue eyes lambent with desire, her breath coming in shallow pants.

"I want you again," Breed said.

"I know."

"Let's get out of here," he said. "Let's go do something."

"I thought it was too dangerous to go anywhere," Grace said, her gaze fixed on him.

"Show me around your property." He needed to get out of here or they were going to end up in bed again.

"All right," Grace said.

Breed grabbed her hand and headed for the front door. "We can start with that creek behind the house. Where does it go?"

"It ends—or begins—in a pond," Grace said as they headed down the front porch steps. "You can swim in it during the summer."

"Then it's the perfect temperature right now to cool me off," Breed said.

"You'll freeze!" Grace said as she led him down a well-worn path through the underbrush. "That water comes up from an ice-cold spring, deep underground."

Breed realized he was still holding Grace's hand and let go of it. "You lead the way."

"The pond is one of my favorite places," she said. "A few turtles hang around in the cattails along the banks, and mallards stop there when they're migrating."

"This property is a great place to visit," Breed said, taking in the lush, wildly tangled undergrowth. "But how could you ever live here full-time? It's pretty far off the beaten track."

"When this is all over—when Vincent Harkness has paid for murdering my mother—I plan to be a private investigator. I'll travel where I need to go and then come back here."

"You're presuming Vince Harkness killed your parents. What if he didn't? Then what?"

"He did it," Grace said with certainty. "No question in my mind."

Breed hoped she was right. But he'd learned that rarely was anything certain where criminals were concerned.

They came to a bridge and she said, "We need to cross over the creek here."

"This wood looks like it was hewn with an ax," Breed said as he ran his hand along the ragged rail that framed the bridge over the creek.

"It very well might have been," Grace said.

They stopped on the bridge and Grace leaned over the rail to watch the water rush along the creek. "Tell me," she said, "are you planning to stay with the FBI when this is all over? Will they keep you on after you've consorted with a criminal?"

Breed's mouth curved in a rueful smile. "That depends entirely, I think, on whether Vince Harkness turns out to be a villain."

"So you've got something to prove here, too," she said. "Presuming you want to stay with the FBI. Do you?"

"I think I can do some good," he said.

He spent the next fifteen minutes, while they walked along the overgrown trail to the pond, expounding on how the FBI was a force for good against evil.

They had to bend low to get beneath the branches of a live oak, and when Breed stood up, he found himself at the edge of a tranquil pond. He whistled his appreciation.

"Yeah," Grace said. "It is beautiful, isn't it? I fell in love with the house even before I found this. I suspect from the trail that leads here that the old man who owned it before me must have come here often. And the construction of that old bridge suggests people might have been coming here for more than a century."

She turned to face him and said, "I like being part of the history of this land. I like that people were here before me . . . and will be here after me."

"Does that mean you want—plan—to adopt kids?" Breed said.

Grace lowered her gaze and walked away from him. "I wouldn't want to adopt a child unless I could make a home for him or her—with a father. And I don't think that's going to happen."

"Why not?" Breed asked.

She sat on a fallen tree trunk that had obviously been used before as a bench. He saw her gaze was focused on a snapping turtle sunning itself on a rock.

"Are you telling me you don't ever intend to get married?" Breed persisted.

She picked up a stone and threw it into the pond and watched the ripples flow outward to the banks, before she finally said, "I could never trust a man not to turn out like my father."

"Not all men hit women," Breed said.

"So you say."

"I have never—in my entire life—struck anything weaker than myself."

"I wasn't talking about you," Grace said.

"You can understand my confusion," Breed retorted. "Your statement seemed to include every male of the species. Which would include me."

"I said I don't mean you."

"How did I get excluded?"

She was quiet so long, he thought she wasn't going to answer him. "I don't know," she said at last. "I feel safe with you."

Breed realized, as he listened to her telling him that she trusted him—a woman who trusted no one—that he didn't feel at all safe with her. He was losing the battle to keep his distance, both physically and emotionally. Maybe he'd been alone too long. Maybe it was the similarity in their pasts. Maybe it was her need for him, which fed his need for her.

He didn't understand what was happening. Or maybe he did, and just didn't like it.

He didn't trust a woman not to abandon him.

She didn't trust a man not to hurt her.

They were two people who would have been doomed to spend their lives wandering alone. Except they'd found each other.

"Grace," he said as he held out his arms. "Come here."

Tears welled in her eyes as she lifted them to him. "I'm afraid, Breed."

"Afraid I'll hurt you?" he asked.

"Afraid I'll love you," she answered.

"Would that be so bad?"

"A disaster," she said as a tear slid down her cheek.

"Grace," he said. "Come here."

Grace rose. And stepped into his arms.

31

Breed spent the day holding Grace. And loving her. And trying to convince her that she should stay behind when he went to Twin Magnolias, once it got dark.

"It's safer that way," he said. "I wouldn't want anything to happen to you."

"I have the right to come," she argued. "And I'm good at getting in and out of places without getting caught."

"Just how many burglaries have you committed?" he asked.

"How many isn't relevant. The fact I've never been caught is what's important. I won't slow you down. I won't get in your way."

"If you won't stay, then I guess I won't go," Breed said as he finished the bowl of chicken noodle soup from a can he'd warmed up for their supper.

Grace looked at him with suspicion. "I thought this was important."

"It can wait until Jack gets back to me," Breed said.

They'd cranked up the generator earlier in the day so they'd have hot water, and Breed said, "How about a bath before bed?"

Grace's blue eyes twinkled as she said, "Sure."

The claw-foot tub was enormous. At first, Grace sat facing away from him, between his bent legs, which gave him total access to her body.

Breed washed her hair. Then she turned around onto her folded legs and washed his. He caressed every crevice in her body. She carefully bathed every appendage on his.

They laughed. They made love.

Bedtime came and went, and they were both still sitting in the living room, Grace in the rocker and Breed in one of the burled wood chairs he'd pulled closer to the fire.

"That's the third time you've yawned in the past fifteen minutes," he said.

"I can't imagine why I'm sleepy," she teased.

Breed smiled, but he felt sick inside. He was about to betray her trust. For her own good, of course. He doubted she'd see it that way. But somebody had to protect her. And the truth was, he might get caught at Twin Magnolias. Shots might get fired. If she came along, he would be too distracted watching out for her to take care of himself.

She had to stay. And he had to go.

"Good night, Breed," she said as she rose from the rocker. She was dressed in the too-large terry cloth robe she'd put on after they'd made love in the tub.

Even after the long day together, his body responded to the sight of her by hardening. He stood and said, "I'd like to come to bed with you, Grace. May I?"

She had a way of looking up at him from beneath lowered lashes that was both shy and seductive. She didn't answer with words, simply held out her hand to him.

Breed clasped her hand in his and followed her into the bedroom.

She crossed to the opposite side of the bed before letting the robe slide down her shoulders onto the floor.

He felt his breath catch and said, "I can't take my eyes off you, Grace. You're—"

"Your turn," she said. "Take off your clothes."

He yanked his shirt off, then unbuttoned and unzipped his jeans and shoved them down along with his shorts, which left him naked. And wanting.

She crossed the bed on hands and knees, like a sleek jungle cat.

He was standing close enough to the bed that she could reach him with her mouth.

Breed pulled the ponytail in her hair free and wrapped his hands in her long black curls, closing his eyes as her mouth closed around him.

Moments, or minutes—a lifetime—later he cried, "Wait!"

But his hands were tangled in her hair. And her hands were wrapped tight around his buttocks as his body arched in ecstasy.

It felt like she swallowed him whole.

When Grace released him, Breed reached down and pulled her up into his arms and kissed her. And tasted himself.

His limbs supported him only long enough to get the two of them prone. He pulled her close, his breathing unsteady, his body trembling, and said, "That was—"

"A gift," she whispered. "Close your eyes now. Sleep."

And he did.

Breed woke with a start, half expecting to find Grace gone. But she was lying peacefully sleeping—exhausted—beside him.

He felt damned lucky to find her there. After all, if he could plan to wait until she was asleep and sneak out, she was perfectly capable of planning the same thing.

He slipped out of bed quietly. Even so, Grace grumbled and turned over, hugging her pillow tight.

He froze and held his breath.

She started snoring. Quietly.

Breed smiled as he scooped up his clothes and left the bedroom. He dressed in front of the fire, which had burned down to coals. He stopped at the door, picked up Grace's backpack, and searched through it.

And found the diary. Which he took.

His pickup was in the barn, which meant he could probably start it without waking Grace. It was dark in the barn and he left the barn doors open for the extra moonlight. He settled in the driver's seat and reached for the keys.

Which were missing.

Breed couldn't help grinning. Grace had obviously anticipated his move. And tried to thwart him. No wonder she was sleeping so soundly. She probably had his keys tucked under her pillow!

Unfortunately for her, he'd learned a thing or two working on North's ranch about starting a pickup without a key. He searched out the ignition wires, freed them, crossed them, and heard the roar as the engine turned over.

He didn't wait to see if the noise woke Grace. He hit the accelerator and heard rocks fly as he headed down the dirt track for home.

32

~

Grace had felt Breed slip from the bed and breathed slowly and steadily through her mouth, in case he checked to see whether she was asleep. She wasn't about to let him leave without her.

Which was why she'd swiped the keys to his truck.

She was sitting up in bed when she heard the front door open and close. She hurriedly got out of bed and began dressing. When Breed came back to ask for his keys, she intended to be ready to go with him.

Then she heard the roar of the truck engine.

It took her a moment to realize what it meant. Half dressed, she ran out into the living room. She saw her backpack lying unzipped near the front door and felt her heart skip a beat. She dropped to the floor beside it and riffled through it once. And again.

The diary was gone!

Grace yanked open the front door and raced onto the porch. The barn doors were wide open.

She leapt off the porch and ran for the barn shouting, "Don't you dare run away! Come back, you bastard! Come back here!"

Breed's pickup roared down the road, accelerating as he passed by, leaving her coughing in a swirl of dust.

Grace swore loud and long, using every bad word she'd ever learned in Giddings.

It did no good.

Breed Grayhawk was gone. And he'd taken the only proof she had that Vincent Harkness was a murderer.

Tears stung her eyes and nose. "How could I have been so stupid?" she wailed. "I never should have trusted him!"

She was pretty sure he'd be back. She just wasn't sure whether he'd bring the FBI with him.

Grace slowly climbed up the front steps and walked back into the house, closing the door behind her. She stared around the empty living room as though she'd never seen it before.

Everything reminded her of Breed. Especially the quilt draped over her rocker. They'd made love on it again in front of the fireplace.

She grabbed a corner of it and dragged it along the floor behind her to the bedroom. Once there, she fell onto the bed and wrapped herself up tight in it.

Maybe tomorrow she'd put on some tennis shoes and jog the 13.8 miles, as the crow flies, to the main road. Right now, she needed sleep.

Making love to Breed Grayhawk had worn her out.

33

~ ❦ ~

Breed could still hear Grace shouting, *"Come back, you bastard!
Come back here!"* He was sure she'd known the effect that particular
epithet would have on him. He tried not to let it bother him.

He should have known she was faking sleep. Especially when he
found the truck keys missing. Maybe he should have stopped and
picked her up. But there were good, solid, logical reasons for leaving
her behind. He still felt like hell for doing it.

Breed knew Grace was going to be more than a little pissed
when she discovered he'd taken the diary with him. But despite
his growing feelings for her, he didn't trust her any farther than he
could throw her.

And he knew she wouldn't run without it.

With the diary tucked inside his shirt, Breed headed straight for
Twin Magnolias. He took a farm road cross-country to his ranch and
parked his Dodge Ram a half mile from the ranch house, in the shel-
ter provided by a stand of cottonwoods at a livestock water trough.

He was grateful for the moonlight that made it possible to see
where he was going without a flashlight. He walked a hiking trail he
and Jack had found that led through the pasture toward the house.
Along the way, he imagined the places he would station agents, if he
were setting up a surveillance and had only two or three agents to
command.

He stopped behind a mesquite fifty yards from his kitchen door.
The narrow trunk didn't fully hide him, but it broke up his profile,
making it hard to identify him as human. Through the light in the

window, he saw Jack working at the kitchen sink. To his surprise, Jack's parents were sitting at the kitchen table.

The one thing he was sure he didn't have to worry about was an agent inside the house. Because of Vince's need for secrecy, he wouldn't have gone to a judge for a search warrant. And despite the government's broad reading of the Patriot Act, Breed knew Jack wouldn't have let the agents inside without one.

Breed's eyes moved along the terrain looking for anomalies and found two government-type vehicles parked beyond a slight rise behind the house, where they would be hidden from the road. Which meant at least two agents were here, maybe more.

Breed discovered one agent standing in the bushes by the kitchen door when the man took a drag on his cigarette and the tip of it flared.

Sloppy, Breed thought disgustedly. *He knows better.*

But he also knew these men personally. Maybe they wanted him to see them. Maybe not everybody wanted him caught.

Of course, he wasn't willing to test that theory by exposing himself. He moved slowly and stealthily around to the front of the house and had no trouble locating the second agent, who was hidden behind the trunk of the magnolia tree at the right-hand corner of the porch.

Breed had never intended to enter by either the front or back doors. Both entrances were lit with motion sensors—mostly to frighten off deer that ate the flowers he and Jack had planted (he'd put in blue hydrangeas and bachelor's buttons, Jack had opted for yellow black-eyed Susans and orange marigolds) to make Twin Magnolias feel more like a home.

Maybe it was the motion sensors that had made the agents relax their scrutiny, since they were counting on the lights to go on and reveal Breed if he showed up.

Breed crept toward an area on the side of the house not covered by the two motion sensors, an entrance the agents wouldn't expect to be there, and which he'd already ascertained wasn't being watched.

Behind an overgrown lilac bush, which Jack had been haranguing him to cut out, was the entrance to a root cellar. Judging from the mason jars they'd found down there, the cellar had once been used to store food. Nowadays, it served as a storm cellar, in case of a tornado.

Breed knew the cellar was unlocked, because the part to fix the broken latch was sitting in the bed of his pickup. He was worried that the angled horizontal wooden door would squeak when he opened it, so he inched it open just far enough to squeeze his body down inside. He let the door back down as slowly as he'd opened it.

He was in!

There were a few small windows letting in minuscule amounts of moonlight, and Breed had to move slowly because the cellar was still cluttered with every piece of junk they'd found in the house but hadn't wanted to throw out.

He nearly had a heart attack when he tipped over a table. He caught the table, but a piece of farm equipment fell to the concrete floor. Fortunately, it was mostly leather and the only sound was the jingle of harness chains.

Breed breathed a sigh of relief when he got to the top of the stairs that led into the kitchen.

Until he realized the door was locked.

He listened at the door and heard Jack's voice. His angry voice.

"Breed is my friend, Dad. This is his home as much as it is mine. If he shows up here you will not inform the FBI agents hiding outside. You will keep your mouth shut."

"And you call me a criminal!" Jack's father retorted. "I never harbored a fugitive."

"Frank," Jack's mother said. "Please come upstairs with me. It's time for bed."

Breed heard Jack's father argue a little more, heard Jack swear, then heard his parents' footsteps on the creaky stairs. Breed waited until he couldn't hear them anymore, then knocked softly on the cellar door from the inside.

Jack opened the door with his SIG P226 in hand. "I heard a noise downstairs and hoped that was you."

Breed pointed to the gun and said, "But you weren't taking any chances. Is there something wrong with one of your parents? Why are they here?"

"They're staying here for a little while. It's a long story. I'll tell you all about it later," Jack said as he set his gun back in the holster sitting on the kitchen counter. "What are you doing here? You know the FBI is watching the house."

"I plan to be gone before first light. I need to use my computer."

"Where's the girl?" Jack asked, looking over Breed's shoulder.

"She has a place in the hill country. I left her there."

"Alone?" Jack said incredulously.

"She's in the middle of nowhere, with no way to leave except on foot." He reached inside his shirt and came out with the diary. "And she isn't going anywhere without this."

"She can call one of her friends to come get her," Jack pointed out acerbically.

"Nope. She's already given them other marching orders."

Jack arched a questioning brow.

"If you don't know, you won't have to lie to the FBI." Breed stayed by the door to the cellar, out of the way of the windows. "I thought you were going to check out the whole 'nitrates in the van' situation. Are you done already?"

"There is no situation," Jack said, leaning back against the wall opposite the cellar door with his arms across his chest. "I made a couple of phone calls and found out—"

"Who spilled the beans."

"Charlie."

Breed thought of Charlie Dawson, an older, experienced agent who'd seen it all. "What did Charlie tell you?"

"There was no ammonium nitrate fertilizer in the van. Just peat moss."

"Peat moss?" Breed asked in disbelief. He grinned. "Peat moss."

"Apparently stolen from a local Home Depot."

"There's no law against possessing peat moss," Breed said.

"The van was stolen, too."

"Could have been left in front of her house by anybody."

"Why are you so happy?" Jack asked.

"It's going to be a lot easier to convince the FBI that Grace isn't a terrorist if there's no bomb to explain away."

"She's a parole violator," Jack reminded him. "Which means she's going straight to adult prison to serve out the rest of her sentence when she's finally caught."

"Maybe not." Breed headed down the hall toward the study with Jack on his heels. From the doorway, he pointed to the shutters in the study and said to Jack, "Can you close those for me?"

Jack made eye contact with the FBI agent outside who was concealed behind the magnolia tree, then shut the blinds in his face. He turned to Breed, who sat down at the desk and booted up his computer. "What is it with you and that girl?"

"If I can prove she was never guilty of the first crime, that she was framed, I'm sure the courts will work something out on the parole violation."

"You just met this woman. What makes you so sure she's innocent?" Jack said.

Breed held up the diary and said, "This book."

Jack shook his head. "All that's going to prove, if anything, is that Vince killed his wife's lovers. It isn't going to help the girl."

"If I can prove Vince committed serial murders across state lines, it'll give me the evidence I need to get someone at the FBI to listen to me."

"Who did you have in mind?" Jack said.

Breed's smile was feral. "Vince's old Quantico buddy—Craig Westwood."

34

Vincent had never been so frustrated. Or so furious. Tuesday morning already, and it was as though Merle Raye Finkel had disappeared from the face of the earth. Again.

Vincent sat in his office behind his cherrywood desk with the door closed, waiting for his phone to ring. For someone to catch sight of Merle Raye Finkel. Or Breed Grayhawk. He was gnashing his teeth because he wasn't sure how much longer he could keep this investigation under his control.

The more prolonged the hunt for Merle Raye Finkel, the more chance one of the JTTF agents would let the cat out of the bag. Vincent could just imagine that glory hog Craig Westwood stalking into his office and announcing, "I'm taking charge, Harkness. And oh, by the way, you're relieved for gross dereliction of duty. Hand over your weapon and credentials on the way out."

Vincent gritted his teeth. He could feel time running out, like the proverbial sand in an hourglass. But he'd already done everything he could think of to do.

Yesterday morning, he'd brought each of the Victims for Vengeance into the JTTF office and interrogated them one at a time. The bitch was smart, he'd grant her that. No one knew where to find Merle Raye Finkel. No one knew how to contact her. They had to wait for her to contact them.

Which was why Vincent had put tails on every one of them and traces on all their phones. He hadn't thought that was such a good idea with Breed's friends.

For one thing, Breed's best friend was a Texas Ranger. His other best friend, his niece, was the governor's daughter-in-law. Vincent had been wary of doing anything that could come back and bite him on the ass.

He'd reasoned that if he simply followed the trail to Merle Raye Finkel, he would find Breed, as well. He just hadn't been able to find the goddamned girl. Yet.

He wondered if the bitch had killed Breed and disappeared. It would serve Breed right if she had.

Yesterday afternoon, the Victims for Vengeance had all taken off in different directions. He'd been forced to make a decision and had taken the risk of calling in the special agents assigned to the Austin office to help follow them.

It turned out the Victims had gone to their respective family homes or to friends' homes, which were spread out across Texas.

Not one of them had contacted Merle Raye Finkel.

Meanwhile, Vincent had involved a lot more people in his conspiracy. Who were running around chasing their tails. For nothing.

Stephanie was leaving on a business trip to Lubbock tomorrow. She would be back Thursday night and would want to write in her diary. He didn't have time for this bullshit. He needed that goddamned girl to show her face. To cough up his wife's diary. And disappear again.

With a little help from him.

The girl wasn't his biggest problem, though. Even if she surfaced, her accusations could be explained away, especially if Stephanie's diary remained buried.

The problem was Breed Grayhawk.

Breed had seen Vincent threaten the girl. Had heard him ask for the diary. Knew, or at least suspected, that he'd left the van in front of the house. The van full of fertilizer that contained no ammonium nitrates, something the lab had immediately discovered.

Vincent smiled at the deception. There hadn't been time to dig up the real thing. All he'd needed was the illusion of danger.

The van supposedly full of nitrates—a bomb intended for the president—would have been reason enough to kill the girl. He could have said he saw the dozens of fertilizer-type bags in the van and logically presumed the worst. The proof would have come later that it was no such thing. But by then the girl would have been dead. Too bad. So sad.

Except Breed had gotten in the way. And ruined everything.

Vincent needed a way to neutralize Breed and make it look like the girl was responsible. Then, when he killed the girl, his problems would be over.

What he couldn't understand was why Breed hadn't gone to some other law enforcement agency by now with his accusations against Vincent. Breed must know that Vincent had no way to act on the threat he'd made to "harm those Breed cared about." Breed had the diary. Which was damning. And there were plenty of dead bodies to lead the way back to Vincent, if anyone cared to look.

So why hadn't an accusation surfaced? What had happened to Breed Grayhawk?

35

Breed sucked in a breath and held it as he surveyed the dirty dishes in Grace's sink. The papers that had apparently been shoved off the table and now littered the kitchen floor. The quilt on which they'd made love—more than once—which lay in a pile on the living room floor.

He headed into the bedroom and found the bed unmade. He picked up the pillow she'd lain on and smelled it. And found her scent. And felt himself harden.

He dropped the pillow and left the bedroom. "Dammit," he muttered. "I should have taken her with me! I should have known better than to leave her here alone."

There was no sign of Grace.

He'd been so sure she would stay and let him help her prove the truth. He had the diary. It was the best piece of evidence—maybe the only piece of evidence—that might establish why Vince Harkness had murdered her parents. Where the hell had she gone?

"So you came back."

Breed bent and pivoted, the Glock appearing in his hand, and found Grace standing in the doorway he'd left open. She was wearing the same cutoff T-shirt, hip-cut jeans, and white tennis shoes she'd had on the last time he'd seen her dressed.

She was poised to run on the balls of her feet, her hands clenched in white-knuckled knots. "I didn't think you'd come back alone. I was expecting the FBI to be with you."

"How can you think, after everything—"

"Cut the bullshit," she said in a harsh voice. "Just give me back the diary and get out."

"Don't you want to know what I found out?" he said as he slipped the Glock back into his boot.

He could see she was torn. At last she said, "Where's the diary?"

"Outside in my pickup."

She turned and marched out the door and down the front steps, Breed following after her. She reached into the open window, retrieved the diary from the seat, and feathered through the pages until she found the newspaper article.

She huffed out a breath of air, then turned to him with the diary clutched against her breasts. "Were you able to confirm how many men in Stephanie's diary were murdered?"

Breed could almost feel the stab of the barbed-wire fence she'd put up between them. If she'd ever trusted him, or started to trust him, she was over it.

He knew he should be grateful she was backing off. Because the only thing he'd thought about the whole drive back here was making love to her again.

Someday, this would all be over, and they'd go their separate ways. Better to back off now.

"I guess nobody was looking for a serial killer," he said as he began walking down the path that led to the pond. "Or someone would have noticed what was going on."

She hesitated for a moment and then moved into step beside him. Keeping her distance, of course.

"Bar brawls and robberies outside bars are pretty common, especially around big cities," he said. "Nobody connected the dots. And there were a lot of dots out there."

"How many?" Grace said, hop-skipping to keep up with his strides.

He slowed his pace to match hers. "I found twenty-four."

"Another busy little bee," Grace said.

"Yeah. I *found* twenty-four. That doesn't mean there weren't more. Local law enforcement might not be hooked into ViCAP or might be behind on submitting reports. I may not have found all of the murders he's actually committed.

"By the way, two of those twenty-four were 'solved.' That is, there was enough circumstantial evidence to convict some other poor SOB of the crime."

Grace arched a brow. "I certainly know how that feels. When was the last time one of Stephanie's lovers was killed?"

"Friday night."

"*Last* Friday night?" Grace said breathlessly.

Breed nodded.

"Then, when Harkness came home and caught me in his house, he'd just killed someone?" Grace asked.

"You were damned lucky not to get caught!"

Grace hugged the diary tighter against her chest and walked faster. "Why would he come back to the house when his family was at their cabin on Lake LBJ? Why not go there?"

"He called me Saturday from the cabin, so he did rejoin his family," Breed said.

"But why go home first?" Grace persisted.

"To clean up? Stabbings must result in a lot of blood."

Grace shook her head. "He's too smart to bring that kind of blood evidence into his home."

"Maybe he came home to drop off something he picked up from the victim. Something he kept as a trophy celebrating his kill," Breed speculated.

"Why would he do something like that? Why keep something that could link him to a murder?"

"I don't know. Some serial killers do keep souvenirs, though."

"I couldn't be that lucky," Grace said. "Anyway, if Vince is keeping something, he's not keeping it in the house. I went through it carefully and—"

"Did you check the garage?"

"I didn't have time."

"The garden shed?"

"No," Grace said.

"What about the attic?"

"I didn't think there was one," Grace admitted.

"So Vince might have brought something home with him that he got from the victim," Breed said. "Or he might just have stopped at home to take a shower. And whatever he took from his victim—if anything—might be hidden at his cabin on Lake LBJ."

As they'd talked, Grace had slowly lessened the distance between them, so they were walking nearly shoulder to shoulder. Breed could feel her heat. Could smell her scent. And wanted her.

He was equally aware that if Grace felt anything, she was careful not to show it. He stopped when they reached the bridge.

Grace leaned over the rail and stared down into the creek running beneath it.

Breed watched her. And concentrated on keeping his hands off the curl at her nape that had slipped out of her ponytail and his lips off the sheen of sweat that had trapped the strand of hair against her flesh.

"Was there any item consistently taken from the murder victims in Stephanie's diary?" she asked, either oblivious to the ridge in his jeans or purposely ignoring it.

He tore his eyes away and started walking again. He heard her footsteps on the bridge following him.

"They were all robbed—of wallets, watches, and any other valuables," he said. "I suppose to make the murders look incidental to a robbery."

Grace hmmed to herself. "I wonder what Vince might be keeping to commemorate his murders. Watches are bulky. Can't count on everyone having jewelry. Their wallets? Too big. Something in their wallets, maybe?"

"Maybe," Breed agreed. "Or he's taken their watches and rings and other valuables and has them in a safety-deposit box some-where."

"Do you really think so? We could search his house for a key," Grace said excitedly, running ahead of him, and then hop-skipping backward so she could see him as she talked.

"That's breaking and entering."

"Yeah. And I'm pretty good at it," Grace said.

"Except, Vince knew you were there." Breed's brow furrowed in thought. "I've been wondering about that. How did he know it was you—that is, Merle Raye Finkel—in the house? Did you leave finger-prints?"

"I wore gloves."

"So there's video surveillance in the house," Breed mused.

"I cased the house before I burgled it," Grace said. "I didn't find any evidence of outdoor video surveillance."

"Maybe there's a camera in the bedroom," Breed suggested.

Grace stooped to pick up a stone from the edge of the pond and skipped it over the water. "Taping sex with his wife?" Grace said, her nose wrinkled in distaste.

"Not necessarily," Breed said. "He might have hidden a camera in the bedroom to make sure Stephanie wasn't bringing her lovers home with her."

"I see," Grace said. "Which would explain why it runs all the time. And he would know who I am, because I went to prison for two of the murders he committed."

Breed lifted a brow. "I never thought of it like that. But it is kind of odd that he'd remember one glimpse of a kid nine years ago, dur-ing a visit to your father. And since you were tried as a juvenile, your picture wouldn't have been put in the newspaper or plastered all over TV."

"So we're going to break in and see what we can find that Vince might have kept from his victims?" Grace said, skipping another stone across the pond.

"No."

"Why not?"

"I think I'd rather do this legally."

"What do you mean?"

"Look, Grace, with Stephanie's diary, and the information I collected off TCIC, NCIC, and ViCAP, I can get a judge to give me a search warrant for Vince's house. That way, whatever I find can be used as evidence against him in court."

"That doesn't solve my problem," Grace pointed out.

"Which is?"

"Proving that he killed my parents to hide his part in the Cancer Society Murder. If you do a legal search, the police are going to get involved. And lawyers. And Vince isn't going to admit to anything."

"You're never going to get a confession out of him, Grace. Assuming he murdered your parents."

"He's the only suspect I've got."

"That doesn't mean he's guilty."

Grace looked at him with stricken eyes. "Please don't get a warrant yet."

"I think it's time."

"What if you get a search warrant for the house, and Vince isn't keeping anything there? What if he's got his trophies—which we're only speculating exist—in a storage unit? Or in a safe-deposit box with the key hidden somewhere you can't find it? What if you can't find any actual evidence to link Vincent Harkness to the murders in the diary?" Grace said.

"I'll get as broad a search warrant as I can."

"I thought you were a fugitive. Along with me," Grace said angrily. "How are you going to get a judge to issue you a search warrant without getting arrested first?"

"I'm going to ask my father—King Grayhawk, that is—to act as an intermediary for me."

"I thought you hated him."

"I do. But Jack and I talked it over last night, and while there are a couple of others who might be able to help me out—most notably my brother-in-law, Clay Blackthorne, who's a federal judge—my father is the one most likely to do what I ask without a lot of questions."

"Why would he be so helpful?" Grace asked. "I mean, if you've been estranged from him all your life."

"What I didn't tell you last night is that King has apparently had a change of heart. I heard—" He'd heard through Kate, but Grace didn't know who Kate was, and the explanation of his relationship to her was too complicated to give right now. "I heard through the grapevine that King believes he made a mistake kicking me out. He wants a chance to make up for all the years we didn't have together as father and son.

"He'll help me, all right," Breed said, unable to keep the bitterness from his voice. "Because he thinks I'll be grateful."

"But you won't?"

Breed looked her in the eye, rage making his voice rough, and said, "You don't get second chances with me."

Grace shrank from him, even though he hadn't taken a step in her direction or threatened her in any way. It was the first time she'd let him see the fear she must always have lived with as a battered child.

He would have reached out to comfort her, except he felt sure the gesture wouldn't be welcome. In the end, he opened his arms to her anyway.

Hesitantly, she stepped into his embrace, resting her head against his heavily thumping heart, and put her arms around his waist.

Breed figured he probably owed her an apology for sneaking away last night and leaving her behind, but he still didn't think he was wrong. So he just held her.

Then Breed had another, less pleasant thought. He'd said he didn't give second chances, and she'd flinched as though she'd been struck.

What if they'd shared something more significant last night than merely fantastic sex? What if she cared, a little, for him? What if how he felt about her mattered to her?

Breed looked down at the woman in his arms and suddenly wondered what Grace Caldwell might have done while he'd been gone that she thought he wouldn't be able to forgive.

36

<hr style="width:10%" />

"I've been invited to a tea party this afternoon for a select few governors who showed up early for the NGA Annual Meeting," Ann Wade said. "I'd like to show off my grandsons. I want you to have them at the Speaker's Residence at the state capitol by four o'clock."

"Four o'clock is two hours from now," Kate said into the phone, as she watched her sons gamboling in the backyard with Jack and their new black lab puppy, which they'd named Harley, because he moved as fast as their dad's black Harley-Davidson motorcycle.

"You have plenty of time to get the boys showered and dressed and drive the hour up here from San Antonio. Traffic on I-35 shouldn't be too bad at this hour of the day. Don't be late, Kate. There'll be a lot of photographers here, since this is the first time the Speaker's Residence has been open since that controversial million-dollar renovation earlier this year."

The two-thousand-square-foot apartment on the second floor of the Texas State Capitol where Ann Wade had asked Kate to bring the twins had been built when the "sunset red"—it looked pink—granite capitol building was constructed in 1888.

When the state legislature was in session, the Speaker of the House needed to be available at all hours. Hence an apartment inside the capitol, where he could catch a few winks of sleep. The newly renovated apartment had the distinction of being the only residence in the country located inside a capitol.

"I don't think Lucky and Chance would sit still at a tea party," Kate said. "Wouldn't you rather—"

"I don't ask for much," Ann Wade interrupted. "Just bring them, Kate. Or better yet, send them with that bodyguard. I know how you hate official functions."

"All right. I'll bring the boys," Kate said. "I'd also like some private time to speak with you this afternoon, if that's possible."

"I won't have more than a few minutes."

"That's plenty," Kate said. "I'll see you at four."

Kate had thought of little else the past two days except what she was going to do about J.D.'s demand for money.

Before she asked King for help, she wanted to talk with Ann Wade and see if there was any way J.D.'s mother could talk her son out of extorting money from his wife. And, if not, to ask whether Ann Wade would be willing to contribute some of the blackmail money J.D. had demanded to keep her grandsons safe from her son.

"Hey, Mom!" Lucky called. "Come play with us!"

"It's time to come in," Kate called to her sons. "Ann Wade wants you boys to come see her this afternoon."

"We want to go horseback riding," Chance said as he and Lucky skidded to a stop at the open sliding glass door. The puppy leapt up and tried to lick Kate's face.

"I'll take him," Jack said, grabbing Harley's collar.

"Thanks," Kate said, avoiding Jack's gaze. When Kate had first seen Jack the morning after J.D. confronted her, her behavior had been abrupt, bordering on rude. She'd been embarrassed and uncomfortable and hadn't been able to meet his eyes.

Jack had found a moment alone with her yesterday to ask, "What's wrong, Kate? Are you having second thoughts?"

She'd wanted to blurt out the whole, terrible mess her life had become. But the thought of Jack and J.D. going at each other with fists—or bullets—left her with acid in her throat.

"I just need a little time, Jack," she'd said. Not that time was going to make any difference. J.D. was alive. Which meant she was no longer free to love Jack.

Jack had given her the space she'd asked for, but he'd watched her with worried, concerned eyes.

Which only made her fall more hopelessly in love with him.

Kate ducked her head to avoid his gaze as she ushered her sweaty, smelly, smiling sons inside. Her announcement, "I'm afraid horseback riding will have to wait until tomorrow," was greeted with loud groans.

Kate used the rambunctious puppy as a reason to step away from the sliding glass door, so Jack wouldn't brush against her as he entered the kitchen.

"You boys head for the shower," she said. "Ann Wade's been invited to a tea party, and she invited us to come, too."

"Aw, Mom," Lucky griped. "Do we hafta?"

"You have to," she said.

After the boys had raced down the hall to their bedroom, Harley bounding after them, Kate turned to Jack and said, "The twins have a command performance this afternoon with their grandmother at the capitol. Your presence is requested."

"Of course," Jack said.

When Kate turned to follow after the boys, she nearly tripped over the calico kitten, named Scratch, because that's what she did every time the boys tried to pick her up. Jack put out a hand to keep Kate from falling, and she felt an electric shock. She jerked free, realized how Jack might interpret her reaction, and tried to make it seem like part of her fall. She scooped up the kitten as she recovered her balance, to keep from turning and reaching for Jack.

She was afraid to be alone with him, because she wanted so much to be held by him. She didn't think she could talk to him without breaking into tears. She could see no way out of her dilemma, no way to explain to Jack why she was rejecting him. She'd been so close to paradise. And the devil had snatched it away.

"Please, Kate. Tell me what's going on," Jack said in a low voice. "Ever since—"

"There's nothing wrong," she said brightly, turning her back to him to set the kitten on the floor near its food bowl. She watched as Scratch sniffed at the expensive canned cat food—guaranteed to tempt even the pickiest eaters—then lifted her tail and headed imperiously down the hall toward the boys' room. There was going to be trouble in a minute when the kitten and the puppy crossed paths, although Scratch had proved she could hold her own.

"Look at me, Kate."

She forced herself to turn around and look at Jack, keeping her gaze as neutral as she could. He reached out with a calloused thumb and traced the dark circles under her eyes.

"These weren't here two days ago," he said. "What's wrong? Is it me? Is it what we did? I know I'm not divorced yet, but I'll be free—"

She put her fingertips to his lips to cut him off, and he kissed them. She snatched her hand away and saw the hurt look in his eyes. She wrapped her arms around herself and moaned.

"What is it, Kate? What the hell is wrong?"

She met his gaze and said, "It wasn't anything you did, Jack."

He tugged her arms free and held her hands in his. "It's that bitch you have for a mother-in-law, isn't it? What has she done now?"

Kate was so tempted to tell him the truth. That J.D. was alive. That she was no longer free to love him. And might not be free for a very long time, if J.D. had his way. But she was afraid of what Jack might do. Afraid he might search out J.D. and confront him. Which could only end badly.

It was better to let Jack think her mother-in-law was making her miserable. Because most of the time, she was.

"Ann Wade always finds a way to make life more difficult," she said at last. "Right now, I need to be ready to leave here in less than an hour, and I haven't even showered."

"I'm here for you, Kate," he said.

"I have to go get ready," she said, pulling her hands free and almost running down the hall.

"Kate!" he called after her.

She almost didn't stop. Something in his voice made her turn around.

"I love you," he said.

Kate fought back a sob, then disappeared down the hall without a word in reply.

An hour later, Kate headed back down the hall dressed in a sleeveless black sheath, with conservative pearls around her throat and in her pierced ears, and wearing nylons and three-inch black heels. She was herding the twins, like recalcitrant calves, ahead of her.

She found Jack sitting at the kitchen table. His dark eyes looked wounded.

She tried to keep her voice businesslike as she said, "We're ready." But she couldn't keep her chin from quivering. She saw that he noticed. And that he was biting his tongue to keep from saying anything about it.

He rose and said, "Let's get on the road." He put one hand on each boy's head and aimed them toward the front door, leaving her to bring up the rear.

She wanted to call him back. She wanted to ask for his help. But this was something she had to do herself.

It had taken Kate a long time to grow up. She'd learned the hard way—during nine years of marriage—how to stand on her own two feet. She was a mother, with two children who were her first priority. She needed to protect Lucky and Chance. Her own feelings and desires came a distant second.

She caught up with Jack and her sons as he was buckling them into the backseat of his Ford Explorer, which he was using to chauffeur them around. He opened her door and closed it after she was settled. He didn't look at her as he opened the driver's-side door and got in.

Kate forced herself not to feel hurt. It was better this way. She had to keep Jack in the dark until she could figure out a way to get free of J. D. Pendleton.

37

~

Kate was proud of Chance and Lucky. They fidgeted silently on chairs in the dining room of the Speaker's capitol residence, devouring cookies from gold-trimmed china plates balanced in their laps while adults milled around them with teacups and saucers in hand.

When they'd arrived, Ann Wade had paraded the boys around like prize calves at a 4-H fair, accepting the fawning compliments of the VIP visitors as though she herself had bred and groomed the twins, who were wearing white oxford cloth shirts, tiny navy blue suits, and regimental striped ties. Kate had been happy to stand in the background, waiting for the crowd around Ann Wade to clear, so she could have a private word with her mother-in-law.

Kate was astonished when Grandpa King showed up, since he didn't usually attend events like this when he could avoid them. As she watched, Jack approached King, who greeted him as though Jack were the person he'd come to see.

Their conversation continued for almost a minute before King shook Jack's hand, whirled on his booted heel, and left the tea party without greeting another soul.

Kate crossed quickly to Jack and said, "What did you say to Grandpa King? Why did he leave?"

"It's better if you don't get involved in this," Jack replied.

"I'm already involved in whatever is going on, since I figured out that Grandpa King came here just to see you. What did you say to him?" Kate asked.

"Breed has decided to ask his father for a favor. King is on his way now to meet with him."

Kate's eyes went wide. She'd been trying for as long as she could remember to get Breed to make nice with King and had failed miserably. And now Breed was making overtures to his father? "What does Breed want with King?"

"Breed's in trouble, Kate."

Her heart skipped a beat. "What's wrong? What can I do to help?"

"Breed has to handle this on his own."

"You say 'on his own,' yet he's asking King for help."

"He needs something only the governor can give him," Jack said.

"Which is?"

Jack smiled. "Persistent, aren't you?"

"I am when people I care about are in trouble," Kate said. "What's going on, Jack?"

Jack looked around to make sure no one else was close enough to overhear, then leaned close and said quietly, "Breed believes his boss is a serial killer."

"What?" Kate exclaimed.

"Shh!" Jack warned when several heads turned at Kate's outburst. He took her arm and led her to a corner of the room, where he said, "Breed has evidence that Vincent Harkness has likely murdered at least twenty-four men with whom his wife, who's apparently a sex addict, had carnal relations."

"I know Vince and Stephanie. And Brian and Chloe are such wonderful kids. I just can't believe it!"

"It is pretty unbelievable," Jack said. "It also seems to be true."

"Breed worships the ground Vince Harkness walks on."

"He might have in the past," Jack agreed. "I don't think the feeling lasted much past the moment when Vince suggested to the FBI that Breed was conspiring with a terrorist to set off a bomb at the LBJ Auditorium tomorrow, when the president is making his keynote to the governors."

"What?" Kate realized she'd spoken too loudly again, turned her back on the VIPs in the room, and whispered urgently, "How long have you known about all this? Why didn't you tell me what was going on sooner?"

Kate felt a hand on her shoulder and turned to find Ann Wade standing there. The hand became a claw as Ann Wade said harshly, through smiling lips, "You're becoming a distraction, Kate. I suggest the two of you take the boys, who've begun throwing powdered-sugar lemon drops at each other—and you can imagine how that is affecting their navy blue suits—and leave."

"I need to speak with you before I leave," Kate said.

"I don't have the time—"

"This can't wait," Kate insisted.

"Fine. Talk," Ann Wade snapped.

Kate turned to Jack and said, "Will you excuse us, please?"

Ann Wade didn't bother to hide her impatience. Once Jack had walked away she said, "What is it, Kate?"

"J.D. showed up on my doorstep—alive and well—asking for money. He's threatening to kidnap Lucky and Chance if I don't give him a quarter of a million dollars."

"Fuck a duck."

Kate was startled into making a sound that was half laugh, half sob. She'd never heard Ann Wade swear, because the consummate politician was always careful not to be caught saying anything indiscreet. And the epithet seemed particularly inappropriate to the seriousness of the situation.

"What is it you expect me to do about it?" Ann Wade said.

Kate sobered immediately. "You're his mother. Can't you talk to him?"

"I'm done talking to him."

Kate took a deep breath and said, "Then would you help me pay him to go away and leave us both in peace?"

Ann Wade grimaced. "I already gave my 'dead' son a quarter of a million dollars to disappear without telling you he was still alive. It seems he ignored his promise to me and sought you out anyway."

Kate felt her face blanch. "You were going to let me go on believing J.D. was dead, when he's alive?"

"Why not?"

"Because I would have been a bigamist when I married again!"

Ann Wade arched a perfectly plucked brow. "You already have another father in mind for my grandsons?"

Before Kate could stop herself, her gaze shot to Jack.

"Oh, no. No. Not him," Ann Wade said as her blue eyes narrowed on Jack. "He can do nothing for my boys."

"They're *my* boys," Kate said fiercely. "And Jack can be a father to them. Which is more than your son ever did."

"Let's not be throwing stones, my dear. I seem to remember you were anxious enough to marry my son."

Kate had no comeback for that. "J.D.'s going to keep coming back asking for more and more money from both of us. Isn't there something you can do to stop him now?"

"The truth is, I don't think J.D. will be alive long enough to come back for another payment."

"What do you mean?" Kate asked.

"He's gotten on the wrong side of the Mexican Mafia. I think they're going to find him—and express their displeasure—long before he goes through the half million we'll have given him. I presume you'll come up with your share of the money he needs to disappear?"

Kate stared at her mother-in-law with dawning recognition. "You're scared of J.D. Of what he might do or say. You can't control him, so he's a loose cannon that may come back and shatter—"

"We'll both be better off when J.D. is dead!"

Kate looked into Ann Wade Pendleton's icy blue eyes and said, "It's unnatural to care so little for your own flesh and blood."

"I care very much for my grandsons," Ann Wade said. "They're my hope for the future. After all, it's become almost a tradition for family dynasties to occupy the White House."

"Chance and Lucky aren't—" Kate bit her tongue. She would

not—could not—give this vicious woman the kind of power she would have if she knew who'd really provided the seed that had split and grown into Chance and Lucky. There would be time enough later to thwart Ann Wade's ambitions for the boys she believed were her grandsons. "Fine. I'll handle J.D.'s demand for money on my own."

"If there's nothing else you need from me, I have people to see."

Ann Wade had already taken two steps before Kate said, "There's just one more thing."

Ann Wade turned to look at Kate over her shoulder. "What is it?"

"Leave Jack alone. Or else."

Ann Wade turned back to Kate, her fingers tightening on the handle of her half-full teacup, the saucer rattling under it. "Are you threatening me?"

"I know you, Ann Wade. I don't want you ruining Jack's life. I don't want him getting kicked out of the Rangers. I don't want you causing him trouble of any kind whatsoever."

"Or you'll do what?" Ann Wade said in a voice dripping with disdain.

"I'll make sure the press finds out about J.D. Not just that he's alive, but that you paid him to disappear. And that you don't care if the criminals he's been working for find him and kill him."

Ann Wade's eyes narrowed to slits. "I intend to be the next president of the United States. I don't intend to let anything—or anyone—get in my way."

Kate met her gaze and said, "We all do what we have to do."

"You're a fool," Ann Wade said as she set the teacup and saucer down on a nearby credenza so softly they didn't make a sound.

"Maybe I am, but—"

"To reveal what you care about most," Ann Wade said. "Now I know where to attack if I want to hurt you."

Kate stared aghast at her mother-in-law. "You wouldn't—"

Ann Wade suddenly stepped into Kate's space, so close Kate could feel the other woman's breath on her face. "I won't go after your precious Jack McKinley, my dear. Unless you give me a good reason to do so." Ann Wade smiled and took a step back. "I trust we understand each other?"

Ann Wade was gone before Kate could swallow past the lump of terror in her throat.

38

Breed stared across the booth in the dark, neon-lit bar at King Gray-hawk. He tried to see himself in the older man, with his deep-set blue eyes, strong, straight nose, cleft chin, and silver-streaked black hair. But there was little, besides their over-six-foot height and straight black hair, that connected him physically to the man who was sup-posedly his father.

"I appreciate you meeting with me," Breed said. His voice was civil, but inside he was struggling to control his resentment. He'd en-dured a lifetime of slights as a result of being rejected by this man at birth. He reminded himself he was here to help Grace. For her sake, he was willing to put up with a lot.

"I'm glad you contacted me," King said. "What can I do to help?"

It galled Breed to be asking for anyone's help. He found his fa-ther's eagerness to help him—at this late date—revolting. But the thought of the trouble Grace was going to be in, if she couldn't prove that Vince had killed her parents, kept him in his seat.

"I need you to get the regional FBI SAC, Craig Westwood, to come see you at Twin Magnolias. Alone. I plan to be there when you meet with him."

"Why?"

"You don't need to know that."

"What if I insist on knowing?"

"Insist all you want," Breed retorted. "I'm not here to beg or plead or cajole. You can help me or not, it's all the same to me. In fact, I'd rather find another way—"

He was already on his feet when King reached out a hand to stop him. "Sit down. I didn't say I wouldn't help. Give me the man's name and number and I'll arrange it."

"Just Westwood," Breed said as he sank back into his seat. "No one else."

"No problem," King said.

"It may be more of a problem than you think," Breed said. "Westwood is managing the FBI end of security for the president's visit tomorrow. He isn't going to want to walk away from that for a meeting with anybody. Not even you."

"What's this all about, Breed?" King asked.

Breed struggled with whether or not to explain more to King. He decided it couldn't hurt. "Friday night, I met a woman named Merle Raye Finkel—she's calling herself Grace Caldwell now. Grace was convicted of murdering her parents and spent eight years in juvie. When she got out, she went hunting for the man who committed the murders. She may have found him."

Breed met his father's gaze and said, "I think the guy who really murdered her parents is an FBI agent. My boss."

King whistled soft and low. "That's quite an accusation, my boy."

"I'm not your boy," Breed said quietly. "You lost the chance to be anything to me when you threw me out."

"But you are my son," King said.

Breed felt dizzy. He shook his head in denial. "You can't be sure of that."

"DNA doesn't lie."

"I've never—"

"I took a beer bottle you drank from at the Fourth of July celebration at North's house. There was enough saliva to provide a DNA sample. You *are* my son."

Breed felt light-headed. He reached for his beer and saw his hand was shaking and stuck it under the table. It didn't make a difference. Not really. The dark years of his childhood could never be erased.

"I made a mistake," King said, keeping his voice so calm that

Breed found it aggravating. "Not long after you were conceived, your mother told me that if I didn't pay more attention to her, she'd find someone who would. When you were born, with those silver-gray eyes and that copper skin, all I could remember was her threat.

"I loved her. And I was jealous. And enraged that she'd taken another man to her bed."

"She never did," Breed said. "She told me she never did."

King sighed. "She told me that, too. I didn't believe her. Which is why—"

"I'm not here to discuss your mistakes," Breed interrupted. "I'm here to get help for a young woman who's had even more bad breaks in her life than I have. Which is saying something, because before I hooked up with North when I was sixteen, I had a damned shitty life. I—"

Breed cut himself off and glared at King, daring him to speak. He didn't want sympathy or empathy or even an apology from his father. He just wanted King's help on this one thing. After that, he didn't care if he never crossed paths with King Grayhawk again. He'd managed to grow up without a father. He sure as hell didn't need one now.

King eyed him speculatively, then said, "What do you suggest I say to this FBI SAC to get him to show up at Twin Magnolias?"

"Tell him I've been in contact with you. And that I've been saying some pretty outrageous things about my boss, Vincent Harkness. For instance, that he's a serial killer."

King raised an inquiring brow, but Breed continued without confirming or denying the facts of what he'd said.

"Tell him I've been defending this woman named Merle Raye Finkel, who's a convicted double murderer, who I claim is *not* a terrorist who's trying to kill the president, even though I say my boss is hunting for her. Tell him you're embarrassed to have your misguided progeny—you can call me your son, if you think it will help—associating with a murderer who's a suspected terrorist. Tell him you want me exonerated, in exchange for telling the FBI where I'm staying with Merle Raye Finkel."

"Is that true? Are you associating with a suspected terrorist trying to kill the president?" King asked.

"I've told you all I'm going to tell you," Breed said. "Do you want to help me or not?"

"I'll arrange the meeting with Westwood. Just tell me when and where."

"Set it up for tonight. After dark. My ranch house. You can tell him you're staying at Twin Magnolias while you're in town for the NGA Annual Meeting."

"Actually, I'm at the Four Seasons," King said.

"You can move this afternoon. There's a guest bedroom on the main floor at Twin Magnolias."

"Where is—"

"Don't pretend you don't know where Twin Magnolias is," Breed said with a sneer. "The banker who sold the place to Jack and me told us you'd inquired about the viability of us running the property as a quarter horse ranch."

King's forthright gaze made it clear he felt no remorse for such an intrusion in Breed's life. "Are you going to be arrested for this? Are you going to prison?"

"Not if I can help it."

"If the FBI is hunting for this woman, don't you think it might be a good idea—"

"Tonight. After dark. My ranch house," Breed repeated as he stood up.

"Could we talk about this?" King said, reaching out to forestall him.

"We're done here," Breed said curtly. "If you have any more questions, they'll be answered tonight."

39

～

Grace was lying on her couch with her hands behind her head, forcing herself to remain calm, even though, at that very moment, her fate was being decided at some distant place.

Breed had left a couple of hours ago to meet with King Grayhawk. If that meeting went well, Breed had hoped to meet after dark with the regional SAC, Craig Westwood, at Twin Magnolias. She'd wanted to be at that meeting, but Breed had reminded her that Westwood would likely arrest her first and worry about sorting out the truth later.

Grace glanced at her watch. It was 6:07 p.m. How long before Breed returned? How long before she knew whether her yearlong search for Allie's killer was at an end?

Grace thought she was hearing a cricket at first. The sound was chirpy. And far away. And there were spaces between the chirps.

Which was when she realized it wasn't a cricket, it was the phone she'd tossed into the garbage after calling the bagel shop yesterday morning.

Grace was off the couch in an instant, and an instant after that had ripped the flip-top off the garbage can and was rooting through leftover food and plastic wrappings and tin cans for the phone. Once she had the slimy thing in her hand, she realized it might be dangerous to answer it.

But what if it was Breed, calling her to say Vince Harkness was under arrest? What if it was Breed, warning her to get out of the house? What if it was Breed, telling her he was in trouble and needed her help?

After all, who else could it possibly be? Who else would know how to get this number, which could only be recovered from the bagel-shop caller ID?

Grace flipped open the phone and said, "Hello? Breed?"

"It's me, Grace. Troy."

Grace felt a stab of disappointment. And a stab of fear. "What's wrong? What's happened? Why are you calling me? How did you get this number?"

"I called Todd at the bagel shop, and he gave it to me," Troy said, answering her last question first.

"What phone are you using to call me, Troy?" Grace asked.

"My cell," he said. "But I'm calling you from my home in Dallas."

"Hang up and go call me from a pay phone," Grace instructed. "The FBI is probably tracing this call as we speak."

"I haven't seen an FBI agent since I left Austin, Grace. Aren't you being a little paranoid?"

"Look, Troy, this is no joke. Hang up your phone."

"But Grace, this is important. There's a bomb—"

Grace had already hung up. Her heart was in her throat. She stared at the cell phone in her hands, then threw it on the counter and quickly washed her hands, as though the phone had been covered in blood, rather than marinara sauce.

How could Troy have been so careless? How could she have been so stupid as to answer the phone? She knew better. *She knew better!* What if the FBI had a trace on Troy's cell? Had she been on the phone long enough for them to find her location?

Was Vince Harkness already on his way?

40

"Did you get it?" Vincent said anxiously. "Can you locate the closest cell tower to the call?"

"We've got it," Steve said. "Troy McMahon called a throwaway phone number, and the call was connected through this tower here," Steve said, pointing to a map that showed towers for every cell phone company with service in South Texas.

"I want to know who owns every piece of property within the service area of that tower," Vince said.

"I've got that," another agent said. "Every property in that area is owned by an individual, except this seven-hundred-acre parcel here, which is owned by an offshore corporation." He pointed to the location of the corporate-owned parcel. "We're searching for the human at the other end of a bunch of shell corporations, but we haven't gotten a name yet."

Vincent tamped down the excitement he felt. The owner of that parcel was going to turn out to be Merle Raye Finkel. When her identity was confirmed, the JTTF agents were going to want to be in on the takedown. Which meant that if Vincent wanted to get there ahead of them, and silence her, he was going to have to get started now.

"I want SWAT on call," Vincent said. "In case this turns out to be our suspect."

"After all the work we've done, aren't we going in after Merle Raye Finkel ourselves?" Steve asked.

"Apprehending suspects is what SWAT does best," Vince said.

"They'll kill her. And Breed," Steve said. "That's what SWAT does best."

"You're a campus cop," Vince said with a sneer. "Do what you're told, or I'll get someone who will."

Vincent waited until Steve turned his attention back to his computer before he said, "I want to know if there are any dwellings on that seven-hundred-acre corporate-owned plot. If so, I want you to text the GPS coordinates for them to my phone and e-mail them to my home and my office, so I'll be sure to get the information wherever I am."

"I really didn't think we'd find her," Steve said.

Vincent patted him on the shoulder. "You need to have more faith in the talented agents of the F–B–I." Then he turned and headed out the door.

"I wouldn't know about that," Steve muttered behind his back. "I'm just a campus cop."

41

"All right, Governor Grayhawk. I'm here. Alone. Where is Agent Grayhawk?" FBI Special Agent in Charge Craig Westwood said. "What is this terrorist threat your son seems to want to investigate on his own?"

The two men were settled into aged leather chairs situated next to each other in front of a crackling fireplace in the Great Hall at Twin Magnolias.

Breed had arranged for Jack to keep his parents upstairs and out of the way, and for Jack to make himself scarce as well. Breed wasn't sure how Craig Westwood was going to react when he heard what Breed had to say.

Breed stepped into the light from a darkened doorway and said, "I asked my father to invite you here, sir. I'll tell you what you want to know. But first we need to talk."

Breed saw King's eyes widen. It was the first time Breed had referred to the old man as his father. He hadn't even realized he was going to say it until the words were out of his mouth.

By the time Breed focused his gaze back on Westwood, the FBI regional SAC was standing in a classic shooting stance and had his Glock 22 pointed at Breed.

Breed put up his hands and said, "Vincent Harkness is a serial killer. He's been murdering his wife's lovers. I've printed out reports of murders that correspond to entries in his wife's diary. The reports and Stephanie's diary are sitting on the table to the right of your chair."

"Stay where you are, Governor," Westwood said as he backed up until he could see the papers Breed had mentioned. "And keep your hands where I can see them."

"The pink silk book is the diary," Breed said.

Westwood focused his penetrating gaze on Breed and said, "How did you get involved in this? I thought you and Vince were friends."

"I'm not any happier about this than you are," Breed said.

Westwood stared at Breed a moment more, then crossed to him and said, "Remove the gun from your boot and put it on the table. Do it slow and easy, so I don't feel the urge to squeeze this trigger."

Breed was careful to follow Westwood's order, because he didn't doubt the experienced agent would shoot him if he didn't do exactly as he was told.

"Put your hands against the wall and spread 'em," Westwood ordered.

"I don't have—"

"Do it!"

Breed hadn't been frisked since he'd practiced it with other recruits at the FBI Academy at Quantico. Westwood was thorough, and when he was done, he gestured with his Glock to the cowhide chair across from the leather one where he'd previously been sitting.

"Get comfortable, Agent Grayhawk. It might take me a while to go through the material you collected."

Before Westwood slid his Glock into his holster, he turned to Breed's father again and said, "Governor, if you tell me you're not armed, I'll take your word for it. Although I'm going to look like a damned fool if you shoot me down later to save your boy, here."

"I'm not armed, Agent Westwood. I'm just here as a facilitator, to get the two of you together, so my son can make his case," King said.

Westwood sat down in the leather chair in front of the fire and picked up the TCIC, NCIC, and ViCAP printouts Breed had collected.

It was hard for Breed to sit still, but he made himself do it. He kept his gaze focused on Westwood, so he knew when the regional SAC had finished perusing the material.

Westwood shuffled everything into a neat stack and said, "Vince committed all these murders?"

"I believe so, sir."

"How did you discover this?"

"I recently met a woman named Merle Raye Finkel, who was convicted of killing her parents. Two murders which I believe, but can't prove, Vince actually committed."

"How did you meet this Finkel woman?"

"Grace—she calls herself Grace Caldwell now—found me, sir." Breed didn't bother explaining Grace had found him at a bar. And had had sex with him the same night. "She's the one who showed me the diary, which she stole from Vince's house."

"She's a thief?"

"Ever since she got out of juvie a year ago, Grace has been hunting for whoever murdered her parents. The trail led her to Vince's home, where she found the diary.

"Vince discovered the diary was missing and has been trying to find Grace ever since to kill her—and destroy the diary.

"I wanted to show you what I've found, to see if you'd be willing to ask a judge for a search warrant for Vince's house here in Austin, his garage and the garden shed behind his house, his car, and his cabin at Lake LBJ, including the boat he keeps there," Breed said.

"You really think that if Vince Harkness has been smart enough to commit twenty-four murders over"—Westwood checked the papers Breed had provided with the diary—"nine years, in eleven states and the District of Columbia, without getting caught, you're going to find anything in his homes or on his property to prove his guilt?"

"Some very smart killers have made some very dumb mistakes," Breed said.

Westwood flipped through the diary. His lips became a thin line as he read a passage. "Twenty-four of these encounters ended with the murder of Stephanie Harkness's lover?"

"Yes, sir," Breed said.

"Where's Merle Raye Finkel now?" Westwood asked.

"I've been keeping Grace safe from Vince," Breed said. "Her father was an Austin PD homicide detective investigating the Cancer Society Murder mentioned in that newspaper clipping. Grace speculated that her father suspected Vince of the murder, and that Vince killed Big Mike Finkel to shut him up and stop the investigation from moving in his direction."

"You have proof of any of this?"

"No, sir," Breed said.

"What about the threat to the president's life your father mentioned. What is that all about?"

"That was merely a way to get you here, sir. But you should know that someone—I believe it was Vince—phoned in an anonymous tip to the Austin FBI specifically naming Merle Raye Finkel as a terrorist who planned to bomb the president when he comes to town. Vince has had the entire JTTF office hunting for her over the past three days."

"Vince hasn't said a word to me about any suspected terrorist," Westwood said.

"Vince isn't hunting a terrorist. He's using the resources of the Austin JTTF to hunt for a woman who can point to him as a serial killer."

"Have you told me everything?" Westwood asked, steepling his hands under his chin.

"Vince also planted a van, supposedly full of nitrate fertilizer, in the driveway of the house where Grace Caldwell was living."

"A truck bomb? Are you telling me—"

"It was peat moss," Breed interrupted. "A ruse, so Vince could justify shooting Grace."

"How do you know he was planning to shoot her?" Westwood said.

"I was hiding in a closet when Vince came to the house where Grace was living to confront her about his wife's missing diary. He intended to kill Grace once he got it back."

"How do you know that?"

"I heard him threaten her. I saw him pistol-whip her. When I showed myself, Vince ran. It wasn't until later, when I called in to the JTTF office, that I realized Vince had left a van in the driveway that supposedly contained ammonium nitrate fertilizer. Vince had made sure it looked just real enough to give him an excuse to shoot Grace."

"It seems the best way to resolve this is for me to take Merle Raye Finkel, aka Grace Caldwell, into FBI custody."

"No," Breed said.

"I wasn't asking permission," Westwood said. "I was ordering you to turn her over to me."

"I can't do that, sir."

"Why not?"

"She's a fugitive. She violated her parole," Breed explained. "If she's in custody, the Texas authorities are going to arrest her and send her back to prison and throw away the key."

"You're harboring a fugitive?" Westwood said.

"I'm keeping an innocent woman safe from a serial killer who wants to make her his next victim," Breed replied.

"Are you expecting me to approve your unorthodox and unprofessional behavior?"

"I contacted you because Vince is at the top of the FBI food chain in Austin. And I needed a bigger gun."

"All right. Fine," Westwood said. "I can get a search warrant. It might take a little time. Someone will have to verify the diary belongs to Vince's wife."

"She's signed every one of the entries, if that helps," Breed said.

"Is this everything you've got?" Westwood asked, tapping the diary and printouts with a forefinger.

"Yes, sir," Breed said.

"I'd like to talk to the girl," Westwood said.

Breed shook his head. "Not until I can be sure she isn't going to end up in jail."

"I doubt Vince is going to confess to her parents' murders," Westwood said. "The girl needs to surrender herself if she's violated her parole."

"The circumstances—"

"Which side of the law are you on, Agent Grayhawk? It's time to make a choice."

Breed hesitated, then said, "I'd have to choose Grace, sir."

"I was afraid you were going to say that. Special Agent Grayhawk, consider yourself under house arrest."

"What?"

"I've brought enough agents with me to make sure you don't leave. They'll be posted around the house with orders to shoot if you stick so much as your little toe over the threshold."

"That wasn't the deal," Breed said angrily as he rose to his feet.

"I never agreed to anything," Westwood said, standing and gathering up the papers and the diary.

"I need to be there to protect Grace. Vince knows she has—thinks she still has—the diary. He wants her dead."

"All right," Westwood said. "You're assigned to keep the girl in protective custody. Call her and have her come here. I assume you can reach her."

"I need to go to her."

Westwood shook his head. "That isn't going to happen."

"But Grace—"

"I'll let you know when I get the search warrant. Is there anything else?" Westwood asked.

"Nothing, sir," Breed said.

King stood, and Westwood reached out to shake the Wyoming governor's hand.

Westwood nodded to both men, then said, "It's been interesting, gentlemen."

A moment later he was gone.

Breed grimaced. With any luck, Westwood would get the search warrant by tomorrow morning and find something to link Vince to the murders of Stephanie's lovers. Maybe Vince could be persuaded to confess to the murder of Grace's parents in return for a few hundred less years on his sentence.

"Tell me about the girl," King said. "It sounded like she's important to you."

Breed was surprised by King's perception. And annoyed by his question. "Grace is . . ." Breed struggled to find a word to describe how he felt about Grace and finally said, "Special."

"If you love her, don't dick around," King said. "Marry her."

Breed watched in silence as King turned and headed down the hall. "I'm tired," he said. "I'm going to bed."

He stared at his father's back. *Marry her?* It seemed like strange advice. Until Breed remembered his father's history. When King Grayhawk had been a young man, he'd hesitated in proclaiming his feelings for Eve DeWitt, and another man had stolen her away. Which was how the lifelong feud between King Grayhawk and Jackson Blackthorne—who'd married the woman King Grayhawk loved—had begun.

"I hear you, old man," Breed murmured. "I hear you."

He just wasn't so sure Grace would be willing to go along.

"Breed! Phone call!" Jack called from upstairs.

Breed headed toward the stairs as Jack came running down with the phone held out in his hand.

Breed took it and asked, "Who is it?"

"It's Steve from the JTTF office."

The hairs stood up on Breed's neck. He had to clear his throat to speak. "Steve? What's going on?"

"He's found her, Breed. Vince has the GPS coordinates for the only dwelling on a seven-hundred-acre piece of property owned by an offshore shell corporation. I assume that's where Merle Raye Finkel is hiding out. He's got a SWAT team standing by and a two-hour head start. If you want to save her butt, you'd better get her the hell out of there."

"Thanks, Steve." Before hanging up the phone, he said, "Why are you helping me?"

"There was nothing but peat moss in the van, for Christ's sake. And I don't like the son of a bitch."

42

Grace had been expecting Troy to call her right back. But he didn't. She had paced the living room in agitation, waiting for him to get to a pay phone. Something must have happened, because two hours later she was lying in her bed staring at the ceiling, still waiting for his call.

Grace jumped when the throwaway phone she'd put on the bedside table rang again. She stared at it warily. She wondered if the FBI had traced the number already, and whether it had been an exercise in futility having Troy make his call from a pay phone. Maybe they'd already arrested Troy, and they were making him call her to get her location or set her up somehow.

She sat up and chewed a hangnail as she listened to the phone ring for the sixth time.

Grace hadn't forgotten the last word Troy had said before she'd hung up on him. *Bomb.* She knew he wouldn't have called her unless he had something important to tell her.

And either the damage was already done and the FBI had her location, or they hadn't had time to trace the call and Troy could safely call her on the throwaway phone. Grace just wished she knew which supposition was correct.

She decided she would be better off knowing why Troy had called. She picked up the phone, which she'd wiped clean of marinara sauce sometime during the two hours she'd been waiting for Troy to call back, and flipped it open.

"Grace?" Troy said.

"It's me, Troy."

"Thank God, Grace! You wouldn't believe how far I had to go to find a pay phone. Then an old friend of mine showed up at the 7-Eleven and started talking, and when he finally left, I discovered the damned phone was out of order and I had to go somewhere else to—"

"Troy—" Grace said, wanting him to get to the point.

"I was afraid you wouldn't answer the phone, Grace," he said, "and I've got something really important to tell you."

"What is it, Troy? What's going on?" she asked, perching on the edge of the bed.

"I wasn't sure what to do," Troy said. "That FBI agent who interrogated me, Mr. Harkness, said a lot of stuff about you being a terrorist. He told me I'd be arrested if I said a word to anyone about the questions he asked. So I haven't.

"I realized none of what he accused you of doing could be true, you know, because you've been through so much in your life, and if you were really mad at the world and wanted to blow things up, the Victims would know. I'd know. So I didn't believe it, Grace, but—"

"Thanks, Troy," Grace said. "For the record, none of what Mr. Harkness may have said about me is—"

"I think my roommate might be thinking about blowing up the Texas governor," Troy blurted.

Grace rubbed her forehead, which suddenly throbbed. "That sounds pretty farfetched, Troy."

"I mean it!" Troy said. "I never thought too much about Harry being a National Guard vet, you know, and losing his legs to an IED—that's an improvised explosive device—in Iraq. How he might feel about that, I mean.

"But Harry said something before I left for Dallas that I've been thinking about ever since, and I'm afraid maybe he's going to do something bad. Like incinerate the governor."

"So call the FBI," Grace said, "and tell them what you know."

"What if I'm mistaken? I mean, I wouldn't want to subject an innocent person to the kind of grilling that FBI agent gave me and the rest of the Victims. It was awful! What if I'm just seeing a terrorist where there isn't one, because of all those questions that agent asked me about you?"

The call had gone on so long, the phone in Grace's hand was getting hot. She knew she was being as paranoid as Troy had accused her of being, but she wasn't comfortable talking this long on the phone.

"I've got to get off the phone," she said. "Can you tell me—in the fewest words possible—what makes you suspect Harry wants to blow up the Texas governor?"

"When I was leaving town, Harry stopped me at the door to our room and said, even though he isn't a member or anything, that he really believed in what the Victims for Vengeance were trying to do. That he'd been thinking a lot about losing his legs and who might really be responsible. And he was finally going to do something about it. 'Get me some justice from the governor,' he said."

"How do you make the leap from that conversation to Harry setting off a bomb?" Grace asked.

"It wasn't only that conversation," Troy said. "It was other conversations we've had, too."

"Can you hurry this up?" Grace said, staring at the second hand moving on her watch. "What else?"

"Like how Harry wrote a letter to the governor asking to get out of deploying with his Guard unit because his mother was sick and needed him to work on their spinach farm. But the governor turned him down."

"That's it?" Grace said. "That doesn't seem like enough—"

"His mom had an accident trying to make tractor repairs Harry thought he should have been there to do. She died. Harry was waiting to get sent home for her funeral when his deuce and a half—that's his army truck—drove over an IED and he lost his legs. Because of his injuries, he couldn't work the farm, and the bank foreclosed. Harry's at UT to retrain for a job he can do from a wheelchair."

"That's bad, all right. Sad, even. But why blame the governor for everything that's happened to him? Soldiers are injured serving their country. That's just how it is."

Grace heard silence on the other end of the line.

Finally, Troy said, "I don't know, Grace. I just heard Harry say he was going to get him some justice from the governor, and with all that FBI agent's talk about a bomb, I thought—"

"It isn't that easy to put together a bomb," Grace pointed out.

"Oh, yeah, I guess I forgot to mention, Harry was always bragging about all the explosives he swiped from the ammo dump that he managed to get sent back to the States. Grenades and C-4 and stuff like that."

"Why didn't you say that in the first place?" Grace looked at her watch and realized that if the call was being traced by the FBI, she was shit out of luck, and the thing to do now was get as much information from Troy as she could, so she could pass it along to Breed.

"Where is Harry now?" Grace asked.

"He's attending classes, as far as I know."

"That sounds pretty normal, Troy."

"Yeah. But he hasn't answered the phone in our room since last night. And Harry doesn't have a lot of outside activities besides classes that would keep him away from the room for very long."

"Maybe he's just been out every time you called."

"I've been calling every fifteen minutes for the past twelve hours. I'm worried, Grace. I like Harry. I don't want him to ruin his life by doing something stupid."

"Troy, are you sure you wouldn't rather just call the FBI?"

"I don't want to cry wolf," Troy said. "I feel enough like a fool just mentioning all of this to you. I mean, I'd know it if Harry was crazy enough to set off a bomb, wouldn't I?"

"I think you must have some doubts," Grace replied. "Otherwise, you wouldn't have mentioned any of this to me."

"Yeah," Troy said quietly. "I guess I do. Tell me what to do, Grace."

Grace wondered if the JTTF would believe Troy if he accused

Harry, since they apparently considered the Victims for Vengeance a bunch of radicals. They might think Troy was pointing a finger at Harry to take the heat off Grace. But surely they'd investigate Harry. Especially since the president was coming to town tomorrow.

"Contact the FBI, Troy," she said. "That's the only responsible thing to do. Harry will have to take his lumps. After all, he isn't totally innocent if he stole munitions."

"What if the FBI doesn't believe me?" Troy asked. "Can't you do it, Grace?"

Grace snorted. "You think they'll believe me?"

"What about Breed? He's an FBI agent. He'll believe you if you tell him. Would you tell him for me, Grace? Please?"

Grace made a face, then said, "All right. I'll tell Breed everything you've told me. He knows enough people to make sure the FBI doesn't discount your warning. Good-bye, Troy."

Grace snapped the phone closed, wondering whether the FBI, Vince Harkness particularly, now knew where she was and whether she ought to get out of the house—leave her home—while she still could. If they had located her, she wondered how quickly the FBI could get here from Austin.

Pretty quickly, and quietly, with a SWAT black helicopter, she realized.

Grace grabbed her backpack—minus the diary, which Breed had with him—and began stuffing clothes in it.

How far could she get on foot in the dark if she just walked away? she wondered. She was nearly fourteen miles from the nearest road. She'd have to hitchhike once she got there, since she didn't have a car hidden anywhere. Because she'd never really thought anyone could find her here.

Grace heard a noise in the kitchen and froze. Her gaze locked on the bedroom door, which she hadn't bothered to close when she'd come in here. She tiptoed over to it, slid it almost closed, then looked through the crack, certain she was going to see Vince Harkness on the other side.

She was astonished by what she saw.

Grace opened the bedroom door and walked out. "You scared me to death! What are you doing in here?"

The raccoon sat on its hind legs on the kitchen table and looked up at her, a leftover blueberry muffin from her supper in its paws.

"How did you get in here?" she said with a grin of relief, looking around the living room for a window missing a screen.

Which was when she realized the front door was standing wide open.

43

"I need to get back to Grace," Breed said. "I have to warn her that Vince has found her."

"How are you going to do that?" Jack asked. "I heard Westwood. Twin Magnolias is crawling with FBI agents. You start shoving them around to get out of here, and you can kiss your career good-bye."

"I don't give a damn about my career," Breed said. "All I care about is Grace."

"You've known the woman for less than a week. Are you willing to throw away everything you've worked for, everything you might have in the future, to save a convicted felon?"

"Hell, yes!"

"Then you'd better get moving," Jack said with a smile.

Breed retrieved his Glock from where Westwood had left it on the end table. The regional SAC had obviously expected him not to try to escape the perimeter of FBI special agents who surrounded the house.

Which was his first mistake.

"Out through the storm cellar?" Jack said.

"Right," Breed said.

"Give her a kiss for me," Jack said.

Breed's face was grim. "I just hope I find her alive."

Breed had his first unpleasant surprise when he shoved open the door to the storm cellar and found an FBI agent standing there waiting, his gun trained on center mass.

"Back inside," the agent said.

"Fine, fine," Breed said. "Just let me—"

Which was when Breed grabbed the agent's wrist, shoved the Glock away from his body, and swung his other fist at the agent's chin, knocking him out cold. He eased the man to the ground, then took the agent's gun and stuck it in the back of his own jeans.

Escaping house arrest. Assaulting a federal officer.

Breed had made his choice. There was no turning back now. He moved swiftly and silently back along the route he'd taken when he'd come to Twin Magnolias the previous day. It was not necessary to assault any more federal officers.

He found his pickup near the stock trough where he'd left it— thank God—when he hadn't been sure what kind of reception he'd get from Craig Westwood. He hot-wired his truck again and headed cross-country.

Which was when the panic set in.

He was an hour away. Vince had a two-hour head start. Which meant Vince was already there, or would be very soon. Breed's pulse pounded in his temples. He gripped the steering wheel to keep his hands from shaking.

Vincent Harkness was once again stalking prey. And Breed had absolutely no way to warn Grace a killer was on the way.

44

"Hello, Stephanie," Grace said. "I must say, I wasn't expecting you to drop by for a visit."

"I'm amazed you recognize me, since we've never met," Stephanie Harkness said. "And I'm not at my best." She shoved absently at strands of golden blond hair that had slipped from the gold clip on top of her head. She was wearing a zippered black velour jumpsuit and black suede flats.

"Ever since you got out of juvie, I've been afraid you would come looking for me," Stephanie said. "It hasn't been easy finding you to settle matters between us. Unfortunately, I'm just a hop, skip, and a jump ahead of Vincent and an FBI SWAT team. I picked up the GPS coordinates for this place from Vincent's office about the same time I overheard him telling his minions where to find you."

"Maybe you'd better leave," Grace suggested. "So you don't get caught in the cross fire."

Stephanie made a *tching* sound in her throat. "It'll be ages before they make their move. While they're 'coordinating their assault on the house' I decided to come take care of you myself." She gestured with a .45 caliber Glock 30 for Grace to move away from the open doorway toward the center of the living room. "Cute raccoon. Is he a pet?"

"The raccoon? No, he's wild," Grace said, wondering how Stephanie could be so calm. "He must have come in when you left the front door open."

Stephanie glanced toward the open door. "Oh. I was being careful, closing it quietly, and the latch must not have caught." She was staring at the raccoon with a little more alarm. "Is it dangerous?"

"You could always shoot it," Grace said, fighting hysteria.

Stephanie laughed. "I suppose I could. But that might look a bit odd, if you stopped to shoot a raccoon and *then* committed suicide with your father's gun—to avoid being captured by the FBI and sent back to prison."

Grace's breath caught in her throat. "My father's gun? You're holding the weapon used to kill Big Mike and Allie? *You* killed them?"

Stephanie shrugged. "I didn't have any choice. Your father figured out that Vincent had killed Harvey. He was going to arrest Vincent and ruin all our lives. I couldn't let that happen. I am sorry about your stepmother. That was an accident."

"What about ruining my life?" Grace cried. "What about ending the life of a good woman, my stepmother?"

"I told you I'm sorry about that. But if it comes to a choice, I'm sure you understand that we're always going to choose to save ourselves. The strong survive. The weak perish."

"Vince knows," Grace said, grabbing at straws, looking for anything that might help her survive this encounter.

Stephanie frowned in confusion. "I believe he thinks Cecil Tubbs killed your parents. And I made sure Cecil Tubbs wasn't around to keep telling his version of the truth."

Grace couldn't believe what she was hearing. And realized Stephanie wouldn't be telling her any of this if she didn't think Grace would soon be dead. "Vince knows about the diary," Grace said desperately.

The blood left Stephanie's face so suddenly, Grace thought the older woman might faint. When the gun wavered, Grace decided to grab for it.

Just as Grace reached out, the Glock steadied in Stephanie's hand and she said, "If Vincent knows about the diary, he's chosen to keep it to himself. So long as he doesn't speak, and I stay mum, we can maintain the status quo."

"The *status quo*?" Grace nearly shrieked. "Your husband has been methodically killing off your lovers. That's the *status quo*!"

Stephanie's chin quivered, and the Glock in her hand wavered again before she grabbed it with both hands and said, "Unfortunate collateral damage. The important thing is that our family remains intact."

"Oh my God!" Grace said. "I can't believe what I'm hearing. You can't be that selfish. You can't be that stupid! I'm not the only one who knows what Vince has been doing. Killing me isn't going to do anything but get you sent to death row for one more murder."

"Who else knows?" Stephanie said.

"Breed Grayhawk, for one."

"I think Vincent intends to eliminate that threat himself," Stephanie said doggedly.

"At this very moment, Breed is talking to the San Antonio SAC, Craig Westwood. Giving him your diary. Telling him everything."

"No," Stephanie said, shaking her head. "That isn't possible. My diary is at home, in—"

"In the closet. In a shoe box."

Stephanie looked at her with horrified blue eyes.

"I stole it last Friday night. I've had it ever since."

"Then how could Vincent—"

"I don't know how he figured out I stole it. Maybe he checks it every night to see who you've been entertaining and found it gone."

Stephanie's eyes widened.

"The point is, your husband has apparently known about your diary for a very long time. And kept his knowledge a secret from you. But Vince knows what you are, Stephanie. He knows what you've done."

Stephanie was shaking her head and saying, "No no no no no no no."

"Yes yes yes!" Grace shot back. "It seems you've been keeping your secret lives secret from each other all this time. You're a promiscuous sex addict. And your husband is a serial killer."

Stephanie moved so swiftly that the barrel of the Glock was already in her mouth before Grace realized what she intended.

"Oh no, you don't!" Grace stuck her finger behind the trigger to keep Stephanie from firing the gun and sending a bullet through her brain. "You kill yourself with this gun, and the cops are going to say I had it all along, that we were fighting, and I killed you. I need you to admit what you did. I need you *alive!*"

"I want to die," Stephanie mumbled around the barrel of the Glock, tears streaming down her powdered face. "I need to die!"

"Not a chance," Grace said, pulling hard on the gun, finally jerking it free from Stephanie's mouth, chipping one of her front teeth. "You're going to face the music. You're going to see what it's like to be torn from your family and spend your days and nights locked behind bars and razor wire. You're going to suffer the way you made me suffer!"

Stephanie was still struggling to retrieve the Glock, but Grace was obviously the stronger of the two. Eventually, Grace freed the gun from Stephanie's hand.

And aimed it at her heart.

It was so tempting to pull the trigger. So tempting to make sure justice was done, rather than rely on a legal system that made mistakes. And made deals.

Grace realized, as she stood with vengeance in her grasp, that she wanted her life back more than she wanted vengeance.

Suddenly, from outside she heard, "This is the FBI. Come out with your hands up."

"That's Vincent," Stephanie said. "If you're going to shoot, you'd better do it now. Because in a few minutes, you're going to be dead."

45

Grace quickly extinguished all but one of the kerosene lanterns that were making the house glow like a firefly in the night, and that one she turned down low. She stayed away from the open windows so Vince wouldn't have a target to shoot at.

"Vince can't really believe I'm going to step outside," she said, staring out into the shifting shadows created by the night wind moving through the branches of the live oak overhead.

"You've seen this on TV a thousand times," Stephanie said. "You know how it's going to end. You might as well give up now."

"How did you plan to get away?" Grace asked. "I mean, after you shot me, how were you going to escape without getting caught, considering the SWAT team you believed was on the way?"

"I planned to be done and out of here before anyone arrived. My car is hidden about a mile down that dirt track you call a road," Stephanie said. "Now we're both stuck."

"Maybe not." Grace stepped over to one of the two open windows on the back side of the house, popped out the screen, and set it on the floor inside. She peered out, looking for movement. And saw nothing. But that might just be because no one out there was moving right now.

She thought of Breed and wondered where he was right now. Had he finished his business with the FBI regional SAC? Could he possibly be on his way back? Would he arrive, like the cavalry in a Western B movie, in the nick of time?

Grace was very much afraid, this time, that she wouldn't be able to save herself. And she didn't want to die.

"I'm going to have to tie you up," Grace said.

"You expect me to just—"

"Sit down," Grace said, aiming her father's Glock at Vince's wife and shoving a dining room chair in her direction. The raccoon was upset by the noise and dropped off the table with an unnerving, chittering complaint.

"That thing is going to bite me!" Stephanie cried.

"Sit down!" Grace ordered.

Stephanie whimpered, eyed the raccoon hiding under the kitchen table, and sat.

Grace headed for the kitchen drawer beside the sink and pulled out a roll of silver duct tape. She strapped Stephanie's wrists together in front of her, then taped her chest to the back of the chair, and finally secured her legs to the chair legs. Grace did a haphazard job, but the tape only had to hold long enough for Grace to get out the window.

"Any last words before I tape your mouth shut?" Grace said.

"Don't leave that thing in here with me," Stephanie begged, eyeing the raccoon.

Grace swore in disgust and said, "It's not going to hurt you if you leave it alone."

"You won't get away, you know," Stephanie said, looking up at her. "Vincent will catch you. And now your fingerprints are on the weapon you supposedly used to murder your parents."

Grace stared at the Glock she'd set down on the kitchen table. She felt like sobbing with frustration. She knew now who'd murdered her parents. Knew who'd framed her and left her to rot in juvie. But there was no way to prove Stephanie was guilty.

She needed Stephanie to confess on tape. Or in writing. She needed tangible proof she could use to convince a court of law that she was innocent of her parents' murders.

There just wasn't time now to get it.

Grace had to get away. So she could come back to fight another day.

She pulled off a long strip of tape to seal Stephanie's mouth. While she was ripping the tape from the roll with her teeth, she heard a sound behind her. She saw Stephanie's eyes go wide and quickly shoved the strip of tape over the older woman's mouth as she turned to meet the next threat.

Vince Harkness stood in the doorway, a familiar Beretta aimed at her head.

Grace reached for her father's Glock.

Vince stopped her by saying, "Be my guest."

Grace looked up and realized she would be shot the moment she had the gun in her hand. "I suppose if I leave it there, you'll put it in my hand the moment I'm dead anyway, and say you killed me in self-defense."

Vince shook his head as he moved into the room, closing the front door behind him. He crossed to the table and picked up her father's Glock.

"Nope. I'm going to shoot you, all right. But it isn't going to be in self-defense. I will have been trying to prevent a homicide."

Grace suddenly noticed Vince was wearing gloves. He aimed her father's .45 caliber Glock 30 at Stephanie's head and said, "Since you will have just murdered my wife."

Stephanie's eyes went wide, her eyes spurted tears, and she began to cry—angrily—behind the tape.

To Grace's amazement, Vince's eyes also brimmed with tears.

"I'm sorry, sweetheart," he said, his voice breaking. "I've always loved you. But you haven't left me any choice. Think of it as a sacrifice for the children. They need at least one of us to come out of this scot-free. By now, that goddamned Westwood has your diary. With you dead, it can be argued that *you* murdered your lovers."

As he put the gun to her head, a tear dripped down his cheek.

Stephanie was struggling against her bonds, crying and shouting behind the tape that covered her mouth, obviously not willing to make the sacrifice for their children that Vince was demanding.

Grace realized the authorities would believe she'd done the murder, because her fingerprints were on the gun—the same gun that had been used to murder her parents. "Maybe Stephanie has some final words she wants to say," Grace suggested, looking for any way to postpone the inevitable and give the cavalry time to arrive.

Vince hesitated, then yanked the tape from Stephanie's mouth, snatching out bunches of her hair, to which the tape was stuck on the sides of her face.

"Goddamn it to hell!" Stephanie screamed when her mouth was free. "What do you think you're doing, Vincent? I'm not the one who should be making the sacrifice, if one needs to be made. I'm not the one who killed Harvey and started this whole ball rolling!"

"You were the one fucking him in the closet," Vince retorted in a voice that was deadly calm and furiously angry. "And making the beast with two backs with every hairy ape you could find."

"I was spreading my legs for them because you couldn't be bothered to satisfy me," Stephanie shot back.

Grace edged toward the open window, certain they were so intent on each other that if she moved quickly and quietly, she might be able to throw herself through it and escape.

"Not so fast," Vince said, whirling to aim her father's service weapon at her.

"If you shoot me with that gun, it's going to be hard to argue self-defense, or anything else," Grace pointed out.

Vincent lowered the Glock and raised his Beretta. "You're right. Luckily, it doesn't matter in which order I shoot the two of you. You might even prefer to go first. Less anticipation of the unpleasantness to come."

"I'll testify for you against Vincent," Stephanie said to Grace. "I'll tell the truth about everything. Just save me!"

"She can't save you, Stephanie," Vince said, taking a step toward Grace, aiming his Beretta at her heart.

He suddenly yowled in pain and began batting at his leg with the gun in his other hand. The unexpectedness of the assault—and his shock at the sight of the raccoon under the table that was attached to his calf—caused him to forget, for an instant, about Grace.

It was enough.

Grace yelled in excitement herself when she realized Vincent had stepped on the raccoon's paw, and that the raccoon had bitten—was biting—his leg. She launched a devastating karate kick at Vince's lowered head, putting the whole weight of her body behind it. The tremendous blow to his temple stunned him, and he toppled to the ground.

The raccoon let go to avoid getting crushed and scurried back under the table.

Grace wrenched both guns from Vince's lax hands while he was semiconscious and tossed them out of the way. She recovered the roll of duct tape from where she'd dropped it on the floor earlier and quickly taped Vince's hands behind his back.

He groaned as he began to regain his senses, and she frantically wrapped tape around his legs, first at the ankles and then at the knees.

Breathing hard, elated at her success, Grace said to Stephanie, "I accept your offer to testify against your husband."

"I don't owe you anything," Stephanie snapped. "You didn't save me. That silly raccoon did!"

"I can leave you here or I can take you with me. Which is it going to be?" Grace said.

"I see no reason to go anywhere with you. A wife can't be compelled to testify against her husband."

"It seems your husband trusted you so much to keep your mouth shut that he was going to kill you to keep you quiet. Go ahead and stay here. I'm sure Vince can arrange another 'accident' for you before the FBI gets around to questioning you about your husband, the serial killer."

"All right. You win. I'll go with you," Stephanie said. "Get me out of this chair."

Grace retrieved both her father's Glock and Vince's Beretta and stuck them in the waistband of her jeans, then found a steak knife and freed Stephanie from the chair. "I'm warning you. Do what you're told, when you're told. One lapse, and I'll leave you behind and let your husband deal with you."

"I'm not going to make trouble for you."

Grace eyed Stephanie suspiciously. She didn't trust the woman. She never would. But she needed her cooperation.

Grace had burned all her bridges when she hadn't shown up for that first meeting with her parole officer. Suddenly, she saw a real possibility that she might be able to prove her innocence. She just had to get Stephanie to confess again, when there were witnesses who could attest to what she'd said.

First, the two of them had to get the hell out of here.

By the time Grace had freed Stephanie, Vincent had regained consciousness and was yelling behind the tape.

"Take that, you bastard," Stephanie said as she kicked him viciously in the ribs.

Vince groaned and curled into a protective ball.

"Stop it!" Grace said. "Save your energy. We're going to need it to get out of here. Vince has a SWAT team on the way—he probably intended for them to bear witness to your murder and my suicide. The sooner we're out of here, the better."

Vince was shouting behind the tape Grace had put over his mouth, but she didn't waste her time trying to figure out what he was saying. She turned out the last kerosene lantern, then opened the front door and scanned the underbrush and the road beyond.

And saw two vehicles stopped on the road where the underbrush ended and the clearing around the house began.

"Damn, damn, damn!" Grace swore. "SWAT is out there already. I can see them getting out of their vehicles."

"Open the front door all the way and let the raccoon out," Stephanie said. "Maybe that'll keep them distracted—and confused—long enough for us to go out a back window."

Grace realized it wasn't a bad idea. She let the front door drift entirely open and waited for the wild animal to make a break for freedom.

The raccoon stayed under the table.

"Now what?" she said softly.

"Here," Stephanie said, tossing Grace the rest of the blueberry muffin the raccoon had been eating on the table. "Use this."

Grace threw crumbled bits of blueberry muffin across the threshold and out the door, then tossed the rest of the muffin onto the front porch.

She waited. And waited.

"This isn't working," Grace hissed.

"Shh," Stephanie said softly.

The raccoon was on the move.

46

~

"What have you done with Grace, you bastard," Breed demanded, his hands wrapped around Vince's neck.

"That bitch kidnapped my wife!" Vince said, struggling to free himself from Breed's stranglehold.

"Stop it. Both of you," Craig Westwood said from behind Vince's cherrywood desk, in an office bright with the morning sun.

Breed heard a round being chambered and glanced in Westwood's direction at about the same time Vince did. Westwood had his Glock aimed at the ceiling, but he repeated his warning. "That's enough. Sit down. Now."

Breed saw the hard line of Westwood's mouth and the narrowed eyes and knew the SAC wasn't bluffing. He released Vince and took a step back.

Vince rubbed his throat and scowled, then grabbed one of the two chairs in front of the desk, readjusted it, and sat down.

Breed crossed to the window, leaned against the ledge, and crossed his arms.

"How did you find the girl?" Westwood asked Vince.

"I had a trace on all the members of that radical group Merle Raye Finkel organized, the Victims for Vengeance. One of them called her, and the JTTF traced the call."

"How did your wife get to Finkel's house?"

"Steve called me from the office with the GPS coordinates. I presume Stephanie overheard me when I called SWAT and gave the GPS coordinates to them. She's got a GPS in the car."

"Why would she go there?" Westwood asked.

Vince leaned forward with his elbows on his knees, his hands clasped between them. He looked up at Westwood and said, "I don't know."

"He's lying!" Breed said.

Westwood shot Breed a look that shut him up, then reached in his briefcase and brought out Stephanie's pink silk diary, which he set in the middle of the desk. "Do you think your wife might have been looking for this?"

Vince sat up straight and cleared his throat. "What is that?"

"Don't pretend you don't know," Breed snarled.

"I don't," Vince protested.

"It's your wife's diary, Vince," Craig Westwood said. "Recounting her sexual liaisons with a great many men who have coincidentally turned up dead."

"What are you suggesting?" Vince said, playing the amazed and betrayed and horrified husband to the hilt.

"I can't watch this," Breed said with disgust. He turned to Westwood and said, "He's lying. He's known about the diary for a long time. That's why he came after Merle Raye Finkel in the first place. She stole it, and he knew it would link him to the murders."

"I went after Merle Raye Finkel because the FBI got an anonymous phone call saying that she intended to blow up the president."

"Which you probably made yourself!" Breed said.

"If you can't control your mouth, you can leave," Westwood told Breed.

At that moment, Breed's cell phone rang. He retrieved it and checked the caller ID. He didn't recognize the number, which meant there was at least the possibility that it was Grace. If it was, he didn't want to answer the call here. "Excuse me, sir," he said. "I need to take this call."

Breed was halfway to the door when Vince said, "It's her, isn't it? That Finkel bitch."

"What's your problem?" Breed flared.

"It's from her," Vince accused, crossing to intercept Breed. "Ask her what she's done with my wife!"

Westwood held up a finger and gestured Breed back into the room and Vince back into his chair. "Who's the call from, Agent Grayhawk?"

Breed stood in the doorway debating whether to make up some lie. But it was too easy to get caught. He finally said, "I don't know, sir. I don't recognize the number."

"Come back in here," Westwood said. "Let's see who's calling you. Put it on speakerphone."

Breed crossed back into the room, set the phone on Vince's cherrywood desk, and pressed the speakerphone function. "Grayhawk here," he said.

"Breed? It's me."

Breed picked up the phone. "Grace? Are you all right?"

"I'm fine. I'm worried about someone tracing this call, so I need to make this quick. Are you somewhere you can talk privately?"

Breed glanced at Westwood, then at Vince and said, "Yeah. Sure. Where are you, Grace? I'm worried about you."

"It's not me you should be worried about," she replied.

"What have you done with my wife?" Vince bellowed.

"Shit!" Breed and Westwood said almost simultaneously. Both of them glared at Vince, who looked chagrined but not cowed.

"Did she hang up?" Westwood asked.

Breed glanced at the phone to see if Grace had disconnected the call. He gave a sigh of relief when he saw she was still on the line. "I'm sorry, Grace," he said. "I'm here with Vince and the regional SAC, Craig Westwood."

"With *Vince Harkness*? And the *FBI*? You told me you were alone! I can't believe I trusted you. Again!"

"Please don't hang up, Grace," Breed said urgently.

He heard silence on the other end of the line. And felt sick to his stomach.

"Like I said," Grace continued in a curt voice, "it's not me you should be worried about. I called to tell you Governor Pendleton's life might be in danger. Check out Troy's roommate, Harry Gunderson. According to Troy, Harry's a veteran of the Iraq war with a grudge against the governor. Harry supposedly shipped a lot of bomb-making stuff back to the States when he finished his tour of duty."

They listened for more. But there was no more.

"She broke the connection," Breed said as he closed his cell phone and met Westwood's piercing gaze.

"She didn't tell us what she's done with my wife," Vince said.

Steve charged into the room and said, "Got her!"

"Where is she?" Vince asked.

"Within a one-mile radius of the LBJ Auditorium." He paused and added, "Where the president is speaking tonight."

"Maybe she's the one with the bomb," Vince said. "Maybe she's trying to shift the blame. Again."

Breed bit his cheek to keep from making a retort. The truth would come out. When the FBI executed the search warrant a federal judge was signing right now, a team would show up at Vince Harkness's front door. The search would be more than thorough. The team would pore over every square inch of Vince's home. Surely, some piece of evidence linking Vince to the murders would turn up.

"What about this Harry Gunderson?" Westwood asked. "Do we know anything about him?"

"I've met him," Breed admitted. "He rooms with one of the Victims for Vengeance, Troy McMahon. Gunderson is in a wheelchair, so he should be easy to track down. And conspicuous if he shows up at the LBJ Auditorium toting a bomb."

"Unless he's got an accomplice to deliver it for him," Vince said.

Breed caught the glance Westwood exchanged with Vince and realized the regional SAC was beginning to believe Vince's insinuations about Merle Raye Finkel. "Grace isn't an accomplice to anything," he said. "She just told us about a threat to the governor, for Christ's sake!"

"So we would be hunting for Gunderson instead of her," Vince argued.

"Grace is *not* a terrorist," Breed said. "I'd stake my life on it."

"It's not your life that's at risk," Westwood said at last. "It's the president and the nation's governors and a lot of innocent citizens. It's time to contact Homeland Security and the Secret Service. Let's get out an APB for Merle Raye Finkel. Post her mug shot on our Web site on the Internet and get it aired on TV—Special Bulletin. Don't wait for the evening news. We need to find this woman before it's too late."

Breed realized he'd lost the battle to convince Westwood that Grace was innocent of everything—including the murders of her parents. He wished he knew what had happened at Grace's house last night. The SWAT team had found the house abandoned and Vince taped up like a Christmas package on the floor.

The only one left to tell his version of the story had been Vince. And he'd been very convincing when explaining everything to his old buddy Craig Westwood.

Breed hadn't lost faith in Grace, even if she'd lost her trust in him. But he was confused by the facts he had.

Had Grace kidnapped Stephanie Harkness? Were the two women together? And how had Grace found out Harry Gunderson planned to blow up the Texas governor?

Breed suddenly realized he had the number Grace had called from recorded on his cell phone. If he got to a pay phone in a hurry, there was a chance he could reach her before she followed her usual habit and threw the disposable phone away.

47

Grace was still in shock after her call to Breed. She was walking along back alleys near the secret apartment Stephanie Harkness kept in Austin for her in-town liaisons with men, which was where they'd ended up last night.

Grace had been appalled when Stephanie admitted during their drive to the apartment that she'd engaged in even more sexual encounters than she'd recorded in her diary. "After the Cancer Society Murder, I never wrote in my diary about the in-town hookups," she'd told Grace. "Because they were too numerous—too brief and too boring, actually—to recount."

Grace had been so caught up in the events of the evening, and her escape from the FBI with Stephanie, that she'd forgotten all about Troy's warning until she'd woken up this morning. She almost hadn't called Breed, because even Troy wasn't sure Harry was a genuine threat.

But she wasn't a murderer, no matter what the world said, and she would have felt responsible if she didn't pass along Troy's warning and something happened to Governor Pendleton.

Grace had left Stephanie locked in the third-floor apartment bathroom, a chair braced against the door, while she went for a walk in order to buy a throwaway phone and make the call to Breed.

Grace still couldn't believe Breed had lied to her. Not only had he not been alone, but *Vince Harkness* had been standing right beside him! She should have known better than to trust Breed. She should have known not to let down her guard.

Grace wanted to curl up in a ball and cry. But that would have meant admitting how much a man she'd met just a few days ago had come to mean to her. Grace put a hand to her chest, which actually ached.

She was glad to be walking in an abandoned alley, so she could say aloud what she was thinking. "You're a fool, Grace Elizabeth Caldwell. You know better than to trust a man. You know better than to let yourself care."

How could she have forgotten the hard lessons she'd learned from Big Mike Finkel as a child? How could she have forgotten the reinforcement of those lessons at Giddings?

"Love isn't worth the risk," she said. "It—" She sobbed and put a hand to her mouth to stop the raw, animal sounds coming from her throat. She swiped angrily at the tears that brimmed from her eyes.

"Love isn't worth it," she said through gritted teeth. "Because pain is the payoff every single time!"

Grace swiped her sleeve across her runny nose, then hunched her shoulders up to her ears to release the tension in her neck. She was back on her own. With a job to do.

She still had to prove her innocence.

Which she would do when Stephanie Harkness told her story to the right people. At long last, Allie would have justice. And Grace would be free.

All Grace had to do was figure out who the "right" people were. Which wasn't as easy as it sounded.

Vince Harkness had long tentacles that stretched into local, state, and federal law enforcement. So far, he was managing to keep from looking guilty to the people who mattered. And if Vince couldn't be proved guilty of all those murders, fingers were going to be pointing back at Stephanie.

Which made her a much less reliable witness to Merle Raye Finkel's innocence.

Grace hoped Breed had managed to get a search warrant for Vince's house. The sooner it was executed, the better. Because now that Stephanie had disappeared, and the diary was in FBI hands, Vince was liable to cut his losses—and dispose of whatever evidence of his crimes he might have kept—sooner, rather than later.

So maybe after it got dark tonight, when all eyes and ears were on the president, she would do a little more breaking and entering. Grace suddenly smiled through her tears. She didn't even have to "break in" to Vince's home.

Stephanie Harkness had a key.

48

Kate was at the stable with the twins when her mother-in-law called to remind her of another command performance by Lucky and Chance, this time at the president's meet-and-greet before his keynote address to the governors. Kate glanced at Jack, who was on the other side of the outdoor riding arena watching the boys. Guarding the boys. Because Ann Wade had ordered it.

Kate wished she'd told Ann Wade a long time ago to go to hell. She wondered if it was too late to do it now.

"When the president's around, the press is around," Ann Wade continued. "I can get a lot of mileage out of being photographed with my grandsons. It will remind everyone how my son died serving his country."

"But J.D. isn't dead," Kate reminded her. Her husband was probably so certain she was going to pay him off that he was already sunning himself on some sandy beach in South America. Meanwhile, she still hadn't bucked up the courage to talk with Grandpa King.

"Just bring them," Ann Wade said.

"They're going to be exhausted when we get done here. They've got a project due for school tomorrow that isn't finished. And I'm tired. I've had a very long, very difficult day."

"Welcome to my world," Ann Wade said. "I'm counting on you, Kate. Don't disappoint me."

Ann Wade hung up before Kate could argue further.

"Trouble?" Jack said, appearing at her shoulder.

"Just Ann Wade being Ann Wade," Kate replied as she snapped

her phone closed. She'd spent a heartbreaking morning doing physical therapy at Brooke Army Medical Center—called Bam-C for its initials, BAMC—with a young soldier who'd lost his left leg in Iraq. She didn't have any emotional energy left to fight with her mother-in-law.

"Anything I can do to help?"

"She wants Lucky and Chance at the president's meet-and-greet tonight, so she can get a campaign-worthy photo of the twins standing on either side of her while the president shakes her hand."

"Then you'll want to leave the house by six instead of seven?"

"I guess so." Kate yearned to be held and comforted by Jack, but under the circumstances, that wasn't fair to him. "Thanks, Jack," she said in dismissal.

He stepped away without another word.

It was Jack's job to shadow the boys, but since Kate spent all of her spare time with the twins, it meant he also shadowed her. He hadn't said a word to her—except in the line of duty—since he'd told her he loved her. Kate knew he was waiting for her to make the next move, but she felt paralyzed.

Sooner or later, she would have to tell Jack the humiliating truth. Her husband was still alive. He was blackmailing her. He'd threatened to kidnap her sons. He'd worked for, or with, the Mexican Mafia, who might be hunting for him. And he'd faked his own death and deserted his post in wartime.

Which reminded her of the young man she'd met today, who'd served with honor in Iraq and paid a very high price for defending his country.

Army Private David Allen Jones, age nineteen, former Uvalde High School Coyotes lineman, voted half of the Best-Looking Couple his senior year, whose parents owned a mohair goat ranch, had been scheduled for a physical therapy session with Kate at 11:00 a.m. this morning at BAMC. He hadn't shown up.

So Kate had gone to him.

There was no sound from behind the colorful, showerlike curtain that surrounded the third bed in the hospital room on Four West, the amputee ward at BAMC.

Kate slipped behind the curtain, which was the only privacy the patient had, and said, "I missed you in PT today, Private Jones."

"What's the point?" the young man muttered, remaining prone on his side, facing away from Kate. "It isn't going to help my leg grow back. Or give me back my eye."

Kate knew the youthful soldier's story. Over the past six months she'd been working at BAMC, she'd heard accounts of her patients' injuries that differed only in the details.

Private Jones had also lost his left eye, where his face had been slashed to the bone by shrapnel from an IED—which she'd learned was an improvised explosive device—along with his left leg below the knee. He'd already started wearing a glass eye imprinted with the flag of the State of Texas, which was one of the options he'd been offered. He'd admitted to Kate with a rueful smile that the red, white, and blue colors in his eye socket made his girlfriend squeamish.

Kate was pulled abruptly from the recollection of her day by Lucky, who shouted "Look at me, Mom!" as he cantered by in the outdoor corral.

"Slow your horse to a trot, Lucky," the instructor said.

"Lucky, listen to Miss Simmons." Kate kept her eye on Lucky until he slowed Big Doc to a trot. Chance already had Little Doc at a steady trot, but he looked stiff and uncomfortable in the saddle.

Stiff and uncomfortable.

Like Private Jones this afternoon. He'd been lying in bed on his right leg, with his shortened left leg resting atop it.

"You need to do your exercises to get in shape for a prosthesis," Kate had said. "Why haven't you wrapped your stump?"

Soldiers were taught early to wrap their stumps, or cover them with a rubber cap, to shape their wounded flesh to fit the amazing prostheses that were being developed for returning vets.

"My father needs an able-bodied man to work for him on his mohair ranch," Jones said bitterly. "Not a cripple."

"You've seen the men who come back here to visit," Kate said. "They have prostheses so good they can run marathons."

"I don't want to run a marathon," Jones said, sitting up and pivoting so his leg and his stump hung over the bed. "I want to walk like a normal, two-legged man. That isn't going to happen. Ever again!"

Kate didn't argue with the soldier. She simply said, "I have no intention of asking you to walk today. I just want you to do a few exercises right here in your bed."

Kate had met Private Jones's hazel eyes, her hands on her hips. "We can do this the hard way or the easy way. It's up to you, Private."

"Why don't you just leave?"

"Not until you wrap your stump and do your exercises."

The young man sighed in resignation. "They warned me you were like this. Fine. Do your worst."

Kate had smiled at him and said, "You'll be dancing with that girl of yours in no time, David."

She'd spent another half hour with Private David Jones, putting him on his stomach and having him do leg lifts, then on his side, then on his back. She ran him through a series of exercises designed to keep the muscles in his legs and back strong. When she was done, beads of sweat had formed on the young man's forehead.

And on her own.

Kate was so very tired. Emotionally and physically exhausted. She didn't want to take her sons to a political dog-and-pony show tonight.

She suddenly realized Chance was no longer trotting his horse in a circle, he was walking him directly across the corral toward her. She stepped up on the bottom rail of the corral and leaned over so she could speak to her son when he reached her. "What's wrong, honey?" she asked.

"I don't feel good," Chance said. "I think I'm sick."

Kate realized Chance's cheeks were flushed. She reached out and put the back of her hand to his forehead. It was clammy. "Where does it hurt?"

"My stomach," Chance said. "It aches."

The instructor had walked over to check on Chance, and Lucky followed her on horseback.

"We're going to have to cut the lesson short," Kate said. "Chance isn't feeling well."

"Aw, Mom," Lucky said. "I was having fun."

"Your brother is sick," Kate said. "We need to get him home and into bed."

"I'll take care of the horses," the instructor said.

"Thank you so much, Sandy," Kate said.

A few minutes later, she had the twins buckled into the backseat and was headed for home, with Jack following in his Ford Explorer to make sure they had no trouble along the way.

Lucky complained incessantly about having to leave the stable early.

Chance was so quiet, Kate was worried that he was even sicker than he'd admitted.

"Chance?" She glanced at him in the rearview mirror and didn't like what she saw. "Are you all right, sweetheart?"

"I think I'm going to throw up," he said.

"Ick! Don't do it on me!" Lucky said.

"Do you think you can make it home?" Kate said.

"Yeah, I think I—"

"*Ew, eerp!*" Lucky said as Chance vomited all over the backseat.

Kate pulled the car to the curb and hurried around to open the door for Chance, unbuckled his seat belt, and helped him out of the car. He immediately leaned over and threw up the rest of the contents of his stomach on the street.

Her son was crying, saying, "I'm sorry, Mom. I thought I could make it. I'm sorry about the car."

"Don't worry about it," Kate said, thinking of how the smell of vomit never came out of the upholstery or the rug in a car. "I'll clean it up later."

Kate was relieved to see Jack's Explorer coming to a stop behind her car. A moment later, he was standing next to her, holding out a clean, pressed handkerchief to Chance.

J.D. would have run ten miles at the mere mention of vomit.

Kate chastised herself for making the comparison between the two men, but it was hard not to.

When Chance took the handkerchief to wipe his mouth, Jack put a comforting hand on the boy's shoulder and said, "Guess those ten tamales at lunch were a bit too much."

"*Ten* tamales?" Kate said. "What were you thinking, Chance?"

Chance, who seemed to be feeling significantly better, said, "I had to, Mom. Buck Betters said he could eat more than me. So I had to eat more than him."

She turned to Jack and said, "You allowed this? You're supposed to be watching them!"

"I figured this was a lesson Chance could learn for himself," Jack said.

"Yeah," Chance said with a sheepish grin. "I should have stopped at nine."

Kate stared at her son, aghast. She turned to Jack, who smiled and then chuckled. Kate threw up her hands and said, "I give up!"

Lucky had gotten out of the car and said, "It stinks in there, Mom."

"I'll give you a ride home," Jack said, "and come back and clean up your car."

Kate started to argue, then shut her mouth. She didn't think she could take the smell of vomit the rest of the way home. And she welcomed Jack's offer to spare her a dirty job. "Thanks, Jack. Can you give us a ride this evening, too?"

"No problem. Wish you didn't have to go?"

"It's just a little tough to manage on a school night," she said.

"If we're going to see Manway tonight, does that mean we can skip our homework?" Lucky said.

"Absolutely not." Kate was startled to hear Lucky call his grand-mother *Manway*. It was the best they'd been able to pronounce *Ann Wade* when they'd been babies. But Ann Wade didn't like the name, and at her request, the boys had stopped using it. Until it had popped out just now. Which just showed her how upset Lucky was about Chance being sick.

"Can I still go, Mom, even though I threw up?" Chance said.

"You *want* to go?" Kate asked.

"Sure," Chance said. "There's always food around whenever we see Manway."

"I can't believe you can even think about eating," Kate said.

"Now that I got rid of all those extra tamales, I'm hungry," Chance said.

"I don't believe what I'm hearing," Kate said to Jack.

"He's a growing boy," Jack said with a laugh.

"Will you join us for supper?" Kate asked.

Jack had already started to refuse when Kate said, "I want to thank you in advance for cleaning up the car. Please say yes."

Jack glanced in the rearview mirror, and Kate realized he was checking to see whether the boys were listening before he said quietly, "You've been giving me the cold shoulder ever since—" He cut himself off. "You can understand why I might not think I was welcome for supper."

"I'm sorry about that." Kate glanced out the window and swal-lowed hard over the sudden lump in her throat. "But . . ."

"But you're not going to tell me what's wrong, why you've backed away. Or why you haven't responded to what I said to you."

"This is *not* the time to be discussing this," Kate said, glancing over her shoulder at the two boys in the backseat.

"They're busy. They can't hear me when I say I love you, Kate."

"Please, don't say that, Jack."

"Why not?"

She was too tired to be careful. And too angry to be discreet. Still, she whispered her answer. "Because J.D. isn't dead."

Kate watched as Jack gripped the steering wheel so hard his knuckles turned white. He glanced at her, then back at the road, then at her again. "If he's not dead, where the hell is he? Where the hell has he been for the past year?"

"Shhh!" Kate warned, glancing in the backseat. The twins were busy playing a mean—the loser got a pretty good pinch—game of rock, paper, scissors. "J.D. showed up on my doorstep Sunday night and asked me for money so he can disappear again."

"Where is he now?" Jack asked.

"I have no earthly idea."

"What's going on, Kate? How could the military make a mistake like that, burying the wrong man?"

"J.D. faked his death," she said. "Apparently, the Mexican Mafia is after him. Something to do with gambling. He threatened to kidnap the twins unless I give him a quarter million dollars, which he plans to use to live in South America."

"Surely you're not going to—"

"I'm paying him, Jack. And that's final."

Except it would be Grandpa King who'd provide the actual cash. Jack didn't know anything about how bad her personal finances were, and she wasn't about to tell him how J.D. had gone through the millions of dollars in her trust fund.

"What happens to us now?" Jack said.

"I'm still married, Jack."

"J.D.'s legally dead," he said through tight jaws.

"Yes. But I know he's alive."

She saw Jack struggle with the reality she'd been facing ever since J.D.'s return. There was no future for them.

"If I know J.D., he'll be back for more money," Jack said at last. "And when that son of a bitch shows up, I'll be waiting for him."

49

~

"I want you walking the floor here at the LBJ Auditorium until the president's speech is done and he's gone, Agent Grayhawk," Craig Westwood said. "Get out there and make sure Harry Gunderson isn't part of this crowd."

"Yes, sir." Breed was standing fifty feet from where the president of the United States was greeting constituents behind a velvet rope, the perimeter of which was ringed by Secret Service agents.

Breed hadn't once glanced at the president. He was watching Vince Harkness, whose house hadn't yet been searched—no man-power to execute the search warrant, because everyone was working the president's visit—and who therefore was still on active duty as an FBI agent. Breed wasn't about to give Vince the opportunity to sneak away and destroy whatever evidence he might have stashed in his home in Austin.

Both of them had been threatened with suspensions, pending the outcome of an internal investigation, but since Breed had actually seen Harry Gunderson, he'd been ordered to work the presidential event. Westwood had been keeping Vince by his side all day. Breed wasn't sure whether the regional SAC didn't trust Vince, or whether he just wanted his help dealing with the hordes of local law enforcement in attendance.

"The Secret Service swears every man or woman here in a wheelchair has been vetted, and none of them is our suspect," Westwood said. "We need to keep a sharp eye out to make sure Gunderson doesn't slip through the cracks."

"Yes, sir," Breed said.

Westwood turned to Vince and said, "Do we have the photo from Gunderson's military ID yet?"

"Not yet," Vince said.

Gunderson's University of Texas ID photo showed him with long hair, a mustache and beard, and glasses with lenses that had reacted to the light and darkened so much his eyes weren't visible. It wasn't much use in helping the FBI or Secret Service to identify him the way Breed had said he looked now, with his blond hair cut short and without any facial hair. The FBI had requested his military ID photo, which hadn't yet come through.

"Why wasn't this man identified as a threat sooner?" Westwood said.

"He's never threatened anyone—including the governor—in the past," Breed said. "He wrote a very polite letter to the governor asking to be relieved from Guard duty."

Westwood frowned. "It makes us look sloppy."

"We aren't," Vince said sharply. "We weren't."

"Well, let's make sure this son of a bitch doesn't come back to bite us in the ass," Westwood said. "You come with me, Vince. Agent Grayhawk, check the exits again."

Breed saw the quick, wary glance Vince shot him. Vince was the son of a bitch Breed was most worried about. He was sure that the moment Vince got the chance, he was going to make a run for his house to destroy evidence. And if he couldn't manage that, he'd take some escape route to a country without extradition that he'd planned long ago.

"How are you, son?"

Breed jerked reflexively when he felt a hand on his shoulder. He turned and glared at his father—hard to accept the truth of that fact—and watched him drop his hand. "I'm on the job," he said curtly.

"I figured as much," King said. "Have you seen Kate and the twins? I wanted to say hello to them."

Breed gestured with his chin toward the area near the president where Jack was watching over them. "Over there."

"Son, I wanted to say—"

"Having the same blood doesn't make me your son," Breed said in a harsh voice. "It takes more than planting a seed to—"

"Shut up and let me talk," King interrupted.

Breed's eyes narrowed. He wanted to turn and walk away. He wanted to ignore the powerful old man who stood in front of him. But once he looked into King's aggravated eyes, he couldn't look away.

"I'm dying," the old man said.

Breed felt his heart skip a beat.

"I don't want to waste what little time I have left fighting with you."

"What do you expect from me?" Breed demanded. "What possible—"

"I don't expect you to forgive me. I'd like it if you did," King said, "but I'm not waiting with bated breath for it. I just wanted you to know that I regret what I did to you and your mother. And that you'll have an equal share of my estate when I'm gone."

"I don't want—"

"I know," King said. "You don't want my money. It's still yours. Give it away, throw it away, burn it. That's up to you."

"You can't bribe me with money to forgive you," Breed said. "I'll never—"

"You're more like me than you think," King said. "Proud. Stubborn. Ruthless. I've said what I came to say. Good-bye, son."

"Dammit, I'm not your—" Breed didn't finish the sentence, because King had disappeared into the crowd.

50

~

Jack didn't like the crowds in the lobby of the LBJ Auditorium, which was on the lowest level of Sid Richardson Hall at the LBJ School of Public Affairs. His eyes were constantly moving, looking for anything or anyone that might be a threat. It was hard to keep track of the exuberant boys, who literally hopped, skipped, and jumped from one place to another, excited by the hoopla.

Jack knew the area was as safe as Homeland Security, the Secret Service, the Austin PD, the FBI, and the protective details of the governors of the fifty states, three territories, and two commonwealths could make it. But when you were responsible for guarding the lives of people you loved, you tended to go the extra mile.

This morning, the governor's protective detail, which included Jack, had been informed that the FBI was investigating the possibility that a disgruntled veteran might make an attempt on Governor Pendleton's life—with an explosive device of some sort—during the opening night festivities.

When Jack had confronted the DPS sergeant overseeing Governor Pendleton's protective detail, concerned about the warning, he'd been told that the Secret Service had been over the premises with bomb-sniffing dogs, with bomb detection devices, with the literal fine-tooth comb. There was no bomb. Ergo, no threat to the governor.

Jack hadn't been satisfied. "Just because the Secret Service didn't find a device doesn't mean one can't be brought in tonight."

"Look, Jack," the sergeant said. "I've been doing this a lot of years.

The governor is never a hundred percent safe. There's always the chance some crazy will get past all the precautions we take."

He settled a hand on the SIG at his waist and said, "Because the president is speaking here tonight, there's more security per square foot at Sid Richardson Hall than Governor Pendleton normally has any of the other three hundred sixty-four days of the year. Believe me, she's safer attending the president's keynote than she would be anywhere else in the state."

Jack's fears had been assuaged. But he was especially alert tonight to anything out of the ordinary, ready to hustle Kate and the twins to safety at the first sign of danger.

Because President Coleman was there to present the keynote, Democrats and Republicans both had come out of the woodwork, along with the twelve hundred NGA meeting attendees, to schmooze and press the flesh and, like Ann Wade Pendleton, be photographed with him. The scene was chaos. He and Kate and the twins had difficulty making their way through the crowd to Governor Pendleton.

"You're here. Finally," Ann Wade said when they met up with her. She was standing near the president with the governors of several states. They were joined a moment later by Governor Grayhawk.

"Ann Wade told me the boys were coming," King said to Kate. "I couldn't resist a chance to say hello."

"Hi, GeePa King!" the twins said in chorus, throwing themselves at his legs and hugging him.

"How are you?" Kate said, leaning in over the boys to give her grandfather a kiss on the cheek.

"You look tired," King said, perusing her face.

Jack hadn't expected Kate's grandfather to be perceptive enough to notice. Or concerned enough to mention it. Ann Wade certainly hadn't.

"I need to talk with you," Kate said. "Are you free—"

"Not tonight," King said apologetically. "How about if I take you out for breakfast tomorrow morning?"

"Thanks," Kate said. "I'd like that."

Jack was surprised when King reached out to brush a strand of hair behind Kate's ear. It was the sort of tender gesture he would never have expected of the powerful man.

"If you're tired, why aren't you and the twins home getting ready for bed?" King asked.

Kate reached up to tuck the same wayward strand more securely behind her ear as she explained, "Ann Wade asked me—"

"I asked her to bring Lucky and Chance tonight, so they'd have an opportunity to meet the president of the United States," Ann Wade said.

King glanced in the direction of President Coleman, who stood in an alcove surrounded by Secret Service agents, who were directing and limiting contact with him. "Good luck getting anywhere near the president tonight."

"I have a timed appointment to greet him," Ann Wade said, glancing at her diamond Patek Philippe watch. "Which was why I wanted you here with the boys fifteen minutes ago, Kate."

"Chance was sick—"

"I don't want to hear excuses," Ann Wade said. "My photo op is three minutes from now." She looked the twins over and said, "Straighten your tie, Lucky."

Jack nearly reached to help, as a parent would. He forced himself to stand back while Kate leaned down and straightened the tie for her son.

After she was done, Kate turned to Ann Wade and said, "Chance was sick earlier today. If he tells you he's nauseated, believe him."

Ann Wade lifted Chance's chin with her forefinger, peered into his blue eyes, and said imperiously, "You will not be sick, young man. At least, not for the next five minutes. Are we clear?"

"Yes, ma'am," Chance replied.

Jack glanced in the direction of the president, wondering if Chance would make it through the excitement of the next few minutes without throwing up again. He was sure the Secret Service had a plan for every eventuality. Even a sick little boy.

Jack's phone vibrated, and he saw on the caller ID as he answered it that it was Breed. He stepped away, searching the room, and asked, "Where are you?"

"Look to your left."

Jack turned and saw Breed standing across the lobby at the exit to the stairway. "Are you all right?"

"Better than I thought I'd be, considering everything that's been going on," Breed replied. "I wish Kate and the kids weren't here tonight. Especially with this latest threat."

"The governor's protective detail got a heads-up this morning," Jack said. "And decided, in light of all the security precautions the Secret Service has implemented for the president's visit, that the danger wasn't significant."

"I'd still be happier if Kate and the twins were safe at home," Breed said.

"Are you speaking as an FBI agent, or a fond relation?"

"Both," Breed said.

"If it's so dangerous, why didn't the Secret Service cancel the president's appearance?" Jack asked.

"It's not the president Harry Gunderson is after," Breed pointed out. "It's Ann Wade. His sudden disappearance from the dorm worries me. Do me a favor and keep your eyes open."

"That's my job," Jack said.

"Finally!" Breed exclaimed.

"What's up?" Jack asked.

"I'm sending Gunderson's military ID photo to your phone," Breed said. "It shows him with a shaved head. The earlier picture the FBI released shows him with long blond curls. He looks like a completely different person.

"Also, Gunderson is in a wheelchair," Breed said, "which I suppose is part of the reason why the Secret Service is so sure they'll spot him if he shows up."

Jack thought of all the amputees Kate worked with at BAMC and said, "Are you sure this guy can't walk?"

"He's missing both legs."

"What about prosthetic limbs?" Jack said. "They're doing some amazing—"

"I wasn't thinking like that," Breed confessed. "Every time I saw him he was in a wheelchair. I assumed he was always in a wheelchair. I'll make some calls and see if he was ever fitted for prosthetic limbs. Take a look at that photo and keep an eye out for him."

When the call ended, Jack checked his photo gallery for the picture Breed had sent. And recognized the face beneath the shaved head. He'd seen it tonight. He just couldn't remember exactly when or where.

But if the FBI's suspect was here, the danger was real. And imminent.

Jack stepped back to Kate and said, "You need to take the boys and leave. Right now."

Kate looked at him with wide, frightened eyes. "They're inside the rope. With the president." She pointed.

Jack realized Lucky and Chance were in the safest place they could be, watched by the eagle eyes of the Secret Service.

He grasped Kate's bare arm and said, "Get as close to those velvet ropes as the Secret Service will let you stand, and stay there till I come for you."

"Jack, you're scaring me," Kate said. "What's wrong?"

"Do what I say!"

He didn't wait to see if she'd obeyed him, simply turned and headed back into the crowd. He needed to find Harry Gunderson. And do it before Governor Pendleton and her grandkids stepped out from behind the safety of the president's velvet ropes.

He hit redial and said to Breed, "He's here."

51

Breed snapped his phone closed and began a methodical search of the faces in the crowd, keeping an eye on the governor, because she was Gunderson's supposed target.

He tried to imagine the form an attack might take, since it would be virtually impossible to get anything metal through the magnetometers at the door, or anything explosive past the continual search of the bomb-sniffing dogs. It didn't matter how many munitions Gunderson might have smuggled back from Iraq. He wasn't getting them in here without getting caught.

So how would Harry Gunderson come after the governor?

It was easy to kill someone if you didn't care if you survived the attack. Was Gunderson that angry? Or that crazy?

Breed looked around the room at the multitude of executive protection and security details protecting the visiting governors. Gunderson didn't have to bring a weapon. There were plenty of guns in the room.

Breed pivoted slowly and realized the place was almost an arsenal. Governor Pendleton was no different than any other governor present. She was surrounded by a protective detail of heavily armed DPS officers and Texas Rangers. All Gunderson had to do was get close enough to take a gun from one of them.

That wasn't as easy as it sounded. No DPS officer or Ranger was going to give up his weapon without a fight. But it wasn't inconceivable, either. There was a false feeling of safety inside the auditorium lobby precisely because there was such good security on the perimeter outside.

Breed headed back toward the small area of the lobby the Secret Service had cordoned off with a velvet rope in order to better protect the president. As he watched, Jack moved in the opposite direction, searching for Harry Gunderson.

Breed was looking for someone, anyone, acting suspiciously. But he saw nothing. Especially not anyone who looked like the man he remembered seeing in Troy's dorm room. Or who walked like he was wearing prosthetic legs. Which he realized might be difficult to detect, considering that the new prosthetic models Kate had told him about flexed so well at both ankle and knee.

Breed watched carefully as Ann Wade shook hands with the president, her grandsons by her side, while a host of photographers snapped flash digital shots to capture the moment from outside the velvet cordon.

Which was when Breed realized that one of the digital cameras wasn't flashing. Maybe the flash was out. But if so, why would the photographer keep on taking pictures when he didn't have enough light to get a decent photo?

Which meant the man standing at the rear of the cluster of photographers wasn't really taking pictures. Breed saw him edging closer to a nearby Texas DPS officer who wore a Walther PPK on his hip, with only a leather strap snapped across it to keep it in the holster.

"Watch out!" Breed shouted.

Two dozen armed men turned in Breed's direction. It was a tribute to their training that not a single one drew his weapon. But almost every one of them freed his weapon from whatever restraint kept it in the holster.

Including the DPS officer standing next to the would-be photographer who Breed believed might be Harry Gunderson.

Breed growled in frustration. The officer had been warned. But he'd made his weapon more accessible to theft by Gunderson. Breed pointed toward Harry as he ran toward the would-be assassin, making eye contact with the DPS officer and shouting at him, "Beside you! Beside you!"

Breed searched for Jack in the crowd and saw him across the room. They were both too far away to avert the disaster he could see happening.

The officer couldn't hear Breed because of the uproar of the crowd, who were trying to find out what was going on, and the organized chaos behind the velvet ropes, where Secret Service agents were hustling the president out of the room by a prearranged exit route.

Leaving Governor Ann Wade Pendleton and Kate's sons, Lucky and Chance, standing behind the cordoned rope all by themselves.

Sitting ducks in a shooting gallery.

Breed waved and shouted at them to get out of the way. But Ann Wade was frozen in astonishment, still watching the president's exit.

And then it was too late. The photographer who was no photographer lowered his camera and turned to glance over his shoulder. A heavily disguised Harry Gunderson stared at Breed with wild eyes.

Breed had never moved so fast in his life.

Harry Gunderson, despite his prosthetic limbs, moved faster. Two steps and he was close enough to slam the DPS officer in the head with his camera. The officer naturally reached up to protect his head, leaving his Walther accessible long enough for Gunderson to wrench the gun from the holster.

"He's got a gun!" Breed heard someone scream.

"Gun!" he heard from another direction.

"Gun!" a woman shrieked.

Breed was afraid to draw his Glock, for fear the numerous lawmen in the room might mistake him for the bad guy and start shooting.

It was already too late to stop the pandemonium that ensued. The panicked mob was running in all directions, like headless chickens, seeking escape.

Breed met Jack's panicked gaze, then watched in horror as Kate slipped under the velvet rope and joined Lucky and Chance, sliding her arms around them and arranging them in front of her, putting her own body between any flying bullets and her sons.

Leaving her in the direct line of fire as the assassin held the Walther he'd stolen in both hands and aimed it at Ann Wade Pendleton.

Breed had no chance of stopping Gunderson before he fired, but it didn't keep him from trying. He was running full tilt, praying that something, anything, would prevent the devastation he foresaw.

It was the manual safety on the Walther PPK that saved the day. Gunderson didn't know it was there, or didn't know how to work it, and couldn't pull the trigger on the semiautomatic weapon. Breed saw the moment when Gunderson realized there was an external safety. The would-be assassin lost another fraction of a second because he apparently didn't know the Walther's safety had to be flicked up, rather than down, in order for the gun to fire.

By the time Gunderson had released the safety, other members of the governor's protective detail, including Jack, were almost on him, and Gunderson was forced to turn the weapon away from the governor and fire at the officers instead. He shot two of them before Jack shot him.

Jack's bullet knocked Gunderson backward, but it didn't put him down.

Which was when it became apparent that Gunderson was wearing some kind of bulletproof vest, something else he'd apparently brought home from the war, along with all those stolen munitions.

Breed's breath caught in his chest as Gunderson turned the Walther back toward Ann Wade—and King, who was standing nearby—aimed the gun with shaking hands, and repeatedly pulled the trigger.

In that instant, Breed realized that all his bluster about not needing or wanting a father was a lie. He'd just learned his father was dying, but he didn't want him snatched away by an assassin's bullet. Blood, it seemed, was thicker than water. He growled in his throat as he launched himself in the air.

He reached King a heartbeat later and shoved him out of the line of fire. He felt a sharp pain in his arm as he turned to tackle the shooter, crushing him to the floor and wrenching the weapon from his grasp. By that time, more officers had arrived, and Breed was glad to relinquish the would-be assassin to another officer, who pulled Gunderson's arms behind him and locked on a pair of cuffs.

Breed had kept his eyes riveted on Gunderson once the shooting started, aware that he would be less effective if he witnessed Kate or one of the boys—or his father—being hit by flying bullets.

He turned back to King, and as he helped his father to his feet, asked, "Are you all right?"

"You put your body between me and that assassin. You saved my life."

"I'd have done it for anyone," Breed retorted.

"But you did it for me. It's a nice memory to take with me to my—"

"You're not dead yet, old man," Breed snapped. "How are Kate and the kids?"

They both turned to look.

"Oh, God," King said.

Breed leapt over the velvet rope that had been set up for the president and saw Jack was there ahead of him. The blood had drained from Jack's face, and Breed put a hand on his friend's shoulder to keep him upright before he turned to look himself— and saw his worst fears realized.

He followed a trail of blood splatter with his eyes and felt his heart catch in his throat when it ended in a dark red pool beside Kate. She was lying on the floor, the front of her blouse covered in blood, her eyes glazed, her head in Ann Wade's lap. Lucky and Chance knelt on either side of their mother sobbing, noses running, tears streaming down their cheeks.

Strobes began to flash, and Breed realized someone was taking photographs of the tragedy. He watched as Ann Wade lifted her head, met his gaze with something like triumph in her eyes, and slowly turned to face the cameras.

52

⁓

Breed rode in the ambulance with Kate to Brackenridge Hospital and allowed one of the paramedics to look at the wound on his arm while the other took care of Kate.

"That's going to need stitches," the female paramedic said as she studied the bullet crease in his arm.

"How's Kate?" he asked anxiously.

"Still unconscious," the male paramedic answered. Then, suddenly, "She's coding!"

The female paramedic left Breed's side and the two of them worked on Kate, using a defibrillator to shock her heart and get it beating again.

"I've got a pulse!"

Breed took Kate's hand and talked to her. "Come on, Kate. You can do it. Just keep breathing. Lucky and Chance need you."

Once they arrived at the hospital, Kate went immediately to surgery, and he submitted to having his wound stitched. As soon as the doctor was done, Breed went looking for Jack and the twins. He found them in the surgical waiting room.

Jack had his arms around Lucky and Chance, who sat on uncomfortable vinyl flowered teal connected chairs on either side of him. When the boys saw him, they jumped up and came running.

Breed felt his nose sting and swallowed hard over the painful knot in his throat. He dropped to one knee and pulled the frightened boys close. "Your mom is a fighter. Don't count her out yet."

"There was so much blood!" Lucky said.

"She couldn't talk," Chance said. "I thought she was dead!"

"Me, too," Lucky said.

Breed met Jack's red-rimmed eyes over the boys' shoulders and felt an unfamiliar tickle in his throat. He stood and escorted the boys back to their seats, where they huddled together with their arms around each other.

He walked aside with Jack, so they could talk without being overheard.

"How serious is Kate's wound?" Jack asked.

"Wounds," Breed said. "She was hit twice, once in the arm, which was a flesh wound, and once in the chest, which is the one that . . ." Breed stopped talking and cleared his throat. "She lost a lot of blood. They had to resuscitate her in the ambulance."

"I couldn't get to Gunderson in time to save her," Jack said in an anguished voice.

"Gunderson would have done a lot worse, if it hadn't been for you." Breed looked around and asked, "Where's Ann Wade?"

Jack grimaced. "She left when the photographers did. She said she'll be back to check on Kate a little later."

"What about the twins?" Breed asked, glancing at the boys. "She just left them here?"

"She's making arrangements for them to stay with her at the Governor's Mansion as we speak. Which is to say, she's out looking for a nanny."

"Where's my father? King, I mean," Breed corrected. "Did he show up here?"

"He was too impatient to sit. He's off driving the nurses crazy trying to find out about Kate's condition. And yours."

Breed saw Jack glancing at his bloody shirt and bandaged arm and said, "It's nothing. A scratch. Did Kate's mom and dad show up yet?"

"They were here, but Libby's crying upset the twins so much that Clay took her to the chapel. I'm supposed to let them know when Kate wakes up from the anesthesia."

"How long will that be?" Breed asked.

"No idea," Jack said, shaking his head. He looked down and saw Lucky tugging on his sleeve.

"I'm hungry," Lucky said.

At that moment, King returned.

"What did you find out?" Jack said.

"The bullet nicked an artery, but the surgeon has repaired the damage. Kate's in critical but stable condition. They'll keep her in the ICU until she's awake."

"How long will that be?" Jack asked.

King grimaced. "There's some concern because the anesthesia should have worn off by now, but she's not waking up. It seems she hit her head on the marble floor when she fell and might also have a concussion."

"But she's going to be all right?" Jack said, his voice hoarse with emotion.

"The doctors think so," King said. "But it might take her a while to get back to her old self."

"Just so long as she's . . ." Jack's voice gave out and tears brimmed in his eyes.

Breed turned away to give Jack time to recover himself, then said to King, "Would you mind taking the twins out to get something to eat?" He could feel his father's eyes on him, but he avoided looking at him, focusing instead on the twins.

"I think there's a cafeteria right here at the hospital," King said.

"I was thinking you could take them someplace outside the hospital," Breed said. "They need something to keep them occupied until they can talk to their mother."

"Sure," King said. "How are you?"

Breed turned and met King's gaze but had to look away from the glisten of tears in his father's eyes. "I'm fine," he said, his voice hoarse with emotion. Then he surprised himself by asking, "How are you?"

"I'm a little shook up." King swallowed hard and said, "I'm not ashamed to admit it was terrifying. I'm just glad you're okay."

"Did the doctors give you any idea how soon we can visit Kate?" Breed asked.

"Not before morning," King said.

Breed glanced at the twins and said, "We'd better figure out what to do with them until—"

"I've made arrangements for the twins," Ann Wade said.

Breed turned to find Ann Wade standing in front of him wearing a mint-green Chanel suit that was stained with dried blood. "Hello, Ann Wade. What did you have in mind?"

"The twins will be staying with me at the Governor's Mansion. I've found a woman to take care of them while I'm giving a panel at the NGA meeting tomorrow. Once that's done, I'll be going back home to Midland and taking the boys with me."

Jack took a step toward her and said, "Who says?"

"Kate isn't going to be able to take care of the boys for a very long time," Ann Wade said. "It's better if they stay with me. It'll give her a chance to recuperate in peace and quiet."

"Kate will shrivel up and die without those boys," Jack said.

"Oh, I really doubt that," Ann Wade said.

"Why don't we wait until tomorrow and talk to Kate and see what she wants to do," Breed said.

"That sounds like a good idea," King agreed.

"Fine," Ann Wade said. "I'll take the boys with me now and get them—"

"I'm taking my grandsons out for supper," King said. "I'll be happy to drop them off at the Mansion once they've eaten."

"Fine," Ann Wade said in exasperation. "Bring the boys by when you're done with supper."

Once the twins had left with King, Ann Wade turned to Jack and said, "I've found someone else to be the boys' bodyguard. You can go back to whatever it was you were doing."

"Thank you, ma'am," Jack said, touching a respectful finger to the Stetson he was wearing. "It's been a pleasure working for you."

Breed saw Ann Wade's lips tighten, since the tone of Jack's voice made it plain that working for her had been a perfect pain in the ass.

When Ann Wade was gone, Breed turned to Jack and said, "What's your plan now?"

"I'm going to stay right here until Kate wakes up."

"I need to go find Vince Harkness," Breed said. "I looked for him when the shooting stopped, but he was gone. It may already be too late to stop him from destroying evidence. But he's not going to get the chance to run. I've had surveillance on his house all day, and I'm headed there now. Call me when Kate's awake. Whenever that is."

"Will do," Jack said.

As he left the hospital, Breed said a silent prayer for Kate. And wondered for the thousandth time that day, *Where the hell is Grace?*

53

~

Vincent could feel the noose tightening around his neck. When the commotion erupted at Sid Richardson Hall, he'd made his break. He had things to do if he wanted to stay out of jail.

So far, he hadn't been arrested, but it was a near thing. Luckily, because of the president's visit, the execution of the search warrant had been delayed for a day. But he figured it was only a matter of time before his houses and grounds were ransacked by the FBI. Which meant it was time to dispose of the souvenirs he'd collected from his victims.

He didn't want to do it.

Vincent was still convinced there was a way to blame all those murders on his wife. If that bitch Merle Raye Finkel hadn't interfered, Stephanie would already be dead. And the problem would already have been solved.

It had been horrible holding a gun to his wife's head. It had taken every bit of willpower he had to do it. He'd been thinking of Brian and Chloe the whole time, how they needed at least one loving parent to survive the cataclysm that threatened to overwhelm them all. He'd already proved he was the survivor in this couple.

Vincent was taking the opportunity tonight, while every branch of law enforcement in Austin was focused on the assassination attempt on Governor Pendleton, to move the driver's licenses he'd collected from his victims to a safer place.

He just hadn't figured out yet where that was.

As far as the kids knew, Stephanie was out of town on business, as scheduled. Earlier in the evening, Vincent had sent them to spend the night with friends, even though it was a school night, supposedly because he was busy with security for the president's visit, and he didn't want them home alone.

The truth was, he'd wanted the freedom to look at his mementos in private before he put them away out of sight, perhaps for a very long time.

He'd laid newspaper on the bed, then set out the driver's licenses in rows, from left to right, beginning with the first murder after Harvey's death and ending with the murder he'd committed less than a week ago.

Driver's license photos were never very good, but Vincent found himself looking at a motley crew. What he noticed, what he'd noticed every time he killed one of them, was how hairy they were.

Thick heads of black and brown and red and blond hair. Bald, but with a bushy mustache. A three-day beard. A ridiculous goatee. Straggly ponytails. Chest hair wriggling out of open-throated shirts like some horrifying alien growth.

The murders he'd committed hadn't put any barbers out of work, that was for sure.

Why was Stephanie so fascinated with hairy men? he wondered. Or was it just that she had sought out the lowest forms of life, men who cared so little about their appearance that they allowed their God-given follicles to grow hair willy nilly on faces and throats and chests and—he shuddered to recall—backs.

Vincent sat on the beige chaise longue in his bedroom and stared at the collection on the bed. And felt sick at heart. How had he gotten so far from where he'd started? He was a moral man. He'd always obeyed the rules. He'd done as he was told as a child. He'd walked the straight and narrow and attended church to learn the Ten Commandments. Still attended church every Sunday, for that matter.

And this was where it had all led.

To a bed covered with licenses identifying the detritus of society. Whom he had killed. Because they'd fucked his wife.

Vincent felt his throat swelling closed with emotion. This would all be so much easier if he were a pathological killer, he thought. Someone without a conscience. Someone who didn't regret what he was forced to do.

Vincent wrung his hands. He wished he could turn back the clock. Wished he could go back to the beginning. He would make different choices, he was sure. How had it all gone so wrong?

Vincent realized he must have dozed off on the chaise longue and some noise had woken him. He sat up, then stood and stared at the bedroom doorway.

Had he miscalculated? Was the FBI here with a search warrant already? He glanced at the bed, his heart beating hard in his chest, knowing the evidence there was enough to get him convicted of multiple homicides. He'd handled each license tonight. Picked each one up and looked closely at it. His fingerprints were all over them. Stephanie's were not.

He nearly bolted through the open bedroom window, but just as he took his first step, he heard again what it was that had woken him.

Female voices.

His wife. And Merle Raye Finkel.

Vincent smiled. And reached for his Glock.

54

Grace had brought Stephanie with her—Vince's Beretta trained on her—to burgle the Harkness residence, because the older woman said she could help Grace figure out where Vince had hidden whatever trophies he might have collected from the murders he'd committed.

Grace had waited until it was dark, and the president's speech was in full swing, before heading out. She felt sure most local law enforcement officers, including FBI ASAC Vincent Harkness, whom she'd discovered was still on the job, would be tied up with security for the president.

Grace had noticed someone in an FBI surveillance vehicle sitting down the street from Vince's house and parked Stephanie's car in the alley the next street over. She and Stephanie had walked back to the Harkness home and used Stephanie's key to come in the back door.

"Vincent was never much one for clutter," Stephanie remarked as she locked the kitchen door behind her and put the key on the hook by the back door. "I'm not sure he would have kept a bunch of stuff from dead guys."

"You're forgetting those 'dead guys' were your lovers. Whom Vince tracked down and killed."

"I guess that makes sense." Stephanie pointed to a small chalkboard on the kitchen wall with writing on it. "Chloe's staying at Janice's overnight. And Brian's at Gary's house, also overnight. That's odd. They're not allowed to stay at a friend's house on school nights."

When she turned back to Grace, her gaze lit on the kitchen counter, and she grabbed Grace's arm. She lowered her voice to a whisper and said, "He's home. Vincent is here!"

"How do you know?" Grace whispered back, holding Vince's Beretta two-handed, aimed at the doorway to the living room.

"He always makes a pot of herbal green tea the moment he comes home from work. And drinks it till it's gone," Stephanie said. "Vincent believes the antioxidants in the green tea will prevent cancer."

Grace glanced at the coffeemaker. Which was on. The glass carafe was half full of pale green tea. "He's home early from the president's speech," she muttered. "Where do you suppose he is?"

Stephanie glanced at her watch. "He might already have gone to bed."

"And not drunk his tea?" Grace said doubtfully.

"It's been pretty stressful the past couple of days. Obviously, he isn't keeping to his normal schedule."

"We might as well find out if he's here," Grace said, holding the Beretta in front of her as she sent Stephanie ahead of her slowly, carefully, and quietly toward the master bedroom.

"What's that mess?" Stephanie said, pointing toward the bed in the master bedroom.

Grace's heart nearly pounded out of her chest. "I think it's driver's licenses. It seems Vince does collect—"

"I most certainly do," Vince said, pressing his service weapon, a Glock 27, hard against Grace's temple. He snatched his Beretta from her hand before she could resist and shoved it into the front of his trousers. "Unless you want to die in a hurry, keep your hands where I can see them."

When Stephanie took a step backward, Vince said, "That goes for you, too, my dear."

Vince reached for Big Mike's gun, which was tucked in the front of Grace's jeans, and set it on top of a nearby chest of drawers. "Well, well. I thought I was going to have to go looking for the two of you, and here you are. Come on in, Stephanie, and join the party."

He gestured with the Glock 27, which had a suppressor attached, and Stephanie reluctantly entered the bedroom.

"I must say I'm surprised to find you with Miss Finkel, my dear."

"What did you expect after you threatened to kill me?" Stephanie snapped. "Grace—that's what Miss Finkel is calling herself these days, in case you didn't know—offered me a deal. I agreed to confess to the authorities that I was the one who killed her parents—"

"You what?" Vince said, visibly shocked.

"Oh, really, Vincent. Sometimes you are so naive. Big Mike Finkel had you cold. He had DNA evidence from where Harvey's teeth cut your hand when you hit him. Big Mike knew you'd killed Harvey, but he'd purposely mislaid the DNA evidence so he could be the big hero. He was going to arrest you. I had to kill him, to keep him from ruining all our lives."

"You did that for me?" Vince said.

"For the family," Stephanie corrected. "I can't believe you're trying to get me to take the fall now for all those murders you committed."

"I told you why I killed your lovers," Vince said. "If you had kept your panties on—"

"Oh, please," Stephanie said. "Don't try to blame your weakness on me."

Grace had heard it all before. Her mind was scurrying to find an escape from the trap she'd fallen into. Vince seemed intent on laying blame elsewhere. Which she was afraid meant he intended to kill both her and Stephanie. He'd already laid out his plan at Grace's house: Kill Stephanie with the .45 caliber Glock 30 that had been used to murder Grace's parents. Then kill Grace with whatever gun was handy and claim self-defense.

When Vince exchanged his Glock 27 for Big Mike's gun, Grace knew she and Stephanie didn't have much time to live.

"Your house is being watched by the FBI," she said. "They're going to hear the gunshots if you shoot either one of us."

"If you're both dead, I can tell whatever story I want," Vince said, aiming Big Mike's weapon at Stephanie.

"What about all those licenses on the bed?" Grace asked. "How are you going to explain them?"

"I'll say I was horrified to discover them in a shoe box in the closet. I should have enough time to wipe them all clean before the FBI gets through the front door."

"So they're covered with your fingerprints right now?" Grace said, eyeing the licenses.

"I was looking through them earlier tonight, since I may not see them again for a while. I was remembering how Stephanie's lovers died. To tell the truth, killing them wasn't much of a challenge."

Vince turned to Stephanie and said, "I did notice one thing, though, that has piqued my curiosity."

"What was that?" Stephanie asked.

"All your lovers were hairy. Every one of them. Why is that, Stephanie?"

"My father was hairy," Stephanie said.

"Dear God," Vince said.

Grace had been watching for Vince to let down his guard. His shock at Stephanie's admission caused him to lower Big Mike's Glock.

And Grace made her move.

She was fit and fast, but Vince was fitter and faster. His balled fist slammed into her jaw. That might have been the end of her, but Stephanie had apparently decided to fight for her life. She attacked her husband with fingernails arched into claws.

Vince had his hands full defending himself, but Grace had no doubt how the battle was going to end. Even together, she and Stephanie were no match for a trained FBI agent.

The battle ended much sooner than Grace had hoped. And the result was every bit as bad as she'd feared.

A .45 caliber bullet from Big Mike's gun ripped through Stephanie's heart. Her eyes looked shocked. Moments later they were glazed over in death.

The deafening gunshot reverberated in the bedroom, and Grace realized, as Vince reached for his Beretta, that she only had moments to live. She knew he was hurrying, because he had a lot to do before the FBI showed up—wiping away fingerprints on the guns, then pressing guns into dead hands to shoot them again so the forensic scientists would find gunshot residue.

And he had all those neatly laid out licenses to wipe clean.

Grace turned her back on Vince and reached out with both hands to swipe the driver's licenses off the bed and send them flying up into the air and around the room in all directions.

"You lousy bitch!" Vince yelled. "I wanted to keep those!"

"Too late now," Grace taunted. "You won't be able to find them all before the FBI comes through the door. And I'd like to see you explain your fingerprints on a murdered guy's driver's license that some technician finds under your bed."

"Pick them up," Vince said through clenched jaws. "Get down on your hands and knees and pick every goddamn one of them up!"

Grace was happy to comply. So long as she was hunting for licenses, she wasn't getting shot. Every moment of life was precious. There was still time for help to arrive.

Not that it ever had. Not once in her life had anyone ever come to her rescue. And she didn't expect it now. Which was why she wasn't able to hide her look of astonishment when Breed showed up at the bedroom door.

He put his fingertip to his lips, but it was too late. Vince had already seen the look of wonder and relief on her face. And followed her gaze to its source.

Vince fired as he turned.

Grace screamed as Breed threw himself sideways and fired back. It took her a moment to realize that Vince's shot had missed.

Breed's had not.

Vince collapsed onto the floor like a puppet with the strings cut. He didn't move. He didn't make a sound.

Grace sat on the beige carpeted floor, her lap full of driver's licenses that now bore her fingerprints as well as Vince's, and started to cry. She let out feelings she'd suppressed for years, sobbing inelegantly, her eyes becoming red-rimmed, her nose running, her mouth opened wide for the woebegone wails that poured out of her.

"Grace, what's wrong?" Breed said anxiously, standing her up and feeling her limbs, looking for injuries "Are you hurt? Are you shot?"

Grace only sobbed harder.

Breed pulled her into his arms and held her close, murmuring words of comfort. "Where are you hurt, Grace? Tell me how I can help you."

Grace swiped the tears away, but there was no comfort to be had. It wasn't grief or relief she felt now. It was deep despair. Because, with Stephanie's death, all hope of clearing her name, all chance of proving her innocence beyond a shadow of a doubt, was gone.

"Grace," Breed crooned, brushing her hair back from her stricken face. "Tell me what's wrong."

Grace looked into his eyes, knowing that soon she'd have to use some of her grandmother's inheritance to disappear again. "I can't prove I'm innocent," she said. "Stephanie confessed to killing my parents, but she's dead. And you killed Vince. So I'm fucked."

"Oh, Grace, no," Breed said. "It's okay. It's all right. You're going to be fine."

She looked at him with stark eyes. "How am I going to be fine? Everyone who could have proved I'm innocent is dead."

Breed left her standing near the doorway and crossed to the head of the bed. He took down the picture on the left but found only painted wall behind it. He took down the picture in the center and found a video camera. He pulled out the camera and retrieved the videotape and held it up.

"I figured out how Vince knew you were here, how he knew it was you who stole the diary. Everything that happens in this room is on tape."

Grace realized what that meant. And burst into tears.

"Now why are you crying?" Breed said as he once more took her into his arms.

"For Allie," she said.

Breed rocked her in his arms. "You're going to be okay, Grace. I promise you. But I wonder if you'd do me a favor."

Grace sniffed and said warily, "What?"

"In a few minutes, this house is going to fill up with FBI agents. Before they get here, would you kiss me?"

"No." Grace looked up at him from beneath lowered lashes and said, "But you can kiss me."

It was a very small step toward trusting a man. A very small step toward letting a woman into his life. Just baby steps, really.

But they took them together.

Epilogue

~

Kate could hear everything happening in her hospital room. But she couldn't seem to communicate that she was awake and aware. Everyone talked about her as though she weren't there.

I remember being shot, Kate thought. *There was a lot of blood and the boys were crying and I could hear shouting and screaming. I remember the glare of the lights overhead when I was on the gurney. But I don't remember much after that. Probably a result of the anesthesia.*

Kate tried to move her mouth. Tried to speak. But her mouth stayed closed. And no sound came out.

For a moment she wondered if she were dead, and it was only her spirit that was hearing everything happening in the room.

But she could feel her pulse throbbing at her temple. And her chest felt as though both twins were sitting on it.

My sons! Where are Chance and Lucky? Who's taking care of them?

Kate tried to open her eyes and look around the room. But she couldn't get her eyelids to move. She told herself not to get upset. She didn't need to be able to see to know Chance and Lucky were nearby. She could always feel them when they were in the same room.

More to the point, she could smell them. And not just when they were sweaty and rank. Their clean hair had a fragrance all its own, and their just-washed skin had a scent she would recognize anywhere.

"Does Mom know we're here?" Lucky asked.

"Does she know we brought her a Christmas present?" Chance

asked. "We put it under the Christmas tree over there in the corner, like you said, Breed. Will she know it's there?"

Christmas? The boys had shaken hands with President Coleman early in October. What had happened to the months in between?

I'm awake. I'm here. Why can't you hear me?

"Mom," Lucky said. "Please answer me!"

"Your mother is—" Ann Wade began.

"Sleeping, so she can get well," Breed interrupted.

Kate heard the irritation with her mother-in-law beneath the gentle voice Breed used to speak to her sons.

"When is Mom going to wake up?" Lucky asked.

"When is she going to open her present?" Chance said.

Kate heard the rustle of denim and imagined Breed going down on one knee and gathering the boys to him, as she so much wanted to do.

"When her body is well, she'll wake up," Breed said. "We just have to be patient and—"

"I want her to wake up now!" Lucky said.

She felt Lucky tugging on her arm, felt Chance on her other side, his cheek pressed against her shoulder.

"Wake up, Mom!" Chance cried. "Wake up!"

"Really," Ann Wade said. "Someone needs to take those two boys—"

"Shut up, Ann Wade," Breed said.

"You're getting a little too big for your britches," Ann Wade retorted. "I don't see—"

"Shut up, Ann Wade," King said.

"Well!" Ann Wade said. But that was all she said. Kate heard the door swish open and closed and realized Ann Wade must have left the room.

Kate felt the boys being tugged away, heard Grandpa Blackjack saying, "Come on, you two. You and your GeeMa and I need to go give Big Doc and Little Doc their presents and give everybody else a chance to wish your mom a Merry Christmas."

And Grandpa King saying, "I'm going to need some help this afternoon putting those brand-new saddles I got you boys for Christmas on those nags Blackjack got you for your birthday."

The room was suddenly quiet. And felt empty, even though Kate knew it wasn't. The hardest thing about being caught in the darkness where she found herself was the fear that she would never get out. Her sons needed their mother. She needed them.

"Honey, your mom and I have a surprise for you this Christmas," her father said.

Daddy! Help me. Make them listen to me.

"Your mom and I are going to give you another brother or sister in the spring."

You're pregnant, Mom? What a wonderful surprise!

"I can't believe I'm doing this at my age," her mother said.

Kate heard the rueful sound in her mother's voice. And the joy. And the sadness.

"I wish I could come see you more often," her mother said, "but the doctor ordered me to bed for the rest of the pregnancy. I insisted I had to see you for Christmas, so he let me come if I promised to stay in this wheelchair."

She felt the warmth of her mother's hand. She tried to squeeze it. She was sure she had. But her mother's next tearful words proved she hadn't.

"Oh, Clay, I can't bear this."

"Don't cry, Libby. Please, honey, you know what the doctor said."

She imagined her father comforting her mother, a strong hand on her shoulder. Protecting her. Loving her. Which only reminded her of her own husband. Oh God, what was happening with J.D.? She'd never paid him off. What if he—

Before she could think more about the catastrophe her own marriage had become, she heard her parents bidding her farewell, her mother sobbing quietly, her father murmuring assurances.

I love you, too, she told them. *I love you both so much!*

When the door had swished open and closed again, Breed said, "I've brought Grace Caldwell to meet you, Kate."

Grace? Kate thought. *Wasn't she the woman who'd murdered her parents? The one who was suspected of being a terrorist, for heaven's sake! What was she doing here?*

"Grace didn't want to meet you until her name was cleared. Remember I told you how she was convicted of murdering her parents? A judge saw the tape of Stephanie Harkness confessing to the crime, and her record has been expunged. The DA agreed not to go after her for violating her parole, especially when he found out she was responsible for helping to clear a bunch of cold cases for the Austin PD. So Grace is a free woman."

"Hello, Kate," a female voice said.

Kate felt a soft, warm hand on her arm.

"It's so nice to finally meet you," Grace said. "Breed has told me a lot about you. I'm sure we're going to be good friends."

Kate heard Breed muttering, "It's damned unfair what's happened to her."

Grace said, "You won't get an argument from me. I've never thought life was fair."

The door swished halfway open and Breed said, "What's up, Dad?"

Dad? Kate thought with delight. *Breed is calling King "Dad"? Would wonders never cease!*

"I wanted to see if you're coming to that family dinner Blackjack organized at your sister's house tonight," King said.

"Grace and I will be at Clay and Libby's around seven," Breed said. "Are you going?"

"I was invited," King said. "So I guess I'm going."

"We'll see you there."

The door swished quietly closed.

Kate couldn't believe how much had changed in just two months. Her mother expecting a baby. Breed and King finding peace. And Breed had a woman in his life.

"You're the first to know, Kate. I've asked Grace to marry me."

Kate was amazed at what she was hearing. *How wonderful! I'm so glad for you!* She grinned. In her head, anyway.

"Grace hasn't given me an answer yet. She says we need time to get to know each other better."

So Grace wasn't leaping into marriage. Good for her! Breed needed a woman who'd keep him on his toes. But she hoped Grace would say yes. It would be fun to help plan the wedding.

Kate was so involved in planning a wedding for Breed that she must have missed what happened over the next few minutes. Because when she started listening again, it wasn't Breed and Grace she heard. They had apparently left her room.

Instead, she heard Jack speaking directly to her, as though she could hear every word he said. She smiled broadly, glad that someone had finally realized she was awake and aware.

When she listened to what he was saying, she frowned. In her head, anyway.

"I've heard that people in a coma can sometimes hear and understand everything you say," Jack said. "I hope you're listening, Kate. Because this is important."

In a coma? I'm not in a coma. Am I?

Kate suddenly felt afraid. It was very dark where she was. It felt like she was in a room with no windows or doors. She felt her way along the wall, looking for a way out. But she couldn't find it. She was trapped. And terrified.

She heard Jack's soothing voice and headed in that direction. And found herself back in her hospital room. Jack was sitting beside the bed holding her hand. Caressing it with his thumb. It felt good.

Kate listened intently to what he was saying, looking for an explanation for the situation in which she found herself.

"The doctors expected you to wake up when the operation was over, after they'd fixed the artery that was nicked when you were shot, and the bullet hole in your arm. The surgery was a success.

Except you didn't wake up. Still haven't woken up after more than two months.

"No one has an explanation for what's happened. The doctors say you could wake up at any time. Or you could stay in a coma the rest of your life. They just don't know."

Oh my God! Kate thought. *I can't stay in a coma forever. I have two boys to raise. I want to marry Jack and have babies with him. Except I'm still married to J.D. Who's still waiting for me to pay him. Which I will do. The moment I can get out of this dark place.*

She heard the masculine gurgle of a man swallowing back tears.

Don't cry, Jack. I'm fine. I just have to find my way out of this stupid room. It doesn't have windows or doors. I know there's a trick somewhere. I just have to figure it out.

"You don't need to worry about J.D. coming after the twins," Jack said. "By now, he's heard what happened to you, so he knows you're not in a position to pay him any more money. And I'm going to be taking care of your boys, making sure they're safe, until you're well enough to come home."

"Don't make promises you can't keep."

Kate recognized Ann Wade's grating voice. She could feel the tension in Jack's hand, because it tightened on hers. But he didn't let go of her, even when he confronted her mother-in-law.

"I don't make promises I can't keep," Jack said.

"I'm the twins' closest living relative—"

"Kate isn't dead yet, Governor. Much as you might like her to be."

"What gives you the right to lay claim to my grandchildren?" Ann Wade demanded.

Jack squeezed Kate's hand again before he said, "I know your dirty little secret."

"What might that be?" Ann Wade said imperiously.

"That J.D. is alive and well and on the run somewhere. He's not a hero, he's a deserter. And a criminal, with connections to the Mexican Mafia, although how he managed that, when they started out as a prison gang, I'd like to know."

"How much?" Ann Wade said.

"What?"

"How much to keep your mouth shut?"

"I want the boys. I'll take care of them until Kate is awake and aware again."

"You're presuming she's going to get better," Ann Wade said nastily. "What if she doesn't wake up?"

"We don't have to negotiate that far in the future," Jack said. "I'm talking about right now. I want the boys to come home with me."

"Who's going to take care of them if they live with you?"

"Breed and I share a house. We can share the care of the twins. And my parents are living at Twin Magnolias right now. They can help."

"You mean your Gamblers Anonymous father and your battered mother?" Ann Wade said snidely.

Kate heard the chair Jack was sitting in screech back. Heard Ann Wade gasp. But she heard no punch or slap from either Jack or Ann Wade. Apparently, Jack had been able to hold on to his self-control.

She couldn't blame Jack for being rubbed raw. Somehow, Ann Wade Pendleton knew exactly where to stick the knife in, and how far to twist it, to make you suffer.

"I presume I will still be able to see my grandsons," Ann Wade said.

"You're welcome to see them anytime. For some reason unknown to me, they love you. You won't be allowed to parade them around in those ridiculous suits and ties for your presidential campaign."

Kate could feel the animosity rolling off her mother-in-law. Her emotions were that powerful. She wondered what Ann Wade would do to hurt Jack. She was bound to do something. Because although she manipulated people herself, she hated being manipulated. She would retaliate somehow.

Kate wanted to warn Jack. *Be careful.* Ann Wade was already thinking up a way to make his life miserable. She tried to move her fingers on the bed. She thought maybe her finger came off the sheet a little.

But Jack didn't see it. He was staring down Ann Wade. Or at least, she imagined he was. She knew Ann Wade was gone when Jack moved the chair back beside the bed and took her cold hand in both of his.

"I hope that didn't upset you too much," he said to Kate. "It had to be done. She said she was going to take Lucky and Chance to her ranch in Midland. I think they need to stay here in Austin, where they can see you as often as they want.

"Your mom wanted to help with the boys, but her doctor told her that her pregnancy is too fragile, that she can't take the extra stress of two more kids in the house. She and your dad agreed that Breed and I were a good substitute.

"The only person standing in the way was Ann Wade. And I've just taken care of that," Jack said.

She heard another gurgle. A masculine sniff.

"I wanted you to know that Lucky and Chance will be living at Twin Magnolias," Jack said. "I'll be bringing them here to see you. And I'll be here every day."

Kate heard the hoarseness in Jack's voice as he said, "Come back to me, please, Kate. We were meant to spend our lives together. I love you. I have for a long time. And I always will."

Kate felt like crying. She was sure a tear slid down her cheek. It felt warm, anyway. But it must have been wishful thinking, because Jack didn't seem to notice it.

I love you, too, Jack, she thought. *Don't give up on me. Give me a little time, and I'll find my way out of this box.*

She felt his thumb brush her cheek. Heard him make a choked

cry. "Wake up, sweetheart," he said urgently. "I'm here. I'm waiting for you. Wake up, Kate. Please. For me. Wake up!"

Kate tried hard to do as he asked. To open her eyes. To speak. To tell him she wanted to be with him forever.

But Kate wasn't able to muster so much as the flicker of an eyelash. She was trapped in the darkness. And she couldn't get out.

Acknowledgments

Writing this novel has been a two-year project, and I owe a great deal of thanks to a great many people in bringing it to fruition.

I want to thank Army Sergeant Rob Laurent (Retired) for sharing his poignant experiences as a wounded combat soldier in Iraq, which became a part of this book, and CW4 "Chief" Perry Bartholow for his insights on how a patient gets from Iraq to a hospital in the States.

A special thank-you to FBI Special Agent in Charge Tom Rice of the Miami field office, who took precious time out during Super Bowl week to answer my questions.

Thanks to FBI Special Agent Roger Peele (Retired) for his insights on the FBI's Joint Terrorism Task Forces on campuses across the country.

I am indebted to Sergeant Rodolfo C. Jaramillo, Headquarters Company, Texas Rangers, Unsolved Crimes Investigation Team, San Antonio, Texas, for sharing his experiences as a Texas Ranger. He's proof of what an elite force of lawmen the Texas Rangers are.

Thank you, J.C., for the DEA background information.

Thanks to Rob Black at the Wyoming governor's office, who took time from a hectic schedule to return my call, and to the Austin Police Department and Texas Department of Public Safety for their assistance.

Thank you, Doug Giacobbe, Judith Rochelle, Jean Jahr, Peter Schreuder, Ray Hannaberg, and Ron Harrison for sharing your knowledgeable friends with me.

Thanks to my sister, Joyce Mertens, for help reviewing the manuscript, and to Billie Bailey, Christy Richardson and Stephanie Dickinson for their help with background research.

I want to thank the Texas State Preservation Board for affording me a private tour of the Texas State Capitol. I especially want to thank tour guide Rachel Sidopulos, who spent several hours wandering every nook and cranny of the Capitol with me.

A very big thanks to the physical, occupational, and speech therapists who shared their knowledge with me over lunch in an occupational therapy room at Exempla St. Joseph Hospital in Denver, Colorado, including Donna Stone, Yvonne Mead, Nancy Sanderlin, Jen Lyon, Cindy Koch, and Shaunna McIntosh. Another big thanks to Beth McGann, a speech pathologist at Tampa General Hospital in Tampa, Florida.

To my friends, who are always there to lend a helping hand, thank you.

If you'd like to get in touch, you can reach me through my Web site, www.joanjohnston.com.